CONSTELLATIONS

Books by Janice Kulyk Keefer

FICTION

The Paris-Napoli Express
Transfigurations

NONFICTION

Under Eastern Eyes:
A Critical Reading of Maritime Fiction

POETRY

White of the Lesser Angels

JANICE KULYK KEEFER

CONSTELLATIONS

Random House
Toronto

Thanks to Ed Carson, David Colbert, Jennifer Glossop for their faith in, and patience with this first novel. And loving thanks to Michael Keefer and especially to my mother, Natalie Kulyk, for looking after my children and giving me a whole summer to write.

Copyright © 1988 by Janice Kulyk Keefer

All rights reserved under International and Pan-American Copyright Conventions.

Published in Canada in 1988 by Random House of Canada Limited.

Canadian Cataloguing in Publication Data

Keefer, Janice Kulyk, 1952–
Constellations

Hardcover ISBN 0-394-22043-9
Quality Paperback ISBN 0-394-22024-2

I. Title.

PS8571.E435C66 1988   C813'.54   C88-093364-X
PR9199.3.K434C66 1988

Jacket design: Brant Cowie/Artplus Limited
Jacket illustration: *Coquillage*
              Acrylic on Board, 1987
              15″ × 18″
              by Michael Halliwell

Printed and bound in Canada.

To the memory of Walter Bauer (1904–1976)

writer, teacher, friend

. . . ultimately, and precisely in the deepest and most important matters, we are unspeakably alone; and many things must happen, many things must go right, a whole constellation of events must be fulfilled, for one human being to successfully advise or help another.

Rainer Maria Rilke, *Letters to a Young Poet*

Autumn this year has brought us satellite dishes like gigantic falsies sprouting from the yards of houses all the way from Trout River to Salmon Falls; has sent storms to set the crucifixes rattling on our bedroom walls, and a pizza take-out to replace the florist's shop which had bravely risen from the ashes of the Countrytime Craft Co-Op. Autumn has also given us Bertrand France, *Parisien, B ès lettres* from the *Faculté des Langues* at the Sorbonne. Aesthete, amateur photographer, grudging civilizer of benighted Francophones, Bertrand is like some luckless rocket launched from the City of Light, and fallen to the brute backwoods of Acadie.

Do you understand that Bertrand is an apparition? A *Français de France*, as we say here: someone whose language, looks, and general skyscraping superiority are like a flaming sword brandished from a transatlantic paradise. He has come to judge how far we've fallen from the heights our ancestors knew, back in the land of wine and cheese, of Rabelais and Louis Quatorze. Bertrand has been catapulted here like some Recording, if not Avenging Angel. And I, for my sins, have been appointed his general guide and comforter.

He is with me now, walking over the rank but green grass outside my house, looking at the one tree the property possesses— a superannuated apple, contorted with wind and long neglect, its leaves prematurely loose, its only sign of life a few fichus of poison-pale, green lichen. We are walking together here because we met in the rock-embedded ditch that serves for a sidewalk, I on my way home, Bertrand on his way to the Post Office several houses down from where I live. I have not asked him inside, but then, he doesn't seem in need of any invitations, not just yet. Behind us the sea glistens—it is early October and on windless days you can still sunbathe behind the dunes along the beach, or even swim in the small lagoon from which wild ducks and blue herons have begun longer migrations than anyone here has ever undertaken.

The sea glistens, dazed with late light, but Bertrand doesn't take the trouble to turn his head. He's shown no special feeling for sea or sun except as agents of those special effects he so admires in journals of photography. He has been in Spruce Harbour for two weeks and swears he's already photographed the few things worth reproducing on glossy or matte paper, 5 × 7, 9 × 12. He has even clicked his camera at my house, a perfect white rectangle behind a split rail fence: painted clapboard, a story and a half, brick chimney. No embellishments of any kind, no bay or bow windows, verandah, gingerbread, flowerboxes: just a rectangular white box with books, a piano, a stereo and some six hundred records from Albanoni to Zimbalist. Bertrand, you see, is the Compleat Aesthete and Intelligentsius: he values these mail-order credentials, the very things that make me suspect, or just plain lunatic by Spruce Harbour standards. The sulphur-yellow willows I planted every few feet along the fence when I returned here fifteen years ago will never grow tall or thick enough to block the prying eyes and noses of my neighbours, but Bertrand needn't know. As far as he's concerned, he can walk in perfect safety up the gravel drive to my front door to borrow or return a book, drink coffee and listen to a record. Except that I haven't yet given him the freedom of my house—that can come later, when he is demoralized enough by fog and crows and fish-plant smells to ask for, and not merely expect, my company. There are rules to this game, whether one plays in Paris or along one of the least picturesque or prospering shores of Canada's Ocean Playground.

Bertrand walks out from under the apple tree, peers down the highway through spectacles which are perpetually smudged, as if there could be no use, here, in keeping the lenses clean, and finally initiates a conversation. His voice is irritated, petulant.

"I really can't understand why you people don't put in any gardens. All this—grass. When there *is* grass, and not just mud or gravel or bog. Why on earth, if you had to come back, come here? They tell me that Chéticamp's at least got a fine setting."

"Of course Chéticamp's prettier—but just as poor. Really, it's not our fault—go ask Père Philippe to give you a history lesson, Bertrand. The Expulsion of the Acadians. You know, Evangeline—"

"Evangeline?" Bertrand sounds perfectly incredulous and I wonder whether he was long enough in Halifax to have passed one of those lingerie chain-stores whose satin or rubber articles sport the name of Longfellow's well-cherished heroine. Do those stores still exist—has it really been that long since I've been in any kind of city to find out? Now it is my turn to change the subject; I talk of Chéticamp and the Cabot Trail (which I have never visited), the schools of dolphins lolloping offshore and, not an hour's drive away, wee Scottish inns offering oatcakes in replicas of Lone Shielings (I have read the tourist brochures). We of St. Alphonse Bay have lobsters instead of dolphins—the sum piece of our good fortune, for otherwise it's as bare and raw as a picked scab round here, the fire of 1827 having destroyed the stands of birch, chestnuts, maple. Only scrub alder, now, and spruce mangy with budworm. "It's not our fault," I repeat, while Bertrand shakes his neat and glossy head. I have a set speech which there doesn't seem much point in delivering to this particular student. If he were looking at me instead of at the scuff marks on his Italian shoes, I would describe how the English hoofed us off our plummy lands round the Minas Basin and then, when we straggled back, graciously gave us the rocks and bogs of St. Alphonse Bay. I'd confide my doubts as to whether the *Anglais* really believed it could be done, making a living here; how it was their clumsy little joke on us, forcing farmers into fishermen and lumberjacks. Or priests, to teach us the docility of poverty. "Who knows," I tell Bertrand, "perhaps they'll strike oil off this coast, and Spruce Harbour will become the Calgary of the East. Till then we're stuck with what little there is around us."

"Rubbish, Claire. It's sheer perversity that made you Acadians settle here—and stay on. That's what I can't comprehend. Your aesthetic sense is about as prominent as a baby toe—look at those puces and limes and turquoises you paint your houses, those obscene black-and-orange, fluorescent butterflies you nail over your front doors. And clothes—everyone in jeans and checkered shirts and ski jackets which stink either of pig manure or herring guts. Look, I've been in the bank at paycheque time on Friday afternoon and nearly passed out in the queue—I *know*. Not three, not two, not one real bookstore, café, cinema, theatre, concert hall within this whole hundred miles of Acadian settlement. Not even a restaurant that can tell the difference between coffee beans and rabbit droppings—that understands *crudités* should be an *hors d'oeuvre* and not a state of mind. And as for that tasteless slime with the even less appetizing name—'rappie pie', dear God—"

"Bravo, Bertrand—and thank your stars. Would you really rather wear a silly beret and carry an even sillier bayonet, and spend a year marching round some barracks in one of the drearier provinces of your *belle France*—or in bloody Germany? Admit it, two years of spruce trees and rappie pie's a small price to pay for a delicate conscience. I presume those are the grounds on which they excused you? Or have you got a weak—heart?"

Nothing I can say gets under that skin. The French government allows its more sensitive young countrymen to exchange the rigours of one year's compulsory military service for a twelve-months' hoisting of the torch of French culture in any third world country once under France's imperial thumb. By this reasoning, Nova Scotia stands on a par with Algeria and Martinique. Yet I can't imagine Bertrand being any more at home on desert plains or coral strands than he is here: he has Paris tattooed on his eyeballs, never mind his heart.

Ah, Bertrand, in your strict navy corduroys and cashmere pullover, your button-down collar on the crackling-white shirt, your absurdly elegant bow tie; with those wire-rimmed spectacles condensing the images of my house, myself, the infirm apple tree and sea beyond us, reducing them to tiny motes in your eyes. If I had any bosom to speak of, I'd almost hug you to it. You will spend one year of a life that has scarcely started, here; will see, touch, hear nothing this place has to give you. I can tell, by the practiced way you stand, the stilted perfection of that English you acquired, as you've already told me, in a British boarding school, that you won't even learn this simple thing—how to relax your gestures and the preconceptions they encode. Right now, for example, you want an invitation: "Come on in and have a coffee, Bertrand. Do let me play some music for you, or better still, let me listen to you talk and talk and talk about Paris." You've only to ask me. But no—you need to confer favours, not ask them.

"Really, I must go, Claire, I've got to get to the post office before it closes—they take forever there; it's scandalous. I'll drop by your office tomorrow—you must have some decent books I can borrow. They told me there was a library at the college, but by what stretch of the imagination *Here's Your Horoscope* and *Princess Diana: A Fairy-Tale Come True* can be called books, I honestly don't know. Cheerio."

And he points the Italian leather shoes already pocked by muck and gravel in the direction of the college, and the little house they've given him there. As he walks off he resembles not the lost child I'd thought him earlier, the homesick boy packed off to some third-rate boarding school, but rather one of those strutting dwarfs Mantegna painted at the court of the Gonzagas—contemptuous not of his own puny size but of the inferior status of the painter who's been hired to set his likeness down. Bertrand France, cast up on the scruffy shores of Nova Scotia, imprisoned here like his countrymen before him, during the Napoleonic wars. And I've been made his jailer; snared by Père Philippe, who could find no one more refined, reliable: "Take care of him, Miss Saulnier, during his stay—make him feel at home among Us. He's Our first *co-opérant*, and We want him to give a good report to the French Consulate, you know."

Well, good father, I will do my best—God knows that's a little more than nothing. Though I don't like babysitting, especially when the child's as tiresome as this one. Still, it will convince the college that I'm earning my keep; it will involve nothing more than lending infinite ear to Bertrand's homesick complaints. And besides, it's a long time since I've had a protégé. It will be another small luxury for me, along with my cognac and chocolate and cigars. And it's not as if there's any danger—he's from a long way off, and if he does take a tumble here, he'll only pick himself up and brush the dirt off his knees before going back to Paris as if nothing had happened at all. Well then, Bertrand. You're stuck here like a canary in a cage—I'll have to teach you to sing something other than "I love Paris" or "How long, O Lord, how long?" You've no more knowledge—and less wonder—about this world outside your skull than a chick inside its shell. We'll have to see what shock or miracle might force you out, all wet and dazed and furiously peeping. Though shocks and miracles have never been the strong suit of Spruce Harbour, Nova Scotia.

WHEN NEXT WE MEET we're in good, or at least numerous company. Though classes have been going for a good week already, we've only just managed to hit orientation day. One hundred and ten students, twenty-six faculty, Père Philippe and his administrative henchmen, have all gathered together in what is surely the most hideous room in Sacré Coeur—the Grande Salle which once had carvings of birds and fish and flowers over doors and windows, but which was aggressively modernized ten years ago. Mock-maple vinyl panelling, slippery on the eyes; febrile orange, heavy-duty carpet, a futuristic chandelier that looks like something pried out of a wrecker's yard, and one hundred and fifty regulation auditorium chairs, on one of which sits a beatifically bored Bertrand.

I teach part-time at Collège Sacré Coeur, built by the Eudist fathers, an obscure teaching order expelled from post-Dreyfus France. The college still has priests at its head, and a sprinkling of nuns on staff. My colleagues are local boys with minimal degrees, joined by the odd bird of passage from Québec. As for our students—they come mostly from local families, though there are always some outsiders, problems sent by their parents for that odour of sanctity and strict seclusion the college still dispenses.

The college survives, even turns a tiny profit, by running French immersion programmes in the spring and summer. They attract a rather different crowd: the slick and sleek youth of Ontario, or worldly Halifax teenagers who can get bursaries from the provincial government to become bilingual here. By May the fogs diminish, the cracked asphalt of the tennis courts is dry enough for lobs and volleys, wild strawberries bloom in the salty fields around the lighthouse, and Spruce Harbour becomes, if not a little paradise, then quite a tolerable purgatory. Our affable *recteur*, Père Philippe, goes off on ecclesiastical sightseeing tours, leaving his morose underling, Père Gilbert, the impossible task of overseeing the immersion classes. Few if any of the students are Catholics, and their teachers—recruited from the unemployed BA's of Montréal, Trois-Rivières, Québec—are positive heathen, indulging as they do in unabashed sunbathing, beer-drinking and casual fornication after classes. I know all this because they spend their leisure hours on the dunes behind my house.

Père Philippe of the royal We, the snowy hair and apple cheeks, has asked the faculty to rise, one by one, and introduce themselves. I have gone through this particular performance at least fifteen times in my life—it does not get any less ludicrous. "Claire Saulnier, music professor and cultural organizer," I say, aware that, even if the students had been paying attention, they would hardly have been able to see me: I stand five feet one in my stocking feet. "Jerry Thimot, sports co-ordinator," says the six-foot-four, blond baboon beside me, and I sink into my chair, making myself as small as I possibly can, hoping no one's noticed my performance, least of all Bertrand. When it is his turn he will rise up like an apotheosis from his splintered plywood seat, proclaiming himself "Bertrand France, *Français de France*." If only he could rise up through the styrofoam ceiling tiles, and scramble back to whatever cruel cloud wafted him here in the first place.

On and on it goes: name, rank, role. "Claire Saulnier." What if I had done it differently for once, stood up on my chair so everyone could see, and shouted out—. What? Claire Saulnier, forty-odd years old, spinster of this parish, Catholic born and bred though no longer to be seen at confession or Mass. Daughter of Félix à Claude Saulnier and his wife Anne (both deceased). Native of Spruce Harbour, township of Vere, Whitby County, Nova Scotia. No need to add on the others: Canada, North America, the World, the Universe—these things have no existence, no reality to compare with that of Spruce Harbour. Few of my colleagues have ever left the province; most of my neighbours have only been as far afield as Halifax, Chéticamp, Isle Madame, where they have family. Père Philippe travels each summer to Paris, Rome, Boston, but on priest's business. Of the men who some forty years ago went off as boys to war, only my father brought back any souvenir more durable than a uniform or patent-vending photograph: a war bride and a war child.

"That you may all use your time wisely and well, We have set down a list of rules to be strictly observed by both student body and faculty. You may look to your professors as your mentors and models, *mens sane in corpore sano*. I will now ask Père Gilbert to read through these rules and to entertain any questions—"

But I've already broken all the Spruce Harbour rules, just by being born over there, of an *Anglaise d'Angleterre*. That is the reason my colleagues give for my being *carnassière*, Acadian for what the French call *polisson* and the English "naughty." Bad in the insistent, uncaring way of certain kinds of children—the ones who must be tolerated even if they're not loved, since they are, somehow, one's own. Despite my English mother, I am taken for my father's child—Claire à Félix—and my peculiarities as a necessary deformity, given my mixed parentage. I speak and write English by preference rather than Acadian or the standard French I literally had whipped into me at convent school in Montréal. Instead of keeping house for my widowed father after my return, I went off to study music in England; by the time I could come back, there was no one to keep house for. And now, long after my return, I continue to spend the little money I earn not on colour TV and video-cassettes, microwave ovens or the more expensive clothes from Sears catalogue, but on books from Blackwells and records shipped from the World's Biggest Music Store on 8th

Avenue in New York. You see, Bertrand, I am not altogether a barbarian.

"And now let us rise and sing the *Ave Maris Stella*—"

Not a beauty, either—what woman is at forty-odd? My mother may have been beautiful as a young woman, but the only photos I have of her were taken after the war, when the persistent unhappiness of exile had stiffened her face and blanked her eyes. Besides, I take after my father's side: dark, sharp-featured, lean— not round and sweet and succulent as the ju-jubes in the huge glass jar at Wagner's store—Spruce Harbour's standard of beauty. Though it's not my ugliness so much as my indisputably unmarried state that's proved me lacking in my neighbours' eyes. They could tell you that my grandmother at least, old Aline Saulnier, got herself a man and had five children drubbed out of her like dust clouds from a carpet. Two survived childhood—my father and a daughter whom I've never seen, who might as well be dead—she is a nun somewhere in Kansas.

Now the registrar, a plump and shortish man with a face like a cross baby, takes the floor to talk about exams and study breaks, the penalties to be incurred for missing classes. Most of the students are asleep in the tepid, dusty light that sways around the room. I sit up a little straighter in my chair so as to get a better look at Bertrand. If he's begun to fascinate me, it's only that he's such a touchstone of the urban, the cosmopolitan—such a caricature Parisian and yet here, now, real among us, forcing connections with those years I spent abroad in London, and my obligatory little tour of France. Perhaps I even walked past him in the Jardin du Luxembourg, perhaps he was one of the small boys in grey flannel shorts and pressed white shirts, sailing wooden boats in the *bassin*. A little boy who's grown into this parody of an educated, well-connected man. Black hair clipped short, parted at the side with perverse exactitude, as though with a razor instead of a comb. I suspect he wears those glasses as much from vanity as myopia—in the same way he wears a conspicuously high-tech wristwatch at which he hardly ever looks. Long delicate hairs creep like Dali's ants around the watchband, well below the cuffs of his shirts; he will end up being the sort of man who keeps a laundress rather than a mistress, and who stipulates the exact amount of starch he wants pressed into cuffs and collars. He is not pretty, or—except for his hands—particularly well made, but lank, with a perpetual stumble when he walks along the ditch which serves for boulevard here in Spruce Harbour.

It is, thank all the gods, over: applause thin as skim milk, students rushing out as if the auditorium were on fire, faculty discreetly making off before Pères Gilbert or Philippe can buttonhole us. Bertrand walks right past me on his way out, but doesn't even whisper a greeting. Did he listen to my one-line summary of who and what I am? Would he even care to know what I didn't say? But he'd as soon ask a real question about me as he would shinny up the dunce-cap steeple of the church and belt out the *Marseillaise* to the crows in the spruce tops.

My office boasts a view of an under-used parking lot; the priests and nuns on faculty have offices inside those college towers that stand out among the scrubby spruce, the telephone wires and sagging bungalows, like hands gesturing forlornly to the power that has created and, as inexplicably, forgotten us. I stare out across the parking lot to the screen of spruce that cuts off the view of the bay. The head janitor, a local boy, passes close under my window—I can see the top of his plastic baseball cap. Dear God, just how will Bertrand France survive in a place where baseball caps and snowmobiles are *de rigueur*? Just what do they expect me to do with him? They didn't tell me that; they simply issued threats as to what would happen if I didn't keep adequate eyes on him. For there have been warnings—''There is not enough money to repair the college buildings, never mind pay inessential salaries.'' I am not about to become, at my age, an unemployed professor, scraping a living from teaching piano to the children of Whitby County's tin-eared elite. I like my life the way it is, the little luxuries connecting me with cities I will never visit, cities full of people I do not wish or need to meet.

WALKING HOME from work along the rutted ditch, dodging exhaust

fumes, I try to see this little world as God would. But no, let's
reduce our sights a bit—as would one of His lesser angels; as
Bertrand would, if he'd only take the plugs out of his eyes. Next
door to the college, in an immense square of concrete parking lot,
looms St. Alphonse Church, an ark in dry-dock. Its architecture
is more Disney than divine, but at least the steeple gives us
something to which we can lift our eyes. The priests have had the
shingles painted a dark grey—during the weeks of mist and fog
the church is the only object that somehow resists dissolution, its
grey acquiring solidity and presence in the soft milkiness that
consumes the air.

Behind the church and college a grove of spruce encloses ponds
and marshes and a small river that drains into the sea beyond.
The first teaching fathers constructed labyrinthine paths through
these woods; you can still find concrete plinths of statues into
which mussel and clam shells have been pressed like giant fingernails. The platform of some rustic shrine rots gently in the
largest clearing, though altar and statues as well as roof and walls
have been carried off to someone's garden or hunting shack.
Enormous crows, some owls and a few blue heron perch in the
spruce tops. Blackflies and mosquitos fur the paths between the
trees as soon as summer comes, so that if Bertrand should find
out about the paths and go looking for wildflowers, he'll return
with swollen face and hands. "Why don't you people put in any
gardens?" Because, Bertrand, the bites we get picking mayflow-
ers, asters or wild azalea itch and sting far longer than the flowers
last in glass jars on our kitchen tables.

To get to the paths in the grove you take a little lane behind the
church, bordered by apple trees and leading to a small wooden
house in which the parish's idiots and handicapped were once
lodged; it has been repaired, repainted, and given to Bertrand,
who knows nothing of its origins. It is Spruce Harbour's collective
joke on him, its return for that blithe contempt Bertrand dispenses
all around, instead of blessings. He tells me the house is not
impossible; at least it's utterly private and, in its primal setting,
a little as he imagines the witch's house in *Hansel and Gretel*,
minus the gingerbread and oven, of course. He sleeps and cooks

upstairs; downstairs is the ''studio'' and darkroom he has con-
cocted with his own supplies and odds and ends pirated from the
college's defunct audio-visual department. Talking of his house,
Bertrand seems almost happy. Not knowing of the bite'em no
see'ems of spring and summer, he has elected the woods as his
Arcadia-in-exile. He's even found chanterelles, he tells me, at
the foot of certain trees; has eaten their peppery orange flesh in
omelettes cooked up *chez lui* on the hot plate provided by the
college.

But Bertrand wouldn't venture farther than the paths winding
through the first hundred yards of the woods. If you scramble
through the tangle of alder and briar where the paths stop, you
can poke your way into open fields—sloping to the sea in one
direction and in the other, down to the fishplant road. Here it is
all furze and heath: thorn trees, naked, sinewy brambles, long
grass that bleaches in winter to pale and brittle gold. Snowmobiles, dune buggies and three-wheeler motorbikes have worn
down a set of paths criss-crossing the fields. There are a few small
fish huts with diamond-shaped windows and shingles scrubbed
grey by salty winds blowing up from the shore. The morning after
his arrival at Spruce Harbour, Bertrand tried to walk down to the
sea; it has already become a legend at the Social Club, the Legion,
the Fish and Game, how this upright man in sleek-soled shoes,
armed only with a week-old copy of *Le Monde*, struggled against
the dunes of rounded pebbles blocking the way to the water,
sinking in a quicksand of fractured Javex bottles, rusty bits of
engines, sticky pools of tar. It took him a week to discover the
dirt road leading straight from the highway down to the crescent
of sandy beach that stretches from the fishplant to the dunes behind
my house, and up to the trailer park half a mile beyond.

I suppose Bertrand's initial misadventures have been all my
fault. I should have taken him on a guided tour of this little world
that's become his temporary prison, instead of sitting back to
watch him flounder. But then he wouldn't concede that there's
anything to be seen, as opposed to suffered in Spruce Harbour. I
could tell him how, when I came back from England and into my
inheritance, I spent whole days reclaiming abandoned territories,

confirming the boundaries of the little world willed to me along with my father's white house, my mother's piano, and my great-grandmother's bleached-out quilts. I could tell him how I walked out, one Sunday morning when the bell was being tolled for Mass, to the fishplant at the very end of the wharf. On holidays, the place has the expectant emptiness of a de Chirico painting, in which one set of shadows menaces another. When I was a child my mother forbid me to go anywhere near the fishplant; she didn't want me to hear the kind of language spoken by the men unloading the Cape Islanders, or the jokes shared over piles of herring guts by girls in hairnets and brine-stiff smocks. Because I was forbidden to play there, I would sneak down on Sunday afternoons for solitary games of hide-and-go-seek between uncoupled trucks in a yard heaped with ruined barrels, split shingles and rotten crates. I would invent my own pursuers lurking behind the giant bags of salt, stiff and heavy as corpses, and when I'd frightened myself into hearing their footsteps or hoarse, excited breathing, I'd run down to the very end of the wharf, to a palisade of silvery pilings so thick you couldn't make your arms touch round them. And I would peer through the chinks at the sea below, or out to the hills that close off the bay, pretending I was on a boat, the same boat that had brought me here, but this time headed in the opposite direction, out to England.

I went only once to the empty fishplant after my return from England, looking for ghosts of the games I had played. I went only once because my mother's warnings had not been so mistaken, after all. Between the abandoned trucks and the heaps of giant salt bags I overheard the hoarse and shallow breathing not of children but of lovers. A generous term for that sweaty tangle of limbs and hair, that necessary heave and press of bodies none too clean, none too fresh. I didn't cry out, or run away, and I didn't watch for any longer than the moments it took to confirm what it was I was seeing. They didn't notice me, of that I'm sure. And I am equally sure of the slow, measured steps I took back from the yard, along the wharf and up to the highway. It wasn't what they were doing, but that they were there at all, in that empty place I'd imagined as belonging wholly to me, to the child I once was.

So I go no more a-roving, but keep to the straight and narrow; to be precise, to this ditch that serves for a sidewalk between the college and my house. If I wanted to I suppose I could calculate how many times I've walked past this string of brand-new bungalows painted those colours Bertrand abhors—colours to bite through the thickest fog: chartreuse, canary yellow, sizzle-pink. Only TV antennae branch above the shoebox houses sporting mail-order American-colonial doors, and those gigantic wooden butterflies that make Bertrand think of Gregor Samsas crucified in metamorphosis. The soil's too sour, the winds too harsh for apple trees or even shrubbery to thrive. Or perhaps it's the diesel fumes that poison all but the alders and burdock, or the transport trucks that career so close to the ditch that only the lunatic or suicidal choose to walk instead of drive, even if only to a neighbour's house or the Kwikway store a stone's throw down the road.

You and I, Bertrand, are the only ones who walk, you and I and those too poor to own even ten-year-old cars or third-hand trucks. The first time we met I offered you the occasional loan of the car I keep shut up in the dilapidated shed behind my house. You didn't bother to thank me, but emphasized, with quite unpardonable pride, that driving wasn't the sort of accomplishment to which you aspired; that you'd never lived in a place where there wasn't a Métro or a fleet of cabs to take you wherever you happened to want to go. What will you do here where there is no city, just houses for mile after strung-out mile, north and south along the coast? A general store here, a bank and post office there, and every so often, Frenchy's used-clothing stores which sell for fifty cents apiece the trousers, nightgowns, shoes, coats, girdles, even wedding dresses that the frantic rich of the Boston states wear twice and then stuff into charity boxes to be sold as rags. The summer students always stop at Frenchy's to pick up tacky evening dresses and mis-matched suits for their cabaret; the fishplant workers go there for jeans, shrunk sweaters and soiled ski jackets (bearing tickets from Banff, Aspen, even Kittsbühl) with which to clothe their children and themselves. Somehow I don't think you will ever patronize the establishment, even if there were whole tablefuls of silk bowties to be found there.

You brushed by me today without a word. You haven't yet come to claim the books you want to borrow, the musical scores you want to teach yourself during the winter nights to which you've already attributed a Siberian severity. You think that if you keep entirely to yourself, in perfect silence and solitariness, you'll be able to conjure up the noise and dirt and stench of Paris, the way people in sensory-deprivation experiments are driven to hallucinate phantasmagorias. It won't work, Bertrand: you haven't the skill, you haven't the vocation for solitude. You might as well acknowledge the sovereignty of this tatty strip of settlement between rough water and matted stands of spruce. Even from your gingerbread house you can hear the two-ton trucks bomb past, or lean out the window to catch sight of planes from Boston and Halifax, floating high above the clouds and fog that hem us in as surely as the hills across the bay. As you've already learned, this is not the sort of place to which you choose to come. You are either born or brought here, and if you stay too long the mists and bleak-boughed spruce and basalt cliffs will take up house inside you. I have known graduates of Sacré Coeur to plunge into despair upon getting jobs an hour's drive up the valley; for them it is a universe away. And those who make it as far as Halifax, or Montréal, or even *outre-mer*—even they make their way back through the devious routes of dreams, or by the deliberate refusal to succeed in exile, as if deportation from their own best interests were somehow in their blood.

A poor, scant place, the tourists think, speeding through to get to the rich green shelter of the valley. Refusing to recognize the blur outside the car window as an equal and opposite reality to that desired one of brochure-bright meadows, pretty girls in fake-folkloric dress under the apple blossom at Grand Pré. One that cancels you out, over and over again, just as the tide erases each day's highwater mark. So that you have to build walls around you, to keep from being flooded away. Walls secured with ropes of blood, the intricately endless fringe of family: lives knotted and extended with each baptism, marriage, funeral and birth. A rope my father severed, marrying my mother, producing a spinster daughter instead of sons. So that I've had to build other walls, quarrying from my own blood and bone a shelter, a defence against everything outside myself, everything I will not allow inside.

"THIS WILL DO—I won't keep it for very long."

Bertrand's standing by the rickety bookshelf in my office, fingering a copy of Rilke's *Letters to a Young Poet*. "It shouldn't be there," I'm on the point of saying—it belongs at home, in my house. That book is one of the few things my mother brought over with her from England. I learned it by heart when I was much younger than Bertrand, I used to recite it to . . . . And now I remember how it got into my office—I have lent it out before, to a former protégé. But who knows—perhaps Bertrand's nursing a vocation for poetry in addition to his passion for photography. Rilke might even teach him a bit of humility, miracle of miracles.

I have courses to prepare, phone calls to make—there's a Halifax string quartet-cum-oboist that seems willing to put on a concert at Sacré Coeur before Christmas. And Bertrand has a remedial grammar class to be suffered through; yet he has come to my office to converse, taking the armchair I inherited from my priestly predecessor, settling himself beneath the room's one poster advertising a British Museum Exhibition, circa sixteen years ago. He prefers my office to the faculty lounge—an overheated storage room with a shabby sofa, an assortment of intimately uncomfortable, moulded plastic chairs, and a coffee machine, though what it produces is undrinkable. Most of all there are our fellow colleagues, who have begun to put up armed resistance to Bertrand. They no longer invite him to sit with them at lunch; they speak their broadest, most salacious *acadien* when he passes them in the corridors; they speculate loud and long about his sexual proclivities. Hubert, the biology professor, someone who knows a thing or two about anatomical possibilities, swears that Bertrand goes out at night and screws sheep. I am not asked for my conjectures. I have taught with these people so long and speak with them so little, and I am so far from being what they think of as a woman, that for them I've as much sexuality as a penholder—or rather less. I have heard Isador lament, in Soeur Angèle, the loss of a fantastic pair of tits; they think it's I who should have turned nun. Delphis, whom I have loathed since earliest schooldays, has suggested to the others that Bertrand and I would make a perfect pair: the *Anglaise* and the *Français de France*. He seems to think I should be flattered at the suggestion, as if I were infatuated with this priggish *Parisien*, as if I couldn't see Bertrand for the spoiled child he is.

He isn't even a child, but a baby—one who's just learned to walk and talk without falling over his feet and tongue, and who keeps twirling his accomplishments under everyone's nose. He volunteers the information that he's twenty-three as if it were a holy wafer to be digested on our tongues: twenty-three, with his Sorbonne degree and an encyclopedic knowledge of the history of photography, as well as firm acquaintance with the masterpieces of Western music, literature and the visual arts. Self-taught, since he admits his family veers toward the Philistine: father something high up in a company, mother the daughter of a minor aristocrat—both heartbroken when he didn't go into business or medicine or law, but chose English literature as a dubious cover for his true passion, photography. He has a small inheritance from his maternal grandmother on which he intends to travel this summer to Texas, to see—

"Helmut Gernsheim's photohistorical collection at the university there—he's done fabulous things." Bertrand goes on to give me the particulars of Gernsheim's career and I interrupt to flick in a few names I know—Cartier-Bresson, Man Ray, Georgia O'Keeffe.

Bertrand purses up his lips. "Of course they're the brand-name photographers. James Jorché and Angus McBean are much more interesting. If ever you get out of this bog and come to Paris, I might try to get you into the *Institut* archives—though I expect to be frantically busy once I get home—if I survive the trip to Halifax airport, that is. Do you know how impossible the railway system is in this country?'' And he proceeds to tell me the story—already much embellished—of his arrival in Spruce Harbour.

"Of course I didn't spend much time in Halifax—I mean it's not the most exciting of towns, and I thought I'd better get straight to Spruce Harbour and settle in. It was a disaster, of course—the stupid taxi driver assured me it was only a short hop to the station from the airport. I think it was thirty dollars he charged me, and how could I argue with him? I'd have missed my train—all two cars of it. Really, it looked like something a child could have set up in a corner of his room. So I get inside and we positively lurch through the utterly monotonous countryside and it starts to get dark—we've been travelling forever, and I have horrendous jet lag. Only twenty hours before I was looking at tapestries in the Musée de Cluny, and now I'm being racketed by a train that should have been scrapped in 1922, listening to drunks discuss hockey scores and being smothered by cheap tobacco fumes. So in desperation—we've been riding for three hours already—I motion to the conductor—his uniform was terribly shabby, just like the train upholstery; you'd never see anything as bad in France, even in the provinces—and I ask him to warn me ten minutes before we pull into Spruce Harbour. He said he would, and seemed inclined to talk. He told me that Spruce Harbour was the metropolis of the Maritimes, ten times the size of Halifax—"

"Oh, Bertrand, you didn't fall—"

"What else was I supposed to do? No one in Paris had the foggiest notion of what or where Spruce Harbour was—and what I saw of Halifax was so small and dreary. Besides, it was pitch black outside the train, you couldn't see anything at all. After the conductor had gone I kept peering out, looking for city lights—and then the bloody train stops and my baggage is being heaved down into—weeds, Claire. Weeds. The bastard grins at me and tells me to watch out for the fast women and muggers on the city streets. Then the train pulls away and leaves me and all my suitcases—the cameras are incredibly heavy, of course—in a vacant lot, a waste field without a house or road or even a telephone pole in sight."

"Liar," I say, looking past him out the corridor where I see a student skulking. "The road's a stone's throw from where the platform used to be; you can still see some of the planks. And there's a house—Anselme Gaudet's—a hundred yards along. Besides, Père Philippe had come specially to pick you up—in his Oldsmobile. It wasn't his fault if he got a flat—luckily it happened just opposite the Petro-Canada station, or he'd have been more than ten minutes late—"

"Twenty. I stood there feeling the mud creep up my shoes, trying to figure out where the stars would be, if the night weren't fogged in. And then I gave up and started to walk—luckily, in the right direction, towards the sea, not the swamp. And your Père Philippe. He's not exactly festive company, despite the fact that he's a dead ringer for Father Christmas. That white hair—surely he must dye it? Do you know he's already inveigled me into teaching immersion classes this spring?"

"Speaking of teaching, Bertrand, you should have been drilling *Français 100* on the use of the subjunctive five minutes ago. I have a student waiting to see me—come on, dear boy—move your ass."

He's nettled as he stands to go. I am the only one he has found it possible to talk to here, yet he doesn't like what he calls the "liberties" I take with his *amour-propre*. But he comes back for more, and I must admit, it amuses me far more than I would have thought possible. There are moments when I find myself watching the awkward tilt of his head, the slight throb of his Adam's apple under the absurd bow tie that must be all the rage in the halls of the Sorbonne, with as much a sense of pleasure as duty. I think we are a little like a maiden aunt with her nephew, the one to whom she used to slip chocolate and dollar bills; the one who's now grown up and off at school, yet who comes to call from time to time, in gratitude for past indulgences.

I shoo him out, and the student enters: a gum-snapping red-head whose brains are as frizzled as her over-permanented hair. I'm supposed to teach her how to play that most exigent of instruments, the violin (Père Philippe has high hopes of a student orchestra). As she executes her scales I debate with myself whether it's time, yet, to ask Bertrand to come for dinner. "Try it again, slowly this time, trying to sound each note perfectly—no, not like that—can't you hear the squeak? It's like a mouse being strangled." I close my ears, keeping eyes on the poster above the armchair where Bertrand had sat: "A Dream of Fair Women: Japanese Paintings and Prints of the Ukiyoe School." A courtesan, falling into the frozen pool of her own reflection. Lacquered hair impaled by ebony combs, mouth no bigger than a bead, letting pass only the smallest words: yes, no. Yes.

WITH BERTRAND'S ARRIVAL I have found myself forced to take stock, gather into the fold of my self-possession exactly what is mine by right or choice—this world I have so dearly bought, prizing its smallness, safeness, its perfect self-enclosure. I am, after all, a woman living on her own without family or friends. I have reached degree zero of independence, and if my colleagues, with their pendulous and itchy groins, and if their bulbous-breasted wives with their oh-so-slappable behinds equate that zero with nothing, it doesn't matter. They are outside, always—and I within impregnable defences: centred. Zero, after all, is a circle, the perfect form, one that can be stretched to comprehend worlds larger than Spruce Harbour.

Sitting here in my white house, my castle keep, I can look out the window and see enclosing me the willow hedge beside the split-rail fence—beyond that the highway on one side, the bay on the other. The only time I need venture out is to go to work—my father, though he left me his house, had run up too many debts during his last years for me not to have to earn my daily bread and dried cod. Saturdays I shop at the Kwikway store for milk and eggs and ground beef, iceberg lettuce and frozen corn. Or when I crave exotica I make an expedition to the Save-Easy at Whitby, bringing back avocados or kiwi fruit like trophies from a big-game hunt. But I do this less and less—living as I do you lose your taste for anything more than serves to keep body and soul together; for anything that takes you too far afield from where you're safe, alone.

"What on earth do you do with yourself here?" That question comes less and less the longer I stay. Only strangers ask it— teachers who put in a year or two at Sacré Coeur before they gratefully find greener pasture; the immersion people who come up for the summers to cram French into their students like too-rich stuffing up a puny goose. "Whatever do you find to do?"

"My work," I used to reply—playing and teaching piano, organizing concerts in the college chapel. Until I realized that they meant what did I do when I was alone, after hours. At first I had all kinds of defences, excuses—and then I realized the best answer was the true one: I talk to myself. Adding something to the effect that, having been an only child, having been orphaned so early and being solitary by nature, I've never found anyone else with whom to carry on as interesting a conversation. Not adding what they haven't yet discovered, that there are two kinds of language: one we speak with others, acquaintances and friends, lovers and family—words to keep them out from the space inside us. And the language we speak to ourselves, to that white and empty space in which words take shape, curling soundlessly within. Nothing like that first raging sound we make outside ourselves, the birth scream. Or the babbling we do, learning to talk another language, separate from the one we've always spoken to ourselves, inside: learning to twist our tongues into sounds a stranger can mistake for speech.

I have chosen this world, this blank, null place, because in it I can hear myself speak to my self. There is so little human inter-ference—only the endless abrasion of the elements, patiently reducing everything down to whatever the first matter must have been. Rock and water, infrequent sun that, acid-like, eats mists and fog, only to be swallowed up again. Even the people are not figures but aspects of the landscape; in their jeans and baseball caps, that odiferous clothing Bertrand despises, they are as natural as barnacles on rock or driftwood logs washed over the sand. Like the peasants in those paintings of Breughel he effects to admire so much. While he struts about in his corduroys and cashmere, as queerly conspicuous as would be an angel in white satin robes and swansdown plumage. An angel looking for someone—anyone—worthy of receiving his Annunciation. For want of a resident madonna, I suppose I'll have to do. Though it's I who should be delivering messages, making the communications only angels can. Telling him about this place, this bare ground on which it's so easy to create and enclose a world.

Though there is a brief summer and a fine autumn here, you dress your mind always for winter, season of endless wind and rain, of snow that blizzards in across the bay, turning sky and sea to one white abstraction. Blowing into drifts across the concrete wells and blistered verandahs, into a gritty powder over the fields and yards whose dead grass pricks through blank skin, giving the lie to any vision of newness, pureness, cancellation, falling snow begets. And you spend the null spring waiting for the too-short summer. Autumn, you watch for signs of winter coming, your eyes mapping a world confined between closed borders: Dürer's patch of turf, but minus the sweet juice and colours. You learn it all by heart—flat, dull stones on the beach; inconsequential blue of a jay's wing in a spruce grove; rich, clogged smells of mud flats exposed by the tide; waves scrabbling to shore.

You come to know these small things so perfectly it is a kind of love, the only kind permitted by the strict enclosure of the bay, the sand flats each tide prints out, only to erase again. You learn to see here all there is to be seen—reality in lower case: minimal. And your life becomes disburdened, divested; the line between being and not-being more and more tenuous, until you've lost all sense of fear as you lose all sense of expectation.

That's what my father must have thought—coming back here after the war, bringing my mother and the small, stiff child I was. My father, who couldn't put enough space between himself and the battlegrounds Bertrand would never recognize as Europe; my mother who, ten years after the war, still woke up to sirens, flames and guns at night. Father, mother and I, alone together in this house walled in by the bay, and the hills across the bay, under a sky like blue ice by day, and littered by night with the debris of some other creation: small, soundless explosions of light. My father, taking me out with him on the back porch when I should have been asleep, trying to teach me the constellations, which I could only see as a mess of stars. Orion, Castor and Pollux, Andromeda—they didn't look like people at all. I couldn't follow his explanations: how this light connected with that to make a line, and you could read the line into a story, if not a shape. And my mother thumping at the window, my mother always cold, wearing a shawl over a sweater, though both the wood stove and furnace were roaring away. Telling him to bring me inside before I caught my death—I can see her mouth through the windowpane, shaping the words I couldn't hear but knew by heart.

She had another way of speaking. She had been a music student in London during the war—met my father in an air raid shelter, married him because he came from Canada, and Canada was to her a pure and perfect blankness. She must have been astonished, infuriated to find cities and factories, and cars full of people: just another set of targets, only a little more difficult to find. She thought my father had lied to her—she would have got on the next boat home if she'd been able to find anything bigger than a scallop trawler: this is what she told me. She spoke another language when she played the Bechstein my father had ordered all the way from England; when she lay with him at night under the quilts made by strangers' hands, dead women who somehow laid stronger claim to her husband than she ever could. For he refused to take her away, to abandon home, to have me grow up anywhere else than in perfect safety, here.

Father, mother and I. And then, one by one, we left—or rather, were sent away, until there was only the white house, white as a dry bone when I came back. And stayed because here there is nothing and no one, perfect silence in which you can learn to hear, faintly, and then louder, louder, your self speaking to your self, as the sea must have sounded in your ears before you were tugged out to birth, when you were happily drowned in the warm dark, and there were no lights, not even the most random scattering of stars to prick your eyes.

"Whatever do you do with yourself here?" They rarely return, the immersion teachers, from one summer to the next. Even though they're at Spruce Harbour at the height of the season, the blue skies, golden sands, glassy water aren't enough to hold them. True, the skies are often fogged over till mid-July, the sands spiky with unbiodegradable Coke tins and aluminum-foil potato chip bags, and any sweet music on these waters tends to be blurts and blats from motorbikes and three-wheelers that ignore the county by-laws to tear up and down the small crescent of sandy beach. The best part of summer is the night sky: fresh, black, stars jostling one another for space to shine, as if every possible galaxy were crammed into this stretch of empty air above the bay. The night sky they probably never see, having their eyes blanked by each other's bodies or shut tight as they thrash between the sheets or behind the dunes.

Perhaps I shall have to interest Bertrand in star-gazing—how else will he occupy his nights, the chaste, inviolable Bertrand? Another item to add to the telephone directory of his accomplishments: constellations to memorize, mythology to dredge up from bygone Greek and Latin classes. A harmless expenditure of time. For what we've named, strung into stories, are just shattered crystals, like the broken glass they put along with iron spikes on garden walls in London: an extra barrier between you and whatever wants to creep inside.

I TAKE THE ANCIENT Volkswagen out of the garage where it's been rusting gently for at least the past month; drive into the parking lot of St. Alphonse Church where Bertrand waits beside the statue of the Virgin stranded in Her asphalt desert, with only a plastic rose and a crown of lightbulbs for company. No need to honk the horn—he runs up to the car and practically catapults himself inside. "What's the rush?" I ask, and he mutters something about students seeing, colleagues and their jokes. If I weren't outside the whole affair, I wouldn't know whether to be flattered or insulted; instead I mimic Bertrand's habitual shrug, rev the engine and take us off.

"Don't get your hopes up too high, Bertrand—we're not in the

Loire, no *châteaux* or *musées des beaux arts*. But there's a pretty enough waterfall at Trout River, and cliffs at Sailor's Cove—two pictures at least.''

On his lap Bertrand cradles, like some well-swaddled nurseling, a camera of peculiarly complicated design, one of those black and brutal-looking German makes, with a whole case of lenses and projecting pieces whose names and functions he regales me with the whole length of our drive. When he's strolling on the boulevards of Paris does he still have this mania for parading his learning, dropping names and numbers into anything resembling a human ear? Or is it like the bow tie he snaps round his collar, just to make him visible—to himself—in Spruce Harbour?

"Look, Bertrand—here's the waterfall we've driven all this way to see. Aren't you even going to get out of the car, or do you intend to keep on muttering about Hasselblads, or whatever? Come on, there's a good boy.''

My high hopes crash as we make our way into the clearing. I can't really blame him for not taking his camera—the sun is brilliant, true, but it glints off a hundred empty beer, vodka and gin bottles. He may not notice the safes glued to the piles of rusty pine needles, but the rush of white water doesn't cancel out the sludge burdening the river, sludge from the sawmill upstream.

"And this is what you go out of your way to show to tourists? Claire, is this a joke?''

We head back to the car and drive off again past sullen houses with rotting porches, disembodied bits of gingerbread amid the smashed machines and rotting rags over the lawn. "Bootlegger's Row,'' I tell him, as if this information excuses the ugliness, categorizes it. This is not my chosen ground, it lies outside my customary radius, although my father knew it well enough—all the babies he delivered, the near-corpses he revived here. *"Wearing yourself out among people who stink of fresh booze and stale sweat—when I need you here, at home.'' "I've smelled worse— you ought to know that.''*

"Where now—back to Spruce Harbour?''

"Bertrand, you sound so hopeful—I'm beginning to think you actually like it at the college.''

"At least I've made my house halfway tolerable—what's this, now—the Evangeline Trail again? Still that moronic Long-fellow?"

"I thought the French were crazy about absurd American writers—you adore Edgar Allen Poe, don't you?"

Wrong move—that sets him off on Baudelaire and Barthes, all the way to the cliffs of Sailor's Cove. He doesn't seem to notice the basalt rocks under the water, making waves like clumsy knives through a victim's flesh. But he cuts his hand while scrabbling along the cliffside path, and one of his beautiful Italian shoes gets soaked in a tide pool. The sea urchin I find for him is scarcely a consolation; he merely fingers the spines and lets it drop back to the rocks. It doesn't even give him the satisfaction of shattering, but rolls casually into the water.

I suggest we go to the Beausoleil Diner to get something warm to drink. A woman with hair like a senile poodle's takes our orders—Bertrand can't make out her *acadien* though her accent isn't particularly strong. He affects not to understand anything but standard French—adds our grammatical digressions, our Rabelaisian *bons mots* to a lump sum of savagery. As he does the coffee—undrinkable—and the root beer, which he considers worse than homebrew, liable to turn him deaf, blind, syphilitic at the first gulp. He has a *petite amie* back in Paris, and she's a health food fanatic who neither smokes nor drinks. Poor smitten suitor follows suit—although his eyes don't exactly cross with longing as he mentions her.

He does accept a cup of tea, nursing it for the next half hour while I talk of the region—where to buy groceries, cough medicine, a used car—

"You seem to have forgotten. I don't drive."

—the quickest way to get to Halifax, the cost of plane fares to New York, Toronto, San Francisco: places I've never been, but about which I collect statistics. He listens as attentively as the stuffed moose over his head; all his energies focus on watching his shoe steam gently on the radiator, or the Elastoplast bandaid the waitress has fetched him crinkle on his hand. A different Bertrand, I suddenly, sinkingly realize—not the egregious egotist who monopolizes my office, but a demoralized one. He has the *cafard* but good—there's a grave risk he'll perish of ennui before the winter fogs descend, hole up in his castle keep in the woods and turn madman, wildman—even poet. And I will hear reproaches, even threats from Père Philippe.

"Bertrand?" What can I offer to cheer him? "Do you want something to eat—a doughnut?"

He shrugs, the kind of ex-imperial shrug Ovid must have given to those inmates of the Transpontine marshes who came bearing gifts of violent wine, crude cheese, to lighten the burden of his exile. Bertrand broods out the fishnet-draped window of the Beausoleil Diner, and finally makes a sad little flourish with his fingers. "Over there, beyond those hills—Boston, if not New York. Bookstores, the Faneuil Market, the Fogg Museum—there's a Helen Frankenthaler exhibit on right now—and we sit *here* just looking out to sea."

"Bertrand—that's not Boston behind those hills—it's New Brunswick. And Fredericton isn't Boston, not by any stretch—"

He shakes his head at me: consummate condescension. "My poor Claire, you've missed the point. You're mouldering along this God-forsaken coast, with only a few lobster fishermen and mink farmers for company, when life is . . . . Life is elsewhere."

I don't mean to make instant confession, but I do. "That's precisely why I'm here, Bertrand. I've had my share of what you call life: the things I can still read about in *The New Yorker* or *Arts Magazine*. As a matter of fact, I was born elsewhere—my parents brought me here, after the war."

"Oh yes—the war." As if the Punic or Napoleonic sort: ancient, unnecessary history.

"Yes, Bertrand—the war that people like my father fought while your countrymen were sitting round drinking Vichy water."

"Honestly, Claire, I can't see what there is to get worked up over. Or what this has to do with the statements I made earlier about your senseless staying on."

"Mouldering was the word you used. And I'm not worked up, Bertrand. Only a little astonished at—let's call it your general ignorance. Wait just one minute—I'm not at all calling into question your overwhelming familiarity with the minutiae of Western culture and society. But as for the larger realities—the connections one occasionally needs to make if one doesn't want to remain in a moral and intellectual nursery. . . . Look, my dear, I wasn't found under a spruce patch, delivered into my parents' loving arms by a seagull—I was conceived in a bomb shelter somewhere in London during the worst of the Blitz—if my parents' stories are true, that is. Romantic, don't you think? All the time I was in London I couldn't walk into the Underground without having visions of thousands of people huddled together in the dark, some shrieking, most silent, and a few, like my parents, making love, making babies, for God's sake, while the planes were shitting death over their heads.''

"Claire, please—there's no call for that kind of language.''

"They never got over it—my parents. My father was one of the doctors who went on into Germany—''

"I know—the death camps, the six million. One has to be careful, you know—that kind of thing has become kitsch. It's been done too many times.''

"My father never talked about what he'd seen—except to say that he *had* seen, and that nothing could ever make him set foot in Europe again. So he brought us here, where there are no sirens or blackouts or barbed wire and nothing ever happens. You know, there must have been some kind of genetic mutation that went on with children conceived during that war. So that we were all born with the imagination of disaster, knowing there is nothing safe, nowhere you can walk without the ground ripping like paper under your feet. That's why I've chosen to stay here—because it's the safest place I know.''

"That's why you don't even set foot out of Whitby County— not even to go to Halifax? Because you're afraid of things that go bump in the night? I could believe that about your parents' generation—I've read Sartre, Malraux, all the rest of them. But it hardly applies to you, Claire. Besides, you did get away, if only to London. What I'd like to know is how you could possibly come back here.''

I wait for a moment, stirring nonexistent sugar round and round the contents of my chipped cup. Then I let the spoon fall back into the tepid coffee and look right through Bertrand's smudged spectacles. "I came back because my father was dying. And because I was his only child, and because he left me his house. Blood ties; you must know something about that kind of love, at least. Or are you even more virginal than you appear, Bertrand?"

I call the waitress for the bill, which Bertrand makes no move to pay. I leave much too big a tip—she did give us a bandage, though, and I want to make up to her, a hundred times over, for the inexcusable boorishness of this person I'm obliged to call my companion. In silence stiff as the singed leather of Bertrand's shoes we leave the diner, and drive through descending darkness which gives a melancholy beauty to the crudely-coloured houses, the stark yards with children's rusty tricycles, sagging laundry lines, dented pick-up trucks. Finally we pull up in front of the Virgin quietly possessing the concrete sea of the parking lot, halo lit for the night, but half the bulbs burnt out. I clench and unclench the steering wheel: a disastrous outing—making confession to Bertrand of all people—stupid, and dishonest too. He saw right through me—though I hope to God he doesn't have the intelligence to follow up his own deductions.

I look cautiously at Bertrand, unwilling to expose any more of myself than I've already done. But he's staring up at the toe of the Virgin; the white rose that curls like some sort of fungal growth under Her foot. On his face is a petulant, puzzled expression. I let my hands drop from the steering wheel into my lap— it's all right then, he's heard nothing, registered nothing but what he takes as my insult to his virility or his conversational charms. He stares at the Virgin's feet, and his stomach begins to growl. I tell him he'll miss supper at the cafeteria if he doesn't hurry. He seems not to hear, then nods his head in the Virgin's direction, curtly thanking me, or Her, or both of us for "the most interesting afternoon." And gets stiffly out of the car, nursing his hand, shutting the door with exaggerated care. I want to call him back, say something to patch up his *amour-propre*, but don't dare, still giddy with relief that I haven't, after all, any breach to repair in my defences. And then I laugh out loud; it's exactly as if we were lovers who've just had their first quarrel. I wait for a while in the parking lot, watching him stomp off into the spruce grove, his body awkward, indeterminate, like a small child's attempt at a straight line.

ONCE BERTRAND has disappeared behind the spruce hedge I pull into the Kwikway store to get milk, eggs, bread—invalid food— with which to make myself a supper. Gustave is behind the counter. Stella, who is working on accounts at the back of the store, looks up to nod a curt hello, then yells at Doris back in the storeroom to check on how many bottles of Minward's Liniment they've got on hand.

I've known Gustave and Stella almost forever, and they have known my grandparents, my father and mother, myself from infancy into early middle age. Gustave is as gruff and bleary with me as he is with everyone. Stella's glacial—she and I had words, once, over an affair of mutual interest. Stella keeps track of resentments as carefully as she does accounts. She hasn't relinquished this particular grudge against me, even though things never did work out the way I'd planned.

Gustave puts my purchases into a carton and shoves it across the counter. Before I can thank him and go he says, "I see you're keepin' company with little shit-face."

News cannot travel this fast—or have there been gossips posted at every parlour window along the shore? I smile. "Just playing mother, Gustave—for Père Philippe. Besides, Bertrand's not such a bad little shit-face—just homesick."

"Up at college they don' talk like that. Say he's stuck-up as a nun's cunt—don' have no time for nobody. So why you takin' care of him?"

"She likes to get them young, remember?" Stella's voice, words she's stored up in the deep-freeze along with the Fudgsicles and Sara Lees.

I pick up my carton, hold it tight against me and smile again at Gustave, as if Stella had never spoken. "I wouldn't stay up nights worrying if I were you, Gustave. I can hold my own against a *Français de France* any day. What have you got against him, anyway—he doesn't owe you money, does he?''

Gustave splits his face into a grin. He and Stella own, among other things, the Belle Acadie Campground up the road, Wagner's Bakery, Wagner's Bed and Breakfast, and the franchise on the Kwikway store. No one in the township is behind more than a week in their accounts with the Wagners—Gustave is six foot three, with a bull neck and hands that could rip a frozen turkey in two; his brother is said to be a master barn-burner.

I'm careful to let Stella see how casually I leave the store, stopping to say hello to Mariette, asking her to remind her mother to come and clean house for me tomorrow, and exchanging a few words with Soeur Marie, who has come in to buy a package of Fisherman's Friend throat lozenges. But when I climb back into the Volkswagen, I feel as conspicuous as if the car bore crêpe paper streamers and a Just Married sign on its rear window. You can no more keep something private in Spruce Harbour than you can keep a lobster from turning scarlet once it's boiling in the pot. *Tant pis*. That it's my job to shepherd Bertrand through this year's fit of melancholia, that I've just told him off, probably the first time in his life someone has told him a truth or two about himself—that won't matter. I'll bet anything that Delbert knows and that the next time I walk into the post office he'll put me through a catechism. Good God, dear God—it's not as though I didn't know the way this land lies.

And even if I never give Bertrand the time of day again, they'll only say—Stella and her cronies—that we're meeting secretly in the library or the woods behind the loony house. Drastic measures—I'll have to make a public show of hospitality, invite him to my house, sit us down in front of the parlour windows so that everyone can see us doing nothing. And coax him out of his depression at the same time, let him talk the paper off the walls— and not say a word. Offer him the use of my stereo and records, my library—but thankfully not my liquor cabinet; my confidential ear, the reassuring mirrors of my eyes: offer them with the same assurance that desert saints braved the multi-coloured demons and winged scorpions sent by a God half gambler, half voyeur. Because I'll be on safe ground, the four walls of home a guardian angel's wings around me. And even if I do give him a random nudge or shove—just to try and shake him up a bit, split his shell, tease him out—he's from so far away, there'll be no one to call me to account. He'll be gone in a year's time, and won't be back. Not he.

I WILL MAKE something out of this remnant of the evening, even if only a hood for the disasters of the day. I will start with a supper of scrambled eggs and toast—nursery fare, remedied by two double Scotches. I leave the dishes for Delima to do tomorrow morning, put the Goldberg variations on the stereo, and listen to Gould talking to himself, talking with the music his hands seem to call, not press out of the keys, until the record stops, silence scratching into its place. Gould plays the way I never dreamed I could; I never had the courage to try, for all my mother's loving lessons, exhortations. Mother, who taught me Neapolitan sixths when I was hardly ready for Baa Baa Black Sheep, had conceived me a prodigy before I turned eight. Instead of bedtime stories she would tell me all about that grand future in which I would return to England, study, establish a career which this time neither war nor marriage—which the worse calamity?—could ruin. "Keep yourself free, don't let them tie you down. Go away, get out of here—go for my sake, for me."

"If you've decided you must go abroad, then go. How can I stop you?" My father, who'd shoved me off to convent school when my mother died, expected me to come back for him grownup, in her guise, making up for her absence. Paying my way to London and my conservatory fees, giving me a living and travel allowance—this was his way of cancelling the guilt he felt over my mother's death, a death that had begun with her voyage out from England. It was also his way of telling me that I couldn't make it on my own, that the very idea of my having a musical career was nothing more than a dead woman's whim, worth humouring for however long it took me to learn the whole chain of mistakes by heart. The way he'd learned his—that in bringing my mother here he had secured for himself another kind of battleground than the one he'd fled at war's end.

Hinx, minx, the old witch winks / The fat begins to fry. A rhyme in the Mother Goose my mother brought out from England along with the volume of Rilke. My father supplied her with her most potent weapon, the piano she used to fill the space between shouting and silence. *Nobody home but Jumping Joan/Father, mother and I.* It should have been enough for them. I should have been enough, the perpetual hostage, a prisoner exchanged again and again until I felt myself split in two, a line of regular gashes from my skull to my feet. I thought the holes would seal themselves up once I got away, but they were always there, father and mother, with their knives out, the knives of their love for me and hate for each other.

Not love, not hate, no name so simple for what they kept between them. If only it could have been one or the other, straight, black lines, white spaces. But it was all confused, spilling over; they kept changing sides, calling truces, meeting in no man's land and trying all over again. For the child who was to have made it all right: a son for him so that she could keep me for herself, make me into her self, the one who'd never got caught by a soldier, never left England, never taken up with strangers. I should have been enough for them. I kept dividing myself, a mirror silvered on both sides, for whatever they wanted to see. And it was never enough. She told me, "Look out for yourself, no one else will. Don't let anyone pull you down—don't you see what it's done to me?" Big with the children who could never get born: complications, my father said, complications, though he was out at all hours pulling babies out of women no stronger looking than my mother; though he'd come home long enough to put death inside her, death in five or six or seven month instalments, till the last one of all, the one she would have carried to term if her labour hadn't killed her. She refused to go to hospital; she refused any other doctor but my father; she refused to give him the sons he wanted but she would never turn him away, never refuse the savage speech of their nights together.

Stick, stock, stone dead/Blind man can't see. There is nothing to be made of this evening, only an end. I try all the doors, rattling the bolts to make sure they still hold. I turn off the silent stereo, extinguish the lights and climb the stairs to my room, quickly, so I don't have time even to look at the locked door across the landing. *Every knave must have a slave.* I fall into bed, but not to sleep. I am swimming round and round, as if dreams were too shallow a pool to drown in. *Hinx, minx, the old witch winks.* Sitting up against the pillows, the little lamp on the night table glowing, I keep a novel in my hands to shove the silly nursery rhyme out my head. But my eyes are on another text, the Rilke I lent to Bertrand, the only book on which my parents' names are scrawled together over the flyleaf, in ink faded the colour of dried blood.

> Try to raise up the sunken feelings of this enormous past. . . . your solitude will expand and become a place where you can live in the twilight, where the noise of other people passes by, far in the distance.

The first thing I did when I came back to this house was to lock up their room. I left it just as it was, with their wedding photograph still on the dresser across from the bed. Framed in eternally tarnished silver, the pair of them ride from a flint-walked church on a gun carriage borrowed for the occasion. I am hidden discreetly under the curtain material she used for a dress, behind the bouquet of roses, blood-red even in the black-and-white of a wartime photograph. Their faces are taut, too keenly focussed, as if they knew even then what their marriage would be like: the rationing of words and embraces, with whole mine-fields to be covered between breakfast and dinner. I remember there was a photograph of them both on the piano bench downstairs, with me between them like an ineffectual white flag. My father must have put it away after my mother died and I left his house—I've never been able to find it. Besides, I can never remember being with them both, together. I was either her prisoner at the piano I hated to play, or else held up in my father's arms to look at the night sky whose patterns I only pretended to see. I ended up trying to do both—playing her music, staring up at his stars because I couldn't bear to lose either of them, and it seemed the only way to hold them, however hurtfully, together.

The lies I told Bertrand this afternoon—really, I'd be quite ashamed of myself if I thought he'd listened to me at all. Conceived in a bomb shelter—metaphorically, perhaps. At least it seemed plausible at that time in my life when it was important for me to figure everything out, account for every moment of the life I couldn't remember. They would tell me nothing—except that her people didn't approve of the match any more than his did. She always said she would never go back, that she had no intention of tripping round London like some gormless tourist, clutching the return half of her ticket to her breast. But where she'd lived before London I never knew—any more than I knew what he saw when he went into the German camps. I have seen photographs, of course, even movie reels, but they don't connect with him— what he was like before he saw the camps, and afterwards, when he came back to us.

There was that bond between them at least, a white conspiracy of silence which I can barely scribble over. I have memories of a garden in Suffolk, not the flowers but the grass under the blanket where she put me down to sleep. I remember waking up beside her in the cabin we shared with three other war brides and their children; hearing the slosh of water over the porthole and suddenly believing what the woman in the upper bunk was saying—that we'd never reach land but just sail right over the edge of the earth. So that I clutched at my mother's arm, shaking her out of her two hours' rest from the seasickness that had kept her up all night, retching into the basin, her face moss-green like her dressing gown. The only other thing I remember of the voyage is the end: my grandmother meeting us at the docks in Halifax, dressed all in black, as if my father had been killed, not married in action.

If he had been there to meet us, would it have made any difference? It seemed years and years before he did join us in this white box of a house, its furniture draped in mothy sheets, damp tarnishing the mirrors and foxing the prints on the walls. My grandmother had moved her clothes and crucifix out—she went to live with the nuns in the convent house at Salmon River, saying she'd come back for one thing—the birth of her grandson. Those words I do remember, and my mother's face, blank as a dust sheet as the old woman left the house. "Never give anything away, Claire, never let them see what you feel—and soon you'll be perfectly safe; you won't feel anything." Did she say it then or a year later when, a week after starting school, I stalked out of the playground one afternoon and slowly, deliberately, stomped all the way home? Because they'd begun to taunt me again about my accent, my clothes, my mother who would not leave the house but sulked inside, the English bitch.

I told Bertrand that my parents stayed here because it was the only safe place they knew. Perhaps it was. But it was also the best territory on which to wage their war: nothing and no one inter-fered, not even the children she couldn't bring to term, that he couldn't deliver. She was pregnant when she died. I was old enough to notice her belly thickening, the awkwardness with which she sat at the piano, how tired she was, impatient with the false notes I played, the theory I couldn't understand. And how she would stiffen when my father came into the room where the piano was, telling her to go and rest—and to leave me be. She would put me through another half hour of Czerny exercises, sight reading, dominant sevenths—and then, putting out her hand to silence my playing, she would take over the keyboard, homing to it, as if it were the one thing she could embrace openly, pas-sionately. And she would play not Beethoven or Schumann but Bartok, Schönberg: a music of naked wires, slivers of glass through my ears.

After she died he never had the piano tuned—I came home from school that first summer away and tried to practise, because I'd promised her I would—but I couldn't bear the sound, as if there were something spongy inside, slackening the wires and rotting the wood. And then I didn't come home at all—because my grand-mother had died and it was no longer a house for a young girl to be alone in. Not with my father, who had drunk steadily for three days after my mother's funeral, and had never entirely sobered up, though it hadn't seemed to make a difference to his patients. They still trusted him with their treacherous hearts and decaying livers, their hands maimed in accidents on trawlers, their wombs scarred with too much childbearing. When I finally came home, too late for his funeral, too late to get and stay drunk, they told me of his kindness, his tenderness, his ministering to them at all hours. None of them said a word about my mother, or seemed to remember that I had a mother at all. Or perhaps they had simply conflated her with me—this *Anglaise d'Angleterre* with her foreign voice and clothes and manner. Staying inside her house all day, sulking, the English bitch.

You got away, at least. But how could you come back? Ah, but you see, Bertrand, I never did get away. At the beginning I thought it would help, going so far away. I hoped I could shut out the shouting and hissing and moaning from their room, from the bed they shared like the roughest kind of speech. So I took my father's money and went to London to make the career my mother never had. And I got sufficient papers and degrees to let me teach at a small Catholic college in rural Nova Scotia—nothing more. How could I listen to the music I was supposed to be playing when all I could hear was their voices arguing, urging me to do the opposite of whatever the other wanted. At the conservatory they told me I could, perhaps, become a decent accompanist—not fine, just competent, if I worked hard enough, though I'd shown no real gift for it. All that time at the conservatory I showed no gift at all, except for isolating myself from the other students and from the city itself, shutting myself up in my bedsit, pre-empting invitations to parties and concerts. Every night I would read till one or two in the morning, drinking endless cups of foul tea, trying to keep myself from the assault of dreams, images going off like mute grenades in my head. The same dreams, night after night: my mother in her coffin, the baby he couldn't get out still locked inside her, just as she is locked inside the red satin lining over the stark wood. Sweetheart roses pinned around the crucifix I refuse to kiss. My father's face like a glass smashed against a wall. And inside the coffin of my mother's body, the baby whose fists I can feel pounding to get out, pounding and hitting at me, as though it were my fault, as though I were screwing down the lid and holding tight.

My father never wrote, though he wired money regularly, once a month, to signal that he was alive still, and that I could continue my exile as long as I pleased. And then, after I had been away long enough to have made some gesture toward earning my keep, he sent a small money order enclosed in a shakily written letter. He said it was for my birthday, for a little tour of France; it was time I saw something of his ancestors' country, used the language he'd spent so much money having me acquire in Montréal. I never wrote to thank him. I intended to rip up the money order and send him the pieces. Even when I boarded the boat train for Paris I put off writing, deciding instead to send him a postcard from Mont Blanc, proving how far and how high I'd climbed since leaving the convent school to which he'd banished me.

Paris, the Loire, the *route Napoléon* to the Alps: it was the standard tour. And I did use his language, which my mother had always refused to let me speak. I had been taught by French nuns, not Québécoises; my speech was correct, formal enough that I managed not to make myself conspicuous on the trains I took. In the shabby *pensions* I pretended not to know any English and owned to a mere smatter of German, so that there was never any conversation to be made, and people left me quite alone. Until I got to Chamonix, where I had to stay for a week until the weather cleared enough to let us see Mont Blanc. And by then it was us: myself and the man who worked in the restaurant of the Hôtel Edelweiss. Not a man, a boy—he may even have been younger than Bertrand. He said he was a student at the University of Grenoble, although for all I knew, all I wanted to know, he may have been nothing more than the permanent kitchen help at a two-star hotel next to the railway station in Chamonix. Every morning we exchanged greetings as he put coffee and croissants on the soiled cloth at my table; at supper he would wait attentively as I dithered over the restricted choices offered on the cheapest menu. And on his afternoon off, when Mont Blanc was still cocooned in cloud, we met in a small town nearby, sat in an outdoor café and ate ice cream, for all the world like two children on an outing, who had stolen away from their governess. I remember I bought a huge slab of Swiss chocolate that we ate while watching an Austrian film about a farm girl named Lieselotte, who, though wooed by a baronet, remained faithful to her true love, Franzi, and his herd of Charollais. And that I rented a room for us at a hotel to which the *Guide Michelin* would not have given any stars at all.

Afterwards, he took the bus back to Chamonix and I returned by train. I packed my bags, sat in the uncomfortable chair by the writing desk, and waited till it grew light enough that I could check out of the hotel. When I bought my ticket at the railway station the clerk told me the sun was shining for the first time in two weeks, that I had a good five hours' wait before my train would pull in, and that I could easily take the cable car up Mont Blanc and be back in time to board the train for Paris. I wanted to tell him that I had no head for heights, but I couldn't find the right words.

In the glass cage, spinning, wheeling over rocks and tree tops, I clasped my hands tightly, containing all that had happened, everything that would not. I wore a short white dress that left my arms and legs bare. I'd forgotten a sweater or even a pair of socks, neglecting the warning signs at the booth where I bought my ticket to go up. The cable car was full, even that early in the morning: Italians, Germans, Swiss, British, Japanese. And a newlywed couple; she had her head buried in her husband's chest as the car bumped and swung past the midway station. All the way up he made comforting sounds, as though she were a baby he were holding against his shoulder, soothing to sleep. It hadn't taken long. We had made no noise. I'd thought that only this kind of silence would finally drown out their voices, distance them. Afterwards, I hadn't let him kiss me. I told him to get out, go away, leave me alone. And all the time I whispered. I was so careful not to make any noise. But I heard them all the same; you couldn't help hearing the shouts and moans from across the hall—it was a very cheap hotel.

The little bride began to cry; she was frightened to death, and her husband torn between tenderness and embarrassment. I didn't catch sight of her face as we left the car and climbed the metal stairs up to the terrace. No one stopped me from going up, though you needed trousers, a parka, mittens. Not a word, either of endearment or contempt, not even the noise of scissors cutting a scrap of silk. *Every knave must have a slave.* The mountains looked brutal under their scarves of snow; my eyes ached with the brightness. It wasn't the cold but my eyes that made me leave the terrace for the restaurant, where I managed to drink half a cup of black coffee before spilling the rest down my absurdly short, absurdly white dress. There was no time to change before the train pulled into the station. I rode all the way to Paris with a cardigan wrapped as tightly as a bandage around me, and I left the dress in the waste paper basket of my Paris hotel room before taking the train to Dover. When I finally got back to London I found the telegram that had been shoved under my door the day after I left for France, the telegram stating the reason of my father's death, and the time of his funeral. And all I could do was throw out the postcard of Mont Blanc that I had bought, but never sent, my last day in Chamonix.

I went away, Bertrand, because my mother's death forced me to leave my father. I came back because my father's death freed me to leave my mother's imagined London; my own failure at the conservatory and at that poor hotel in the little town near Chamonix. You see, I had come into my inheritance, a house that was at last my own. It wasn't till I came back that I learned how to silence their voices, to make them as distant as the green valley floor had been from the cable car jerking its way up Mont Blanc. With the simple turning of a key in a lock, with the building of walls and fences round me, I banished all their shouting and silences.

And I discovered my true vocation, which has nothing to do with music, though I do that well enough, for here. I've discovered that my real gift is for talking to myself, refusing to let myself be spoken by anyone else. I have perfected the discipline required to keep my true self apart and alone, absent from the voice and face and eyes of the Claire whom you see at the college, who lends you a volume of Rilke, and takes you for country drives. If there have been breaches in the wall, I've easily repaired the damage. And besides, haven't I needed to test my defences against any assailants half-way worthy of them? My protégés. But I have let no one inside, no one, no matter what Stella hints, or Delima says. No matter what anyone may think, you are quite safe with me, as safe as I am with you. All that other business is nothing but gossip and stories. I have locked their door, I am home free. The dreams I once had are stick, stock, stone dead: nobody's home but me.

HECTOR COMES IN to get the mail. There are two nuclei of information in Spruce Harbour: Wagner's Kwikway store, and the Post Office. At Wagner's you'll get bright slashes of gossip, like the plastic streamers kids attach to the handlebars of their bikes to flare out in the wind as they pedal fast and faster. Whose truck was parked in front of whose house till what hour last night. Who got picked up for trafficking in the back parking lot of the Social Club at three in the morning. The reasons it couldn't have been an act of God when Joe à Willie's barn burned down last month. Why Calixte Deveau's wife was limping, wearing long-sleeved shirts and trousers right down to the ankle, even though it was hot enough for T-shirts and shorts. Just what kind of a private beach resort it was to which the Thimot boy went down each summer.

News at the Post Office is of a more decorous sort: indirect, yet often more substantial. Delbert has been postmaster at Spruce Harbour for twenty years—he knows who gets welfare cheques and when, who can never pay their electricity or phone bills on time, the number and quality of items anyone can afford to order from the catalogue each month. And, of course, how many and what kind of letters find their way into the metal boxes to which all but the poorest of the one hundred and sixty families of Spruce Harbour possess a key, but to which Delbert owns *carte blanche*. No one has ever, could ever accuse him of opening a sealed letter—postcards, of course, are fair game—but Delbert has twenty years' experience in his fingertips: knows just by the look of the handwriting on the envelope whether trouble is brewing for the recipient; can predict who will be coming or going over the next few months just by the disposition of the letters' stamps or postmarks. When, for example, Hector had been deciding whether to go away to Montréal or Moncton for his post-graduate degree, sending off all those letters to this university, that professor, and a host of registrars, Delbert had known before Hector's own parents that they'd soon be losing their boy. And when Claire Saulnier began to receive all those thick letters from Hector in Montréal, Delbert knew better than anyone else just how great a role Claire had played in Hector's leaving Spruce Harbour, if not in his coming back.

Delbert waves through the glass partition at Hector who is turning the key to his metal mailbox. As he pulls out the wad of coupons, ads, free offers and bills he sees Delbert's big, bland, pear-shaped face like an apparition at the open end of the box.

"So how are you, Hector?" Delbert calls out in his slow, faintly melancholy postmaster's voice, aware of the dignity and responsibilities demanded by his calling.

"That's good, Hector. I'm fine too, thank you." Delbert's greetings and responses, even his observations on the weather, are invariably neutral, unimpassioned; if you were to enter the post office with water sluicing off your coat, glasses fogged, shoes drowned, Delbert would look up from the counter at which he is checking the "return to sender" or "paid" stamps and call out, "It's raining. It sure is raining out there. And how are you today?" If the answer should simply be, "Wet," Delbert will consider it an unwarrantable act of sarcasm and be twice as slow as usual in weighing your letters or pasting on the stamps before giving you your change.

Hector, before he went off to Montréal, had often goaded

Delbert into spectacular displays of foot-dragging—it had once taken him fifteen minutes to post a letter to Moncton. Delbert has ways of putting down the stamps he is licking for you to say a desultory hello to deaf Madame Comeau, or to allow the widow from the old age home down the road to select an attractive assortment of one-penny stamps as a birthday present for her grandchild. You do not lick your own stamps in Delbert's post office—nor do you slap down the exact amount for the postage and walk out—not if you want to dispatch or to receive your mail without undue delay. You wait until Delbert has asked how you are, commented on the rain or snow or fog or wind out of doors; carefully torn out, along the beautifully perforated lines, the required number of stamps; licked them all and rubbed them into place; till he has done his calculations on a precariously hung roll of white paper, asked you to check his addition and then carefully, cautiously, counted out the coins you've laid down—and given you your change.

Since coming back to Spruce Harbour, Hector has tried to allow himself the customary fifteen minutes that visits to the almost-empty post office require, sometimes stretching out the ritual of sending letters just for the pleasure and discipline of Delbert's company. For the first year of his return to Spruce Harbour, Delbert put Hector through a daily catechism.

"You going to be staying for a little while, Hector?"

"Yes, Delbert. I'm home for good this time."

"That's nice. Your family, they will be very happy. You going to be staying till Christmas—it's a nice time for families to be together, Christmas."

"I'm not going to be anywhere else, Delbert. I'm not leaving Spruce Harbour any more. I'm not going back to Montréal."

"Yeah, your mother and father, they're going to be glad to have you home, even if it's just for a little while. Do you like it in Montréal?"

"Too big for me, Delbert—that's why I'm home for good."

"I've never been to Montréal. All those tall buildings. I've seen them on the postcards you used to send home. Imagine Delbert standing there, in front of one of those tall buildings. Well, maybe one day I'll go—on a bus tour. Come and visit you.''

Throughout his second year at home, Hector had been questioned, in Delbert's slow and swaying interrogational style, as to when he was going to settle down.

''Your mother and father, they'll be real happy to see you marry a nice girl and start a family. Yes, it's a nice thing to see young people getting married, having children.'' Delbert always swivelled his eyes to the photo of the Queen on the opposite wall as he said this: the Queen at a perpetually matronly forty, the regal bosom swelling under the weight of medals, ribbons, decorations, orders pinned there. Delbert adores the Queen, a mother of four healthy children, a dutiful wife, a stern but reassuring profile on the stamps he licks and posts off every day.

Before Hector could wave his hand and slip away, Delbert would fix him with his sadly solicitous, wall-eyed stare. ''Maybe you got a nice girlfriend back in Montréal?''

''No, Delbert—at least not a nice—no girlfriend, I mean.''

''Claire Saulnier—you wrote her a lot of letters while you were away. You see much of her now, Hector?''

''Not much. Looks like rain. We'll be getting that storm from New Brunswick. So long, Delbert.'' And Hector would make his escape, reflecting as he drove off in his middle-aged truck, on the benevolence of the postmaster's inquiries, the sheer absence of malice in his out-turned eyes and his deliberative, yet plaintive voice. Delbert has five grown children, is a widower and lives in a small frame house on the station road. Besides his own children, he has sisters and brothers, nieces and nephews, aunts and uncles he calls up on the post office telephone after work, gleaning grains of information to be used in his catechisms of villagers like Hector—people he's watched grow up from scarved, snow-suited sausages into lanky schoolkids, wild adolescents, and then respectable, pot-bellied married men and women. And besides, Hector's mother is a second cousin by marriage of Delbert's—he has a special interest in Hector's well-being, even if Stella did marry Gustave Wagner, whose profanity and crudeness of manner are a source of continual melancholy headshaking to Delbert.

Now, starting into the third year of his return, firmly if

ingloriously settled in Spruce Harbour, living in an apartment he's
fixed up at the back of his parents' Kwikway store, dancing with
all the girls on Friday and Saturday nights at the Fish and Game
Club, married to none, Hector has become the fixed object of
Delbert's attentions.

"Not married yet, Hector."

"Not yet, Delbert. All the pretty ones get snapped up by the
kids coming out of high school. Maybe I should shave off my
beard—I guess I can't compete."

"Not just pretty, Hector. You want a good girl. I've seen some
sad things—but you'll be all right if you get yourself a nice girl.
You don't see much of Dr. Saulnier's daughter?"

"No, Delbert. I fix the sewage system at the college—she
teaches music. We don't see each other."

" 'Cause she's a good woman—quiet, respectable, well-estab-
lished. I know she's older, a bit, than you. I think, maybe she's
a little shy. You know, my Rita, she was seven years older than
me, and we were very happy together. Very happy, Hector. Good
kids, a nice home she made for me. It's sad to see two nice young
people all by themselves."

"I'm not lonely, Delbert."

"Maybe you should go and see her, Hector. Call on her, maybe
Saturday night. Go to the store and get some chocolates—ladies
like chocolate. Sit with her, talk to her. You wrote each other so
many letters when you were away—big letters. She's maybe five,
maybe six years older than you?"

"It doesn't matter, but it's more like nine or ten."

"She's the kind of woman it doesn't show." Behind his spectacles, Delbert's eyes are moist with conviction. "You know,
Hector, that kind of small woman—skinny—they don't let go the
way the big ones do. I think maybe it's eight, nine years between
you? A woman, she needs children to make her happy. My Rita,
she had our last kid when she was forty-six. Nice, healthy baby—
you know our Joey? He's never been a problem—"

"Sure, I know Joey. Look, Delbert, how much do I owe you
for this parcel? I want it to go special delivery to Moncton."

Delbert moves ponderously over to the drawer in which he

keeps the red and blue and green labels, selects a red one, and then another and finally another, returns to Hector's parcel and begins contemplatively to lick the labels, interrupting himself every so often to address Hector.

"The doctor, he was a fine man, and you couldn't find a better doctor. No, you can ask Eddie Blinn or Wayne Robichaud or even Louis à Pierre over to Trout River whether Doctor Saulnier wouldn't come to see you even if you called him in the middle of the night. When Jeanette Gaudet's husband had a heart attack Wednesday three o'clock in the morning—"

"I need that parcel to get to Moncton as quickly as possible, Delbert."

"Pick-up's not for half an hour yet. I was saying about the doctor—he was a fine man, even if maybe he had his problems at the end there, but he never let that stop him being the best doctor on the whole French Shore. So maybe you should call on Claire Saulnier this Saturday night, Hector. Those dances you go to out at the Fish and Game—they're not the nicest girls there, you know? You take them back to your place after the dance— things happen, you don't want to make a mistake and have to get married to a girl you couldn't respect. I've seen it happen—oh, it's a sad thing, Hector. Claire, she's a lady, and her mother was a lady, whatever else you could say about her. Not that I did, I always told Rita, 'We can't judge strangers, especially from *outre-mer*.' Three dollars forty-five cents, Hector. You don't want insurance? Okay, then. But try Saturday night—try chocolate."

IN HECTOR'S MAIL today there is, among the usual assortment of flyers and coupons, a notice that he has received a package— Delbert placed the notice on top of the pile of junk mail so that Hector wouldn't, by mistake, throw it out with the rest. The package isn't anything private—Delbert knows this by the typing on the oversize envelope, the embossed return address: *Canadian Philosophical Journal*. He hands it over to Hector, reluctantly yet quickly, as if the envelope contained some sophisticated sort of explosive. When Hector comes back in a month or so with a similarly bulky envelope to be weighed and measured and embellished with a whole fresco of stamps to be carefully dislodged from their perforations, licked, and pasted down, Delbert will be equally cautious and protective. For now that Hector has been back in Spruce Harbour for two years, Delbert has reclaimed him as a prodigal son, and detects a whiff of rival fatted calf in letters sent from foreign parts.

Once or twice in the first year of his return, Hector had received, under Delbert's wistfully omniscient eye, letters addressed by an obviously female hand, dispatched from an apartment in Notre Dame de Grâce in Montréal. The innocence of the address did not deceive Delbert—he saw in the creaminess of the paper, the sheer abandonment of the handwriting—tilted, extravagantly looped, even the commas sensual—a barbed hook to fish Hector from the placid pond to which he'd returned just when everyone had consigned him to the belly of the whale. Delbert needn't have worried—Hector never delivered to him any envelope addressed to Notre Dame de Grâce. And when the letters in their expensive cream-coloured envelopes stopped coming, Delbert interpreted this as a sign that God and Hector between them had conspired to ease a weight from the postmaster's already over-burdened shoulders.

As for the large, buff-coloured envelopes such as he'd just received, had Hector believed that an explanation of these would soothe Delbert and not trigger off another round of laments and questions, he would have explained that, as a single concession to the urban-intellectual world he had abandoned, as a necessary exception to the firmest of rules, he remained in touch with a friend he'd met in graduate school in Montréal, a woman who now edited a journal to which Hector contributed book reviews. He didn't consider his pieces to be particularly important—he believed the editor accepted them just for the novelty of having a "Hector Wagner, Handyman, Collège Sacré Coeur, Spruce Harbour" listed among the contributors.

Almost no one in the community knew exactly what he had been studying off in Montréal—to his parents, it had been as shameful, as catastrophic to have their only son go off to read philosophy as it would have been to have him do ballet. There had been chairs broken when Gustave discovered that the heir apparent to Wagner's Kwikway and the Belle Acadie Tent and Trailer Park had decided to study the love of wisdom when he could have taken a commerce degree after his Bachelor's at Sacré Coeur. Hector had no desire to be talked about as that brown-nosed Wagner kid who'd skipped grades at school, swept up every prize at Sacré Coeur, and then won a big scholarship to go study in Montréal, only to come home after five years with nothing to show for it. Come home to be handyman at the college and screw the less attractive girls on Saturday nights in a one-room apartment back of Wagner's store.

He climbs into the pick-up truck, which he has on permanent loan from the store. WAGNER'S KWIKWAY is painted on its doors; Gustave thinks it might as well sit in the college parking lot, doing a bit of free advertising, instead of rusting out back of the store. That way even the students would see the sign and stop by Wagner's instead of going all the way to Falmouth to the plaza supermarket to pick up useless fancy food: wholegrain bread, bean sprouts, kiwi fruit. Anything that comes in a tin, Wagner's sells—corned beef, Campbell's soup, sardines—and good fresh meat besides. Gustave's brother regularly slaughters beef cattle and pigs for the Kwikway meat counter. And you'll find cucumbers and carrots, day in day out—frozen peas, ice cream, even Vicks VapoRub and a whole shelf full of cosmetic aids. Not to mention an assortment of Sheik and Ramses, extra-safe and extra-sensitive, on the shelf across from the disposable diapers.

Hector has little occasion to advertise the store at the college—he makes a habit of avoiding faculty members: the priests and nuns who'd once taught him, and who interpret as spiritual pride his refusal to join them on staff; the snotty Québécois for whom the Acadians were a francophone version of Newfoundlanders. Or the occasional decent, elderly professor with whom, if Hector ever spent an hour talking in the faculty room, battles over religion and politics would erupt as surely as worms pop out of the earth after spring rain. As for Claire—she'd made it clear to him, once he'd announced his decision to abandon his doctorate, quit Montréal and come home, that she would have nothing more to do with him. The first time he'd seen her on his return it had been as if she'd had a sign reading TRESPASSERS WILL BE PROSECUTED— VICIOUS DOG—KEEP OUT posted over her face. Now she's relented sufficiently to nod at him in the corridors, had even given him a cup of instant coffee the time he'd come into her office to fix the broken radiator, but she still hasn't broken a silence like sheets of glass piled thick between them. Perhaps it was best this way. At any rate, they'd said all there was to be said between them in their last letters, the ones over whose comings and goings Delbert had so conscientiously presided.

So he didn't know what she thought of his decision not to take the teaching job at Sacré Coeur which Père Philippe had so enthusiastically tendered—even without his doctorate, Hector would be one of the best-qualified teachers on staff—or of his refusal to take over the Kwikway store, marry the nicest of Angèles, Simones or Louisettes, and found his own dynasty. She must have heard the gossip that, like wood ticks in spring, burrowed under everyone's skin to suck out as much juice as was going. Gustave was officially disinheriting Hector, handing the business interests over to his oldest girl, Nadine, who had married Steve Comeau— not exactly a philosopher, as Gustave took pleasure in pointing out, but smart enough to beat the competition. No one knew that Gustave was doing all this on the advice of his son, who felt only profound relief at his father's actions, and was not about to burn down any barns in protest. All the same, Hector felt Claire should at least have inferred all this and somehow signalled her approval of his integrity. Since she believed that his sole aim in life was to ruin every chance at success Fate threw in his way, at least he was doing something right.

He parks his truck in the only available spot—under Claire's window—and takes the back way into the college. His office is in the basement, next door to the combined furnace and laundry room. Tacked up on the door he finds a note from the receptionist at the front office: "Co-opérant complains about fuses in Loony House. Wants someone to come right over to check things out."

IT'S THE SMALL house between the decayed apple orchard and St. Alphonse Church—the house which once was crammed with the severely retarded and mildly schizoid, the children who never learned to talk or kiss their parents, but who spent their hours staring into lightbulbs and through closed doors. Now the loonies, as Spruce Harbour not unaffectionately calls them, are in the psychiatric wing of Falmouth Hospital, and the house has been repaired, cleaned and painted under Hector's supervision for the arrival of Bertrand France, the protégé of Père Philippe. Of course the house was much too large for one person, but it was felt that the co-opérant couldn't simply be thrown into one of the residences. As there was a severe shortage of rental accommodation in the area, and as this particular co-opérant insisted on having a photographic studio set up for him, the college would just have to endure the expense of heating a whole house for the exclusive use of the *Français de France*.

Hector, taking the short cut through a neglected field, stops halfway to the house and looks around him. Early autumn—on the withered trees a few apples show: scarlet, mottled with fungus or the attacks of parasites, but somehow beautiful as they possess their boughs, defying gravity and time. In the alders and spruce, goldfinches still flicker. Hector has trampled down wild asters, clumps of them like fallen stars: dusky purple, like daisies that have lost innocence. Small, simple, inconspicuous things—their courage and beauty in growing here where no one except those who've trained their eyes to look down can glimpse them. If it weren't for the man waiting in the doorway of the house, tapping his toe with impatience, Hector would simply take off through the field into the woods behind the college—spend the day tramping round, looking at things. Why else had he come back from Montréal if not for this?

But the man is calling out to him. Hector takes his time in reaching him, and does not appear to be listening as the man goes on about the lights.

"They flicker on and off at the most inconvenient times. I thought it might be dangerous—God knows how old the wiring in this place is; it would go up like straw if something went wrong, got overheated—do you think you should check the fuses?''

In his broadest *acadien* the handyman replies, ''Yeah, I'll check duh fuses, if ya want. I guess dey're down in duh cellar?''

Bertrand, hands in pockets, follows Hector down the cellar steps; there's no railing and the planks are steeply spaced, but it is a point of honour with him not to appear as though he's afraid of losing his footing. He negotiates the steps and watches the handyman fiddling with the fuses—taking one out, replacing it with a new one he's extracted from the pocket of his overalls. There are no bottles of wine in this cellar, no treasure from rum-running days bricked-up in the chimney, just rusted garden tools propped up precariously against the walls, and cobwebs filming all the window sills. Hector is silent as he works; Bertrand says nothing, but it's obvious he has a case of cabin fever, wants badly to hear the sound of his own voice talking to someone other than himself.

''Finished,'' Hector announces. ''Won't have no more prob-lems now. Wirin's okay—need ta be changed in five years' time, maybe.'' He turns in the direction of the stairs and makes his way up, but before he reaches the landing he hears a curse and a protracted noise of falling. Turning round, he finds Bertrand on his corduroy ass at the bottom of the stairs, in a cloud of the loose dirt which makes up the cellar floor.

Five minutes later Bertrand is sitting in a chair the handyman has drawn up for him—the handyman who has also helped him up the stairs, examined his arm to make sure it is a bruise and not a break, brushed him off and fetched him a glass of water from what has become the darkroom sink. For all of this, Bertrand, pale and furious at the premeditated treachery of things, has uttered a curt ''Merci.'' And Hector, more amused than con-cerned, lets slip, ''Think nothing of it. You know—that's the first time I've ever seen anyone fall up a flight of stairs.'' But he doesn't laugh, not out of concern for Bertrand's *amour-propre*, but because of the astonished look on the co-opérant's face, aston-ishment caused by the fact that this glorified janitor who had previously made all his remarks in a nasal, anglicized Acadian—

Allons checkez le fuse—has just addressed him in perfectly standard French.

"Where did you learn to speak like that?" Bertrand cries, rubbing his elbow and looking up at the dark, bearded man in the mechanic's overalls and plastic baseball cap.

Hector waits for a minute before answering. "Not at school. They made us speak English there. I had a private tutor—and then I lived in Montréal for quite a while."

"Montréal—what in the world were you doing in Montréal? I give up trying to understand you Acadians. Why in God's name did you come back here?"

"None of yer fuckin' bizniss," Hector is about to answer, but the sight of Bertrand nursing his arm, so obviously helpless—a tenant of the Loony House, acknowledged prisoner of Spruce Harbour—makes him suddenly magnanimous. He could have replied that he was up in Montréal checking fuses, but he decides this stranger can handle the truth. "I was studying," he says.

"Studying what?" Bertrand is blatantly incredulous.

"Philosophy." Hector looks as blatantly at his watch—he should be getting back to the long list of things-to-be-repaired-before-the-end-of-the-month prepared by the obsessive Père Gilbert. But Bertrand gestures with his uninjured arm to the other chair in the room, invites Hector to pull it up beside his and begins to talk so quickly, so intensively, that Hector has no choice but to listen. After all, he must assure himself that this idiot's all right; Père Philippe is as proud of his co-opérant as he is of the marble monument he erected to the college's founder. He is out to restore the fallen fortunes of Sacré Coeur by one-upping the New Brunswick competition, and he will no doubt succeed, for behind the rosy cheeks and the hair as fine as new-fallen snow is an intellect that reminds Hector of the radar screens and trawling arms with which the fishermen equip their quarter-of-a-million dollar boats.

"Philosophy? Who? Hegel, Heidegger, Wittgenstein? In Montréal? Are there any Canadian philosophers one should know about? I used to go and hear Lacan and Derrida lecture when I was an undergraduate, even though I was studying English literature. I suppose you wouldn't have heard of them? Oh, you have—

how interesting. You studied philosophy—do you play chess by any chance? I'm dying for a game. The only other person I've really talked to here doesn't play at all. Claire Saulnier—I don't suppose you know her. She's quite an unusual woman isn't she—for these parts. I read a lot of Foucault last year—it's stood me in good stead for my stay here—I honestly can't comprehend why you would have left Montréal—I'm hoping to go there during study break. I understand there's some not-bad theatre there—and cinema. I really want to get to New York, though—I'm planning that escape for Christmas. But you didn't tell me which philosophers you studied—was it for an undergraduate degree? I suppose one doesn't get into specialized work at that level—''

"I did my doctoral thesis—at least two-thirds of it—on Descartes.''

"Oh, Descartes—rationalism, yes. We're taught all that in fourth grade at home. He's rather out of fashion in France just now—I mean there's so much interest in fringe things, off the centre—all that logocentrism in Descartes is so tedious—''

"Actually, I was interested in Descartes because he was so irrational.''

"Pardon?''

"Off his head in a number of ways.'' Hector pulls from the pocket of his checked shirt a pipe and a pouch of tobacco. Suddenly it seems perfectly natural that he should be sitting here with this utter stranger, discussing his doctoral work. Perhaps it was the mention of Claire's name that makes him so defiantly at ease, as if he has to stake a claim to his identity as someone more than just the Dean of Drains at Collège Sacré Coeur. Perhaps he's nettled that while Bertrand has expressed astonishment that anyone could prefer life in Spruce Harbour to Montréal, he seems to have taken it for granted that someone who almost has a doctorate in philosophy should earn a living as a glorified janitor.

"Did you know,'' Hector continues, "that the arch-rationalist whom you studied in grade school was a Rosicrucian—was accused of being a magus who could make himself invisible—and that to refute those charges he paraded round the streets of Paris, just letting himself be seen? And that he dreamt of melons?''

"Melons? But that's—"

"And whirlwinds."

"Ridiculous."

"Exactly. It wasn't till I discovered just how irrational Descartes could be that I decided it would be no great contribution to the sum of human knowledge to write another dissertation on Mr. Cogito. My supervisor didn't approve of me bringing in the melons, you see. Anyway, I gave up my doctoral work and came home. Mostly because there was no great prospect of my getting a job teaching philosophy afterwards—commerce professors are more in demand these days. At least I've got a job here that pays my keep—the alternative would have been teaching one extension course at the Université de Montréal and waiting on tables—which is a tough business in that city. You don't need much to live on here, if you're handy at hunting, digging clams—"

"Digging clams?" Bertrand says the words with an equal mix of incredulity and apprehension, as if Hector is going to seize him by his injured arm, drag him out to the sandflats, and set him to work with a pitchfork.

"Yes, clams. They're a specialty round here—you can find them big as soup plates in some places. Hasn't Claire fed you a supper of fried clams yet? As a matter of fact, I do know Miss Saulnier; she tried to teach me piano once. And yes, I do play chess." Hector gets up from his chair, and though he is not a tall man, no more than five foot eight, he seems to tower over Bertrand. "And if you want to know the real reason I didn't stay on in Montréal, it's because I kept meeting *Anglais* who insisted on pronouncing the 'H' in Hector. Not much future for any philosopher named Hector Wagner, is there?"

Bertrand rises, too. Hector has stopped on the threshold. He's looking at a number of photographs tacked up on the wall beside the door, photographs he hadn't noticed on entering the house, so insistent had Bertrand been about checking the fuses. Black and white: shots of a young girl, and of a woman and a small child—except it seems to be the same model in each of the prints. She looks familiar to Hector—but the chasteness of her pose—madonna, *jeune fille en fleur*—he can't place at all. He stares at the photographs for a long time, so long that he becomes aware of the verbal pressure behind Bertrand's silence: "Well—aren't you going to tell me how good they are?" And they *were* good— too good. It made him feel uneasy, too much like a *voyeur*, and he suddenly resented the fact of Bertrand's having discovered something in Spruce Harbour that he'd never noticed—this young girl, whoever she was.

"That's not bad at all—so you're a photographer, Bertrand? Nice to have a hobby to pass the time. Listen, we can have a game of chess any time I'm free—I'll bring my set to the college. My office is in the basement, next to the furnace room."

"I'll drop in some time. I'm rather tied up at the moment—my little hobby, as you call it, makes rather pressing demands. And I've all that wretched course preparation to do. Plus I've promised Claire to come to dinner at her house—isn't it extraordinary you should know her."

"I'd better warn you—my chess is more than a little rusty."

"Oh, that doesn't matter—one can learn something playing with even the poorest player. Goodbye, then, Hector—. Your last name?"

"Wagner—like the Kwikway store."

"Very good."

"So long."

As he leaves the house and makes his way through the asters, the goldfinches, the crimson rosehips grating on the metallic-blue sky, Hector realizes that Père Philippe's co-opérant hadn't even bothered to introduce himself. But then, he reflects, there's no more need for Bertrand France to pronounce his name than there'd be for Jesus Christ or the Blessed Virgin to do so, should they ever decide to climb down from their white-washed *calvaire* over in the cemetery and show themselves to the faithful. Bertrand was just as unmistakable and familiar a figure to the people of Spruce Harbour; perhaps, after his departure, they'd put up a statue of him in the parking lot or in the spruce grove behind the Loony House, immortalizing in bronze or plaster the spectacles and bow tie, the cashmere sweaters and Italian shoes of the *Français de France* who'd so miraculously descended to them.

ULYSSE BELLIVEAU and Le Grou Thyme Band are on at the Fish and Game Club this Friday night. Hector doesn't show up till late—there'd been an emergency at the college. The female students had been locked out of their residences, since the men had nailed the doors shut after breaking in and stealing all the shower curtains which they'd then draped over the trees at the front of the college, right next to the granite tablet proclaiming "Collège Sacré Coeur, founded by the Nudist Fathers, 1899." (Restoring the vandalized lettering was one of Hector's more urgent tasks.) After Hector had drawn the nails from the doors and removed the shower curtains to their proper places, he'd gone back to his parents' house, eaten the rappie pie and clams and Jello his mother had been saving for him since five-thirty, watched part of the hockey game with his brother-in-law, read a bedtime story to a niece whose parents had gone to a movie in Falmouth, and then left for the Fish and Game with his youngest sister, Aline.

It had been almost pleasant at his parents' house—his mother hadn't expressed verbal disapproval of the fact that Hector, at twenty-nine, still had no wife of his own to make him rappie pie; his father hadn't been home, and little Nicole had not insisted that he read her, word for word, *The Adventures of Huey, Dewey and Louie*, but had let him tell her a fairy tale about the goose that laid the golden egg—a story that was not only more satisfying than the Disney, but a good deal shorter. If it hadn't been for the fact that his mother, in requesting he take Aline with him to the Fish and Game, had thereby committed him to bringing her back at a decent hour—and alone, without any chippie keeping him company in the front seat—Hector would have had nothing but staunchly filial feelings in his heart as he wheeled down the driveway.

As it turned out, Aline decided halfway there that she had a headache and wanted to be dropped off at her Aunt Régine's house—Aunt Régine is only four years older than her niece, and with her husband on an oil rig somewhere off the coast of New-foundland, she needs the right kind of company. Having made the detour and waited to be sure Aline phoned home to explain the situation, Hector climbs back into the truck and drives off the main highway along devious gravel roads until he comes to the Fish and Game. The band is playing—he can feel tinny reverberations in the whorls of his inner ear even before he gets to the porch of the club. Inside, men of forty are playing pool in the corners, while eighteen-year-old boys smoke up in the washroom. The one decent Québécois at Sacré Coeur is arguing politics in a fog of cigarette smoke with three fishermen from La Butte, and assorted couples are drinking at plywood tables pushed up against the wall. No one's dancing. At one table crowded with beer bottles, ashtrays, purses and elbows are the girls of the night— the ones who've been ditched by the men who brought them, or who've sent some Steve or Louis home with a flea in his ear after he'd stumbled back from the can, reeking of vomit. Or they are irremediably plain girls who have come alone, looking for someone as desperate as they.

Things are getting a little close—he's taken each of these girls home with him on a Friday or Saturday night, and more than once. They aren't, despite Delbert's pronouncement, bad girls— for they all know what while it's okay to get in a little bit of fun while they can, they are fated for marriage as surely as the tuna's fated for the tin. And that if a Steve or Louis or Hector slept with a girl, four, maybe five times in as many months, then he was beholden to her; she had a right to expect a ring, a wedding dress with a Southern Belle or Lady Di hat attached, and a bungalow or trailer down one of the inland roads.

Of the six women at the table, it's Marvine who looks up first and smiles at him. She isn't pretty, Marvine, but she has a generous smile that tries so hard to make up for her plump thighs and big bum and the over-permanented hair for which the other women tease her. A huge smile and large breasts of which she tries to make the most by wearing a ''lift-and-separate'' brassière. Hector smiles back, despite himself—an absent, avuncular smile, and passes on to the next girl at the table—he's never cared for big-breasted women. He doesn't mind Marvine's plumpness, but it's the way she tries to serve up her tits like goose eggs, sunny-side up, that always makes her the last one he asks to dance on any Friday night.

Yet it's Marvine who drives beside him in the truck at one-thirty in the morning—Simone had been too stoned, Agnita had made it up with Guy, and Connie and Laurette had decided to leave early. It is Marvine who lies beside him under the Star-of-Bethlehem quilt, Marvine whose unfortunate little rosebud lips he mechanically kisses and who then flops back, arms and legs spread wide so that she resembles a mutated starfish. And who expects him to roll in and out of her like a Fundy tide—which he does, feeling no uncertain relief after he's finished, a physical and mental relief that it will be another six days—perhaps even two weeks, if he can school himself, before he need do this again. "Cartesian dualism," he whispers to Marvine, who's already tumbled into sleep beside him. Hector looks down at her for a little while, oddly moved by the expression on her face, a look she must have worn as a child, expectant and yet tranquil, as if she were certain of waking to possess her heart's desire. He slips out of bed, covers Marvine with the quilt, washes himself as quietly as he can and then gets dressed again. Sitting on a plain wooden chair he smokes a pipe, looking over rather than on the sleeping Marvine, and allows himself half an hour before he wakes her, helps her lumber into her clothes, and drives her home.

He doesn't think of Marie-Claude—he'd been thinking of her, summoning her image as he'd laboured atop Marvine, trying to persuade his senses that it was Marie-Claude's delicate, small breasts pressing against his chest, Marie-Claude's slender hips he held under his hands, her long, lovely legs wrapped round him as he pressed gently and then furiously inside her so that they both cried out together. But Marie-Claude was in Montréal, having refused not only to agree to marry him, but to admit she loved him. He'd asked her to marry him the third time they'd slept together. She'd sat up in bed, lit a cigarette and blown smoke around them. "Look Hector, I like your mind, I like your beard, I like your cock—isn't that enough for you?" Suddenly she'd seemed not five but fifteen years older than he, a woman from another planet. All through the three years of their affair she'd insisted on their having separate apartments—he'd suffered the sexual equivalent of stigmata on the nights she'd phone up to say she couldn't see him. Offering no excuses, explanations, since she'd made it clear from the beginning that she would want, from time to time, to sleep with somebody else, and that he of course was welcome to do the same.

She'd been right, as usual—he hadn't loved her, and he wasn't sure, now, that he'd even properly liked her. Hadn't he been too busy experiencing the novelty of sexual passion to analyse, as he could do now, how he'd been attracted by precisely those qualities in Marie-Claude—her smallness, slenderness, most of all her being so much older—that had reminded him of Claire? The times Marie-Claude was not at home to him were the times he'd written his longest letters to Claire—not about his inability to contend with Montréal women, but about his conviction that he wasn't, after all, good enough—that Claire had been mistaken in encouraging him to go away, in believing in him at all. That perhaps he should come home again.

Listening now to Marvine's riffling snores, Hector shifts his thoughts to Claire, remembering how, a few nights after he'd received his last letter from her, the one washing her hands of him and his lunatic decision to come back to Spruce Harbour, he'd dreamt that he was René Descartes at the Court of Queen Christina. He'd stood shivering in the courtyard at four in the morning as a splendid woman in riding breeches and a plumed hat invited him to get up on horseback with her and gallop away over the frozen Swedish fields. There he'd stayed, a wreck of a man in a thin, grey satin cloak, spluttering, coughing, unable to say yes or no as the queen's horse reared up and she slashed at him with her riding crop, then rode away, her horse's hooves beating like frozen thunder. She'd had Claire's voice and face, and he'd never been able to think of Claire afterwards without feeling a blast of cold air through his lungs.

He really ought to go and shake Marvine out of her doughy dreams. But instead he sits sucking at the stem of his pipe, thinking of his odd meeting with that arrogant little bastard at the Loony House: "Do you know Claire Saulnier? I'm going to dinner at her house next week." Not jealousy—he'd no right to feel that—but incredulity that things had worked out as they had. The things he remembered best about Claire were the long, strong hands that seemed so out of place attached to her small body, and then the beautiful clarity of her voice. Thanks, no doubt, to her mother's efforts and the years she'd spent in England, she had a disciplined way of speaking, no dropping of final "g's" or "t's"—no "wanna's" or "gonna's" or "hafta's." And yet there was an underlying softness in her slow-blossoming smile which had made him believe her beautiful. Even, especially when he'd still been a boy, small for his age and two grades ahead of himself at school, a boy who preferred reading to hockey, though to please his father he'd always signed up each year for whatever league would have him. A boy for whom the little world of Spruce Harbour afforded one great pleasure—canoeing on the tea-coloured lakes hidden in the spruce groves back of the highway. His cousin had shown him how to paddle and steer, and then he'd spent whole days by himself on the lakes, sometimes camping overnight, forgetting all about serving as altarboy at Mass the next morning or manning the counter at the Kwikway store while his parents went off to watch the Gentlemen's League game at the arena.

He'd tried to describe what it was like in the canoe, but Claire wouldn't listen.

"All that business about voyageurs and the song my paddle sings—it's drivel, Hector, boring and useless as those hockey games at the arena, the stink of sweat, that awful synthetic hot chocolate and the rancid butter they smear on the popcorn. You don't need that kind of thing; you're above and beyond all that. Listen to me, Hector—you don't need to care about any of it."

And he had listened. He'd screwed up his courage and gone to her house one Thursday afternoon when he'd known she'd be in—he must have been all of fourteen then—too old to start piano lessons, and yet that's what he'd asked her for. Hoping she'd know that what he really wanted was recognition of his difference from the others. Because she, too, was different. She lived alone, in the big white house with the willow fence; no father or mother, husband or brother or children. The kids at school called her a witch—they spat at her shadow when she walked by, and dared each other to go up to her house at night and rap on the windows.

She never yelled at them; she didn't show by the merest word or shake of her head that they even existed. And that trick had been what he'd really wanted to learn from her.

A tin ear he'd turned out to have—the hands that were so skilled at steering and noiselessly paddling a canoe proved hopelessly clumsy on the keyboard.

"Well, if I can't teach you piano—and you'll never get beyond Three Blind Mice, my poor Hector—I can at least show you how to speak proper French—English too, for that matter."

So he would go to her house, with his parents' grudging consent—he'd argued that the banker's and the doctor's children took piano lessons from Miss Saulnier; why shouldn't he? But instead of playing he would talk, tell her how he understood things, as opposed to the ways his parents or teachers did—and she'd listen to him, correcting his grammar and pronunciation as he went along. Letting him know that it wasn't just his ideas that were different, but the whole cast of his mind, as if his brain spoke its own difficult language only she could decipher. And somewhere along the way he'd stopped being her student and become her reflection, letting her plan and arrange his future as if he had no more volition than an image in a mirror. All the time that he'd been a student at Sacré Coeur there had been a passionate, if invisible complicity between them, even though the lessons had stopped, and he'd been invited into her office only some half dozen times in three years. But he was going to go out into the world as her ambassador, he was going to do great things. And she'd made it clear that she wanted nothing more from him than that he should go as far as he could and never come back.

"There are other places than Spruce Harbour, dear boy—and you'll get to them. There's no reason you couldn't get a scholarship from Sacré Coeur to the Université de Montréal—there's the Sorbonne, too—it's not just a name, people actually go there and study. No, you mustn't even consider Moncton—it's too close, and you have to get away. There's no need to keep wondering what your parents will say—they have no right of possession to your mind, Hector, no more than to your body. Besides, when you've gone away and done important things, become someone other than the heir apparent to the Kwikway store, they'll forgive, even if they never understand you. And don't use me as a model—I went away, Hector, but the reasons I had for coming back aren't the same as yours could ever be. We'll leave it at that, shall we?''

Did she ever wonder how he saw her now, after his time away—was that why she'd insisted he never come back? A small woman, living alone, beginning to grow old. A woman immured, not in herself, but in her fear of herself—you could see it in the hurried way she walked, as if there were someone shadowing her. He'd never known a person so walled off, with so many intricate defences. In her more bitter moments his mother had said things to him about Claire being a crazy old maid, grabbing at a boy because she'd never be capable of getting a man. But even his mother couldn't really believe that—there was no person less sexual than Claire Saulnier. He imagined her body smooth, white as that of an old-fashioned porcelain doll, without any hairs or openings at all. As sexless, in her way, as Bertrand France was in his—a perfect couple. No doubt he was impressed by her, no doubt she trotted out the same stories she'd once told him about her salad days in London, made him free of the books and records and journals she'd once lent him. That volume of Rilke's letters he'd devoured his first year at Sacré Coeur—the first thing he'd done on getting to Montréal had been to walk into a bookstore and buy his own copy. Where was it now—in the cupboard with his papers? Why hadn't he ever got around to building himself proper bookshelves—?

Marvine begins to snore, shifting into shallower sleep—he must get her up and out to the truck. He forces himself up from his chair and walks to the door, opening it so the fine, clear autumn night can arrow in to wake her. Stepping outside he throws back his head and looks up at the stars: crystal spiders dropping from invisible webs, netting him, hauling him up to them, as if he were one with them, as cold and clean and solitary.

Solitary, yes—except for Friday nights. He digs his hands into his pockets, wheels round and re-enters the apartment. And as he pulls at Marvine's meaty legs, there come into his head snatches of the only song Claire had ever succeeded in teaching him to play. A lullaby, set to a verse by Browning or Tennyson, he couldn't remember which: "Stars in the summer night,/(something)/Hide, hide your golden light/She sleeps, my lady sleeps—" Not Marvine but Marie-Claude; not Marie-Claude but Claire; not Claire—then who? Who would have him, Hector Wagner, shot star, Dean of Drains, *philosophe raté*? Who besides Marvine? The girl from Bertrand's photograph, the girl he knew he'd seen somewhere but couldn't recognize?

Seizing the quilt in both hands, twirling it up like a conjurer's silk scarf, he grabs Marvine's arms, on which goosebumps are starting to pop. And then he hauls her dead weight out of bed, pushes her into her clothes, and leads her out under the carelessly splendid stars to the truck with WAGNER'S KWIKWAY stencilled on its doors.

"DOWN IN THE VALLEY where the green grass grows/ I seen Mariette takin' off her clothes." That's what Louis sang every recess when she would be hanging round where the girls were skipping, wanting to join in, even just to hold the rope. But she couldn't because of what Louis said, the others too, but mostly Louis. And the teacher pretending not to hear, but he did anyway. She could tell just from the way he looked at her, as if he might catch something off her, wanted to catch something—. Because she was Delima's kid. She lived in the trailer with Delima and Luc-Antoine, and what else could you expect from a pair like that? Even the nuns didn't want her, Soeur Martine calling one by one all the girls ready to quit high school, asking them whether they had the vocation; all the girls but Mariette, who'd flunked two grades and never even made her First Communion, but it wasn't her fault. If someone would only ask her she'd tell them it wasn't.

Louis hooting at her from his truck—Louis à Pepsi, now, since he got the job at the bottle plant down at Matou. They said no one could buy Coca-Cola any more on the French Shore, he was that pushy, Louis. Going to work each day in a big truck with BELLI-VEAU'S BOTTLES painted on the side, and a picture of a girl with her lips round a Pepsi bottle. Honking his horn at her whenever he saw her pushing the baby in his stroller along the ditch, minding him for Delima who was gutting fish all day at the plant, and off Saturdays cleaning house for Claire Saulnier. *Down in the valley where the green grass . . .* "Double-Fuck yourself Louis," she would've called, but she didn't want the baby to hear her—and he wasn't no baby, he was nearly three, but he was some small. Didn't talk but made lots of noise, enough for Luc-Antoine to swear he'd put a fist through his mouth to quiet him. So she took him out for a walk as much as she could—sometimes down to the wharf to look at the boat rotting away on the stones; to hear the gulls screaming when they dumped out the fish guts. Sometimes along the ditch past Wagner's store, past the big houses, the nice houses with their shingles all painted and new cars in the drive-ways. Houses where the doctor lived, the lawyer, teachers—and all the professors at the college. Past the post office, Delbert waving at her through the window. He was some kind, though they never received mail, just UIC for Delima or Luc-Antoine, but Delbert still waved to her anyway. Around the puddle, the spruce wood, into the church parking lot. Stopping at the statue of Our Lady so Paul could see, telling him, "That's Jesus' mother, she's pretty—she lights up in the dark. When you're bigger we can come down at night to watch."

Frère LeBlanc, fixing the shutters of the priest house—he waves at her too, calling her name, though she doesn't come to Mass. Delima doesn't let any of her kids inside no church, though all of them got baptised—Frère LeBlanc told her that. One time he came to school to talk about First Communion. He was walking back to his car, it was recess and she ran out to the road, ran out to tell him she was sorry, she couldn't make her communion, did that mean she was going to hell? Trying to look through his glasses, fat thick glasses so you couldn't see his eyes, but he smiled, gentle smile and he said, "It's okay, Mariette—at least you've been baptised. When you're older, when you're a big girl and can leave home you'll come to see me and we'll arrange for your communion.'' Now every time she passes him he waves at her and it means she's okay, she won't burn, nor Paul neither, even though Luc-Antoine, he says priests are less use than a chicken's ass, and Delima, she didn't want no more to do with them after Père Gilbert came to the trailer that day and gave her hell for the way she was living.

So, could you give someone heaven? She bends down to lift Paul out of his stroller; carries him on her hip up the concrete stairs and into the church. Nobody but the two of them inside—and the saints against the walls, behind the altar. She carries Paul from statue to statue—St. Peter with the rooster at his ankles, Ste. Thérèse Little Flower of God, John the Baptist wearing a sheepskin round his middle, and sandals on his cold white feet. On little stands: like dolls, only bigger and made out of plaster, not plastic. Plaster's white—their faces white but their hair all smooth and wavy brown, none of the women saints are blondes and that's fine because her own hair's black as a crow, like Delima's, only Delima dyes hers now.

Walking up and down the aisles of the church, under every station of the cross, telling Paul what the priest had come to school to tell them—all about Our Lord and Our Lady. Saving for the very end the best statue of all, one she could look at forever if Paul weren't on her hip weighing her down, making her leg go off asleep. Statue of Our Lady, in a white nightgown with a blue sash. Crown on Her head: gold, heavy. Our Lord in Her arms, a baby like Paul—wearing His own crown, like Hers only smaller. And at the very bottom, right at Our Lady's feet, two women. Girls like her, Mariette—long black hair like hers, dark eyes and skin white as paper. Wearing nightgowns, too, and kneeling down. One of them has chains on her arms—Mariette puts out her hand to gently touch them, black tiny chains fastening the statue-girl into the flames. Orange, yellow, swirly fire—it doesn't feel hot, plaster like snow under her fingers, but somehow the chains, real chains make the fire real, the girl real. Make it her, Mariette.

But not the girl on the other side, the same girl only her arms are free now, folded over her breast and clouds under her feet, not fire. Frère LeBlanc explained it to her one time. He'd seen her staring at the statue, Paul on her hip; he'd come over and patted Paul's head, asking her how she was, and did she know that the statue was Our Lady of Deliverance? Did she know what deliverance meant? All sinners could pray for help to Our Lady— no matter how bad you were, the things you'd done, you could ask for Her help. She would lift you up from the very fires of hell and keep you safe beside Her—you could cross from fire to ice-cold clouds, just like the lady in the statue. Did she understand? Nodding her head, yes, yes Father, I do—thank you. Except she knows what the priest doesn't—some things are too bad for anyone to forgive, some flames aren't orange but black, colour of darkness and you couldn't even see the chains on your arms till you tried to get away but couldn't, couldn't move from the filth you were lying in. So that if maybe she could just change fires from black to this clear, light flame in a skin white as paper, lifting up her eyes and her chained arms—that would deliver her enough.

Paul begins to shift in her arms, to pound weakly against her shoulder. He's hungry—it's time to get back to the trailer, to give him some bread and beans and a can of Coke. Diet Coke, Delima bought—dyeing her hair black and drinking Diet Coke and throwing the tins into the pond behind the trailer. Deliverance, the priest said. But you have to open your mouth, open it wide and call out for Our Lady to help you. And he'd told her, "Not a word, you say one word and I'll smash yer fuckin' cunt up yer asshole." Paul starting to cry, making her cry too, so the candles in their ruby orange golden jars start to blur and shake and she has to get out before someone comes in, someone not as gentle as Frère LeBlanc. "What you doing there, you stealing something? You're Delima's kid, you're not allowed in here."

Can't go back to the trailer, not yet, has to give herself time, doesn't want them to hear her, see her—"*takin' off her clothes*"—. They didn't know nothing, Louis, Albert, Stéphane, Omer—all of them trying to get her to go with them to the Fish and Game, not even take her home but screw her in the woods behind. She'd like to see them try, she wouldn't give them the time of day, that's what Delima told her to say to the kids at school. "Mariette, they're jealous 'cause you're a million times prettier, and your old lady's a million times prettier than theirs— I wouldn't give 'em the fuckin' time of day." Out into the concrete parking lot, the church like some mountain blocking her way— except for the woods behind. She'll go along the path into the woods, you can go in right behind the church, she'll leave Paul's stroller in the bushes and come back and get it later. She'll carry him—he was that small it wouldn't hurt—good for him to walk some, too, his skinny white legs, they should take him to the doctor. Luc-Antoine arguing with Delima: "No kid of mine's a cripple, ain't nothin' wrong with him, woman, you jus' don' take care of him right." Health visitor coming round, snooping, telling them to eat this and drink that, as if they won Atlantic Loto and could buy all the tins off the shelves at Wagner's. Just let her try and take Paul away, just let her try—

Warm for November, even warmer here in the woods, no wind, just sun rubbing against her face and hands, like a hand on her head, priest's hand, blessing. Paul asleep against her, dead weight, soon she'll have to stop and rest, get past the place where the shrine was. Who would do a thing like that? Knock down a statue of Our Lady or Jesus, leaving just what They'd been standing on. Though why They needed anything to stand on she doesn't know. They are perfect, better than angels, and angels, they could fly, they were air and light and you couldn't even see them. Guardian angel on the picture Frère LeBlanc gave her: child with hair curly-gold and a white dress only he wasn't a girl but an angel. Side of a cliff and the angel is in the air, arms holding a little girl's head up, so she won't fall down, down the cliff into black rocks and sea below. Like Louis à Pepsi's friend Paul Thibault, got so drunk last Saturday night he drove right off the wharf and drowned and there was no angel, no priest, just a truck crashing into black water, black fire, what's the difference? Deliverance, deliver me from evil, but how could you lift up your arms to pray if he chained them down?

So many paths, some marked with plastic ribbons on the spruce boughs, different colours, blue like Our Lady's robe or yellow, green. She chooses the blue one, getting lost when the ribbons peter out, path narrowing, alders blocking her way, and brambles scratching. She has to put Paul down for a minute, he's heavy, too heavy, her arms are going to crack off at the elbows. Ground's good and dry—there's a bit with long grass like brown feathers, just lay him here for a minute, he won't catch cold, just for a minute. Lays him down, takes off her jacket to cover him; stretches, turns around and walks off a little ways, just to feel her body move with nothing to weigh it down. Walks a ways and walks right into it. Black and heavy as lead and waiting for her. Even if the ribbons marking the path were blue, Our Lady, there is no deliverance from this.

Long grass snaking at her ankles. She comes up close enough to touch it. Nobody knows who left it here—maybe some drunk like Paul Thibault driving not into water but into some tree. Long ago—different story: same end. Leaving this: car like Delima must have gone riding in when she was eighteen: black, big bumpers, metal rusted away but the black deeper, shinier, as if it had grown in the rain these ten years, twenty years. Brambles, big, thorny, poking up through where the seats had been, inside the steering wheel, where the roof caved in. Brambles shoving their way through rotten metal, thin like a cotton nightdress. Leaves still green on the alders, but the car black, night with no stars, underwater, locked-in, locked-out, shut up. *You keep yer mouth shut* while the water's coming up over you and you can't ever get out. Not her, nor Paul, nor any of them—

Paul? She left him, she left him all alone sleeping there: *shithead little cunt* she was leaving him there when there were hunters out, she should have thought—. They had no right to come into these woods, the priests' woods, but they come anyway, shooting rabbits, pheasants, shooting anything that moved. Christ Jesus— there he was. Asleep still under her jacket where she left him, but with who? Guardian angel, but he doesn't have wings, no long gold curly hair, but shiny glasses and shoes and clothes like out of the catalogue. Like no one she's ever seen round here, never; no one she's ever heard. Saying what? She can't make it out, it's no French she knows, he'll think she's some kind of loony, like the ones used to live in the house by the college. In English, now, easier.

"He belongs to you, then? I don't need to call the police and report a lost child, abandoned baby—a wild child, shades of Truffaut—"

Police—no police, no. "He's mine, yeah. Mine—my kid, my brother, I mean. I just went off for a minute. I didn't mean you should come and find him all alone—I was carrying him and my arms—"

"Please, there's no need to apologize, it's not as if I'm going to confiscate him, no fear of *that*. But I don't think we've met— at least I've never seen you before. Do you live round here?"

"Yeah." Don't tell him where, he's not going to tell no social worker, no health worker, had enough of them coming round, she'll get the shit beaten out of her if she tells him—

"Wonderfully laconic bunch, you people. Don't worry, I'm not going to bother you. I just thought you had a rather mobile face. Quite photogenic. Has anyone ever taken your picture?"

"I gotta go now." Bending to get Paul up off the ground, only he doesn't like it, he's still sleepy, starts hitting at her with his fists.

"Looks like he's quite a handful."

"I love him. He's *mine*." Holding him to her, quieting him, sitting down on the ground with him in her lap. Pushing the hair, too long, too thin, out of his face. Too white face, eyes too big. Mine.

"That's the best speech I've had from you yet. Fine—as I said, I wouldn't touch him for the world. But I do wish I'd brought my camera with me. You'd make a charming study: Backwoods Madonna and Child. Good enough to put in a *tondo*."

Maybe he's a crazy man. Maybe he's one of the loonies, come back looking for his old house. Who is he? Stupid, stupid, she should have known straight off. "You the *Français de France*?"

"The very same. Bertrand France—the instantial universal. Do you mind if I sit down—at a respectful distance—and just look at you? You know, you're the first thing—person, object, whatever—I've seen around here that would make a really good photograph. I've rigged up a studio in my house—it's back there, in the woods—between the college and the church. Perhaps you'd come and let me take your picture sometime? And your brother's—he's got rather beautiful eyes. What *is* your name?''

Her arms relax around Paul—she smiles at Bertrand who's loony no longer, since he's admired her baby. ''Mariette.''

''That's all? Just Mariette?''

''And Paul—''

''Paul, of course. Listen—''

''I gotta get goin'. He's some hungry.'' She pulls herself up, the child in her arms. Bertrand reaches over to retrieve the jacket she's left on the grass; he stands up and drapes it over her shoulders.

''Whatcha do that for?'' He could have thrown it at her—*ya dumb bitch, ya ain't got enough sense to stick up your ass*. He could have made her bend down and get it herself. He puts it round her shoulders like she's made out of plaster, might break if the wind blew too hard.

''Isn't it yours?''

''Yeah—.'' Stupid, she was so dumb, *dumb bitch*. ''Thanks. Thanks a lot.''

''Well then. Do you come here often—into the woods, I mean?''

''Sometimes.'' Paul's getting heavy again—she has to get him home.

''Then perhaps we'll see something of each other. This is my refuge, my retreat—when it's not raining that is, or fogging, if that's what you say. Right then—we'll see about those pictures, won't we?''

Pictures? ''Yeah, sure. I come here sometimes.''

''Good. *Allez, au revoir.*'' Leaves her standing there, looking at him walk off along the path marked by blue ribbons, nowhere near the black car, as if he doesn't even know it's there, only knows the safe way to go. Paul whimpering; she can hear her own belly rumble. ''Okay now, baby, mamma will take you home now, we're going, see?'' Can't talk to her, can't say nothing but smiles up at her out of blue eyes, sea-blue, black-blue, beautiful baby eyes like in a photograph.

DELIMA COMES Saturday mornings to clean house for Miss Saulnier—Saturday mornings, that is, when she isn't feeling either too good or too hung over. Delima is tall and large and her flesh hangs as comfortably on her as an old sweater—increasingly baggy now, as she does less and less cleaning, more and more shiftwork at the fishplant, sitting on the line and gutting herring, mackerel, cod. Delima's part Micmac—her hair was once glossy, iridescent as a raven's wing, just as her daughter's is now. Delima still wears it long and loose, though she's going on forty and looks a good fifty. Long with bangs and a funny pompadour bit perched on top of her head like an Edwardian hat. Mariette has Delima's cheek bones and her eyes, the same giddy slant to both though in Mariette's face there is a soft, unfocussed look—she is seventeen but looks as though she's just stumbled into puberty.

Delima has worked off and on cleaning house and fish ever since Mariette was born. Stellar Seafoods isn't the best of bosses—lousy pay, Delima says—fish scales glued to your skin, pinching as they dry. All the guts and blood you have to stick your hands in, the detergent you have to scour with to get off the slime. And having to wear a hair net—friggin' things always give her headaches, she swears. And if that wasn't enough, a paper cap like nurses wear, and you stink of fish all day and all night long, and all for lousy pay and even then, only when it's in season. So Delima works for Claire, who tolerates her vagaries and pays her a good deal more than the less-than-minimum wage Delima gets at Stellar Seafoods. Throws in lunch, too—ham sandwiches and a glass of beer; all for dusting, scrubbing and waxing the kitchen and bathroom floors, vacuuming the rugs. One person doesn't make much of a mess, and even if it's not much better than gutting mackerel, it gets Delima out of the trailer, away from the shriek of kids and Luc-Antoine.

Whom Claire loathes on sight, but whom Delima delights in

since she's had him with her for twelve years now. Met him when Mariette was five years old and they were living in a slummy apartment over the old Social Club, the one they tore down last year. Met him at the Club and then took him upstairs after too many beers; woke up next morning with Mariette trying to get back into bed—they'd put her onto a heap of old clothes on the floor—and Luc-Antoine climbing all over her. Delima just shook off the two of them and made black tea with plenty of sugar in it and turned on the TV to watch cartoons. They've been together ever since: Delima, Luc-Antoine, Mariette, and the five kids that came after they moved into the trailer Luc bought with the money he made doing roadwork and unloading ships up Whitby way. A big, fleshy man, fingers thick as unfried sausages and blond hair greased, slicked straight back from the head which is oddly handsome, almost noble—like that of a dissolute emperor or bishop.

He doesn't beat her up—Delima swears she'd never stand for that, she'd give him as good as she got if he tried anything rough with her. Belted the kids now and again but that was a father's job, wasn't it? Asking Claire over the glass of beer, and Claire looking back into Delima's ruined eyes, like blackbirds caught in red nets. She said, "I wouldn't know, Delima. I never had a husband or kids—what can I say? My father never lifted a finger against me—but then he packed me off to convent school when I was ten, and the nuns saw to that part of the business." *Singeing my palms with rulers if I made mistakes in my grammar, cried for my mother, my father, home.* Delima shaking her head, pursing up purplish lips. "Holy Jesus save me from them nuns and priests—ain't gonna get near me nor my kids neither. Don't need that kinda help."

But she came once to ask for Claire's, three years ago on a Monday morning when Claire hadn't, by a miracle, any classes scheduled. "She's bleedin' down there—" Delima gestured to her own flabby crotch. "Been bleedin' all night but she wouldn't come ta tell me. Waited till Luc had gone out ta work and the kids ta school and then I find her lyin' with the cat lickin' her face and she's got her arms crossed tight over her belly, and so help me Claire, she looks like friggin' death and Luc, he'll kill me."

On the way to the hospital—an hour's drive, with Mariette stretched out on the back seat, a black garbage bag under her so she won't bleed into the pale blue upholstery, Claire gets the story out of Delima the way you'd pry open a child's mouth to get the penny she's stuffed there.

"Okay, okay, I'm not tryin' to hide nothin'. She got knocked up—wouldn't tell me who—one a' those fuckers on three-wheelers always roarin' up and down the ditch. Can't blame 'em—back from the oil rigs, wanta good time and Mariette, she's some pretty—skinny, maybe, but a looker—couldn't stop nobody from noticin' that, it's a free country, right? So the first thing I know she's pukin' outside the trailer before breakfast—I'm not dumb, been through it enough ta know right away. Took her right up ta Hattie Brown's, up by the falls. Shit, Claire, what'm I supposed ta do? How many ya think we can jam into that trailer—and she won't say nothin', so who'm I gonna drag to the friggin' altar? Or maybe I'll take her up to the nuns at Salmon River and say it's the Holy Ghost that whanged her? I got no time, no money— can't exactly take the kid down ta Boston, can I? And Hattie, she owed me a favour, I helped her outta trouble once. And Luc, he says we gotta get rid of it—who's gonna know the difference, who's gonna care? I don't need no priest on my back and no social worker neither—next time she gets knocked up she'll know enough to say who did it and Luc, he'll go and beat the shit outta the kid till he owns up it's his. He's a good father to her, and she ain't even his own, ya can't say he don't care.

"So I drove her up ta Hattie's. Up at the falls—she's gotta kinda cabin, blanket hung up on a rope between the kitchen and her bed. I sat on the bed and I waited—it was quick, though. She didn't cry, not much. She's a strong enough kid—looks like ya could poke yer finger through her, but she'll stand up ta anythin'. And she knows the way it goes—didn't say nothin' once we got back—she went right off ta bed and I told Luc she was okay, I swear she was till I went in ta see her and there was all the blood, black, it smelled like a goddam hunk a rotten meat. Think she'll be okay?" Delima turned round, her youngest squirming on her lap, to call back to Mariette, "You'll be okay, kid, Claire here says so."

Mariette stayed in Falmouth hospital for two weeks—appendicitis, Delima told the neighbours. Her classmates and teacher sent a Hallmark card with a pretty nurse and handsome doctor on it, telling her to get well soon. Delima came to clean at Claire's house the day after Mariette's return. She was singing, she was so happy, believing in the story Claire helped her concoct; puzzled, more than a little angry Claire wouldn't believe it too.

"Delima, you should talk to her. She must be feeling miserable; these things leave scars, you know. In the mind—"

"Ya know so much, talk ta her yerself. I can't get nowheres with the kid—Christ, it's none a my business. Ya think I was some kinda Easter lily when I was her age? Just lucky, that's all. She'll be okay."

And she was—at least until now. Claire never did talk to Mariette about what had happened to her, because everything Mariette didn't say made it clear this was something words couldn't explain or cure. And she got better, went back to school, dropped out of school, stayed in the trailer minding the kids too small to be at school. And if Delima worried, it was that Mariette was too good a girl, never went out with anyone though there were at least three guys had the hots for her. A real good girl. Until now. Delima puts down her tuna-fish sandwich, unbitten, and fixes Claire with fishhook eyes.

"He a pervert or somethin'?"

"Pardon? Is who a pervert?"

"That little shit-ass from the college."

"Shit—oh, you mean Bertrand."

"Don't know what he calls himself, but he's been messin' round with Mariette."

"Damn—I'm getting so clumsy—that's the third glass I've broken this week. Never mind, Delima, I'll mop it up. What were you saying?"

"Look." And out of the cracked vinyl handbag she's left on the kitchen counter Delima produces a handful of photographs. Black and white. Some taken outdoors against a background of ferns and lichen-scabbed spruce; some against a stark white cloth, inside. Claire grabs them so quickly one of them tears a little. She looks through them and laughs. "Delima," she says, "these could be put up on the church bulletin board. I've never seen anything so innocent. And what's more, they're good."

"What you mean?" Delima snatches the pictures back, holds them up close to her eyes, the better to see what Claire does.

"I mean they're well-done—professional quality, whatever you want to call it. And you say Bertrand took them?"

"She said—after I damn near twisted her arm. Found them under her mattress. What's it supposed to mean, like? I know the kinda stuff they show in magazines—that pig filth they sell up at Wagner's store. But this stuff? Is he fuckin' her or isn't he?"

"Delima!"

"Shit, Claire, yer actin' like he's the friggin' pope. Ya don't think she's good enough for him? Christ Jesus, he don't look like he's got cock enough ta stuff a crack in plaster. She's too good fer him, ya know? She's a damn pretty girl, even if she is on the skinny side. Ya put her in a dress, fix her hair—she'd look like the fuckin' Queen a' Spain. He oughta be fuckin' her silly, even if he's got more brains than balls. And if he knocks her up, let me tell ya, there'll be no Hattie Brown this time, no hospital. Luc'll beat the shit outta him if he don't marry her—and why shouldn't he? Give her a house, kids, make her happy. Christ knows we got no room in that trailer; it's time she started lookin' herself out a man."

"Don't be an idiot, Delima—you're telling yourself a fairy story." Claire gets up from her chair, crouches to pick the broken glass—two neat pieces—off the kitchen floor, and carefully wipes up the spilled juice. Then she turns to Delima, shaking her head and saying gently, soothingly, "Don't make things impossible for yourself—and for Mariette. Bertrand will no more marry your daughter and settle down in a bungalow on the fishplant road than you'll get a job teaching at the college."

"Don't ya be so goddam sure about that. Look, if it weren't for all them christbitten priests there—they'd like nothin' more than a piece a' me—and it ain't my mind I'm—"

"That's quite enough—. I'm sorry, Delima, I just don't want you to give Mariette false hopes. I can swear there's nothing of that kind going on between them. Bertrand's already engaged to be married to someone back in Paris, and besides, he's not good enough for Mariette. You'd better just give her back those photographs and stop the third degree. Leave her be—look, there's still the floor to be done—and the bathroom. I've got a student coming at three—you promised you'd be finished by then." Claire waits for Delima to say something; Delima sits nursing her beer for a while, then looks up at Claire. For a moment Delima looks superb instead of grotesque—a barbarian queen.

"Engaged my ass. We'll just see if Mariette can't get him kissin' hers before she's done. You find out, you talk ta him. Find out what's he doin' with her—what's he gonna do if she ends up in shit creek with no paddle. I want him ta know—if he tries anything fast Luc'll beat his ass right up ta his ears. Tell him, Claire. I never asked nothin' since that last time, long time ago. I ain't asked fer what I could a got—"

"Delima, we've been through all this—"

"What I could a got fer her, not me. Ya, I know. We been through, right through."

"Delima, God knows—"

"God don't have nothin' ta do with this. You gonna speak ta him? Promise?"

"Yes. I'll speak to him. I'll let him know. I'll try."

BERTRAND IN BED, this Sunday morning: no papers to mark, no Mass to attend—he has abandoned the piety of his childhood though he still retains an amateur's interest in ecclesiastical architecture (who else in Spruce Harbour could point to the church's possession of a triforium, ogee arches and a mandorla over the vestry?). No one to make him breakfast or to call up and suggest meeting for lunch, or a concert in the evening. No one, no where.

Bertrand is still in bed because there is, as far as he can see, nothing to get up for. Fog has smothered the entire coast; he can hear the tolling of the buoys, the melancholy wheeze of the fog horn. Were his eyesight better he would be able to see the infinitesimal droplets clinging to the window across from his bed. He has been awake for some time, having made himself coffee which he sips, now, from an ugly ceramic mug (it came with the house) as he lies in silk pyjamas reading old mail: from his mother, his sister Berthe, and from Antoinette.

Antoinette gave him the pyjamas as a parting gift—a very temporary parting, since he would be flying home again less than a twelvemonth after quitting Paris—she would be waiting for him at the airport along with his mother, who happened to be her godmother. All this a trifle incestuous, but no one had raised a finger against it—in fact his mother and hers had schemed at such a union from their children's cradles. Ten years ago he and Antoinette had been pushed into each other's grudging company at his sister's wedding. Ten years, and they were now understood to be "affianced," at least as far as the two families were concerned. He had meant his parting gift to Antoinette to be a ring, but, severely unromantic, she had vetoed that. She'd given him pyjamas (purple and orange stripes, with an Art Deco monogram) because, as she said, silk was the best thing to wear next to your skin—cool in summer, warm in winter. She knew that the Canadian climate was vicious; she'd read her *Maria Chapdelaine*. From him she'd demanded and received a high-tech sports wristwatch, as ugly as it was expensive. She was *sportive*, Antoinette; bored with horseback riding and tennis, she'd taken up racketball, windsurfing, rollerskating—just a phase that would pass, or so his mother had consoled him, once Antoinette became involved with a truly womanly life.

She was also mad about everything American, and insisted on being called Tony, a boon that Bertrand had quite properly refused, especially when talking to Claire of Antoinette de Vigny (leaving it vague whether or not there was a connection with the poet). Granddaughter of the Comtesse de Vigny, *châtelaine* of Commereau, in an old Burgundian town Claire wouldn't have heard of. It wasn't in the *Guide Michelin*—the Comtesse had no desire to be disturbed by tourists in bermuda shorts—though it did get several paragraphs in the *Guide Bleu*. There was no letter for him from the Comtesse, which was understandable, for she was nearly ninety and blind in one eye. But even a mere postcard from the Comtesse—just her signature—would have been worth all these letters strewn over his bed—letters from home.

Letters at least six weeks old and, when not intensely irritating, relentlessly boring. His mother's go on interminably about the filthy weather they've been having in Paris, the inept repairs to the plumbing, the dreadful American films his younger brother watches, and the visit she and Antoinette's mother are planning to a German spa—listing the various ailments she will have treated with mud baths and mineral water. His sister's, on the prim blue notepaper she affected, the one with so many watermarks in it you could hardly read her writing, was a lecture to the effect that he needn't moan so much about life in *Nouvelle Ecosse*—it made *Maman* unhappy, and besides, if he had been not only manly but sensible and done his *service militaire* like everyone else, he wouldn't have ended up in that miserable place with the absurd and unpronounceable name. And that there was no need to blame *Papa* for not having pulled strings that could have got him posted to New York or at least Montréal. Since he'd been so childishly stubborn about studying English and playing with cameras instead of taking up *Papa's* offer to join the firm, who could blame their father for folding his arms and letting his son parachute into a virtual Devil's Island? Bertrand read the letter again for the sole pleasure of observing the infelicities of his sister's style; her diction, he reflected, was as stolid as her shoes—stout, serviceable matron's shoes, impeccable attire for the wife of a kidney specialist and the mother of twins.

Antoinette's letter had lain unopened on his bookshelf for nearly a week. He had not entirely forgiven her for that wristwatch—it had cost him so much more than the modest aquamarine (to match her eyes) he'd intended for her that he'd have to delay until his trip to New York the purchase of the light monitor and lens case he'd been coveting. He drank the last of his coffee—revolting over-glazed banana-coloured mug—and screwed up his eyes at the photograph of Antoinette he'd tacked up on the wall. One of his better efforts, a splendidly simple shot of her sitting on the balustrade above the moat at Commereau. Black and white—you couldn't tell her hair was red; it looked almost blond in the strong sunlight. He'd tried to console himself for the shade of her hair by thinking of Titian's models. It was not, however, that golden red—rich, heavy, voluptuous—but sandy, pinkish; it made him think of the noses of white rabbits. Of course, one did not choose one's future wife for the colour of her hair; one did not flinch at the fact that you couldn't see her eyelashes and that her gooseberry-green eyes were more than a little prominent. And she was an intelligent girl, capable, sensible, except for this mania about fitness. He envisioned a marriage of equals, with Antoinette going off to the *Institut* every morning (she was training to be a film editor) and he off to the *Faculté des Langues*. As soon as he returned to France he'd sit the exams for university teaching; the notion of a lifetime spent with puddingheads in a *lycée* was just too dismal to contemplate.

He thumps the mug back on the night table, hoping he might manage to shatter the clay and thus have an excuse for buying another, less offensive one. But where? Wagner's Kwikway store boasted an assortment of pottery manufactured by the proprietor's wife: Blue Boy plates, Age of Innocence ashtrays, plantholders in the shape of cut-off blue jeans, busts of all the Popes within living memory, all looking more or less the same. And a metre of banana-coloured mugs that could survive the assault of a dozen transport trucks. He'd neglected to buy milk at Wagner's last night—what he had on the windowsill had gone sour, and there was only a box of soggy crackers to breakfast on. He'd get some lunch at the cafeteria—stewed cod and slimy tomatoes, no doubt, and then try to hold out till dinner at Claire's. She'd at last got round to asking him; a poor show of hospitality, but what could you expect from someone who'd lived so long in this place?

Forcing the revolting crackers down, he lets himself think of breakfasts at home: his mother in her pale blue satin robe standing over them all, pouring out *chocolat chaud*, refilling the preserve dish—cut crystal, with a silver spoon—so that no one suffered the indignity of having to scrape out the last bit from the bottom. She never sat down to eat until they were off, his father to his office, he and his brother to school. It wasn't servitude, as he'd tried to tell Claire, but aesthetics—the aesthetics of domesticity.

"To me the very essence of family life is this breakfast scene: the wife standing guard, preserving the tranquillity, the graciousness of the table, with husband and children under her as chicks gather under the hen."

"Bertrand, out of what cave did you crawl?"

A better one than she'd chosen, he'd been tempted to retort—but then, she had just asked him to dinner, and he needed that respite from the atrocities the cafeteria passed off as food, wanted it too badly to risk offending her. If Paris, if *le foyer familial* was a cave, then he'd gladly crawl back to it, out of the mildew that passed for a social existence here. To cancel Claire's remark he picks up Antoinette's letter, sliding it out of its fragile airmail envelope as the fog horn sounds again—slow, sensuous, muffled in the mist that blows like odourless, cold smoke over everything, into everything. "Read Antoinette's letter; read it and you will be back in Paris, and everything the same, safe, sure." But it doesn't work—her very handwriting irritates him: square, large, brisk. Five pages, single sides, the first four dealing with a new health club she'd joined, the weight-lifting programme she'd begun, the exams she'd just passed, enabling her to sit another set of exams which would enable her to sit—. When they went to the cinema she could remember in perfect detail all the cuts and splices; she was a perfect wizard at divining technique, but ask her for the impressions created by the effects—you might as well ask a lamp post, the dog that peed against the lamp post. Shuffling pages he gets to the end, the final, cramped paragraph in which she'd scribbled something about a visit paid to Commereau.

O saisons, O châteaux/Quel âme est sans remords?

In the photograph she is sitting—she is an inch taller than he, and rather more muscular, so he prefers to snap her seated: contained, controllable. Sitting on the balustrade over what they'd call here a *fosse*—how much nicer the English word "moat" sounds; *fosse* always makes him think of *fesse*, of Antoinette's pear-shaped, slightly pendulous (despite all the exercise) buttocks perched on that noble, elegant marble balustrade. She is sitting, arms folded, face placid as the water in the moat below her, water turned into a green sponge by the duckweed the gardener has allowed to fester there. He will have it all cleared out; he will stock trout, as they do at Fontenay—have a copy made of the little punt that has rotted almost beyond recognition in the boat house, its gilt scrollwork and inlaid gunnels blue with mould.

O saisons, O châteaux. In the photograph, Antoinette and the *château* behind her are one, indissoluble as the image and the paper on which it is printed. *Quel âme est sans remords?* His—at least in this particular case, for wasn't it an honourable, a gallant act to have affianced himself to Antoinette and her *château*, and the grandmother who would leave it to her? The title would lapse, unfortunately—Antoinette's uncle had been killed, a mere boy, during the war. Ah, but what magnificent consolation the Comtesse had taken, turning Commereau into a haven for artists of all kinds—painters, actors, writers, musicians. He, Bertrand, would have under his own lock and key rooms that had been lived in, created in, by the likes of Stravinsky, Picasso, Ionesco. Letting Antoinette's letter slip from his hands, he lies back on the lumpy pillows and imagines himself in the Comtesse's quarters at Commereau, with the poem by Valéry, the sketch by Dufy framed and hanging on her bedroom wall, the equivalent of a thank-you note from her prodigally gifted guests.

He is sitting with the Comtesse in her boudoir while Antoinette plays endless sets of tennis with the gardener on the courts behind the stables, courts tastefully screened from view by a thick juniper hedge. The old woman is skeletally erect in her bed, indigo-coloured spectacles over her near-dead eyes, and what remains of her flesh is swathed in batiste and antique lace, faintly rusty in places. He reaches forward to the night table to pour her a glass of ice water from the crystal decanter—pour it with consummate skill, tact, deference—like a head waiter at a five star hotel, Antoinette had once sneered. But then the Comtesse doesn't talk much to Antoinette, and doesn't talk at all to her daughter, whom she considers too frivolous and weak-headed to inherit Commereau. The Comtesse talks to him, Bertrand, and he knows well enough only to listen, interjecting every so often a note of admiring surprise and appreciation. But his eyes, all the time, ahead, focussing on an empty bed and rooms with all the curtains down, windows flung wide open. There would be the sketches and sonnets and autographs to be restored, reframed, hung in the salon where they could be appreciated, or at least noticed by the public— he would open the château to view at carefully selected times. The Comtesse talking, her voice crackling, scratching like an old phonograph record as he leans towards her, to hear her every word—he will preserve the memory of this bewigged, blue-spectacled, lace-shrouded skeleton—he will be marrying not so much Antoinette as the socio-aesthetic ambitions of her grandmother— and why not? Those who can, create; those who can't, keep house for the creators—and charge their own kind of rent.

"So I'll have to go down to Commereau for Easter—*Maman*, of course, is afraid to go without me. The whole affair will be too dismal for words, but Ottilie expects us, and it will only be for the long weekend. Of course, it will be too wet to have a decent game of tennis or even to jog." *Visions of women in long-waisted dresses, swishing through dewy grass, parasols over their marcelled heads, walking back and forth under the flowering chestnut trees of Commereau.* "Of course, you're always in paradise at Ottilie's—really, you should marry her instead of me. I'm always bored out of my skull there. I'm going to ask her to put in a gym—a small one; don't worry—where the old conservatory is. That's one building that will have to be pulled down before too long; the woodwork's rotted right through and the plants are half-dead anyway." *No doubt because the gardener's always off playing tennis with Antoinette.*

He puts down the letter, kicks off the covers of the bed, pokes about with his feet till he secures his slippers (maroon leather) and then slip-slops over to the window. The fog, if anything, is thicker, muffling even the rowdy cawing of the crows. What would Antoinette make of it here? Probably set up a make-shift gym with an exercise bicycle and a Nautilus machine. She had no use at all for the arts, but then, that incredible energy of hers, that self-assurance which made her every physical or moral act as direct and efficient as her tennis serve—. Wasn't it *that* the Comtesse approved in her, the direct link with the husband she'd adored? For the Comte had been an athlete, a sportsman with no use at all for the painters and poets with which his wife festooned her house. Lavishly good-natured, he had given his wife *carte blanche* to invite whomever she would for as long as she liked, as long as one of them could play a passable game of tennis.

If it hadn't been for the fog he would be able to see the tennis courts, their nets still up—really, Hector wasn't as conscientious as he should be—the wire round them was unravelling, their asphalt cracked like a pair of lips in winter. They would have to resurface the courts at Commereau—that much he would concede to Antoinette's tastes. His life in say, eight or ten years from now, this he could see with absolute clarity, fog or no. He would have been married to Antoinette for a good seven years; the Comtesse would have lived to see her first great-grandchild before she died—in her sleep, so peacefully there would not even be a crease in her gown, a glass knocked over from the night table. He would have his post at the Sorbonne (his mother and parents-in-law combined could pull strings enough for that). A flat in the *seiz-ième*—near the Luxembourg, by preference, and an expensive enough car that the commuting to Commereau (three hours if the roads were good) would be a pleasure instead of a chore. Antoinette would no doubt stay much of the time in Paris—he'd have the *château* all to himself. His duties at the *Faculté* would be light and financially rewarding enough that he could set up a darkroom and studio in the old *donjon* and produce dozens of prints—a major exhibition wouldn't be such an impossibility. Monet had done countless versions of the façade of Rouen cathedral; he would produce countless studies of Commereau, at different seasons of the year, at different hours of the day, registering each nuance of the changing light on the golden stone, documenting the proud decay of brocaded chairs in which not only Gide and Eluard had sat but also Rameau and Madame de Staël, if the Comtesse's stories were true. And if he had any luck at all, his children would be photogenic and he could shoot them under the chestnut trees, or sailing boats in the *bassin* in the great courtyard.

The electric clock—ugly buzzing thing like a giant bluebottle trapped eternally against the wall. Quarter to ten—really, he was waking absurdly early these mornings. It was as if the place were so gigantically, so globally dull that even his dreams were perishing of inanition, condemning him to increasingly short and vacant periods of sleep. Quarter to ten. Claire had asked him for five-thirty. An eternity in which to bathe and dress and shave and wait. If only it weren't Sunday—Hector would be in his basement office; they could stretch out a game of chess until late afternoon. If only there weren't that fog, like a bed of slut's wool over everything—he could go for a walk in the woods—perhaps meet up with that funny girl and her brother again. She might not have much to say, but at least she was something to aim his camera at. He should write to his mother, answer Antoinette's note, send off a longish letter to the Comtesse—she'd never be able to read it, but they'd tell her who had sent it, surely. Perhaps Antoinette would read it aloud to her—well, if not Antoinette, then her mother. Quarter to ten. He might as well go back to bed and read.

Cracker crumbs brushed not out, but to the very bottom of the bed; the covers pulled up around him, the volume of Rilke Claire had lent him and a mug of that disgusting Kwikway coffee—it always tastes of mushroom soup—in his hands. Bertrand begins to read a description of the values of solitude. Skipping from page to page till this:

> If your everyday life seems poor, don't blame *it*; blame your-self; admit to yourself that you are not enough of a poet to call forth its riches; because for the creator there is no poverty and no poor, indifferent place—

All very well for Rilke, writing not out of some black hole like Spruce Harbour but from Paris, Rome. . . .

> And even if you found yourself in some prison, whose walls let in none of the world's sounds—wouldn't you still have your childhood, that jewel beyond all price, that treasure house of

memories? Turn your attention to it. Try to raise up the sunken feelings of this enormous past.

Bertrand snaps shut the book, tosses it onto the night table and, defying the weak morning light, the moan of the buoys, the cups of coffee he's manfully downed, burrows under scant covers into a crumb-littered cave. Willing himself back into sleep, trying not to raise up anything whatsoever. Yet the image that insists itself into the stuffy dark is one his mind has dredged up from a treasure house of memories more tawdry than Rilke ever knew. The summerhouse at their place in Chamonix, the summerhouse to which—a bored, disgruntled boy of twelve—he'd gone to read a book in peace. They were always trying to make him go walking in the mountains; they could never just let him be. From his hideout behind the piled-up trellises, hearing noises, voices—turning to see Berthe and her fiancé in a mutual stranglehold on the dusty floor, making bleating sounds as they rocked up and down between the garden hose and the pruning shears. Worse than in the *bandes dessinées* in the adult section of the bookshops—because while those pictures were obscenely clinical, this reality was—ridiculous. Berthe's breasts squashed like day-old buns on either side of Maxim's chest; Maxim's buttocks like balloons blown up to popping point, like beachballs furiously bounced. And afterwards, at the dinnertable they sat across from one another eating *carrottes Vichy*, making excruciating small talk with his parents, while he, Bertrand, was not allowed dessert because he'd insisted on sulking by himself instead of going for a family climb.

Between his thighs his sex lies limp and baffled. What had Dylan Thomas called it? A candle in the thighs? His was more like a flashlight with the batteries gone. What could you expect, here—the women here—. But then, even at home, with Antoinette; she always made him feel as if he were running laps. And it wasn't as if he were *that way*, for God's sake, it was just that he didn't feel at all real when he was making love—that is, he didn't feel anything like desire. And he knew what desire was, had known since he'd had anything in his life worth remembering.

Sunken feelings, never raised except in his own head. To be able to tell them out loud, say them to someone who wouldn't so much listen to, as substantiate them. But was there anyone like that, anyone he could entrust with something so important to him?

He throws back the covers, upsetting his half-empty mug of coffee on the night table. Some of it splatters the Rilke, the rest making an irregular dark stain on his coverlet. Damndamndamn—he'll have to buy Claire a new copy; he can't give it back to her like this. Repulsive dank smell of the coverlet—more dust than wool. Outside fog, inside disorder, nothing to do but listen to the bluebottle buzzing on the wall. He stomps off to the bathroom and runs a whole tub of scalding water, repeating in a stage whisper, "I can't any more, I can't. I've had it had it had it." The church bells dole out the hour—eleven o'clock; only eleven. Six more hours before he can present himself to Claire. He sighs richly, resonantly, but there is no one to hear him. Thuds down inside the cold tin walls of the tub, contemplates, as he soaps himself, the splotched paint—battleship grey—and the ivy-patterned wallpaper peeling from the ceiling; stubs his toe against the bathtub's ugly griffon legs on climbing out.

Since all the elements have conspired against him, Bertrand spends the day marking insuperably incompetent grammar tests and preparing his lectures on classic French literature, for the benefit of students who don't even know *Chateaubriand* as a method of preparing steak, much less as a poet. Much too early he throws down his red pen and grabs his coat and the volume of Rilke from his night table, deciding that the electric clock on the wall must be slow, that Claire will be wondering where he is, and that even if she isn't she must be as terminally bored as he. The impending reality of an audience, the idea that he will actually be speaking to someone other than himself sends him racing down the stairs, nearly tripping over his trouser cuffs. Careless of the glistening mud along the path, he makes his way to the road, that is, to the ditch between the highway and the swampy fields along the shore. He is going out for dinner; he is on his way to Claire's; he will be adequately fed and gladly listened to. Little wings of happiness seem to be lifting up his feet, blurring the area ahead of him, so that he runs smack into her—

Delima, all tarted up in turquoise sweat pants, baggy at bum and knees: puce ski jacket, stained with what looks like engine oil, stitching all unravelled and the padding snowing out. And that puff of hair right over her forehead—he really ought to take a picture of her and send it to Antoinette with the caption: "To make you jealous." Delima winks at him as he apologizes and makes way for her on the path. He'd heard that she had been what they called "the local lay" in her youth. He couldn't believe Delima had had one, or that she'd been much to look at, either. There were lamentably few beautiful women on the French Shore, or at least what he'd seen of it. Claire, at least, had an interesting face. And Mariette, though you could hardly call her pretty, wasn't exactly common. A natural model—she didn't seem to have any idea of that. Lucky for him—in Paris she could charge a healthy fee for what she'd done for nothing in his studio. He must have taken a good thirty shots of her and the little boy. He'd exhausted his ideas of what could be done with her—unless, of course, she'd agree to some nude studies. He'd never attempted it before, and she seemed awfully young—but that's what made the proposition so interesting—the sense of a young body just coming into form, the skin with that elasticity of childhood still, the sense of possibilities—

Which would do her no good at all, stuck as she was in this place, of this place as were the spruce and shacks and dull pebbles on the shore. And was most likely happy to be here, whereas for him every moment spent in Spruce Harbour was a rub against the grain, so that his very senses had become a limb of soft wood rasped against a file, gritty bits clouding, choking his eyes, mouth, ears. If he were to be life-sentenced here, like Hector, what would become of him? Would he start dressing in overalls and checkered shirts, ski jackets and a baseball cap of lurid-coloured plastic? Spend his time at the Fish and Game Club or the Belle Acadie Beverage Room, eating rappie pie soaked in molasses and ketchup and listening to the Grou Thyme Band? Coming home at night to a bungalow with wooden butterflies nailed to the walls like trophies, and inside a Delima, lying like a crumpled sheet on the bed, eyes glued to the commercials on TV even as you shoved her legs apart and blasted into her? He saw it all, knew it all. Poor Mariette—she would only marry someone who would fill her up, use her up with children—hadn't he seen the laundry lines behind these houses: a whole genesis spelled out in diapers, children's overalls, the ubiquitous adolescent blue-jean. Copulating like animals, reproducing themselves not out of will or desire, but just an itch in the groin, an uncontrollable twitch sending penises thumping and stuttering like pneumatic drills breaking up patched and brittle slabs of road—

Like animals. No wonder Claire had never married. What was it Rilke said about the animals? Bertrand fumbles in his pocket for the small, stained volume he carries with him as another person might an umbrella: to feel prepared, protected. Halting there in the ditch he riffles pages in the late afternoon sun till he finds what he wants.

> "all beauty in animals and plants is a silent enduring form of love and yearning"; "the animal . . . patiently and willingly uniting and multiplying and growing, not out of physical pleasure, not out of physical pain, but bowing to necessities that are greater than pleasure and pain, and more powerful than will and understanding."

Bellicose, blasting sound: he jumps to the edge of the ditch just as a huge three-wheeler driven by a hulk of a man in a black snowsuit barrels by. The imbecile had sprung on him out of nowhere, given no warning. If only the place had sidewalks to walk on instead of this *pissoir* of a ditch—they didn't let *débiles* on motorized tricycles onto the sidewalks of civilized towns. Civilized—these *canaille* don't know what the word sounds like, never mind what it means. He walks on, fuming, stumbling, the Rilke clutched so tight in his hand that his knuckles hurt. *Canaille*—they wouldn't even know what the word meant here; they'd say "duh fuckin' dogs"—so much for the language of Rabelais! That imbecile in his outsize snowsuit had been *trying* to run him down, had seen him *reading a book* and had zoomed out of nowhere to blast him to his knees, prostrate. Well, he wouldn't give him the pleasure; he would not just throw himself to the barbarians. Deliberately, decisively, he slows his pace, unclenches the Rilke and begins to read as he puts one mud-smeared shoe in front of the other, looking for all the world like a young seminarian consulting his beviary before Vespers. Each time he stumbles against a rock—and yesterday's rain has scoured more earth out of the ditch, leaving an even greater number of sharp-sided stones exposed—he forbids himself even to scowl. He will be as and how he is, a *Parisien, Français de France*; he will hide nothing; he will tell Claire everything, tell her tonight, and by God he'll show them what the measure is—show them all.

BERTRAND COMES much too early, she isn't able to finish the second volume of Rubinstein's biography she'd picked up after breakfast. She'll have to wait till later tonight when he's long gone (push him out early, set a precedent; this dinner is a privilege bestowed, not a right conferred). Bertrand brings Claire no supplicating wine or flowers, not even a box of the damp-furred chocolates you can pick up for a few dollars at the Kwikway he has to pass to get to her house. She supposes it's enough for him to make her the gift of his person. Well and good; less icing for the gossips' cake. She'll turf him out conspicuously at nine—he'll run the gauntlet of kitchen-parlour windows on his way back to the college, showing his night at Claire's to have been a strictly milk-and-cookies affair. She can already see her colleagues, whispering over Coffee-Mated cups at faculty meetings, Hector throwing her accusatory looks in the corridors.

The sun's still high enough for them to take a walk—the *cassoulet* is nowhere near ready yet. What could have possessed him to come at this hour—excitement at seeing daylight again after the hours of fog? She puts on a jacket over her sweater, tucks her trousers into rubber boots.

"Good God, we're not going wading, are we?"

Bertrand hasn't any boots and you can tell he intends to own none, rubber boots being the first telltale sign of acclimatisation to Spruce Harbour.

"You can go in your bare feet if you like." Claire takes the lead, around the back and along a path threading the spruces, to the dunes.

Brilliantly clear. On either side of them high clumps of asters with wine-dark petals round their centres: night closing round pungent suns. Some evening-primrose, splendidly, vulgarly yellow on their hefty stalks. "Hips and haws," she says, as if reciting from *The Flower Fairies of the Fall*, pointing to swollen rosehips and crimson hawthorn berries, their leaves already curdled by frost. A thin, acrid scent is in the air, the scent of autumn here—no mellow fruitfulness along the shores of St. Alphonse Bay. They climb to the top of the dunes and suddenly the sea appears, blueblack in this light, the hills closing off the bay irradiated so that you can trace the outline of each tree. Around their feet are whole clumps of flowering beach pea, absurdly, succulently pink and purple in the jostling spears of marram grass. Claire closes her eyes, not daring to look at Bertrand's face, hoping that what he sees here, this moment, will redeem the place for him—redeem, as well, her act of staying here. Then jabs herself with asking why she cares what he thinks of this sea or the sky above them—what anyone thinks of her staying on, her standing here with him: *She likes them young, remember?*

"I spent a few summers by the sea. It's a little like Normandy here, you know."

"No, I don't know. Let's move on—it's getting cold."

They go down from the dunes and start to walk along the strip of sand the ebb tide's left exposed: smooth, flat, firm as the skin of a child. Gulls mew and hang in a blue dome over them, making her think of those paperweights enclosing some miniature house or landscape you can eclipse in simulated snow, just by turning the glass upside down. No blizzards here, thinks Claire, following the very lip of the retreating tide, safe and dry in her boots. Nothing can rattle us inside our little dome: shrouded, silent.

The only noise comes from the gulls, in which Bertrand shows a child's delight. Despite his visits to Normandy he obviously has little acquaintance with the garbaging instincts of gulls, the efficient savagery with which they seize and puncture clam shells, ripping out the raw mess inside with beaks brightly yellow as a child's crayoned sun. Walking along, his eyes fixed on the careening birds above, he stumbles into heaps of seaweed, rippled streamers of kelp, and olive bladderweed. Claire helps to disentangle him.

"Look—I'll show you what we used to do as kids"—inventing a childhood filled with gangs of friends, endless hours spent with pails and shovels on the shore. "We used to tear them open, like this, and then dribble the jelly over our fingers." Cold, clear jelly—it stings her skin.

"How—charming?" Bertrand goes a few steps on, stands with his hands in his pockets, waiting for something worthy of him to happen, then finally hunkers down by a rock which barnacles have colonized with their calcified flowers. He strokes the tips of the razor-buds with his fingers.

"I suppose I could photograph these, do a series of close-up shots. It's been done before of course—and really, I prefer taking pictures of buildings, people . . ."

She could say something right now, pay off her debt to Delima— what debt? Delima's imposition on her. Right now, as he's getting up, she could say, "And have you found anyone interesting enough to photograph?" But she doesn't want anyone else on this beach, in this evening; she doesn't want to share, not Bertrand, but this sensation of company, audience; this other kind of speech, in which she likes occasionally to show her fluency.

He's inspecting his shoes to see if they've been scratched by the rocks, by the salt you can almost feel encrusting the air. Then he looks at her, expectant, as if daring her to question him—or perhaps just waiting for his supper. His spectacles reflect the sun that has begun to slide into the small gap between the hills across the bay, like a gold coin into the pocket of some banker's tomb-coloured suit. And then his stomach starts to rumble—he begins to talk of how filthy the cafeteria food is—*déguelasse*—and how he misses, most of all, decent cheese. Overhead gulls hang, shreds of blank paper glued against the air. One star, the wishing star rising, the one she always used to watch for as a child on summer nights when they would put her to bed and she could not sleep.

Bertrand and Claire make their way back along the sand through which rocks are poking sharp black snouts. Bertrand stubs his toe against them—Claire watches his eyes as he stares down at these tiny, petrified icebergs; his lids blink like camera shutters as he fixes the stones in his mind's eye, arranging them in some file of images he has on record somewhere. Does he see her as distinct from the seaweed and sand and rocks at which he peers? Or is she simply part of the restricted view, the surface he's content to take for substance? Take, mistake—his shoes sink in the sand, evening mist obscures his spectacles—he takes the hand she stretches back to him, allowing her to help him up through the quickening dark to the porch steps, to lead him through the door.

And sits himself down at the dining room table while she spoons out *cassoulet* and rice into her mother's china; opens the wine he says he doesn't drink. She fills her glass and watches him eat, feeling curiously like the witch in the gingerbread house, fattening poor Hansel in his cage. Once he's polished off his cranberry pudding and the best ice cream the Kwikway store supplies, Bertrand sinks down into the chintz armchair by the empty fireplace, listening to the record Claire puts on—Bartok's Violin Concerto, No. 1. Or, at least, listens to the opening bars before he grabs at the record jacket, pronounces upon the merits of this or that other recording and declares he'd heard the definitive performance last year in London or Amsterdam. He chatters compulsively throughout the whole first side, so that she doesn't rush to turn the record over. She knows he wants to talk, not listen, that he hasn't the aptitude for silence. But what exactly has he said to Mariette? He couldn't have led her on in any way, made her expect what Delima thinks. For all that he's so arrogant, thinks Claire, he's not malicious—that's the nice thing about egotists, they aren't aware enough of other people's existence to go out of their way to hurt them. And Mariette can't be hurt any more—Claire knows this, even if Delima doesn't. There's no harm, no need to do anything but pretend to listen and then shoo him out the door.

"—a while to get to like Bartok, though of course one doesn't dispute the fact that he's a modern master. Still, one can see that Stefi Geyer would have been as frightened of him as she was of his music. Did you know he wrote that piece for her—she was a violin virtuoso, just a girl, really—but it seems he wrote her passionate letters, as well as music. One would have thought she'd have had the foresight to accept both, don't you think? It must be such a wonderful solution to everything—if you haven't got any particular talent, that is—to be loved by someone who has, to be justified by their gifts.''

"Justified? What a peculiar word to choose." Claire goes over to the corner cupboard, takes out the cognac, two glasses and a package of the Swiss chocolate she has sent down to her from Halifax. Bertrand doesn't protest when she pours him out a glass; his tongue is like a parakeet set free, whipping its wings back and forth, frightened each resting place will turn out to be a cage.

"Yes, justified—you wouldn't understand. I mean that it's different for me, it has always been. You mightn't think it, Claire, but I have been marked out—distinguished—from everyone else—"

Dear God, he's schizoid: delusions of grandeur. Not something Delima would understand . . .

"—my family, my peers, even—but I don't want to bring *her* into it. I can remember exactly when I first knew that I'd been given this terrible gift—"

"Some cognac? I've poured you out a glass."

"—wanting something so badly I would die for it—and still never have it. Not like when you're a child and you want something—ice cream at the fair, a ride on the ponies at the Luxembourg, a cowboy hat—something you know you can talk your parents into getting you. But when you must have something that's utterly beyond your having. Do you know what I mean? Like a child who sees an elephant at the zoo and suddenly has to have nothing less than an elephant for a pet. Nothing else—not hamsters, kittens, even a largeish dog—will do. And who goes on wanting—dreaming of elephants, collecting stuffed and painted, plastic and ivory elephants as the years go on, ending up with a collection he hides away in a trunk—something he could never let even his own children find, but which he can't bring himself to throw away. That's how it is with me.''

''You're into elephants?'' Wanting to sabotage this confession, its unexpected eloquence and intimacy; not wanting to know any other Bertrand than the little pedant in cashmere and corduroy. This passionate Bertrand—he just might be dangerous: to Mariette—to herself. For a split second the thought digs its nails into her—then she pulls herself out of its reach. He hasn't heard her glib little comment, anyway—his story rushes on with the fluency of conviction—how many times has he told it to himself, over and over for want of an audience: a confessor who'll neither violate the secrecy of the confessional nor prescribe any penance? She sighs, pours herself another cognac; Bertrand agitatedly unwraps a square of chocolate, wolfs it, seizes another and continues.

''It's absurdly Proustian, but it's true, it did happen and I can remember the exact moment, circumstances, everything. I was eight years old. My *bonne*—the nanny—had taken my brother and me to the Luxembourg—we rented those wooden boats, you know? The ones you push with a long stick, so they sail back and forth across the *bassin*—you can spend a whole afternoon at it, particularly if your *bonne* has a trashy novel she wants to finish. But on this afternoon it was different, somehow—I was out of sorts—my brother, out of sheer malice, had sunk my boat; my nanny told me not to be a complaining little beast when I came to tell her. I tried to run away, but I couldn't get lost—I knew the garden paths too well, and I was frightened of going out onto the boulevard. So all I could do was wander round in circles, in and out the statues of the Queens of France, the tubs of oleander on the *terrasse*—''

He is getting homesickness mixed up with revelation; this will go on all night. Perhaps if I make some move to gather up the glasses—his still untouched. Or take away the chocolate, most of which he's polished off—

''—where the puppet theatre is. It was in between shows; no one was there, but on a little path behind the pavilion I saw, I heard something I've never been able to forget, that's lodged inside me and that I carry with me like some sort of invisible growth—''

Dear God, here it comes. A couple fornicating in the bushes? A noxious pervert exhibiting himself? Or reaching out cracked hands with claws instead of fingernails, grabbing this tender slip of a boy and making off with him into the nearest public washroom? Not this—I absolutely refuse to hear this—

''You know, a street musician, playing a pipe—a flageolet, all reedy, breathy but, to my ears it was—it was enchantment, Claire: unearthly. You must remember that no one in my family is musical at all; they're Philistines and simply don't understand my feelings. And what I felt, hearing that shabby old man play, was a pleasure unlike any other I'd experienced—stuffing myself on *pain au chocolat*, going up the *téléphérique* at Mont Blanc. In fact, it wasn't just pleasure—I was afraid, too. It was like the moment when you're going up the mountain and the cable car dips and sways passing the cross-bars—the moment when everyone packed inside catches their breath and all you see and feel is the silence of the car, because everyone knows there's nothing but a sheet of metal, a few panes of glass, and a mile of air between them and the rocks below. Such a simple little tune he was playing—it was ice snaking down my back. I couldn't move. I was—can you say transfixed? Yes? Well, I was. I wanted it to go on forever, even though I hadn't any *francs* to toss into the man's cap; when he picked up the few coins people had given him and walked off, I felt—I felt stranded, as if I were an animal left off the ark—and knew I'd been left off. Do you know how that feels?''

''I've been up Mont Blanc in the *téléphérique*, Bertrand—I know how that feels. And it's getting late—perhaps we can finish this tomorrow?'' She leans across to take his untouched glass, but he's impervious.

''I came home at last—found my own way, in a daze—I'm happy to say that my *bonne* was severely reprimanded afterwards. Do you know what I did—the first thing I did on setting foot inside the apartment? I ran to my mother and begged her for a pipe, like the one I'd heard the man play—I didn't know the name of the instrument, but I knew, as surely as I knew my name, my address—that I could make the same sound come out of the pipe. I thought the magic was in the instrument, not your fingers, the way it's the bits of coloured glass and not your eyes that make patterns in a kaleidoscope. I must have asked her a hundred times for a pipe to make music—I must have driven her mad, since she finally relented—she gets migraines all the time, can't bear even the radio on. Well, she took me to a shop to buy a child-sized recorder. I carried it home under my arm as if it were a sack of diamonds some thief might steal away. I wasn't allowed to play it in the house; I had to wait till my nanny could take me to the Luxembourg gardens again.''

Claire sits back in her chair, an empty glass in each hand, rubbing the stems with her thumbs. She may or may not be listening—her eyes are half-glazed, half-fixed on the empty fireplace across from her. Bertrand sits forward in his chair, his hands clasped together, his eyes burnishing the lenses of his glasses.

''She took me two days later—I took my recorder with me, waited till my brother was settled with his boat at the *bassin*, and my nanny had her nose in her book. Then I ran with my pipe to the exact spot where the musician had been. He wasn't there, but it didn't matter. I took the recorder out of its case, put it to my lips, blew into it. A ridiculous tweet-tweet-tweet—no different than the sounds babies make with two-penny whistles. I felt— *anéanti, aboli*. So of course I threw the recorder down to the pavement—I smashed it and smashed it with my foot. The nanny slapped me when she saw what I'd done. *Maman* told my father at the dinner table that night—I remember how he put down his fork, wiped his mouth with the table napkin and looked at her, not at me—as if I were too unimportant even to address. He said, 'You see what comes of indulging this child—you'll ruin his character, and I'll be the one who'll have to pay for repairs. There will be no more idiocy of this sort.' He called it *niaiseries*. So there was no question of music lessons. For a while I haunted that path in the Luxembourg, waiting for the street musician to come back—I was going to beg him, threaten him with knives and pistols to teach me how to play. He never returned—maybe he set himself up in the Tuileries, I don't know.

"It turned out, of course, that I wasn't musical, at least as far as performance went. I took lessons, but it was too late—that was at school in England. My father sent me there when I was fourteen, to learn enough English to be able to manage that side of his business when I left school. It wasn't a bad school—they used to take us up to London every once in a while—to go to the National Gallery, the British Museum, lunchtime concerts. And finally I heard, at a symphony concert, that same tune my street musician had played on his flageolet—only it wasn't the same— it was too loud, too smooth, too cushioned in all the other instruments, the acoustics, everyone else's ears. It meant nothing to me. I felt nothing but the old desire, concentrated like a stone in the pit of my stomach, for something I couldn't have—couldn't make, couldn't be.

"I tried everything at that school. My father didn't know it, or he would never have sent me there, but they had an excellent programme in the arts; they encouraged us to try different things. And I did. Painting, poetry—but all I could produce were competent imitations of the models they set. As for music—I was given up for hopeless, and if it hadn't been for the art master, I'd have been lost for good. Oh, he knew I was a duffer at drawing, but as a last resort he gave me a camera—told me to go outside and take pictures, anything that looked interesting. Of course my first attempts were awful—I overexposed entire rolls of film. I lopped off people's feet and heads. But somehow the feel of that camera in my hands, the sense of it as an instrument, was almost like having that first recorder back in my hands, unbroken. So, I read all the manuals, technical journals. I haunted the local camera shops—and started producing things that weren't so bad. If my father had had an ounce of aesthetic understanding, appreciation, I might have been able to study photography, make it my living. We had terrible rows when I came back to France—my getting a university degree in English was my mother's idea of a compromise. It's all settled, now—I'll earn my living being an English professor and save my soul by taking photographs. It's the only thing that's kept me going here, I might as well confess. In fact, I've done some interesting things—I've found an excellent model.

I might even take a few shots of you, if you don't mind—you have a rather interesting face, you know, Claire? Claire?''

A start and shudder from the armchair—Claire rouses herself, picking up the brandy snifters which have tumbled into her lap. "I'm terribly sorry, Bertrand—I was up late last night—and I'm afraid that cognac hit me like a transport truck. You were saying something about going up Mont Blanc on the *téléphérique*? Oh, Bertrand, you're not offended? Have some more chocolate—you've finished it all? Look, I'm the one who should be offended—that's a two-month supply. You're hopeless, it's all over you—''

And she reaches toward him with a handkerchief which she first licks, then rubs against his cheek, removing the smear of chocolate that makes him look exactly like a greedy child. His eyes are suspiciously bright—he blinks them behind the smudged spectacles, letting her wipe the chocolate from his face as if she were the nanny who had slapped him for breaking his recorder. She has half a mind to confess that she wasn't sleeping, that she did hear his confession—but that would make everything awkward between them—it was no use getting tangled up with other people's needs and desires, trying to help them—she was finished with that. All the same, she feels a ridiculous tenderness toward Bertrand as she puts the handkerchief back in her shirt pocket, a tenderness she cancels by abruptly getting up from the chair and fetching his scarf from the clothesrack by the door. It's nearly eleven—and she'd meant to turf him out by nine.

"It's long past my bedtime. Good night, Bertrand.''

"Claire—I hope I—''

"Really, it's terribly late. Look, you can come back another time—in the afternoon. Come for lunch or something.''

"Claire?'' Just for a moment she thinks he's actually going to touch her hand—give her that little Gallic peck on both cheeks. But his hand goes to his pocket—he pulls out the little volume of Rilke, the one that had belonged to her mother.

"Can I keep this for a while longer?''

"Of course. There's no rush—you've got another few months here, haven't you?''

And then his eyes lose whatever brightness they'd had—slip back to weary, vague indifference: his Spruce Harbour look. The old Bertrand, safe and simple. He shakes her hand the way a child would a rattle, then winds his scarf round his neck and blunders out into a night black and brittle as a June-bug's back. Even before he's disappeared down the ditch, Claire is closing the curtain, bolting the doors, briskly clearing scraps from the dining room table.

"This is why I gave up on entertaining," she says. "Not just that there's no one worth asking round, any more, but all the mess that's left behind—bread crusts, fish bones, forks and knives congealed in puddles of sauce, stains on the tablecloth—napkins crumpled on the rug—you'd think we were a party of twelve. Half a bottle of extremely decent *Rioja* left, though the cognac's as good as gone. And I'll have to carry on, now—I asked him once, he'll be back, he'll find reasons to turn my house into a kind of private lounge. I ought to get a dependant's allowance from Père Philippe. At least Bertrand doesn't drink—that's one expense I'm spared."

She wonders if he's as chaste about life's other pleasures—if chocolate is his only indulgence here. She's heard the girls to whom he teaches Lamartine and Musset call him Bertie behind his back, giggle at the swish of his corduroyed legs as he walks down the college corridors. The only other women on faculty at Sacré Coeur are the nuns who teach Philosophy and Classics, and then the librarian, mother of fifteen and well into her fifties. His tastes don't appear to run to the other sex—to sex at all, in fact. He's in love, she concludes, not with Mariette, nor with his Antoinette de whatever back in Paris, but with this *fin-de-siècle* image he's styled for himself—the *artiste manqué*, the wandering aesthete: I-am-a-camera. "Except that he believes it, has become it and wants confirmation. From anyone who will listen and acknowledge him. Wanted it from me and I refused him, I can't—"

Claire scrapes the remains of the pudding and molten ice cream into the black belly of the garbage bag, wishing she could shove in Bertrand's confession as well. Why couldn't he have stayed on the subject of Stefi Geyer and Bartok tonight—why did he have to expose himself so? Christ, she's tired—the tenderness she'd felt for Bertrand boils over into irritation. Of course he'd made the whole thing up from an adolescent reading of Proust—the first volume only. What was it he'd said? "I bear a mark that sets me apart from other people." Sensory stigmata—she began to feel sorry for his parents, having to put up with all that. Didn't he luxuriate in it, though—feeling special, annointed, different, as though his suffering were some Baroque cloud on which he could float forever over any sharp or pointed rocks. She has a sudden image of Mariette, bleeding onto a garbage bag in the back seat of the car. The doctor, assuming she was family: "Kid looks like a battlefield inside. Well, she won't have to bother about going on the pill, at least. I think it would be best for you to tell her."

Time to put out the lights—she'll wash the dishes in the morning. On the way upstairs she passes the armchairs in which they'd sat, the almost-empty bottle of cognac, the pile of foil and coloured paper wrappers on Bertrand's side of the coffee table. Claire reaches for the foil, crumpling it into a tight ball—it will go with the fish bones into the garbage bag. She reaches for the paper—takes it in her hands, sits down in the chair and smooths the wrappers against her knees. Swiss chocolate, a stupid, sentimental movie, a room in a cheap hotel. An extravagance, that chocolate, sympathetic magic to ward off evil, the evil of possibilities multiplying, rampant, defying the strictest choices the way wood can defy hammer and nails, split apart instead of hold. She stares at the coloured paper which had enclosed the chocolate: photographs of mountains, Edelweiss, grazing cows—innocuous. Good word, that; you must find words to act as slip-covers, curtains, safety-chains. Thinking of Bertrand quitting Spruce Harbour in ten months' time, leaving behind a mountain of chocolate wrappers, a pile of photographs: Mariette as mother-and-child—

She takes the carefully-smoothed wrappers into the kitchen, drops them into the garbage bag, turns out the lights, and goes upstairs past the locked room, into her own. Undresses in the dark and lies herself down in the brass bed she's slept in since she was a child. Naked under the white quilt made so long ago that it's turned the hue of ancient ivory, crinkled, like an old woman's skin. Outside, trucks heave and rumble past, loaded with frozen fish, lumber, milk and vegetables—back and forth between Nova Scotia and the Boston states. She takes a long breath, as though she were about to dive into deep water, spreads out arms and legs into two fans so that she's spreadeagled on the taut sheets, fingers and toes staking the corners. Staked. Beneath the yellowed quilt her breasts press like bulbs smothered under snow. Belly caving in on womb and birth canal—white, infolded, crumpled now that the menstrual blood has drained forever out of her. Bled-out, bone-white, ghost-white inside: room enough for only emptiness itself to take up lodging. Slowly she brings arms and legs straight again, as if she were a dull pair of scissors closing. Falls asleep with thighs locked tight, hands cupped over her opening: fingers pressing silence over locked and hidden lips.

THE NIGHT of the concert brings a storm so fierce there's not a hope of more than ten people showing up. Another aesthetic miracle and box-office apocalypse for which Claire will be held responsible by Père Philippe, who will make his usual courtly speech in two languages to the audience spread out on splintery chairs throughout the Chapel. There have been times when the performers outnumber the faithful come to hear them—at least tonight it's not a mere pianist, but a string quartet and oboe soloist from Halifax.

Bertrand takes the seat next to Claire's, in the front row. He is in a suit, with a knitted vest (his mother's doing?) and a plum-coloured bow tie he could have picked up for a dime at Frenchy's, except that he would never profane the temple of his body with a scrap of silk someone else once wore. Claire is severe in black trousers, a white shirt she made up herself with material ordered in from Halifax. Both have coats draped over their shoulders, because drafts sweep in through the stained glass and under the floorboards in spite of Hector's best efforts to eradicate them. Claire worries, as she always does, whether the performers will

come down with pneumonia and chillblains before they're
through.

"Pretty safe, this selection." Bertrand is skimming the programme: a comfortable Beethoven in the first half, Britten's Fantasy for Strings and Oboe in the second. The oboist would seem
to have an unfair advantage in her name: against a Sue McBean,
an Everett Stokes, a Pauline Deveau and Stephen Tompkins,
"Halyna Radowska" reads like the real thing—Europe—the
"other side." The quartet enters, seats itself, and waits for Père
Philippe, who—elegant, genial, authoritative—walks up to the
podium where the altar used to be before the Chapel's deconse-
cration, and clears his throat. But just as he's about to speak, a
gust of glacial wind rushes through the chinks in the wall as though
to fill up some gigantic balloon.

"How can they play against that?" Claire groans, then answers
her own question. "As every gallant band sent touring through
the regions does—playing that much louder if not better."

Bertrand is tapping his toes and humming the allegro from the
opening movement of the Beethoven. He is in an uproarious mood
tonight, for he's just received consular permission to escape to
New York for the Christmas break—he's already planned the
exhibitions he will take in, operas he'll attend, books he will
buy—even the gently chiding postcard he will send to Claire.
Claire with her warnings: "New York? Every Frenchman's wet
dream of America. You can take Lady Liberty—I'll tune into the
Saturday afternoon broadcast from the Met and listen to you
applauding the quiz panel."

Père Philippe compliments his handpicked audience for sup-
porting the Muse in Whitby County, and proceeds to read the text
Claire has prepared for him. "We are to be rarely privileged
tonight, for not only is the McBean quartet one of the liveliest
performing in the Maritimes today, but its members are being
joined for this performance by a player of exceptional promise,
only eighteen years old, but already an artist of note both in
Canada and in her native Poland." December wind oohs and aahs
through the chapel windows; the stained-glass saints, pasty faces
blacked out by the night, loom over Père Philippe like funerary

sculptures in a dim cathedral aisle. Bertrand shifts in his chair—it shrieks against the highly-polished floor, and Claire raps his knee with her rolled-up programme. The musicians—minus Miss Radowska—take their seats under a chandelier which the now-howling wind sets swaying back and forth, like a vine waiting for the ecclesiastical equivalent of Tarzan.

They play. The audience claps resolutely, dutifully, twelve pairs of hands that have braved a whirlwind, pails of rain to come and hear these messengers make music. They bow, and everyone files out—musicians to the classroom that does for backstage, audience to a corridor that boasts no bar, not even a cigarette or coffee machine, just varnished wainscotting that reflects rain-splattered legs in rubber boots. At the end of the corridor Bertrand holds forth about Boulez and Stockhausen to Claire, who doesn't listen, so preoccupied is she with watching Père Philippe make the rounds, his sleek and dimpled face hiding—forebearance? Resignation? Firm resolution to end this gaping hole in the college's pocket? One student in the audience—two faculty members—the rest are culture-bereft couples who've retired here from Halifax. "Aren't we a stilted little bunch," thinks Claire. "No antic laughter in this corridor, no glasses clinking over discussions of the music we've just heard." "I do what I can," she says aloud, interrupting Bertrand, who is on to Berio and Henze now. "There'll be a reception in Père Philippe's office tonight: coffee and doughnuts from the cafeteria—you'll tag along, won't you? There has to be someone to meet the artists, you know—you can tell them all about modern music—they'll be so happy to hear there's life after Beethoven. Hurry now, we'll have to get back to our seats—second half coming up. Oh, come now, Bertrand, they didn't do that dismally with the Beethoven—Père Philippe, good evening—Bertrand was just saying what a splendid performance it is—don't you agree?"

TEPID WATER in the urn: Maxwell House and Coffee Mate. Packets of sugar with provincial flags stamped on them, colours out-of-sync with the outlines. Passing doughnuts and egg salad sandwiches on a stainless steel tray, a waitress from the cafeteria in what looks like a nurse's uniform with white sweat pants underneath, and a nylon hairnet from which ringlets dribble down her cheeks and nape and forehead. People grouped around a desk crenellated with photographs of Père Philippe's sisters, nieces, nephews; people waiting for the performers to make their entrance. Or rather, for the star performer, since the members of the quartet have already assembled here, faces chalky, arms exhausted, but—Claire sighs, relieved—without shakes or shivers, and making no complaints about the wind or the slight staleness of the doughnuts (left over from the Student Disco the night before).

Halyna Radowska walks in at last on the arm of a short, squat, middle-aged man who might have stepped out of a photograph of the Politburo. Calculated contrast, for the girl looks as dazzling as her playing. She had walked into the chapel after the quartet had been seated—walked with the vacant aplomb of a sleepwalker, eyes fixed straight in front of her, pale braids wound across her head the way children in Russian propaganda photos sometimes wear their hair—though minus the whirlybird bows. Gown like a mute bell swaying round her: gown, not dress, for this outfit has a conspicuously decorative function, though Claire can't tell whether it reminds her more of discarded wrappings from a bridal shower, or the tarnished uniform of a Christmas tree angel. Off-white—through age and improper cleaning—metallic ribbon shot like shrapnel through absurd tiers of flounces, ruffles. Low-necked enough, Bertrand notes, to show her collar bone, but high enough to make it just impossible to tell whether what appears to be a surging bosom is more foam than flesh.

And yet, decide Claire and Bertrand both, the girl carries it off, as though she were a golden thread holding together a motley row of beads. Though she wears violent makeup, though her cheeks seem more rubella'd than rouged, she looks bizarrely beautiful. Père Philippe comes forward with a cup of coffee for her—she shakes her head, and her father explains she only drinks ice water after a performance. The waitress is sent off with a styrofoam cup to the bathroom down the hall as Père Philippe introduces Mr. Radowski, the musician's father and a teacher of mathematics, formerly of the University at Krakow. Mr Radowski makes a curt bow to the assembly, waves away the plate of egg salad sandwiches Père Philippe himself is offering to his daughter, and stares up at the larger-than-life oil painting of the Expulsion of the Acadians that hangs on the wall over Père Philippe's desk. Pregnant silence does not so much fall as stumble over all.

Until Claire, pale as her shirt, walks up to father and daughter, offering congratulations to Mr. Radowski on the performance of Mlle. Radowska. Bertrand follows at Claire's elbow, anxious not so much to speak to the girl as to hear her speak, waiting for the fever-painted lips to open and let out the voice of any North American teenager—gawky, loud, calling back the tray of doughnuts her father had also refused for her, as if they were pomegranates for his Persephone. Her silence seems to have literally entranced him—at last, as the waitress comes forward with the glass of cool water, Bertrand bursts forth in his most fulsome French. "It's been a privilege—and a pleasure, of course—hearing you. You play so expressively, with such—"

"Thanks," says Miss Radowska, as though confirming an announcement of the correct time on the radio. But not to Bertrand—to the waitress. Bertrand stares at her, his face suddenly as flushed as if he were a small boy who'd gotten into his mother's rouge—until Mr. Radowski steps in.

"My daughter, alas, speaks very little French. At school in Poland she is learning German, as well as Russian too, unfortunately. And since we have been to Canada she is occupied learning fluently English. In the time she can spare from her instrument."

Père Philippe's ears prick up—he is so excited that the murky coffee sloshes down the sides of his cup and over his hands. "Ah, then, you must send your daughter to us—we have an excellent French immersion programme—spring or summer—or both. Now that you've made Canada your home, it would be a shame for your daughter not to master our other official language—don't you agree, Miss Saulnier? In terms of your daughter's career, I mean, Mr. Radowski.''

Slanting a smile out long, narrow eyes the colour of buckwheat honey, opening full lips to let a voice husky, rich, as unlike the usual North American bubble and squeak as pumpernickel is from Wonderbread, Miss Radowska finally speaks. ''I think that is a wonderful idea. I don't speak French at all, as my father has told you, but I know how it should sound. And if these people''—she gestures to Bertrand—''can learn to speak it so well right here, then surely I can too.''

Bertrand looks as though someone has just attempted to defenestrate him. ''But I'm not local. I'm the *co-opérant*—I'm from Paris. I've spent barely two months here, surely you can't have—''

Père Philippe overrides him, taking Miss Radowska by a long, bare arm. ''Then you must attend our course, mademoiselle. Here, come and meet Père Gilbert—he's the one in charge of everything to do with immersion.'' And he leads the girl and her father away with the deference due to royalty in exile.

Claire, hiding laughter by pretending to choke on her doughnut, looks up in time to see Bertrand wobble out the door like a bicycle whose tires have been punctured, and are irremediably losing air.

NEW YEAR'S EVE. Hector is at his parents' house eating rappie pie, drinking Screech, and talking politics with his father and assorted brothers-in-law while their women collapse around the TV, having exhausted themselves putting the children to bed, cooking and washing up after dinner, and listening to the shouting going on in the dining room, right under the tapestry-rug of *The Last Supper*. Mariette babysits in the trailer while Delima and Luc make a night of it at the Fish and Game. Bertrand is still in New York. What's he doing there right now? Claire wonders. Surely not Times Square. She almost hopes he'll get mugged, raped, robbed and whatever else can happen to a traveller on a winter's night in New York; it might shake him loose a bit, cut through the custard-skin of his *amour-propre*. Claire herself is keeping contented company with a bottle of Ballantine's, a half-dozen back copies of *The New York Review of Books* and a ten-inch stack of records.

She pulls herself out of the armchair to put on another record—that same Britten fantasy they heard the night before Bertrand went off to New York. She listens hard to the oboe part, and concedes, half-grudgingly, that the Polish girl from Halifax *did* play it as sensuously, cockily, perfectly as any virtuoso. A long sip of Scotch. What on earth is the girl doing with the McBean quartet when she should be off at the Royal Academy or the Juilliard? And then Claire remembers the outrageous but frumpy dress the Polish girl had worn, the stone-jowled duenna of a father, the salary he'd be making as a recent emigré. And Père Philippe had visions of her studying French here—had mentioned to Claire just before the holidays that he'd mailed off a pamphlet advertising the College Immersion Course to Miss Radowska, or whatever her name was. "As likely she'll come back here as our little Mariette will entice Bertrand into connubial bliss in a trailer on the fishplant road," decides Claire. "Or that he'll lure her into his bed instead of his camera lens."

She frowns. Forgets the Britten, sitting up straight in the sagging chintz chair, making herself remember that she's said nothing to Bertrand—and that she's lied to Delima. Or at least, hasn't indicated that there's a gap between the message Delima burdened her with, and its actual delivery to Bertrand. "I am not, not, not Mariette's keeper—I wish Delima would get that through her skull. Might as well try to split a coconut with a nail file. And I am not responsible for Bertrand, either, no matter what Père Philippe may think. For all I know or care they can fuck each other silly in their little witch's hut in the woods—God knows it would at least do him some good. And it can't harm her—not now. Though I can't tell that to Delima, because being Delima she'll tell Mariette, and there's no way she can handle that: not now—not yet."

Neither can Claire—without another glass of Scotch. What was that doctor's name? Didn't matter—he wasn't *acadien*; wouldn't know her or Mariette; that she wasn't, as he'd assumed, the girl's aunt, if not her mother. What good would it have done to tell him?

What good would it do to tell anyone, now? Perhaps it was for the best—given that Mariette was, after all, Delima's daughter, even if not Luc's—she had that in her favour. Besides, Bertrand was interested in the girl merely as a model, a pleasingly angular object for his lens. If she had said anything to him that night he came for dinner, he would have—what? Broken a bottle over her head? Bertrand, aesthete *abandonné*, take up with a girl who reeked of dried fish and most likely couldn't spell her full name? No, that would be much more Hector's style—since he seemed so determined to humiliate himself. Forget Hector, he didn't exist anymore except as a mistake erased. Bertrand—what would he make of the New York women, ripe as he was for a fall from that snotty innocence of his? That oboist, God bless her, look how she'd levelled him with her comment on his French—''pretty good for a local boy''—something like that.

Claire smiles, lying back in her chair, the record and the Scotch going round and round her head. That concert, the goddawful reception afterwards, Mariette, Bertrand, Miss Warsaw 1953. Herself, in nunlike black-and-white while Père Philippe showed himself a peacock in his Harris tweeds. ''That little waitress, waiting so patiently with her tray, serving us all—only she had Mariette's face, or else Mariette has hers; it's getting all mixed up. And that Polish girl, who reminds me a little, a very little of Hector, before he came back—when he was so fierce to get away. Hector in the front row—he should have been wearing a dinner jacket—he'd carry it off so well, he wears even his overalls with distinction. Should I have asked him back to the reception—did he feel slighted? Does it matter? Tired, must go up to bed.'' Hector, Mariette, Bertrand, little Bertrand in his bow tie and cashmere sweater, Bertrand at the podium, turning pages for that Polish girl in her tarnished bridal dress while Hector watches the performance. And in the wings, Mariette, with a leaden tray of ice water; Mariette, frilled cap on her head and perfectly naked: small slit between her legs black as a bruise—deep, spreading, her skin white as the bones sharpening below—

Crazy-quilt, confused, confumed: Claire shakes herself like a spaniel jumping from a puddle. Needs air, needs light, the tokens of sobriety—or else face the fact that here she is on New Year's Eve, alone and drinking herself into an irresponsible scramble of names and faces and knowing. She grabs her coat from the hook by the kitchen door and goes out onto the porch. Cold night, crystal sky—she hears in her head those first bars of Stefan George's poem, the one Schönberg put into his string quartet: "I feel the air of other planets . . ." She throws back her head, pressing the very skin of her eyes against the frozen sky: so cold, so clear, an infinite scatter of stars, looking like a bottle of milk thrown against a wall of ice, drops freezing even as they scatter. Tintoretto's painting, "The Origin of the Milky Way": goddess with milk spurting from breasts into empty air as her children are snatched from her. Not Christ's blood but mother's milk streaming in the firmament. Too far; frozen hard as stones—we can never drink it. Are what we are, unnourished children fallen to earth.

"Where we burn out," she whispers to the dark. "Slow or quick—that's the only choice. And I swear I'll go slow, so slow I won't even feel myself burning. *Stick, stock, stone.*"

2

Hector decides it's time to let Bertrand lose.

"Check."

Bertrand's fingers close round his doomed king. You can watch his eyes darting to the white and black squares left empty on the board: illusory exits—temporary safety. He doesn't play a bad game of chess; it's just that he tends to be over-protective, to hold back from making the reckless moves which might, if he kept his head, lure his opponent into losing his. This time, however, there is no choice but surrender. He looses his fingers from the little wooden crown, grimaces, moves his king into—

"Mate. But a good game—you've forced me to go back to my copy of *Chess for Champions*, Bertrand. Would you like a coffee now?"

"You've only instant? Well then, yes—I need something to keep me awake. How can you stand it down in this dungeon? The heat is unbearable, and the thumping of those pipes next door! Surely you can do better than this—"

"This" comprehends the cracked plaster of the walls, on which a patina of new dust forms over old dirt; a plain wooden desk scarred by saturn-rings from coffee cups, ink bottles, Pepsi tins. On the wall a calendar from Wagner's Kwikway showing, above crudely and incorrectly reproduced dates, a twentyish honey-blonde cultivating an infantile air. Braids drawn over her shoulders, a prim white blouse with a Peter Pan collar: unbuttoned, so that the impossibly golden, fluffy, rotund chicks she holds up merge with the impossibly golden, bulgey breasts inside the starched cotton blouse. It is the calendar which simultaneously repels and attracts Bertrand—the photograph is in such patently kitschy taste it's positively classic. Yet there's something about the confusion of downy chicks and breasts that mesmerizes him, so that he stares at the calendar while Hector dumps some atrocious edible-oil product into his mug. Stares and sighs.

"Your type? You go for rustic buxom blondes? Why didn't you tell me earlier—I would have taken you with me to the Fish and Game." Hector swings his feet, in their workman's boots, up to the desktop, narrowly missing the chessboard. He disregards Bertrand's silence, as pointed as an over-sharpened pencil. "What do you do for women here, Bertrand? I'm sure Père Philippe will have warned you off the students—did I ever tell you about the Lothario from Chicago they hired as a sabbatical replacement one year? They had to pay him a full year's salary to get him to leave after three months. He rented that blue house across from Claire's, threw all-night parties for the students, had a portable drugstore as well as a bar. I've always regretted he left before I did my time at Sacré Coeur. He taught philosophy—we might have got along. The story goes that he tried to seduce Claire—might as well have tried to shell a lobster with a spoon."

Bertrand puts down the coffee he's scarcely touched, thumps it down on the desk so that it sloshes over the sides of the cup and leaves yet another pale ring on the varnish. "You take a lot of liberties, don't you?"

"And you sound like a Victorian clergyman defending his sister's virtue from the hired man. What's Claire to you, Bertrand—or is she your cure for thorns in the flesh?"

Bertrand sits with his spine straighter than a flagpole, his spectacles intensifying the blaze in his eyes. Hector perfects an exaggerated sprawl—were he to tilt back any further in his wooden swivel chair, he'd do a back flip into the furnace room. Neither man says a word; their silence has the consistency of hardening cement. Suddenly the pipes begin to pound: manic, deranged, with a wheezing and growling as if they were some gigantic fat man shaking the bars of an iron cage. Hector brings his chair back a fraction. Bertrand permits himself to fold his arms. Then Hector shrugs—an excellent imitation of Bertrand's state-of-the-art Parisian shrug—and deflects his question.

"You know who has the best of it round here? The frogs—spring peepers. Wait till spring—you'll hear them every night for a month—high-pitched noises like sawed-off squeals when they mate. Just think of it, Bertrand, millions of frogs in every marsh and pond of *Acadie*, fucking their little feet off come April. You'd better watch out—it's contagious."

Slowly stroking his bow tie, Bertrand shakes his head. "Actually, I'm as good as engaged to a girl at home—a real beauty—like a Titian painting—would you know what I mean? The granddaughter of the Comtesse de Vigny. Quite a figure in her day—she had a *salon* like something out of Proust. Marcel—you read him at university? I see. Well, then, you can keep your fat blondes at the Fish and Game, Hector. Actually, it's rather funny, but I don't seem particularly troubled by what you so poetically call thorns in the flesh. This whole place is so dreary, so closed in, all this fog and rain we've been having. It's ten times worse since I went to New York—if you must know, I was sorely tempted the last day of my visit there to hop on a bus to New Orleans and never come back. The women here might as well be spruce trees as far as I'm concerned. As for Claire—she's just company, though I must say I might have done worse. I'm not surprised that your gangster-professor from Chicago paid court to her—she's rather attractive in her way, don't you think? What we'd call a *belle laide*, a woman who carries herself as if she thought she were beautiful, and almost convinces you she is. At least I can talk to her."

"About what?" It's Hector's turn to sound huffy, hostile, as if he were some discarded lover accosting his rival.

"Oh, art, politics, all kinds of things. She's an exceptionally knowledgeable woman, for these parts—"

"For any parts. You know, Bertrand, you should be a little more careful."

"Careful? Of what? Not—you really don't think people will think that I—that we—that's too absurd. She could be my mother."

"Bertrand, this is the French Shore. She could be your

grandmother and people would still talk if the two of you exchanged more than a few words in the Kwikway store. Anyway, I'm not thinking about your reputation—it's more your—. Look, I'm concerned about your well-being—''

"And who sounds like the Victorian uncle now? What have you got against Claire? How do you know her, anyway? She never mentions you.''

"Why should she? I'm dead and buried in Montréal as far as Claire's concerned. Ever since I decided to come home, she refuses to have anything to do with me—not because I screwed up on the doctorate, but simply because I came back. Look, Bertrand, the point is that Claire's a meddler. She prides herself on being self-sufficient, solitary, but she can't stop herself from correcting people's lives, interfering to save them from themselves—maybe to save herself. But she's a random kind of meddler—she has a nasty habit of taking people in and then, just when they're most in need of shelter, locking her door against them.''

"You seem to think I need Claire—I mean, for more than a decent cup of coffee and the occasional meal. My dear Hector, I certainly don't need someone like Claire to 'save' me. You don't seem to have thought this through—that it might, after all, be Claire who needs me. And that I'm the one who'll slam the doors shut—on Spruce Harbour and every one of its inhabitants, once my time is up.'' Bertrand rises from his chair and stands against the wall, hands thrust in his pockets. He looks calmly, benignly down at Hector. "You see, I'm Claire's link with—the great world, the other side—what she once was, or at least wanted to be. I gather she studied in London—had plans for a career as a concert pianist—at least that's what Père Philippe told me—she isn't exactly forthcoming about herself, is she? Actually, that's what I admire in her—she isn't one of those irritating people who oppress you with the state of her mind and heart each time you sit down for a bit of conversation. No, my dear old chap, you needn't worry about Claire and me. I don't mean this unkindly, but if we were in Paris I wouldn't go out of my way to give her the time of day. Naturally it isn't a matter of physical attraction—it's just that, after so many years here, she's bound to be—limited, intellectually speaking—you know. Although, as I think I mentioned, I find her rather striking. I've even asked if I might photograph her sometime, but she hasn't taken to the idea. Luckily I latched on to an excellent model shortly after I arrived here. Look, I'll show you—I'm sending these off to the *American Journal of Photography*.''

He turns to his satchel, takes out a padded manilla envelope and extracts half a dozen photographs, all of the same model. Sometimes alone, sometimes with a small child. Hector looks at them closely, taking each one into his hands.

''Well, what do you think?''

''I've seen ones like these before—at your studio.''

''But what do you think? Rather effective, that contrast of light and shade, wouldn't you say? I mean, it's not the usual hackneyed thing. Of course it helps that she's got such dark hair—and white skin, though I'll guess it's because she's anaemic. What is it—do you know her?''

''I do now. I sometimes see her pushing a kid in a stroller along the ditch. Her mother—''

''Oh, I don't want to know who her mother is. I don't even want to know who or what she is—it would spoil everything if I were to find out she's some waitress in the rappie-pie take-out, or a fishplant worker. You see, I discovered her—in the woods behind my house. She seemed a little—wild, you could say. I mean, as if she could have grown up out of the ground along with the grass and the ferns. I've tamed her—she was awfully shy at first. Rather charming—imagine finding a *jeune fille en fleur* in the backwoods of *Acadie*. Anyway, you can see what marvellous photos I've gotten out of her.''

Hector drops the photos to the desk, carelessly, so that one falls to the floor and Bertrand has to scuttle after it. ''Little shit face,'' Hector thinks, watching Bertrand search for the picture, pulling it gently, slowly, so as not to scratch it against the dirt underneath the desk. Repeats over and over Gustave's name for Bertrand, coined the day the *Français de France* walked through the door of Wagner's store and demanded *dentifrice*. And when Gustave had asked what the hell *that* was, Bertrand had said ''toothpaste'' in the tone of voice you'd use with a person who was not only slightly deaf but imbecile as well.

"Really, Hector, you could be a little more careful." Blowing the dust off the photograph, putting it back with the others into the manilla envelope. Before he can finish, Hector has switched off the lights. Bertrand can just make him out by the door in his overalls and ski jacket, the baseball cap in his hands. "You might wait a moment—"

"I've got work to do outside. Why don't you run along to Claire's?"

"As a matter of fact that's exactly where I am going—as soon as I've posted these. If Delbert will let me, that is—I have to spend at least a quarter of an hour discussing the weather with him every time I go in there. No wonder your Canadian postal system is so inefficient. Claire's asked me for dinner—and not rappie pie, either. What you people see in potato-porridge and clam juice I really can't fathom." He leaves the office, turning in the opposite direction to Hector, opening the basement door and heading up into the lighted corridors.

"Go fuck a sheep—if one'll have you!" Hector calls out against the clanging pipes. Bertrand wouldn't understand, even if he'd heard. He rams the cap on his head, jabs his hands into his overall pockets and walks up and down the dark, evil-smelling basement corridor. Thinking of Claire and Bertrand, Bertrand and the girl in the photographs, the girl he has seen every day in the ditch as he drives to work. She has a name—she is Mariette, she's Delima's girl, Delima's and any one of a dozen men along the French Shore. Although—. But he stops there, kicking open the basement door and running off into the parking lot where his truck, at least, is waiting patiently for him, its doors deliberately unlocked.

HECTOR DRIVES BACK to his apartment, boils up some instant soup on the hot plate, and makes a supper out of it and the submarine sandwich left over in the refrigerator of the store. Brushing the crumbs off the table, he then extracts his typewriter from under his bed, brings out pens and paper from the closet, and sets up the shoeboxes which serve as a makeshift filing cabinet. On Monday morning he must mail off a review of a new biography of Descartes for his friend's journal. It will mean another long session with Delbert, who makes special occasions out of small packets, and seems consciously to choose twenty five-cent stamps rather than the dollar one, just for the protracted pleasure of sticking them all on. While he interrogates Hector, of course. In another age he would have been one of the more successful agents of the Spanish Inquisition, wearing his prisoners down with the simple, gentle gravity of his persistence.

"And how are you today, Hector? I didn't see you at Mass on Sunday. Weren't you feeling well, Hector? You know, it's not so good for a man to stay away too much from his church. No, it's not good at all. Especially if what keeps him out late on a Saturday night is something he should be telling his priest about on Sunday morning."

It isn't a particularly interesting biography—it is not a necessary book—not the way his own would have been: *Whirlwinds and Melons: The Dreams of Descartes. Ergo,* he could still write it —his thesis was three-quarters completed, historical and psychological contexts established, with only the analysis of three dreams to tackle. The whirlwind would be no problem—his own interpretation's water-tight, even if unorthodox. It's the other two— the apparitions of the Thunderclap and the Spirit of Truth—which need careful integration into the system he's worked out. He sits staring at the typewriter, the half-started review, then gets up and flings himself down on the bed, looking up to the black blanks under his eyelids. Why couldn't he fall asleep and be wakened by a demon's thunder or the descent of some angel-faced spirit, showing him the way to heaven or hell, it didn't matter which, just an exit from this impasse. Dean of Drains at Sacré Coeur, the highlight of his existence a chess game with the impeccably tight-assed Bertrand. He thinks of him with Claire, right now, eating *coq au vin, coquilles St. Jacques* together, sitting in the overstuffed armchairs and discussing that world of which Bertrand has elected himself emissary. The great wide world for which Hector à Gustave Wagner hadn't been good enough, for which Claire had never forgiven him.

He opens his eyes into the molten brightness of the unshaded lightbulb, dangling on its thick black cord from the ceiling. In the comics he'd read as a child, lightbulbs appeared by a character's head to signal "idea!" Well, here was his grand scheme to come back to Spruce Harbour on his own terms—nobody's fool, nobody's protégé, but his own man at last—here it was strung up, suspended from the gallows of the ceiling. He'd taken the job as handyman because he'd thought it would be good to occupy his hands while he worked out things in his head, egg-head disguised by the impregnable shield of the baseball cap. But he'd done nothing on his book, had spent his less than abundant free-time patching things up with his parents, driving up and down the coast road with tapeplayer blaring, hanging out at the Fish and Game—

"I don't feel particularly troubled by what you so poetically call thorns in the flesh." Arrogant little prick, little prude—he deserved whatever he had coming from Claire. *Sauve qui peut*; he'd done his bit, delivered warning. But to the wrong person. He ought to have been talking not to Bertrand but to the girl—Delima's kid, Mariette. Tell her not to let herself be used—though would she understand the uses to which the chaste Bertrand could put her? Turning her into an object under a lens, a finite number of poses which could exhaust her, erase her. How could she be made to understand that—she spoke the same language as a Rita or Marvine: Bertrand was no fucker, she was safe. Unless, on the other hand, she wanted just that, what that lonely tableful of girls at the Fish and Game wanted from him: so many fast fucks that there'd be an obligation to marry, to settle down in a trailer and raise a laundry line of diapers forever after. What else was there to do in Spruce Harbour? What else had his ancestors done but, like Noah and Co. after the flood, multiplied, multiplied, multiply. . .

Hector jumps off the bed. Over the jeans and shirt he's wearing under his discarded overalls he pulls on a sweater—rummages in the dust-clotted corner of his closet for a tie. Combs his hair in the spotted mirror over the bathroom sink, remembering how

Claire had once told him he looked a bit like François Premier—
or was it Henri Quatre—with his black hair and beard. Who gives
a shit—let her drink burgundy with Bertrand for all Hector cares.
He'll get quit of them, clear of them, this night at least. Singing
to himself, stuffing all the cash he has on hand into his wallet,
grabbing his leather jacket from the hanger and leaping into the
Kwikway truck, enroute for . . .

Not the Fish and Game. Not even the Legion Hall at Whitby.
He drives fast up the shore, past all the houses and halls in which
people who know him, all about him, are drinking beer and
dancing and playing pool; drives till he leaves the shore well
behind him and is into the valley, the neat, whitewashed valley
towns, tourist towns, cluttered with signs like "Drive carefully,
we love our children" and "Apple Blossom Capital of Canada."
Six-thirty. He can get to Halifax well before ten if the roads are
clear. No sign of any snow—one of those mild February nights
which whet your appetite for spring just as another blizzard's
brewing.

He has a friend in Halifax, an old friend from Sacré Coeur
who's been asking him to come up and see him ever since he'd
heard the news of Hector's return. Stéphane Dugas—ran his own
computer company in Dartmouth. Hector had never taken up the
invitation to come and stay—their reunion would be a little too
much like an enactment of the parable of the idle and the indus-
trious apprentice. But if he simply dropped by this evening—and
accepted the offer of a bed for the night—just to walk city streets—
a sidewalk, for Christ's sake, just to feel a sidewalk under his
feet—see different sorts of people, city people. Maybe go to a
movie, maybe a club, maybe get utterly stoned and forgo the
reunion with Stéphane, who the hell knew—. But out. Away, for
Christ's sake.

Not even stopping for coffee at the Okay Diner in Paradise.
Barrelling right through the valley, tapedeck on: *Così fan Tutte*.
Threading the maze of the Micmac rotary—why *that* name, why
such a cretinous use of a people's name?—past the Micmac Mall.
Heading into Dartmouth—he'll just stop by Stéphane's, see if the
bugger's in. An apartment—you'd think if he was as successful

as people said he'd have a house by now. On the northwest arm,
or on Bloomingdale Road, with the plastic surgeons and corpo-
ration lawyers. But no, a two-bedroom apartment in this shabby-
looking six-story: The Dartmouth Arms. Hector brightens visibly
as he parks the truck and walks up cracked concrete steps. Waiting
for Stéphane to answer the buzzer, he peers through the glass
door into the lobby where a couple are arguing. January–May, or
else father and daughter. Wearing serviceable but out-moded coats
that are clearly someone's castoffs—they have a sad and sagging
air about shoulders and hems. The girl's blonde hair wound tight
around her head. She is hugging something to her chest—a kitten?
A video-cassette?

But then Stéphane's voice over the intercom—mild surprise, no
great joy or irritation. They never were very good friends—they
hadn't been friends at all. Why had he come? By the time he's
pushed open the now unlocked door, the girl and her father have
disappeared. Instead of taking the elevator, Hector runs up the
three flights of stairs, head reeling at the smell of disinfectant—
this hallway could be the lab of Pasteur or Lister. Over-zealous
janitor, he thinks—worth his weight in Mr. Clean. Apt. 309.

Ten minutes inside and he realizes that Stéphane is covering up
a profound lack of interest in Hector's company with the excessive
warmth of his hospitality. Still, Hector stays an hour or so, three
beers or so, hearing the news, offering none. That Stéphane is
getting married in three months' time—an elementary-school
teacher who grew up in Salmon Falls: Alice à Joe à Charles à
. . . . He talks about his company, which Hector pretends not to
have heard of. Has bought a house in the South End—they're still
renovating it—will rent out the top two floors and live in the
bottom, just for now. Pay for itself—rents sky high in Halifax—
Hector would have a time of it if he moved here from the shore.
Just what was he up to there? Worked at the college—well, now,
always knew you were the professorial type—

Hector gets up to use the bathroom, counting the cracks in the
plaster behind the toilet. He examines his eyes in the mirror—are
they really bloodshot or is that just the effect of the pink-shaded
light? Goes out to shake Stéphane's hand and wish him well; he

apologizes for having to drink and run, but— "friends I have to see uptown." Back in the lobby—no trace of the quarrelling couple; Hector feels bereft, abandoned. Stéphane's beer on a nearly-empty stomach. Crosses into Halifax to get a meal—ends up at a sub-sleazy place on Barrington; stares at the scorched hamburger and fat-laden fries, realizing he cannot eat, his guts are knotted up. Panic when he walks Barrington, Spring Garden Road, alien concrete under his feet, streetwalkers foul-mouthed, accusatory as he passes them by—not that, not here and now. Stores shut but everything lit up inside in pale, poisonous fluorescence: silk shirts and cashmere sweaters; pearl necklaces, gold signet rings; fur coats worth more than the yearly wages of a Delima or Marvine at Stellar Seafoods. Kids peering in the windows, shoving him off the sidewalks; students from the universities, the technical college. Feels a hundred years old, ragged, stupid next to them, knowing he'll never again be one of them.

Taking refuge, Hector lines up for the late show at the repertory cinema: a film he'd seen years ago in Montréal. He has to wait twenty minutes to get in; silent, overhearing conversations all around him, subjects he had the words but no longer the convictions to handle. Who were these people? What world was this? Wagner's Kwikway, Delbert, Mariette, himself—they'd have no more reality to these people here than the celluloid the technician was threading through the projector. But they were just as real; you didn't fall off the edge of the world once you quit the city limits of Halifax. As if Halifax existed for the inhabitants of Montréal, or Montréal for the *Parisiens*, or Paris itself for the people of Spruce Harbour. Just as the credits start unrolling, Hector rises from his seat, suddenly, irrevocably, ploughing through the coats and feet out into the last of the night. Claustrophobia, euphoria: needing fresh air, wanting air salt-scoured, so clear you could sit, not in some smoky cinema but outside, on the beach or in the back of your truck, watching whole constellations revolve across the sky.

Back in his truck, in the companionable emptiness of the 101, headed for home. *Don Giovanni* this time, but he doesn't hear any other words or music than sweet home sweet home sweet

home. And as he quits the valley for the coast, as he leaves behind
the English settlements one by one till he comes to the fluorescent
sun set/rise painted on a billboard saying *Bienvenue en Acadie*,
it comes to him, certain, definite as a stone in his hand. Spirit of
truth, celestial revelation. All this time thinking he'd come back
because he wasn't good enough. When it was the city itself, the
university, the being apart and away that wasn't good enough.
For him. Something Claire wouldn't have fathomed—couldn't
have. Something that put him far, far beyond anything Claire
could give him: candlelight suppers with Kwikway frozen peas
in the *boeuf bourguignon*: civilized company, for Christ's sake.
He'd rather walk the ditch with Delima's kid, discourse on the
weather with Delbert. This whole past year a self-inflicted wound:
right royal asshole to have prostrated himself like that before his
own grandiose sense of failure. Working as a frigging janitor, for
Christ's sake—living in that shack at the back of the store, driving
this mobile billboard. He hadn't even taken his canoe out of his
parents' barn, hadn't once thought of getting a house, building
himself a house—something just big enough for himself and his
books, with a shed for the canoe out back—lake edge, inland.
Lake filled with loons, still water shaken by loon laughter at once
expression and derision of desire.

   Château Hector. The very suburbs of sentimentality—and why
not? Banish the *Acadie* of Tastee Freeze and Kwikway stores;
trailer parks and beverage rooms, satellite dishes, mini-bikes.
Make up his own Arcadia; fishing boats out on the bay. Wild
strawberries by the lighthouse: berries big as your thumb, succulent, small seeds prickling as the pulp slips down your throat.
Asters, golden rod, hawthorn; and summer or winter the night
sky webbed with stars telling their stories over and over into your
eyes. *If you trust in Nature, in what is simple in Nature, in the
small Things that hardly anyone sees and that can so suddenly
become huge, immeasurable; if you have this love for what is
humble and try very simply, as someone who serves, to win the
confidence of what seems poor: then everything will become easier
for you, more coherent and somehow more reconciling. . . .*
   Three in the morning by the time he rolls down the highway

into Spruce Harbour. Grey indecision of sky just before dawn. Lights on in some of the houses—births or deaths: acute, substantial reality. Past the church, the inexhaustible illumination of Our Lady of the Parking Lot. Past the dark towers of the college; he would see if he couldn't move up a story or two from the basement office, see if he couldn't do a little teaching, maybe finish the goddam thesis, maybe build himself a house. Hector Wagner, *philosophe et professeur titulaire; père de famille nombreuse*, the very suburbs of sentiment but—why not? If Claire could make her own little world here—in the teeth of everything— why shouldn't he?

Pulls up with a spray of gravel behind the store. Flings himself down on the bed where he's spent his nights fucking the local girls as casually as he might have blown his nose; lightbulb dangling naked overhead—he has lived in this dump for a year and let that damn thing dangle over him. An allegory. They would be starting things up in the store in four hours' time—he should crowd in some sleep before—but his mind's running like a tap. Money he's saved—nothing to spend it on in Spruce Harbour, no signet rings, designer furs or suitcases to buy. Build himself a cabin: A-frame. He's seen ads for land around Deer Lake—soon as it was light he'd drive round, look things over. . . .

Hector lies back against the scrawny pillows, studiously happy, like a child with a new set of blocks defining the world. Setting the borders here and here and here: sealing himself safe inside.

"I DIDN'T *NEED* you to take me home—so why should I be grateful that you came to the concert? Professor Vilnos would have driven me home with the others. I *hate* taking the bus—and having to miss the party. It's Friday night, Tahta—can't I just pretend to be like all the others?"

"Like the others—they're just a bunch of hoodlums,

delinquents in the making. And you didn't need to miss the party—
I would have taken you—''

''But I didn't want to be *taken*. Who else has their father chaperone them to a party at their music teacher's house? Mrs. Vilnos is serving tea and cakes—there's nothing depraved about that, is there?''

''There's no need to make a public spectacle of ourselves—someone's in the vestibule—''

''Then he can't hear us. Besides, I doubt if he's fluent in Polish.''

''And your mother will be waiting up for us—''

''Up? It's only ten o'clock, *Matko Bozhe*—''

''Halyna, there is no need to take the name of Our Lady—''

''*Bozhe!* All right then, let's go.''

They push open the dead-green door labelled ''Superintendent'' and disappear from the eavesdropper's view. Once inside the apartment, Halyna stomps to her broom-closet of a room, carefully puts away the oboe case she's been clutching to her bosom all through the argument, and undresses. One of cousin Sabina's castoffs—a size too small, the ''silk'' obviously synthetic, and the colour—a kind of cloudy-chocolate—looking definitely, deliberately mouldy next to Halyna's fair hair and skin. She kicks the dress into a corner of the room—the tiny closet's already filled to bursting—and puts on her lumpy quilted dressing gown. There will be a cup of cocoa waiting for her in the kitchen, and a plate of poppy seed biscuits—while everyone else is drinking tea with rum and eating strudel at the Vilnos' house! And what's more, what really hurts, making music, improvising quartets, trios, duos in every corner of the house. She should have gone, even if she had to drag her father with her—and yet if she didn't put up this stupid, hateful kind of scene, how would they ever learn to let go of her? No, she had to do it this way—make things so unbearable for them they'd have to let her make her own way.

Maria comes into her daughter's room, clucks her tongue at the dress balled-up on the floor, picks it up and smooths it out, looking for a hanger as Halyna sulks on her bed, combing out her braids. If Sabina were to see how the girl treated the dresses she gave her—gave her out of the goodness of her heart, even if she seemed never to hand down anything that was quality, or even remotely flattering to the girl. But then, that was Sabina—

—who wasn't even Sabina, but Sue, now that she'd been so long in Canada. Her father had been smart, got the family out of Poland in '38, the last possible moment. All the war had meant to him was the chance to build up his business, a restaurant-cabaret for lonely service men awaiting shipment overseas in dull, dry Halifax. Highly illegal of course—and therefore highly profitable. So that Sabina-turned-Sue could be sent to university where she met and married Tadziu Bobrowski who, once he'd graduated from Dalhousie Law School, had become Ted Bobrow—and thus ridiculous in Polish *and* English at once.

And yet prudent, too, for he'd invested Sabina's dowry in a six- story apartment building in Dartmouth. So that when Russian tanks appeared in the streets of Warsaw, and it became expedient for those who had family in the West to get leave to visit them, Viktor, Maria and Halyna ended up not only with a roof over their heads but work to hand, once their visitors' visas had become refugee cards. None of which had been promised when Maria had first received Sabina's food and clothing parcels, her letters—in curiously archaic, adulterated Polish—begging them to come and pay a long visit to the cousin Maria had never seen in her life. Possible, but not certain, for there was the fact of Tomasz and his wife and their two small children, whom Sue and Ted had pointedly not invited for a visit; the Bobrowskis were "comfortably situated" but certainly not wealthy enough to sponsor two families. It was Halyna who had begged and pleaded with her parents to accept Sabina's offer, and to leave her brother and his family behind, to sustain, by their continued residence in Warsaw, the fiction of eventual return to a free Poland. Halyna had come to the West, land of freedom and opportunity, only to find herself chained by her parents' grief and anxiety. Having lost their son, their grandchildren and daughter-in-law, they weren't about to let Halyna loose to roam the streets of Halifax, or to fly off to New York or London for the sake of a career, as that criminal, Vilnos, had advised her to do. What did he expect them to say? How did he expect her to support herself? By waitressing—or worse?

Maria hangs up Sabina's dress in the bathroom, hoping the steam from the shower will make the creases fall out. She's relieved that Halyna has come back with Viktor after all, that she hasn't stayed for the party—that man Vilnos has to be watched like a hawk—and thus forebears from scolding her daughter for her carelessness with the dress, her rude silence, her stubborn refusal to touch the cooling cocoa in the kitchen. They couldn't keep her forever, but she was only eighteen—too young, years too young to leave, if not her parents, then the family.

Tadziu had been generosity itself, installing Viktor as superintendent of the Dartmouth Arms, Maria as maintenance, giving them the apartment and a monthly allowance—small, it is true, but any more would seem like charity. And now this plan of Sabina's, to have Halyna stay with her daughter, Gail, while she was at the *Conservatoire* in Montréal. Stay free of charge, helping Gail with the three children, all under school age, and occasional housework, but all the same, in a family environment, a nice house in a good area, safe from the dangers of a shared apartment with other musicians—"no better than a brothel," Sabina had warned. If only Halyna hadn't been so cool—sullen even, when the idea was proposed—and in Sabina's presence, too. "Why Montréal—why not Paris, or Munich?" was all Halyna had said. The matter had to be resolved quickly—the scholarship (awarded by the Ladies' Auxiliary of the Polish-Canadian Friends of Freedom Society) depended on Halyna's being able to find her own accommodation, and, as there was no money for that, she would have to accept the room at her cousin Gail's house (no cousin: an employer, Halyna had snapped). If only she would see reason, take up the scholarship, graduate three years later with her Teacher's Certificate. Sabina said she could make good money teaching in a public school, even a high school right here in Halifax; things would be so much easier for them if there was another salary— they could send more parcels to Tomasz, they could even sponsor him and his family for a visit. . . . Maria thumps back to the kitchen, where her husband is drinking a small glass of slivovitz and devouring the poppy-seed cookies she'd left out for Halyna.

"I can't get a word out of her—Viktor, you try."

"I tried all the way home from the concert—all she did was complain, complain—about how strict we were, how interfering, how hard we were making things for her by not taking out Canadian citizenship so that she can't get the right kind of scholarships, how we're spoiling her career—"

"Career!" Maria sniffs, picking up Halyna's now-icy cocoa and sipping it as slowly as if it were scalding her lips. Such ambitions, this daughter of hers. If *she* had any say in the matter, Halyna would become a nurse or a nun—the only good career for a woman. To be abasing yourself, carrying a cross or bedpan for a husband whom you hardly saw by day, and who cut into you like a knife into a loaf of bread by night. Or for children who first sucked the milk and then the blood out of you, getting mixed up in things that did no one any good, only harm. But to sacrifice yourself to a disembodied Spirit of Medicine, or the chaste, weightless embrace of the Man of Sorrows—that was the only happy life for a woman, Maria knew. Knew and could not find the means to tell her daughter, who'd been born to her long after she'd had Tomasz, after the miserable years of barrenness which were God's punishment to her for something she knew she must deserve, even if she could not identify. The daughter who was supposed to be the comfort of her middle age had turned out to be only a thorn, a whole crown of thorns.

Viktor sighs, as if underlining her thoughts, rises from the table, washes his hands at the kitchen sink, and makes his way to bed. It's tiring for him—does Halyna ever think of that? Exhausting for a man his age to be shepherding his only daughter through whole plains of wolves—and after a hard day's work, too—work which God knows they're glad to have but which, all the same, is demeaning for a man who once taught mathematics in one of Krakow's better high schools. And Halyna had told him he was trying to do her out of a career—what *right* had she to do so, after her father had lost his own career to come here for *her* sake? *Matko Bozhe.* Maria crosses herself and pours a finger's breadth of slivovitz into her cup. Why such a daughter? Born with an aptitude not for piety and obedience, but for music. Maria drinks down the slivovitz and closes her eyes, surrendering to a not unpleasurable despair. She feels a little as the Virgin must have done when Her child began to show a disputatious, independent spirit, preferring to converse with the rabbis in the temple rather than hold His mother's hand on the long road back to Nazareth.

Maria pulls herself out of her chair, puts the bottle back in the cupboard—on the top shelf, out of Halyna's sight—and washes up the few glasses and plates. The hot water comes out in little drips—Halyna, running the shower—she would disappear into the bathroom for hours, careless of whether the fuel bills went sky high—*she* didn't have to suffer the Bobrowskis' interrogations at the end of each quarter. She showed no signs of wanting to suffer anything. Viktor didn't know the half of it. She, Maria, had had the daily raising of a child who could sing before she could talk, sing tunes she'd heard over the radio or on the street. Who had taken up, not a respectable instrument—piano, violin—but the oboe. A girl who hadn't played with her dolls in the usual way, bathing them, washing and ironing their clothes, dressing them up—but who took them out only to arrange them in a semi-circle round her as she sang or played arpeggios on her recorder.

"Halyna!" Viktor, trying to get into the bathroom that Halyna has locked. "Halyna!" A girl who shows none of the respect she owes to her father and brother. This is what makes Maria afraid as she scrubs walls and tends the rubber plants in the lobby; afraid even as she'd been angered, earlier, by that hardness Halyna had shown as a child—refusing to run to her mother for a bandage and a kiss if she'd fallen and scraped her knee, but simply getting up from the ground and playing twice as hard, oblivious to the trickle of blood ruining her dress. Between Halyna and her brother—had there ever been any true affection? Even if they were ten years apart—shouldn't that make her look up to Tomasz, admire him? But Halyna had done nothing but argue with him as soon as she was able—not even argue, simply tell him she thought it was all stupid, his politics, his fiery speeches. Not stupid because dangerous, but because she couldn't bear to have him monopolize the conversation at the table; to be told she couldn't practise because Tomasz and his friends were having a meeting in the kitchen.

"Good night, Tahta." Kissing him as if that would erase all the bad temper and pouting; looking demure, devout in her long white nightgown—like a ten-year-old imitating an angel. Maria stands with her arms folded, watching the scene from the kitchen doorway: Viktor patting his daughter's cheek, a cheek all fresh and rosy from the warmth of the shower. If she didn't get her way by shouting at him, she tried by petting him, and it would have worked if Maria hadn't been there to interfere. "Good night, Halyna—I hope you haven't used up all the hot water—your parents might like to take a shower, too, you know. And did you take the dress out of the bathroom before you—Halyna, it's wringing wet, and the dye's dripped out onto the bathmat—can't you be just a bit more careful? Viktor, tell her to have some common sense—"

"Halyna, your mother's right. Now off to bed, you've had a tiring day."

Flouncing off to bed, without even a peck for Maria's cheek, as if *she* hadn't had a tiring day, swabbing windows, lavishing whole bottles of Mr. Clean on the corridors. What for if not the girl's good? Maria gave up—but not in. Halyna would be brought to see reason; they would have to make things so tight, so uncomfortable here for her that she would do anything, everything to reach the haven of Gail's house in Montréal. Why not Paris indeed? As if Paris weren't full of Polish refugees trying to pick up their lives again—as if Halyna were something special. Maria hurriedly brushes her teeth, battles her way into her shrunken nightgown, crawls into the narrow bed beside Viktor who's unsuccessfully feigning sleep. He's taken out his teeth and so she has him at a disadvantage—all he can do is grunt yes or no.

"Viktor, listen. She can't go on delaying, trying everyone's patience—that scholarship will go to someone else. She said tonight that she refused to have anything more to do with it if she had to stay at Gail's? Yes? What if we tell her she can go away in the spring—to that Catholic school, to learn French—that's all she could talk about before Christmas. There'd be no harm in it—

she said she could get a bursary for it—and she'll need the French if she's to study in Montréal. We'll tell her she can go in June, and she'll accept the scholarship and we'll handle the problem of where she stays once the time comes. Do you agree? Yes? Good. We'll tell her tomorrow morning—and if she doesn't agree, you'll have to beat some sense into her. Do you hear, Viktor—Viktor?'' But his snores are no longer simulated—he's beyond even grunting now. Never mind—she has won her point. Maria folds her hands over her breast, beginning her nightly prayer to the Virgin. ''More blessed than the Cherubim, Glorious beyond compare with the Seraphim''—falling asleep as the image of the Virgin from the icon over her bed converges with the bald, happy, earring'd face of Mr. Clean.

3

Bertrand, shaving one Saturday morning near the end of April, peers out of his bathroom window and remarks to himself how the absolute clarity of this light unmakes the fishplant at the end of the wharf—smashes and flattens its yellow buildings into cardboard cutouts flicked onto a blue background, like the paper shapes Matisse cut out and pasted in the release of his old age. But Mariette, waking at six o'clock the same morning would have seen, had the trailer possessed a window clean enough to show it, only mist mouthing all but the nearest objects. That it was a fishplant and no paper cutout down the road she could tell from the briny smoke that always crouched in her nostrils. What Mariette hears, once Paul has left off crying for the cornflakes and watered milk she's soon given him for breakfast, is the noise of birds tearing away at the mist as if it were some tightly woven cloth to be unravelled. She hears her mother and stepfather snoring in the double bed behind the plywood partition; the rest of the children are quiet, curled up tight in dreams, like wood lice prodded by a finger.

She and Paul sleep in the small annexe Luc-Antoine shoved onto the trailer some years ago—it's cold in the winter, and whenever storm winds blow, Mariette thinks the whole annexe will be wrenched away, tossed like an old, crumpled milk carton over the spruce trees into the sea. But in summer it is the best place in the world, because you were away from the others—even if you could hear every shout or curse or slap, you didn't see it. And the light comes in through the cracks between the boards like a long white hand stroking her eyes open, and she can pretend she's like that queen in the fairy tale Claire once told her: the queen cast away to sea by a cruel father in a large chest, with her baby in her arms. Washed far away by the waves to another kingdom, rescued and set free and let to live again, just she and her baby and the kind rescuer.

In the fall Luc-Antoine gets up almost as early as she does, to go hunting with his buddies. Once he even brought back a deer—it had been so young, though, there'd been hardly any meat on it—Mariette couldn't have eaten it even if she'd been much hungrier than she was. Deer looking so sad and stiff and small splayed out on the roof of Luc's truck. Days when there's work for him on the highways Luc has trouble getting out of bed, shoving his thick body into overalls and padded nylon jacket, pulling his cap down low over his forehead, visor almost slicing off his eyes. Delima would get up after Luc had gone—there wasn't room enough in the trailer for them all to move round at once. And when Delima's left for the fishplant, Mariette rounds up the kids, sees they're dressed and fed and put on the school bus in time. Little Paul she carries aslant a hip that's no more than a knob under a scarf of skin. When everyone's gone, she puts Paul in the bashed stroller and they go for their walks, down to the church or past the pond on which white ducks swim circles, waiting to be killed for someone's freezer, for new ducks to come swim circles and be killed.

Walks him up and down the road till it's time to go back to the trailer for lunch—bread and tinned beans, or jam sandwiches and Diet Coke. And when he falls asleep, she'll watch TV, the screen smaller and duller than a dirty goldfish bowl. Game shows whose rules and strategy she can't make out, only the splendour of the prizes—sofa suites and bedroom furniture, home entertainment centres, computers, all revealed by ladies with hair and teeth bright as stars, dresses that whish over them as they point to the prizes and smile at her, Mariette, sitting on a plastic crate in the trailer. Or shows whose doctors and nurses, husbands and wives aren't like people she knows but a separate species, like the suffering saints and angels printed on the holy pictures the priest gave them once at school.

And when school is over and the kids shoving out from the bus, she'll watch from the doorway of the trailer while they play in the dirt outside, watch in between making supper for everybody. Luc and Delima will stop at the Social Club for a beer before they come back—then they'll all cram inside the trailer and eat salt cod and potatoes, or else weiners and creamed corn for a treat— from Wagner's store. And she'll clean up the dishes after supper, pumping rusty-coloured water into the sink, then scrubbing the kids' faces with a worn J-Cloth and making them brush their teeth and hair—there are always notices from the Public Health about head lice and scabies and nutrition. She knows just how to find nits and wash the kids' heads in the foul-smelling soap the Health Visitor brings. And then they'll all watch TV again, till Paul falls asleep in her arms and she'll take him into the annexe and tuck him into the pile of old sheets and shirts on the floor, then fall asleep beside him, dreaming in a foreign language of images and sounds that have no connection at all with the days of her life.

Delima yells at her all the time—"Why don't ya get off yer butt and go find someone ta take ya out? Ain't natural, a girl yer age, sittin' mopin' at home when she could be out havin' fun. Ya wanta be a nun or somethin'? Wanta end up like that bitch I clean house for, got no more juice in her than a Pilot biscuit, by Christ?" Delima says. Delima is her mother; you should love your mother and obey your father. Luc wasn't her father, not her real father, Delima said. She likes it when Delima comes home from the club and hasn't drunk too much, only enough to make her feel good and happy, hugging Mariette, singing, "Stand by Your Man," and "Ruby"—these are Delima's favourites. But Mariette doesn't love her, not the way she loves Paul, or Paul loves Mariette. Better than he loves Delima who doesn't like him because he's too thin and too slow and can't talk or walk like he should, like the Health Visitor says he should. Delima doesn't understand. When she'd found those pictures he'd taken and given to her— they were hers, her own to keep—and Delima had said those things, thinking she knew what they were doing, thinking she knew everything when all that time she hadn't, she hadn't looked or listened, even when Mariette had tried to tell her but without saying a word—not one word. She knew things Delima didn't know she knew.

Like when she was small and Delima would take her with her when she went to clean Claire's house, telling her to go play on the beach or sit down on the chair with her doll and pretend she was watching TV—Claire didn't have a set—till she was through. How Mariette would wait till Delima had finished the downstairs and gone up to the bedrooms—and Mariette would come up the stairs slowly, quiet as a snail (Delima hated it when she made noise, would give Mariette a smack across the mouth if she'd been singing too loud, or knocked a bottle off a shelf) and stand beside the doorway, head curled round till she could see inside. See Delima opening Claire's drawers, handling the clothes inside. Or in the bathroom, opening bottles of green and pink and yellow coloured stuff that made you smell sweet, smell like the pink saltwater kisses looked in their glass jars at Wagner's store. Delima looking in Claire's mirrors, dabbing the sweet stuff under her arms, opening her shirt to squirt it, rub it between breasts that hung soft and heavy, nipples almost as long as Mariette's thumbs.

She didn't think to blame Delima for going through Claire's things; she just liked to watch her mother alone, when she had her to herself, the way she never could when Luc-Antoine was around. They'd made her sleep on the floor, away over by the sink; she'd cried and Delima had hit her and then she'd just lain wide awake, sucking her thumb and waiting for them to finish wrestling behind the plywood partition that hid the double bed from her view. And then the babies had started coming; first they'd share the bed with Delima and Luc, and then one night Delima would give the baby to her to mind while she and Luc went out to the club. She'd carry it round in her arms, singing Delima's songs to it and the ones Claire taught her, brushing so softly the little bit of hair the baby had, feeling with her fingertips that soft spot where the bones hadn't grown across. Feeling always a little sick inside when she touched it, yet full of love for the small thing in her arms, even if it smelled sour and had spots over its face and cried and cried till she learned how to warm the milk up on the stove and not give it cold, the way Delima did.

Lying down with the baby snug in her arms, hearing its heart beat the way it must once have heard Delima's when it was living inside her. That first baby—the first one that lived, after the two Delima lost. Once she'd seen her mother sitting in her nightgown on the bed, watching TV; seen right through the skimpy material to the mound of belly where a shape pushed, swimming just like the fish you could see off the wharf at high tide. Mariette had climbed slowly up to the bed, careful not to block Delima's view of the TV, had put out her hand to her mother's belly, and Delima hadn't slapped it away, had pressed Mariette's hand down so she could feel the fish swimming and spinning inside. "Busy little bugger, eh?" Delima had said. "Listen, kid—it's the one good thing about bein' a woman—makes ya feel some good, like the sun itself's risin' up inside ya." Smiling at Mariette, as though this were their baby, Delima's and Mariette's, and Luc-Antoine had nothing to do with it, nothing.

She would wait till the baby had fallen asleep, then uncover it and look. The rash all faded from the sleeping skin, the small belly full, swollen like a balloon. Breathing so slow she would be scared it was dead; she would have to put her face close, close so she could feel the tickle of its breath against her skin. Baby's breathing like the tiny feathers that leaked out from the pillows; white feathers from ducks that had gone to the freezer. Uncovered, the baby looked just like the pictures of Baby Jesus Frère LeBlanc had shown her in the church, except Jesus, He was fatter, had big sausages of fat round His belly and legs. But the way He'd lain in Our Lady's lap, all quiet and still, like a boat in harbour—that's how her baby looked in her lap. And she'd bend down and kiss the baby right in the middle of his chest where his heart was and cover him up again, thinking how strange it was that so small and perfect and still a thing should come out of Delima—that it was Luc who'd put it into her.

And then all the other babies came, the ones Mariette would rock in her arms the way she'd done the first one—rock in her arms as the others crawled all over the trailer while Delima did or did not get supper. The ones Mariette would take to bed with her to comfort them when they woke hungry in the night while

Delima slept, snoring, worn out from looking after the others all day long. Mariette would have to get up quick so Luc wouldn't wake and shout at the baby, waking the others; would get right up no matter how cold or hot it was in the trailer and heat up the milk, rocking the baby in one arm, then giving him the bottle and getting him to belch. And change him—so sore the skin looked, raw, and the health visitor telling Delima to put egg white on it. Delima snorting to Mariette after the nurse had left, "I don't got money to fool round with friggin' egg whites; she think I'm nuts or somethin'?" But Mariette had seen at Wagner's a shelf full of medicines, and a tube with special cream for babies on it—had bought some with money she'd made from collecting bottles on the beach. And it helped the babies some, but didn't help her at school, being up all night with the baby, hushing it so no one would hear and get mad. She'd been failed a grade; they'd put her into the slow learners' class—he'd called her stupid, said no kid of his would be that dumb. "Who'd ya get her off, Delima?" he'd roar. "One of the loonies up by the college?" And Delima would roar back, "Guy a whole lot smarter 'n you. Cleaner, too. He was somethin', he was really somethin'." And if Luc-Antoine were feeling good, he'd go over to where Delima was working by the sink or stove and rub his hand over her belly, saying, "You're the one that's somethin' "—pushing his hand between her legs and grabbing her hard so that she'd yell, "Fuck off, Luc—can't ya see the kids are watchin'?" But she wouldn't be mad; she wouldn't stop him, she couldn't—

Mariette didn't spy on them, it was just that you couldn't help hearing the moaning and thumping on the bed behind the plywood partition. Hearing them wasn't the same as looking, though she'd crept up that one time, the first time, to see what was hurting them both so much, and had seen two people drowning, each one trying to drag down the other and were somehow fastened together, nailed down like Jesus on the cross, and she'd shut her eyes and crawled back to her bed, pulling the blanket up over her head. In the close, thick dark, telling herself a story to make a space around her, between herself and the bodies drowning in that bed: a story like the ones Claire told her a long time ago, when she used to come to her house with Delima. So long ago it was like a story itself.

Once upon a time, a long time ago, Delima goes to clean house for Claire Saulnier. Mariette is seven years old and should be at school, but gets sick a lot and stays home in the trailer while Delima comes and goes. Today she's better and so walks with Delima to Claire's, sits down in the big armchair, holding her doll in one arm and pressing with her hand tight between her legs, hard. And Claire comes in to make lunch for them; she comes home every time Delima cleans, maybe because she wants to keep an eye on things, or because she wants company. Claire walks into her house and the first thing she sees is Mariette in the armchair. And shouts at her, "Don't do that. Stop it right now. Don't you know it's bad to put your hands there?" Mariette had taken her hand away. Claire standing over her, shaking, saying, "Why were you doing that?" And she answers, "Because my cunt hurts." Claire looks as if her eyes were caps ready to pop off a bottle; she calls for Delima to come downstairs, and they make Mariette pull down her pants and show them.

At the doctor's she feels so bad. He is nice to her; he doesn't hurt her, but he's mad at Delima, says people like her shouldn't have children if they can't even keep them clean. They stop at the pharmacy on the way back—Claire wouldn't let her go inside, so she stays in the back seat with Delima who's smoking cigarette after cigarette, throwing them away half-smoked, still lit like she always does when she's angry at someone she can't tell to piss off. Claire comes back with a white paper bag—they drive back to her house and, while Delima eats lunch, Mariette and Claire go upstairs to the bathroom. Claire fills up the tub and undresses Mariette without even letting her fingers touch her skin, makes her step inside the tub. Brings her the doll she'd left behind in the armchair, and things from the kitchen to play with—a plastic bottle and some cups—pours in something that makes the water cloudy, that makes it so she doesn't hurt anymore. Her voice is low, gentle, and her hands, too—lifting Mariette out of the water, wrapping her in a towel thicker and warmer than the blanket she sleeps in at the trailer, showing how to rub the cream the doctor had given her into the sore place to make the soreness go away. Claire makes her do it all by herself, so she'll know what to do when she gets back home. And shows her how to wash out her underpants, saying if she keeps herself clean it won't hurt her anymore. And all the time Delima's downstairs, and it's like Claire is Mariette's mother. Claire who washes Mariette's clothes and puts them in the dryer so they come out warm, soft; Claire who tells her a story about a girl no bigger than her thumb, a girl who's made to live under the ground and escapes on a swallow's back, a swallow like Mariette's seen flying over the duckpond in summer, so it must be a true story. And the best part is that even though the girl travels far away and marries the prince, she never grows any bigger than your thumb.

For a long while Mariette goes every week to Claire's with Delima, Saturday mornings, and while Delima cleans house Claire talks to Mariette, takes her for walks, tells her stories. Takes her up to her own room and brushes out her hair, putting it in braids for her and shows her in the mirror how pretty she looks, her face and Claire's together inside the mirror: silver pond with faces floating like strange birds. A long time ago, when the only real place was Claire's house, not the trailer, Claire would tell her stories and keep anything from hurting her. Waiting and waiting for Claire to say to Delima, "I'll keep her here; don't worry, I'll take care of her." Except that she never did, never said anything to keep her all that long time. Till Delima said she couldn't go with her to Claire's anymore; she needed her at home. And then the baby was born, the one that lived, and Mariette learned how to keep it and care for it, and all the babies who came after.

Until the morning Delima found her behind the trailer, found her retching up her very bones and blood, and then took her off to Hattie Brown's. She said it wouldn't hurt, but it did. Hurt so much Claire came to take her away, but it was too late then; she couldn't help her, no one could help her, not even Our Lady who could deliver the girl chained in fire. Bright fire, not like hers: black, smeared, like charcoal, like the logs they burnt on the beach. Claire driving her to hospital, asking questions she couldn't answer: doctors, nurses, social worker. Out of hospital and no more questions, no more anything till Delima told her, "He's knocked me up again, goddam his balls. Last thing I need, Jesus, I swear I'm gonna get my tubes tied soon as the kid slides out. He wouldn't sign no papers last time, but this time I'll tell him, you don't sign no papers, I'm not comin' back ta you, not me nor the kid neither. Let him put that in his goddam pipe and smoke it."

And Delima came back with Paul, gave him straightaway to Mariette as if he were her baby, the one Hattie Brown had pricked like a balloon inside her. And she looked after him as she looked after all the others, staying up nights, failing her grades at school, and it didn't matter because they let her leave school. She was old enough, and now Paul was hers; he loved her, he was hers and she wouldn't give him up, not to Delima or any health visitor, not even to go live at Claire's. And some day, maybe soon, she'll get married, but not to Louis; she'll marry someone who'll take her and Paul to live in a big white house like Claire's, and Paul will be like the baby Jesus in Our Lady's arms, will grow no older, no bigger, and she will carry him always with her, white dress and veils and never any fire, only a crown of small white stars around her head, stars instead of flames.

THIS SATURDAY MORNING, near the end of April, Mariette takes Paul in his stroller down to the wharf, lets him throw stone after stone into the water, deep water, scum floating on top—they pour acid from the fishplant; Delima tells her, "Don't you never touch that water; it'll burn yer hand off." Mariette holds on to the hem of Paul's jacket so he can't get away from her. Mist starting to clear—she can feel the sun working as if each bit of air were laundry to be shaken out and hung on the line to dry. Coming on warm at last—spring peepers started up the night before, the marsh beyond the pond full of them rubbing legs together, cheeping, fizzing noise like gingerale makes under your nose. Paul keeps picking up stones and chucking them into the water, rising smooth against the pilings—she picks up a stone, too, a rough-edged grey lump, lets it fall from her fingers. Stupid, ugly stone, but where it breaks the water, perfect circles spread, circles on circles till she can't count them all. Suddenly Paul throws a whole fistful of stones, makes the water hiss and jump. Makes her think of the peepers, the soft, wet stillness of the night before. Did he hear them, hear them from his house in the woods? She could show him, the way she'd shown him where the mushrooms grew, the orange ones that he said he liked to eat. Her stomach crinkles inside her—too early for lunch, but she's so hungry. Paul too. She gets him to come back inside the stroller by promising him bread and jam— he holds up his arms to be lifted—he doesn't like to walk any- where; he's old enough to be running round everywhere, but his legs are so crooked and thin—. The health visitor had made him an appointment at the hospital in Falmouth, but Delima didn't take him; too far to go, and what was some fancy doctor going to tell her about her own kid? He was lazy, that's all. Mariette spoiled him, carrying him everywhere. But she had to; he cried when she made him walk; his legs hurt him, she could tell. But she wouldn't say anything to the nurse, because they'd take him away, that's what Delima said.

Flock of gulls over the oozy muck where the tide had gone out. Stroller rumbling over the dirt, Paul laughing, making shouting noises—and the gulls rise up, blizzard of wings, jabbering, shriek- ing overhead. And the boat—tipped on its side, rotting slowly from tide to tide for as long as she could remember. Once she'd walked up close to read the name painted on its stern: *Lady Fair*. Pretty name—that's what he'd call a boat if he were a fisherman, though she can't imagine him with his spectacles and the beautiful watch with the numbers flashing green on the dial, in a boat jigging cod.

Back at the trailer she gives Paul and the other kids lunch— Delima's at Claire's, Luc at the Social Club. The kids settle down to watch TV. Paul is falling asleep right there on the floor in the middle of them. Mariette covers him with his blanket—she was going to take him with her into the woods, but she won't now he's sleeping. Asks Tina, the second oldest girl, to keep an eye on him when he wakes up—she's going out for a couple of hours, just walking—she'll be back in time to start supper.

A jay splashes the air as she climbs the hill, its wings blue as Our Lady's eyes, as Her dress, but the jays eat the other birds' eggs—if she'd had a rifle in her hands, she'd have taken a shot at it. But the bird disappears into thick arms of spruce, and she has to be careful following the paths, choosing the right one. Easy to get lost, go round and round and never come out. Sun's full, round belly overhead, so warm Mariette undoes her jacket and the collar of her shirt, unties her long black braid so the hair lopes over her shoulders as she walks. A bird begins to call, not the crows, big as chickens, roosting in the sprucetops all winter long, but one of the small gold birds come back from the south. It perches on an alder twig: small as it is it weighs the twig down, making it shake like a finger, warning, scolding. Wind bristling through spruce needles, filling the hollows of her throat, lifting her hair from her shoulders, like wings. And the sun rushes back from behind a cloud, tumbles down onto a burdock, so its spines are flush with light, a burning bush, heat and light catching her, sticking fast like the burdock barbs into her clothes.

She could turn here and go back, but she doesn't want the trailer, close and hot and dark. She could go on to the church—can see the top of the tower poking out of the spruces. It'll be locked—they're scared of people coming in and stealing things from the museum, the gold cloth and crystal cup. Or she could take this path, marked with blue plastic streamers, the path that goes to the college, to his house. She hasn't seen him for so long—he'd gone away, and been sick when he got back, and then when she'd finally seen him again in the woods, he didn't ask her to come and let him take her picture the way he did before. But maybe he was sick again—maybe he was sick and all alone in the house, and she should just go and see, was he all right?

Blue plastic streamers marking the path. Many of the smaller spruce and tamarack are dead, struck silver, tufts of milky green sprouting in the clefts of branches. Squirrel twitching its tail on a bough right over her head, clucking, chattering till she walks on, quickly, so no one can follow her, into another clearing. Still and cool, sun throwing needles like darts to the ground. So still she can hear nothing: ocean, voices, breath itself. Somewhere outside the village, the college, the church: Our Lady in the Parking Lot, Her big blind eyes sailing over the trucks on the highway, over the graves fenced in by spruce and swamp. All gone, everything sucked up by silent mouths of moss and old man's beard; wintergreen that her feet, in their heavy workman's boots, are bruising as she walks.

She wants to sit down, take off her boots and throw them away where she'll never find them again. Walk barefoot over spruce cones, alder twigs, mosses like small green stars pricking up from the ground, stars that don't scare her because she can bend down and stroke them; they are rooted here where she walks, in the earth she crouches over. Bird calling—twang in his throat, taut wire strummed. She closes her eyes, presses fingers tight into the starry moss, then brings them up to her face, smelling bitter freshness, scent spreading like water over her face. When she stands up at last it's as if she's rising to the surface of a pool in whose black, slippery weeds she's been tangled almost forever, long enough she's forgotten the use of light and air. Some black pond choked with reeds and mud putting soft loose hands up her legs to pull her down, inside. Rising up and out, everything dripping like black water off her body, out ears, eyes, mouth, down her breasts and belly and thighs; from the small slit between her thighs.

Until she was washed white, white like in the photographs he took of her: sitting with Paul in her lap like Our Lady and the Baby Jesus, even though she had no robes, no stars. Just her jeans and checked shirt, hair braided down her back, a rope Paul could hang on to, pull himself up with, stronger than her arms. The girl in those photographs wasn't her, was too white and clear, but he didn't seem to know—he kept taking pictures until he said there was nothing more he could do with her. But he hadn't even seen her, hadn't looked, only pushed the camera back and forth around her with his hands that never touched her: large hands, and long fingers. Body long and thin, too, not like the men who go off fishing, lumbering, working on the roads in overalls and steel-toed boots.

It's so hot, her feet are sweating inside her boots: she would, she would sit down and take off the hot, heavy boots. Sheltered here—like walls around her, sun pouring into the clearing like water bubbling from a kettle. Takes off her socks, too, stretching out her legs, wriggles her toes, then lies back on the moss and spruce needles, scent splashing round her. Narrows her eyes, stares up at the small circle of open sky over her, then closes them and lies still, even when ants begin exploring her wrists, her open palms and ankles. Can feel the press of small stones and twigs below her through the thin shirt; sun and sky so warm, so soft over her, undressing her and she's lying soft, warm, still as the moss beneath her. Shutting her eyes, tight: sun like a stone making circles inside her—

Crow barks—noise of cloth tearing: harsh, black, beaked: "Down in the valley where the green grass grows, I seen Mariette, takin' off her clothes." Pecks her eyes open: she sits up, puts hands to her head, feels twigs and needles tangled there, tears them out, out. Just because she's Delima's kid, Delima's, but not his. Everyone saying, it, knowing it, even Claire, and Frère Le-Blanc. Everyone except him; he doesn't even know her last name; he's different from all of them, never lifted even a finger—. His hands clean, white, as she'd be if only he touched her. Lacing up the heavy boots, stumbling to her feet, running, running without looking, alder twigs like little whips at her legs as she goes to find him, ask him: black fire, white stars, deliverance.

BERTRAND SHUTS the door against the streamers of light and air she lets in. "Mariette, what are you doing here? I thought I'd told you—are you all right?"

"I'm okay." She's out of breath, as if she's been running—flying: black eyes like ink splotches on a crumpled sheet of paper. She must be in some kind of trouble, though why she's chosen to

come here—. And Claire's expecting him—he should have left
ten minutes ago.

"Look, Mariette, I was just on my—"

"Can I maybe have some water? Please?"

"Of course. I'll have to get a glass from upstairs. You might
as well sit down."

When he returns she isn't sitting anywhere, but standing by the
work table on which are piled copies of *Photography Today, The
American Journal of Photographic Art, Camera,* and *A Concise
History of Photography.* She's looking through *Camera: A Special
Issue on the Nude.*

"Mariette?"

She whirls round, the magazine dropping from her hands. "I'm
sorry, I didn't mean no—"

He bends down to retrieve the copy of *Camera* from the floor.
"Oh, it's perfectly all right. I just didn't know you were interested
in photography, that's all."

"I don't—." Her face is tight, as though the skin's a mask tied
round her. "They're like the ones in Wagner's store."

"What is?"

"Them pictures." She points to the magazine in his hand.

"Oh, come now, my dear Mariette. Can't you see the difference? No, let's forget that—do you want this water or not?"
Exasperated with this inconvenient annunciation—the Spirit of
Spruce Harbour—keeping him from a comfortable afternoon at
Claire's. *Them pictures.* She takes the water from him, but her
hands are shaking so much the water splashes on to the magazines
on the table—she tries to mop up the few drops and ends by spilling
the whole glass.

"I'm sorry, I'm sorry. I didn't mean—"

"Oh for heaven's sake—look, it's all right, just let me clear
this up." He takes a handkerchief from out his jacket pocket and
tries to repair the damage—it's too late; the pages of the different
magazines are glued together. "*Merde.*"

"Yer mad at me." She's looking up at him as if her whole
body's inside her eyes, tortured. He's never seen her look quite
like that; it reminds him of the expression of the girl in Munch's

painting—*Puberty*. Remarkable how much she looks like that girl. Interesting to take her picture, even just her face, the way it looks now.

"Are ya mad?"

"Angry? No, it doesn't matter. Why don't you sit down—I'll get you some more water."

"No. I mean, I might spill it. I'm sorry, I shouldn't a come. I'm just makin' a mess—"

"Sit down—it's all right. I haven't seen you for a long time, you know." As if it were her fault, as if she'd been keeping away from him, and he missed her. Minded.

He's pulled up chairs for both of them and they sit facing each other. She has the empty glass in her hand—he still holds the special issue of *Camera*. She can't keep her eyes off the cover: close up of a breast, enlarged so that each shivering pore of skin seems mountainous. Raises her eyes to his face, drops them to the cover—back up to his face. Her own the colour of tomato soup; she can feel it burn—

"Really, Mariette—it's art, don't you understand? My God, have you never seen pictures of Adam and Eve?"

He's mad at her again. He thinks she's dumb, *dumb cunt*, what they all want—does he? Mad at her because she's never let him— he'll never let her come back now, he wants—*Down in the valley where the green grass . . .* "Do you want me?"

"Want you to what?"

"Do you?" But she answers her own question, starting to unbutton her shirt, pulling the cloth slowly, gently from around the buttons, as if she were afraid of hurting them. He stares at her for a moment, then takes a long sip of the water he'd brought for her.

"You mean you want to pose for me—in the nude? I—we really ought to have someone else in the room—these things have to be done properly; there'll be the devil to pay—but I don't suppose anyone will—. Wait, Mariette—we'd better go upstairs."

On her face the same consuming look, her eyes feeding on something inside her as she sits on the bed, unlacing her boots, unzipping her jeans. He's shocked at how quickly she is naked before him, how small, how straight her body is, the delicacy of small veins mapping her skin. Like a doll, a store mannequin, *good girl*, letting him arrange her body so that she's sitting not on but against the bed, legs tight together, locked, her shoulders hunched so that little caves appear above her collar bones. Crossing her rigid arms at the wrists so that one hand rests on top of the other; cupping her knees and shading with the inverted triangle of her arms, the small, dark mound of hair crouching between her thighs. Her arms, held straight and stiff, do not cover her breasts, but seem to expose them all the more: small, stretched flat across the ribcage, nipples like eyes sealed up in sleep.

"Perfect. Don't move—this is marvellous." She looks up at him now, expectant, but not anxious any more, as if waiting for a gesture, a word to cut the cord wiring her body in that stiff, strange pose.

"No, Mariette—not like that—I want you to look like you did downstairs—what were you thinking of, then? Come now, this is important, you must co-operate. Try to think of something you don't like, something that—frightens you, makes you feel anxious, even a bit ashamed. A nightmare you've had, or something terrible that could happen to you."

He's fiddling with her hair, keeping it from falling too far forward, moving back and forth with the camera. Her face, which had been white as candle wax darkens suddenly, becomes suffused, almost sullen with a rush of blood. "That's it—exactly— good girl." *Click.* Her eyes like targets. *Click*, as he comes close, shoving the camera at her, over her, into her

one hand over her mouth, the other between her legs, opening them like a pair of scissors; she is shaking her head under his hand without a sound, without a word, each shudder a scream inside her where no one can hear where he is shoving himself into her, ripping her open from cunt to throat, jamming his tongue into her mouth till she gags, feeling her body retch under him as he digs deeper, harder, exploding, bullet exploding, bits of twisted metal scattered through blood sky inside, hunter's bullet. You wanted it, don't tell me no different, you been askin' for it and all I done was give ya what ya been prayin' for; you tell anyone

I'll kill ya; she won't say nothing, she promises, she won't say
one word if only he'll leave her alone now, no more, please

"Mariette? I said that's all; you can get dressed now. I'll wait
for you downstairs."

She hears his feet, light on the stairs, looks round her and slowly
finds the dirty puddle of her clothes where he has shoved them
out of the way. Pulls them on slowly, carefully, buttoning up to
the neck, braiding her hair down her back and then walks down
the stairs, boots like chains on her feet. Doesn't look at him, even
when he tells her how perfect it's been, how he wishes he could
pay her for modelling, but after New York—he knows she'll
understand. And that perhaps it's best if they don't say anything
to anyone else about this session—so narrow, so foul-minded,
people around here—look at her own response to that issue of
Camera. "So not a word, all right? It'll be our secret. *Not a word.*
Good girl."

SHE WALKS HEADLONG through the woods, taking any path, not
knowing, not caring where it takes her, just walking, walking so
quick it's running, round and round the paths marked with blue
streamers, legs stiff as planks, trying to find the way home but
she can't; she can only run with her breath and her heart screaming
inside her, warning her, but nothing can help. She finds it all the
same. Spruce with dead branches like spikes, aimed at her, leaves
and moss and twigs underneath her feet, but furred with the dark,
winter dark creeping, burrowing into everything. And in the
centre of the clearing, the black car, brambles, giant thorns punc-
turing what's left of the red upholstery. They should burn it, pour
gasoline and torch it so the flames would roar and sparks crackle,
blood drops sizzling, exploding; burn it so nothing was left but a
scorch on the ground, scar that grass and moss would smooth
over, seal up. But they left it there, rotting slowly, forever. Black,
dank fire consuming nothing, black car going nowhere. There is
nowhere to go.

Because there is nothing, nowhere, she backs out of the

clearing, follows the paths round again till she comes out at the edge of the fields. Takes the rutted lane between the briars, down to the edge of the fishplant road. Full-stop; end-stop. Two ways to turn: up to the highway, down to the trailer. Claire's house on the highway, the doors shut. Louis on the highway, honking his horn at her. Louis à Pepsi yelling, "Delima's kid," Delima's, Delima's, not his. Delima and Luc in the trailer, drowning in their bed behind the plywood wall: didn't she want it, pray for it, but they cut it out of her, just a black mess of blood left inside.

Behind the fishplant she sees the long chain of hills enclosing the bay: a huge arm, barring her. Light so fierce she can make out every fissure in the basalt cliffs, every slash in the spruce cover, his arm pushing out, thin, tattooed: belting her, posing her, shoving her. Down.

4

"I thought I'd just die, Marcie, just up and *die*. I mean he really meant it, and there we were alone together. I was jello after two seconds, just *jello*. Stu, he—"

Halyna forced herself to keep waving out the window as the train pulled away. Long after her father would have left the station platform, she was still watching—not the scenery out the window but the glass itself, as if she expected the reflected images of father, mother, apartment to quiver there: bemoaning, admonishing. She fingered the thin gold chain where it fastened at the back of her neck—it was so long the cross hung down where no one could see it. Between her breasts—over her heart insisted her mother, stubbornly inaccurate. Halyna blessed the extortionate price of a return ticket from Halifax to Spruce Harbour, the five hours it took to go some three hundred kilometres. Had the ride been cheaper, shorter, one of them would surely have come with her to settle her in—

"Let me tell you, he was jealous. I made a point of letting him know there were real *live* French *men* teaching there. French from France. Latins—*you know,* Marcie. The Absolute End. As lovers, of course. Oh my God, Marcie, you don't think anyone really goes there to learn French, do you?"

But that was why—after her campaign, first of enthusiasm, then of intense indifference—her parents had agreed to let her go, though it was her money, not theirs that was paying her way. Money she'd earned by doing laundry for the tenants and cleaning their apartments—most of which went for her music lessons, but a portion of which she'd saved and which, added to her bursary, made it possible for her to carry out the plan first suggested by that priest after the concert. No one had said anything about real French men at Sacré Coeur, least of all her father, who'd gone on and on about the priests and nuns running the language school as if their daughter were to be immured, not immersed there. It didn't matter. When she came back at the end of June, proficient in French, she would resume her music lessons, her apartment-cleaning, her recital playing and her refusal to clean house and wipe noses in suburban Montréal.

Past Bedford Basin and the silly little belvedere built by the Duke of Kent for his fat French friend—squashed now between the highway and the tracks. Hadn't they been lovers, passionate lovers though he was bald and beefy, and she well past her prime? Past the expensive houses built to look like summer cottages—who lived there? Doctors, dentists, businessmen—lawyers like cousin Ted. One of the doorways was blocked by tricycles and a child's wagon. Halyna put a mental "X" through these. She didn't like children; she hadn't particularly enjoyed being a child. Trees invading the gliding window, branches barely in leaf—the end of May and still too cold to go outside without a coat. The dun-coloured coat squashed into the rack overhead was a hand-me-down from cousin Sabina; her suitcase was stuffed with clothes that cousin Gail couldn't wear anymore, that were unsuitable for a mother of three. Just as unsuitable for a girl of eighteen, reflected Halyna, remembering how her mother had spent the whole night starching and bleaching high-necked blouses, ironing frumpy skirts and headscarves, so that she'd have something to wear to Mass at Sacré Coeur.

No more houses or highways; they were into the country at last, sliding between low hills thick with tapering trunks of birch, branches in tender, translucent leaf. It was like Poland here, like the countryside through which she'd travelled on her summer visits to her grandparents' farm. Halyna put her hands to the top of her head and began unfastening the tightly-wound braids. Her mother would no doubt be at church already, praying for her daughter's safety. And what would her father do now without his daughter to accompany into town for music lessons—as though her teacher were some ravening beast instead of an invariably courtly fifty-four-year-old. She grimaced, remembering the bus rides back to Dartmouth, her father submerging her into long sombre conversations in Polish about Poland, so that she wouldn't forget. The only effect of these conversations had been to make Halyna conscious of the other passengers staring wildly at them, wondering if they ought to call the RCMP.

When she thought of Poland now it was in the way you think of a dead person you once loved, whose features become blurred, then vacant, and finally flash with a surreal clarity in and out of dreams random as falling stars. At school she hadn't the clothes, the makeup, the video-cassettes, the little bags with pills or powders that would endear her to her peers. Her only friend was a girl who'd recently emigrated from Hong Kong and whose parents were as fiercely Catholic as hers. As for boy friends, she'd never been able to understand the North American idea of a girl's having some sweaty, pimply, sluggish-brained fellow to hold hands with while walking down corridors. Or to fumble under your sweater during spares or flub you with a member luckless and mechanical as the arm of a slot machine, in the back seat of the family car. Halyna wasn't interested in having a boy friend—she wanted a lover.

"Don't do it, Laurie, it's not worth it. I'm telling you—mine got all frizzy and then flat—I ended up looking like a dead poodle. So no more perms—see, I'm growing it all out."

Halyna raked her fingers through her long, fine hair, spreading it over her shoulders. It was still too bright outside for there to be any reflection in the window, and she couldn't bear the thought of making her way down the jolting, smoky corridor to the toilet, just to peer at herself in a dirty little square of glass. She'd braided her hair for her father's sake. If she had dared she would have put on the old school tunic she'd worn in Krakow; the hem barely reached the place where her thighs began to round. He wouldn't have seen the joke, though. He'd put his hands on her head and given her his blessing before they'd left the apartment, invoking the protection of the Virgin, the saints, all angels and the Pope, as if he were sending his daughter off to Sodom instead of to a school named after the Sacred Heart of Jesus. She wondered at the sexual optimism of the girls in the seat ahead of her. Real live French men at Spruce Harbour—with mustachios, no doubt, and pomaded hair. The only people she remembered from the concert had been the two priests and that woman who'd organized the whole affair—she was the only one who'd seemed to know the first thing about the pieces they'd played. And then that silly fellow with the spectacles and bow tie. He'd taken offence at something she'd said—she couldn't remember what. No matter, he'd have a fine time with the girls in the seat ahead.

Windsor, Kentville. They were into the Annapolis Valley as the sun began to set, reflecting off the farmhouse windows so that each pane of glass blazed up: seraphim roasting in the glory of God. Halyna watched the evening sky deepen from azure to plum; she even poked her head out the carriage to find the evening star when the train halted midway for the cars to be uncoupled. She wondered how saints and sinners could look up into the sky as though it were an enormous window through which you might catch a glimpse of God moving in a distant room. To her it had always seemed a mirror, not a window: silvered glass whose images were the reflections of our desires, needs and fears. And where her pious mother saw only the mild face of Mother Mary, Halyna made out jostlings of Thrones, Powers, Dominations— the power blocs of Heaven. Heaven was here—but across the ocean, away from her parents, her narrow bed in the basement apartment.

Her fingers tightened on a leather bundle in her lap. Not a purse but the case in which she carried her oboe, the farewell gift of her teacher in Krakow who had warned her that if she was getting out she should go to the places that mattered—London, New York, Paris. And she not even in Halifax, but, dear God, Dartmouth. She shook her head and her thoughts, closed her eyes and went through the obbligato in the B minor Mass she was to play in the Atlantic festival in July. But the train had finally picked up speed and was jolting from side to side like a deranged cradle. She put her hand to her stomach; she would be ill if she didn't fight it down, she would *not* be ill here, in front of all these strangers.

She opened her eyes, looked out the window and saw—instead of low fields and lazy, looping river—her own face or ghost of that face, its outline blurred and doubled.

"Want another Coke, Laurie? I'm just going to the can, be back in a sec, okay? Sure you don't want another bag of chips?"

Halyna watched the girl flounder down the aisle, bashing into the backs of seats, laughing loudly at each toe she trod on, every elbow jostled. The girl was fat, her face peppered with pimples, but the friend, Halyna guessed, was thin, pretty, rich—she was clamping headphones on, you could hear the tinny buzz of the tape she was playing, the cruelly monotonous thump of the bass: da-da-dùm, da-da-dùm, da-da-dùm. No other combination, no other rhythm—the crash of that fat girl through the stubby jungle of her life: da-da-dùm. The fat girl lumbering back, laden with silvery inflated bags of potato chips, the seat in front of Halyna giving a panicky jump and click as the girl plopped herself down. What would Marcie do while her pretty friend was off at the beach fucking Frenchmen? And what would she do, Halyna? What had she ever been able to do?

In Krakow, when she was twelve, sneaking out of the crowd of girls with whom she'd walk home from school. Making a rendezvous at the park with the boy from the neighbouring apartment. They had slipped into a bed of ornamental bushes. Burrowing, hiding themselves away from all the boots and shoes trotting serenely by. Clothes still buttoned tight, they'd furiously rubbed bellies together, the way he'd sworn he'd seen his parents do at night. Nothing had happened at all except the soiling of her clothes, and dust specks lodging in her eyes.

In the textbook for Family Studies Class at Cornwallis Collegiate: the line drawings of tubes and sacs and organs. "Orgasm is a little like the moment just before you sneeze." Something Kleenex tissues could take care of.

In the laundry room in the basement of the Dartmouth Arms, putting the tenants' wash through the machines—Mr. da Silva from the fifth floor coming up from behind while she was rinsing something at the sink, putting his podgy baby hands around her breasts. She hadn't cried out; she'd let his fingers make their joyful, frantic squeeze and then—she'd taken his hand in her own cool, strong fingers, lifted it to to her lips—and bit till the blood came. Watching him back away, nursing his hand, eyes bright with puzzled tears like a baby slapped by its mother.

Whereas love was different from all this, vastly different, as the ocean is from a puddle, mountains from a slag heap. When the poets spoke of it there were always rushing torrents, roses bursting open to the sun: transcendence, transfiguration through a passion single minded, single hearted. And sadness, too, sweet delicious sadness—Pan chasing Syrinx and she running quicker than the wind, turning herself into a reed in the stream and yet he'd plucked her after all, played his music through her. Why did they make Eros a brat of a cherub or a thin-hipped, spindle-shanked boy when he was really shaggy, an earth-coloured brute whose one desire was mastery, power over the pursued? Why wasn't Eros a woman, like those Venuses she'd seen reproduced in the artbooks in the Public Library—hefty women lolling on mounds of dishevelled silk, buttocks and breasts big and pink as the hams her grandparents strung from the rafters of their kitchen? Women who could take a boy like that stick-limbed Eros from Picadilly Square and crack him like a hazelnut between their thighs, or brush him away like a mosquito that's sucked its fill?

And certainly different, another planet from what that fat Marcie would no doubt be doing on Friday nights while Stu turned Laurie into jello. Feeling yourself up, they called it—dialling your own number. She had tried that—holding her breasts, moving her fingers down to the curiously puckered lips of what the Family Studies textbook had called the pubis, but what the olders girls at school in Krakow had called Venus' mound. Perhaps it had been the thought of her parents asleep a stone's throw away in the cramped apartment; perhaps it was her own impatience, but all she had felt was the warm, familiar weight of her own flesh in her hands—hair and skin more secretive perhaps, but no different than any other part of her body. Nothing like the passion of concentration and release that came from playing the most difficult music—Bach, say—making melodies jump through a dizzying multiplicity of hoops and still sound sweet and whole and true.

"Not diet pills, Marcie. You know: *those* kind of pills. Of course I did—look, you can't be too careful."

Be Careful. Careful not to stain your clothes, tear your dress, talk to strange men. How then could you make anything happen? Halyna stroked the scratched leather of her oboe case, the one possession of hers that neither her father nor mother would touch without her permission. Inside the maroon velvet lining was the slim vial of pills she'd got from the Dartmouth Well Woman Clinic that afternoon she'd skipped school. She'd been taking the pills for a month now, ever since it had become certain she would go off to study French at Sacré Coeur. Next to the pills, more as a talisman than anything else, lay her only other valuable, her passport, stolen from the suitcase under her parents' bed, the suitcase they would open only to prepare for their return to a free Poland.

Not just pleasure, certainly not romance, but power—that was what she wanted. Not power over someone, but power to understand, master the feelings inside her, the way she did when she was playing music. Aesthetics and Erotics, they must feed into one another: the body's power not suppressed, as her mother would have it, but released, fed back into the music, breathed into the very instrument. Bach—look at Bach. Sixteen, eighteen children? A lifetime of cantatas and copulation, the one fitting into the other just like your fingers when you clasp your hands. She'd read somewhere about how sharks, if once they stop swimming, stop breathing, too. That's what playing music was like for her; that's what loving—not just having sex, but making love, must be like. If she could only find a lover. It would change her forever, she would never be her parents' child again; she would be herself, with her music and her love like wings, brilliant, sturdy wings carrying her over every hurdle till she got what she wanted, where she wanted to always be—

Whitby. Scattered lights across the water: a clutch of parents, husbands, wives, children waiting to greet the travellers descending from the platform. And all she wanted was the chance to get off this inchworm train into blessed empty space—no one waiting for her, watching over her, expecting things she'd no desire even to pretend to give. She stretched out her legs, checked her watch— still another hour to go. Marcie was snoring. Laurie had put her headphones back on and was humming, off key. Halyna seemed to see her parents' faces before her, pale and scarred as this full moon, like another lamp reflected in the windows. They wanted her to come here to learn enough French to be able to manage in Montréal; they wanted her to study for three years and then take a job teaching in grade school, making money to bring Tomasz and his family out of Poland. In three years' time she would be twenty-one, too old to launch any dazzling career as a soloist, too young to be a member of any distinguished orchestra or chamber group. If you played violin, cello, even flute—she pursed up her lips in dislike of that fleshless, silvery instrument—then you had a chance: people would take an interest in you. Barbarians who couldn't tell an oboe from a clarinet, the Swingle Singers from the Berlin Philharmonic. There was only one way—to get out, away. From the family in Dartmouth, Montréal, Krakow; from the redundant virginity she was lugging around with her like a valise stuffed with a thousand different constrictions—the crustaceous brassières her mother made her wear, the chastely capacious underpants, the lectures, pleadings, threats. "Your body is the temple of your soul, your purity a treasure it would be sin to sell cheap. You are our only hope, our only reason for going on— if you get yourself into trouble you can walk straight into Halifax Harbour; we are your loving parents and you will do nothing to hurt or shame us."

The car began to rock less violently. A long, clownishly melancholy whistle blew into the darkness ahead. The conductor called the stop: Spruce Harbour. Giving a little sigh at the perfect impossibility of her expectations, Halyna followed Marcie and Laurie down the steps and practically into the arms of the teachers sent to meet them. But what she heard, in the strange and empty space she'd come to, was not Père Gilbert's fulsome greeting in our two official languages, but magic. A curious, delicate chorus from the fields all round them, as if bubbles in blown glass were rising up and bursting in her ears. *"Des grenouilles,"* said a voice nearby. *"Puis-je vous aider?"* She surrendered her baggage, except for the oboe case which she clutched under her arm, and entered a car parked in the middle of nowhere and nothing. And then she rolled down the window to hear, as long as she could, that disembodied, effervescent choir, closer, yet no more reachable than the constellations pricked out overhead.

"EXCUSE ME for disturbing you. Père Gilbert sent me—he thinks you might be able to find me a practice room."

A blonde girl in a white dress, a runaway Renoir framed in the doorway of her office. Claire puts down the papers she's been sorting, frowns and then, as quickly, smiles.

"You did come, after all? I'm amazed. It's Miss—"

"Radowska. Halyna Radowska. And you're Claire Saulnier, aren't you? I remember meeting you the time of the concert, last year. You teach music here?" Halyna sits down in the chair Claire has motioned to—sits carefully, knees primly together, clutching her oboe in her lap.

"I wouldn't call it teaching music—I just make sure my students don't do too much damage to the instruments. I suppose I'd be a pianist if there were anyone to perform with here. But that's entirely beside your point. You want a room to practise in—where they won't hear you, is that what Père Gilbert said? Have some tea? The kettle's just boiled."

Claire busies herself with measuring out Earl Grey from the cannister into a porcelain tea pot—no Red Rose or Brown Betty for her. This pleases Halyna—she likes the look of this office, the austerity of book-crammed shelves and institutional oak tempered by the Japanese poster on the wall. She likes the look of this woman, too, the brown eyes as alert as a child's in a face blank and lustreless as old paper. Likes the way she smiles at her, offering fragrant-steaming tea out of china cups on a lacquer tray. Making no pretence of scolding Halyna for not speaking French—as she was honour-bound to do, according to Père Gilbert—but addressing her in easy, friendly English.

"A practice room—there *are* a few of them on the fourth floor, but they're terribly hot and stuffy. The roof's not properly insulated, you see. The maintenance man's supposed to be fixing that—but he's still on holidays, I'm afraid. I don't see why you can't use a classroom, but then Père Gilbert's fanatical about locking them up if they're not in use. He's frightened someone might come in and steal all the chalk. You could practise in my office, I suppose—except that nothing's soundproofed in this building, and the secretaries are right next door. I suppose the residences are hopeless? Stupid question. And no one understands that you have to practise several hours every day; they imagine that just because you're here learning French you should let your music drop, right?"

"You understand? I was beginning to lose hope that I'd find anyone round here who would."

Halyna says this with just the right combination of ingenuousness and calculation, thinks Claire—she's a professional, all right. But she's also pleasanter company than Claire's had for a long time—a change from Bertrand, whom she's already learned by heart, and who has begun to bore her beyond all measure with his continual complaints about the rigours of immersion teaching and life in residence. Though she hasn't put any sugar in her tea, Claire stirs the cup for several minutes, deliberating. What if she introduced a new member to their little company, making up a trio instead of the endless duets? Wasn't it part of her job to distract and entertain Bertrand with whatever means she had on hand? And what of this girl? Surely Père Gilbert would concede that Halyna Radowska was as much of a rare bird in these parts as a *Français de France?* What of the report *she* would make of Sacré Coeur? Didn't that have to be taken into account? Claire smiles to herself, remembering how deftly Halyna had punctured Bertrand's pretensions at that dismal concert. What other kinds of salutory damage could she do? On the kind of impulse she knows she should suppress, Claire puts down her cup of tea and leans a little towards this charming, self-possessed girl in the absurd white dress.

"You could practise at my house, if you like. Afternoons would be best—I'm generally out teaching students then. Besides, there's the piano, which I imagine you could make use of? And it's quite close by—you could walk. You should ask permission of Père Gilbert, though—he likes to have a finger in every pie, if that's not too messy a way of putting it. No, of course not—I'm as selfish as the next person—I wouldn't have offered the invitation if I'd thought it would inconvenience me. But as a matter of fact, I feel responsible for you, Miss—Halyna, then—and do call me Claire—since I'm the one who first invited you to Sacré Cœur for that delightful concert. Look, why don't you come over tonight—you're free to do what you like in the evenings, aren't you?"

"There's supposed to be a discothèque—but I can easily get out of that. Where is your house?"

"Right on the highway—there are no house numbers here but—. Wait, I've a splendid idea. I'll ask Bertrand France—you must know him, he's one of the immersion teachers—to come over as well. For coffee, say eight o'clock. He can bring you— will that be all right?"

"I don't see why not." A smile flickering on Halyna's lips. "You're very kind."

"Not at all. But you'd better just go and clear things with Père Gilbert. *Allez, au revoir.*"

"IF YOU HOLD your eyes—like this," and he puts his palms up like shutters at the sides of his face, "then it's a bit, a very little bit like looking out at the Mediterranean—don't you think?"

Halyna, lying stretched out on her stomach, chin propped in her hands, nods without trying the experiment. Knowing that Bertrand, by cutting out the scraggy spruce, the wind-blistered lighthouse and the shingled outhouses on either side of them, has reduced the view to a square of sundazzled water: any sea, any sky.

"Of course in Poland you wouldn't see much of the sea, would you? It's silly of me, I suppose, but I can't help imagining you all as a nation of Conrads, fantasizing escape by means of something you've never seen. Of course you've read Conrad?''

"I don't know whom you mean.''

"Joseph Conrad. You know, *Heart of Darkness, Typhoon*—I once wrote a dissertation on *Typhoon*. Surely every Pole has read *Lord Jim*?''

"And why should every Pole read *Lord Jim*? I didn't, not until I came to Canada. I did read some of Jòzef Téodor Konrad Naleçz Korzeniowski for English class, at school in Poland. I didn't really care for it—except one early book about an old man and a house he builds for himself and his daughter on an island in the South Seas. And his daughter runs away with her lover instead of the man her father's chosen for her. I liked that one. God, it would be wonderful to be in the South Seas right now—the sun's so cold here—look, I've got goosebumps.''

"Korzeniowski, of course.'' Bertrand is thoughtfully chewing on a stem of long grass—he either hasn't heard Halyna's words, or is sternly ignoring the stretch of bare, rounded arm she's offering him for inspection. He looks out to the hills across the bay. "Did you know Conrad spoke French better than he did English? He lived in Marseilles for a long time. He could have stayed on in France and written his novels there—in French of course. I really can't see why he chose to go to England.''

"You don't like England?'' Halyna is sitting up now, cross-legged beside him, one beautifully rounded, pale-gold kneecap no more than a hair's breadth from his fingertips as they idly flick at the blade of grass.

"England? Oh, it's pretty enough in parts—rather amusing, though unbelievably old-fashioned. I went to school there for a few years. My father thought I'd stay and work for the family firm—in London. But I couldn't. Paris is really the only place to be, if one's at all interested in the arts—if you're a European, of course. New York is—unbelievable in its own way. A terribly exciting city—if that's all one wants. But Paris—and I'm speaking objectively here—you can't say that Paris isn't—''

"I can. I can say it.'' Halyna almost hisses out the words—

there is such passion in her voice that Bertrand's compelled to sit up, take note. "I've never been to Paris. We passed through Vienna and London on our way to Canada—London's grey and dirty and damp. And I've been to Warsaw, Prague, Budapest— for recitals and competitions. But never Paris. And I've got to get to Paris—I've got to. One of the world's best oboists lives there, Marcel—"

"Yes. Duclot. I've often heard him perform. But of course you must come to Paris sometime. I might even be able to show you around—"

"You might?" There's a little blade of mockery in Halyna's voice, but Bertrand hears only deference, shyness, abashed expectation. He looks at this girl sitting beside him, hugging her knees, her blonde hair ribboning out behind her in the wind. They are within a few feet of the cliff edge: below them only air and the swollen roar of the sea. He moves back a few cautious inches, hoping Halyna will follow suit. She doesn't.

"What kind of bird is that—look, there, hovering over the cliff. What's its name?"

Bertrand shades his eyes with the copy of *Parlons Français* which he's brought along just in case Père Gilbert comes strolling by in his cassock and clerical hard hat—unlike Père Philippe, he doesn't affect contemporary dress, and this placates Bertrand— he like his priests to look, if not act, vaguely medieval.

"Don't you know its name?" Of course he doesn't—he can recite every street and alleyway in Paris, but as for a kind of tree or bird in this place where he's already spent nine months . . . Hopelessly unobservant: she's wasting her time. She lunges to her feet and walks right to the cliff edge while Bertrand makes clucking noises. Legs wide apart, firmly planted in the earth, Halyna looks out through salt-stung air to the blue hills across from them. She can feel him watching her, his eyes on her bare arms and legs, on her white cotton dress. One of Gail's hand-me downs—sleeveless, full-skirted, buttoning up to the chin, though Halyna has to leave the top buttons undone since otherwise she can't breathe: Sabina's daughter is a good size smaller than she. No longer in fashion, this cut or style of dress—the other girls in the immersion course wear oversize T-shirts, short shorts in neon colours, or else elaborately cut sweat-suits which would have fallen down to their ankles had they once tried to do more than lounge in them. Big plastic necklaces and zigzag earrings: shock-wave hair and metallic makeup, almost as painful to Halyna's eye as their squeals and giggling are to her ears: "Bone-jooor, shay-ree. Savvy-voo kwa? Say *tray* gross."

The boys are worse. Some of them into their twenties, but ape-like in their speech (you couldn't call it conversation) and their moves. Spending their time outside the classroom playing base-ball, drinking beer smuggled onto campus, and talking, in Eng-lish, about screwing girls. Père Gilbert, of course, wouldn't know what was going on: the Coke-and-cheesies sex in the spruce groves behind the dunes where there were more condoms than spruce cones littering the ground. Besides, some of the immersion teachers weren't much better than their students—among them Bertrand stood out like a dove among crows. "Bertie," they called him—"the Virgin Mary." Halyna had had the fun of watch-ing Laurie-from-the-train have her most-practised manoeuvres on "a real live French man from *Paris*" crushed by Bertrand as if they'd been so many cigarette stubs under his heel. Though, as Laurie had complained in the residence lounge to Marcie: "He doesn't smoke—not even tobacco. He doesn't drink, he doesn't swear, he doesn't screw. Christ, Marcie, if that's French, then I'll take a hundred per cent Canadian every time."

A flock of cormorants suddenly rush down over the water, their ugly long necks straining towards a huge rock which the ebbing tide's exposed. Surely he'll give a sign, signal his intentions? It's been a week, already a week since the start of the immersion—since he'd escorted her to Claire's that evening, stiff as a chap-erone, refusing all suggestions of cognac and cigars (Halyna had been offered nothing more decadent than milk and sugar for her coffee). This morning in class she'd looked up at him from her seat in the second row and found his eyes already on her, his pale skin suddenly inflamed, like the rind of a radish. And she'd realized what she'd done to make him blush so—she'd been absently exploring the gold chain that fastened round her neck, veering down from her collar bones to the deep cleft between her breasts—she'd been pulling the cross up, fingering the gold still warm from the skin it had pressed against. When their eyes had met he'd coughed and pretended to be looking at the fat girl in the seat next to her, making Marcie stand up and give a little speech as to which she preferred, opera or theatre, and why.

"Halyna—it's late, we'll have to be going."

Here she was, standing alone at the cliff edge, her skirts billowing against her legs, hair streaming out behind her. The cormorants have vanished from the rock, plummeting like stones into the sea. She bites her lips, full lips, scored with tiny lines, stippled, like the tip of her tongue.

Of course it's late, too late; she wheels round on him, declaiming in Polish, "Mother of God, you mooning idiot, do I have to strip to the skin and threaten to throw myself off the cliff before you'll do so much as hold my hand?"

"*Comment?* No, don't bother translating—it sounds marvellous, whatever it is. A line from Mickiewicz? Yes, of course, let's get going—Halyna! Do wait up. I can't run in these shoes."

She slows her pace until they're walking side by side along the path to the college, her skirts sidling against his trouser legs. Somewhere a bird cries out—two notes, high-pitched, melancholy, like a rusty gate swinging absently back and forth in the wind and never latching.

EVERY AFTERNOON, from four to five-thirty, Halyna spends at Claire's. Even easier done than said. After a short interview with Père Gilbert, and a lengthy confession of the most trivial sins she could fabricate, Halyna had secured the priest's permission to practise at Mademoiselle Saulnier's: she'd sworn to speak nothing but French there. Bertrand had rather nervously accompanied her for a pleasant enough hour at Claire's. They'd all chatted over coffee, and then Claire and Halyna had discussed the qualities needed for the perfect practice room. They'd decided on the sunroom in which she's playing now.

She has a view of spangled water over grassy dunes, the fish-plant, with its buildings like tumbled sugar cubes, and the hills that wall in the bay. You can open the sunroom windows, letting in the wind which almost always blows along the shore, chasing mosquitos and raising gooseflesh on sunbathing tourists. Claire is usually off teaching, but sometimes holes up in her study, preparing next year's courses or concert schedules, and marking the theory papers of her gaggle of piano students. Halyna prefers it when Claire's in the house with her, it gives her the illusion of an audience, and she always plays better when she knows someone else is listening. Besides, it's not the sort of house you'd want to be alone in, too long. It's old enough that its timbers creak with every breeze, and even on the mildest of days little gusts of wind will shriek along walls and windows. Except for the sunroom, the house has few windows, so that on a scorching mid-day you feel yourself imprisoned in a cold and roomy darkness. How can Claire live alone here, with so few connections to the ordinary world outside?

At five-fifteen Halyna puts down her oboe and joins Claire in the kitchen for tea and talk—unapologetically English—about music and musicians, teachers, competitions, orchestras. Though for the last fifteen or so years she's clung to Spruce Harbour the way a barnacle cements itself on rock, Claire seems knowledge-able, Halyna concedes. And confides. Little by little over this week, she's told Claire practically everything: her parents' plans for turning her into a grade-school music teacher; the scholarship to study in Montréal—when she's not being an *au pair* and clean-ing lady for her cousin Gail; and her determination to get out of Canada altogether, and not to New York, either. Everyone went to New York; it was crawling with violin– or flute– or oboe-toting emigrés. Paris on the other hand—that was where the Nadia Bou-langer-of-the-oboe was to be found. But most of all, Halyna con-fides to Claire her desperation that she will never, never find the means to get away from home.

''Why don't you just pack up and go?'' Claire is leaning back against the kitchen wall, lighting not a cigarette but a slender, gold tipped cigar. The fragrance of the tobacco somehow combines with the smile on her lips, making Halyna think, ''She must have been quite beautiful once—she is still attractive. I wouldn't mind looking like this in twenty years' time, being like this—on my own, needing no one.''

''No money,'' Halyna sighs. ''Oh, I know I could do what other musicians do—give lessons, even get part time work—as a waitress or a secretary. Do you think I'd take dictation well?'' A small, acidic smile. ''But I'm still a Polish citizen—oh, I'm grateful that we could come to Canada, but I'm not going to spend the rest of my life—my musical life—here. Maybe Swiss or French or German citizenship would be more useful. If you want to be a soloist you have to be based in Paris, or London. That's where the music is, and the important musicians—the ones I want to play with. But you know all that, you studied in London, didn't you? And then there's my family. The only way they'd let me out of their sight is if I entered a convent—or got married to a rich Polish Catholic who'd adopt them as well. They've told me that if I were to go away on my own they'd throw themselves off the top of our apartment building, right into Halifax harbour—and of course they can't swim.''

Claire is folding her serviette into smaller and smaller squares as Halyna speaks; when it is finally so small and thick she can fold it no more she frowns, throws it into the last inch of tea in her cup, and addresses Halyna.

''I had a family too, and I left. It was as hard for me as it'll be for you. Oh I know—you've told me all about your brother back in Warsaw, family this, family that. True, my mother was dead— but that meant my father was all the more alone when I left: alone and not in the best of health. You must understand that I was an only child of—curiously protective parents. My father didn't stop me from leaving, he even drove me all the way to the airport. Sent me money to pay for my lessons and the rent on my bedsit— and died of a massive stroke before I could get back to see him one last time.''

''Oh—I'm sorry.''

''Of course you're not. It wasn't your father—it wasn't your fault. And it's really none of your business. Except that if you really want this career of yours, if you really want to be a musician instead of someone who occasionally plays music, then you'll be heartless and ruthless and hellishly single-minded. No one and nothing will get in your way. And you'll go—as I did.''

''But you didn't stay.''

''No. I wasn't good enough. You are.''

''Claire?'' Halyna puts out her hand over the empty plate, touches Claire's. It feels cold as metal in January—she pulls hers back, and all the time Claire's watching her, eyes looking clear, fixed, precise as a doll's. Then Claire changes her face with the subject; smiles, lights another slender cigar.

''How's our friend Bertrand? I haven't seen him since that first night he brought you here.''

That first night, with Bertrand practically playing the part of her chaperone—so worried someone might see them walking together, and then so huffy when Claire had talked to her and not to him. Asking questions about Halyna's family, her music, her life in Krakow: questions that made the answers she gave sound distinguished, intriguing, different from how things really were. So that even Bertrand had stopped sulking and actually listened to her for a moment before he cut in with comments of his own on everything aesthetic under the sun.

''Bertrand—oh he's fine, I suppose. I don't get to see that much of him.''

''Do you want to?'' Claire is leaning forward, chin in hand, inviting another confidence, one that Halyna isn't sure she wants to give. Père Gilbert had warned her about sticking to music with Claire Saulnier, nothing but music. Père Gilbert's head is full of rosary beads, all rattling around.

''Why shouldn't I?'' Halyna parries. ''At least he's intelligent. And cultured—that's an awful word to use, but you know what I mean.''

''Oh, I do know—I've received a postgraduate degree in the Modern European Mind from Bertrand France over the last six months.''

Halyna isn't sure of her ground—should she join in Claire's smile, wink, shake hands? Is she, however absurd it may seem, a little bit of jealous of Claire, this woman who has a good twenty years' experience on her, and has probably had as many lovers— though where in Spruce Harbour would she find any one to suit her? Is Bertrand burning a weak little torch for Claire? Is that why he's so stubbornly chaste with her, Halyna? Taking her home from Claire's house that night, leading her off under a sky whose stars were like perfume sprayed from a crystal atomizer. She'd purposely left her sweater behind at Claire's—had started shivering, but Bertrand hadn't put his arm around her—he offered his jacket. Which she'd taken, digging her hands into the pockets and finding the little leather-bound volume of Rilke he'd secreted there. She'd asked him to lend it to her—if only to have an excuse to get into his room on campus, to give it back.

"Do you like Rilke?" she asks Claire, who jumps a little at the non sequitur.

"Rilke? Why on earth do you ask that?"

"Bertrand lent me his volume of Rilke's letters. Do you like Bertrand?"

"My dear Halyna, one doesn't like Bertrand, one suffers him— like the visit of a self-important angel, one who's got a certain clout, however minor he appears. My job doesn't exactly hang on my putting up with Bertrand, but I am expected to entertain him—in properly spinster-aunt fashion, of course. He's not that bad. I'm quite fond of him, actually. I shall miss him when he goes back to Paris. Speaking of missing things, aren't you due back for your meal at the cafeteria?"

"Yes. But I'd much rather talk with you."

"Another time—I've got to get some practising in—besides, Père Gilbert will miss you. Perhaps even Bertrand will miss you. You're blushing—oh, Halyna, don't tell me you're interested in our very own *Français de France*? Seriously, you can't be chasing after Bertrand France?"

"You're right—I will be late. Thanks for the tea." Halyna pulls herself back from the table, stands up and stretches the way cats do after a long nap—and is gone before Claire can change her mind and call her back.

"SO HOW ARE YOU TODAY, Hector?"

"Fine, Delbert—and you?"

"Oh, the arthritis is acting up a little—you know how it is. You had a good time on your holidays? Your mother, she said you were off in the woods somewhere; you go very far, Hector?"

"Just out and around. With the canoe. I'd like this to go air mail, please—that's London, *England.* "

"You're sure that's where you want it to go, Hector?"

"I'm sure, Delbert. Yes, I know that's pretty far away. No, I'm not going—just the parcel. No, I don't know anybody in England—it's nothing personal. No, it's not—look, if you really want to know, it's the name of a publisher."

"Is that right? A Publisher." Delbert pushes out his lips, preparatory to licking the stamps. He's chosen an array of wildflowers and butter churns and Christmas angels—leftovers from previous Special Issues. It is clear to Hector that Delbert doesn't believe him, is waiting for a retraction or explanation. "A publisher of books, boring academic books, not like the ones in the Kwikway store."

"I see. Pretty far away, all the same, eh, Hector? You planning to go away to study something again?"

"No, Delbert. I'm staying right here. I even bought some land—on Deer Lake. That's where I went canoeing."

Delbert's eyes become unduly bright, like Christmas lights. "That's real nice, Hector, your parents will be very happy. Every man needs a house for himself."

"Not really a house, Delbert—just a cabin, almost a shack—"

"So he can get things ready for the day when he marries, starts a family. Is it a big house you're building, Hector? Four bedrooms, five, maybe?"

"You're sure you've got the right postage on that parcel? No, I didn't mean to—of course you know exactly how much, I just thought—it's not often you get someone with a parcel going overseas. No, I'm not going off on a trip. I've just taken my holidays, Delbert."

"That's nice, Hector, a man needs a holiday. You want to stay in good shape, especially now, at this stage in your life. Just a minute. I'll get you your change. And how are you today, Claire?''

"Fine, thank you Delbert." But she looks strained, played out.

"I'm just giving Hector his change. He's sending a parcel out to London, England. Maybe you know the place it's going to in London. You lived in London a long time ago—"

"I'm afraid I don't know it, Delbert. There's a parcel for me?"

"I'm just going to give Hector here his change, and then I'll get your parcel. It's from that store in New York. Must be a sight to see, all those skyscrapers. Me, I don't like to travel much. I like it right here. My Rita, she used to say, 'Why'd we even buy a car when the only place we drive to is church, and we can walk there anyway?' But you been driving your car around quite a bit these days, Claire. I saw you going down Falmouth way this morning.''

"Delbert? My change?"

"I'll just get Miss Saulnier's parcel, Hector, and then I'll count out your change. It's a good thing they built that hospital in Falmouth—a good thing. Your father, Claire, he always used to say that's what we needed here, a hospital—isn't that so? Well, I bet poor Delima's glad we got a hospital so close—better than going all the way to Halifax. But even so, it's a sad thing, a sad thing about her girl. Even if it wasn't an operation this time, still, you don't like to see a young person like that go into hospital. Depression, that's what I heard. Such a nice girl, the way she always took care of those kids, eh? Maybe you went in to see her today, Claire? Sure, you go down to Falmouth to do some shopping; you call in at the hospital, see if anyone from the French Shore's laid up. Go and say hello. That's nice, people appreciate it. She look okay when you saw her? You just sign here, on this line, that's right. Here you go, Hector: five dollars, forty-seven cents. You want that insured?''

"No, Delbert, that's okay—"

"I don't know, when you're sending something so far away, I think it might be a good idea. Delima was there at the hospital when you went?"

"No, Delima was cleaning the house for me. Thanks, Delbert—I'd better run, I've got someone—"

"A real shame. Hector, you're sure about that insurance? She going to stay in there a long time you think?"

"Really, I don't know. I didn't speak to the doctors, I just stopped by and said hello to Mariette. I must run—"

"She look okay? They said she hadn't been eating anything for a long, long while. She was just a bag of bones, that's what I heard. Does she look better now?"

"She looks as well as can be expected. They've given her some kind of medication—it makes her look different; her face looks a little puffy. I don't know, Delbert. Goodbye."

Hector follows Claire out of the post office, Delbert watching through the window as they walk together down the ditch, pause, talk a little. That's nice, he thinks. Nice to see them talking together again, like old friends. Maybe Hector's told her about the house he's building. Nice house, out in the woods, by the lake. Good place to raise a family. I told him he should go and see her. Friday, Saturday nights. Give the Fish and Game a rest.

"Hello Lucien. And how are you today? Your wife's feeling better? How long she going to stay in hospital? Well, that's how it is for those operations. You been to see her this week? You going today? You know Delima's girl, she's in hospital too. Claire Saulnier just went down to see her. Maybe you should go in and say hello to Mariette, too—that'd be a nice thing, she must be feeling lonely—"

By the time Delbert has given Lucien his pension cheque, Hector and Claire have vanished—he doesn't know when they left, or whether they went their separate ways, or if they got into Hector's truck and rode off together. Maybe they've gone to look at the house Hector's building in the woods off the Evangeline Trail; maybe they're talking right now about important things. He could phone Delphine down by the turnoff to Deer Lake—she'll be able to tell him if the Kwikway truck goes past; whether there's a passenger in the front seat; how long before the truck drives past again. Maybe he'll phone Delphine.

HECTOR HAS BEEN in his office for some twenty minutes before Claire knocks at the door. He drove there in his truck—she has walked, to divert Delbert's suspicions. Her temper is not altogether good—it is ludicrous, stupidly clandestine to have such a meeting, as if they're conspirators putting together part of a puzzle that doesn't belong to either of them. But she knocks all the same at Hector's office door. If someone should see her she can always say that she's gone to complain about the broken glass in her office window; about getting a new set of bookshelves, about—

"Coffee?" Hector offers her the same instant and coffee white he'd given Bertrand a couple of months earlier. She doesn't want anything, but tells him, "Please." It will take away some of the awkwardness of this meeting, the first real conversation they have had since Hector's return. Conversation about third parties: safe ground.

"I didn't know you and Bertrand were—such good friends," Claire begins, her voice pleasant but precise. She doesn't bother to even play at drinking her coffee, but simply holds the cup in her hands, as if its heat could melt something still glacial in her response to Hector.

"As good friends as the two of you seem to be? Maybe better— since I gather he didn't show you this."

Hector opens the central drawer of his desk; draws out a large manilla envelope. He's about to remove whatever's inside, but changes his mind and hands the envelope to Claire.

She sits with it in her lap, unopened. "You knew he'd made friends with Mariette?"

Hector leans back carefully in his swivel chair. "I only knew that she'd modelled for him—but for photos that Père Philippe could have displayed on his desk: Madonna-and-Child stuff. Portrait studies: 'The Age of Innocence'—like the ashtrays my mother mass-produces for the store."

"And this?" She gestures to the envelope, undecided whether to open it or to put it back on his desk.

"See for yourself. He left it for me as a kind of peace offering, while I was off on my holidays. We'd had a falling-out back in the spring."

"Oh?" She fingers the envelope, turning it over, staring at its buff blankness.

"I got pissed off with him, and let him know—not in so many words. As a matter of fact, it had to do with Mariette—the way he'd talked about her, taking her picture. As if she had no other existence than on a roll of film. As if she ought to be grateful to him for—I don't know, for capturing her with that shitty little camera of his."

"It's a bloody expensive camera, if you want to know."

"What has that to do with anything? Aren't you going to look at it?"

"Of course. I don't see what all this secrecy's about, though—"

Claire wants to shut her eyes. For the model in this photograph she holds in her hands is not nude, but naked: shamefully exposed. A child still, though her body bears the signs of womanhood: small breasts, dark mound of hair shielding her genitals. On the face an expression of fear—not of something she didn't want to know. But fear of something that has already happened to her, that she can't stop happening again and again. Claire doesn't shut her eyes but instead, slides the photograph back into its envelope and gives it to Hector as though it were something infected—the dressing from a wound. Shakes her head, as if to say there's nothing to be said about the photograph, except that she wishes she hadn't seen it at all.

Hector slides the envelope into his desk drawer, slams it shut. "Horrible, isn't it? As if the lens were skinning her. The best photograph he'll ever take. And the worst thing he'll ever do."

"Just what did he do? I can't believe he'd have put a finger on her—"

"He didn't have to, did he? Christ, Claire, just because she's Delima's kid, you think she doesn't have—what shall we call it—finer feelings? Doesn't feel hurt at being exploited, abused, even if it's only by a fucking camera?"

"Mariette's been through worse things than this, Hector. She got knocked up, had an abortion, complications—the whole damn thing—all at the age of thirteen. Pretty, isn't it? Bertrand didn't know—he doesn't know anything about this place, the kind of things we do here to amuse ourselves in the long winter months—''

''Or the things we don't do to keep certain things from happening—right, Claire? Don't blame it on this place—you think things like that don't happen in those big beautiful cities you were always telling me to fly away to? Always trying to foul your own nest, aren't you, Claire? You think the fisherman or truck driver who knocked her up when she was thirteen is ten times more of a shit than your friend Bertrand, with his spectacles and corduroys?''

''He's not my friend. And neither are you. I don't have to sit here and listen to this.''

''Anyone who could keep clicking a frigging camera at someone who looks at him like that—. Christ, no wonder the kid's in hospital.''

''What do you want, Hector? You want Delima to sue Bertrand and the Kodak Film Company for damages? Whatever's got inside Mariette now isn't something Bertrand's responsible for. And it's nothing I'm responsible for, either. Look, Hector, I like Mariette. I've known her since she was a kid, but she's my cleaning lady's kid, not mine. I agree, it's an awful picture, and a brilliant photograph, and that Bertrand's somewhat lacking in sensitivity-to-others. But there's nothing we can do about this. Or anything else.''

''He should know what he's done—or at least what's happened to her.''

''Of course he should know. But do you think he'll acknowledge anything—except the fact that he's managed to take a superb photograph using a local model? What did he say when he gave you this?''

''He didn't say anything, he left me a note—to the effect that he'd submitted the enclosed picture to an American journal, and that it had just been accepted for publication. An important American journal—of course he stressed that. I'd teased him once about his little hobby of photography—he wanted to show me how good he really is.''

''He gave you the picture?''

"It's a print—he has the negative."

"I don't suppose anyone from Spruce Harbour subscribes to any important American journals of photography? No one else will see it—Mariette will never see it."

"She'll never stop seeing it."

"Why this sudden concern for Mariette, Hector? It wasn't you, by any chance, who knocked her up all those years ago?"

He looks as though he'd like to throw the dregs of his coffee in her face. "No, it wasn't me. If you'll remember, I was away at the time—I had this rendezvous with destiny in Montréal."

"All right, Hector. I'm sorry, I don't know what I'm saying. I've had an exhausting day. I've got to get back home, think this over. I said I'm sorry—I don't know what you expect me to do—but I'll take the photograph—take it up to Falmouth and show Mariette's doctor, if you like, though it won't do any good; she still won't say anything."

"What about Bertrand?"

"Bertrand? What about him? Oh come now, Hector, do you want to call him out—pistols under the spruce trees at dawn. With Delbert for your second. You're talking as though she's your sister—"

"And you're not?"

Claire gets up from her chair, rubs her arms, as if she's cold—turns toward the door. "My God, Hector, you're really taking it seriously, this business of your return to Spruce Harbour. A one-man band, revenger-and-redeemer. When you've been back as long as I have, you'll learn to take things less dramatically. That's one of the virtues, the supreme virtue of a place like this—nothing you do or don't do can possibly make a difference to anyone—least of all yourself."

"You're wrong, Claire. And I'm the last one you should say that to."

"Are you, Hector? Whatever I once told you—but let's not go into that. We were speaking about Bertrand. I'll see that he—knows something about what's happened to Mariette. But I can't promise you that he'll care very much. Perhaps you should let me have that photograph?"

Hector gets up from his desk and stands facing Claire in the oppressive, oily heat of the furnace room. "Don't misunderstand—about what I just said. I don't want to go into all that either. Surely it's time we at least called a truce between us?" He opens the drawer of his desk, extracts the envelope and holds it so that Claire has to take a step forward to secure it.

"Thanks." She retreats toward the door, tucking the photograph under her arm. On the threshold she tilts her head at him, considering.

"All right, then. Truce, Hector. And if you're so concerned about Mariette, why don't you go up to Falmouth to visit her? It'll give Delbert something new to talk about."

She leaves his office as coolly as if she has a limousine waiting for her outside. Yet as soon as she's climbed the basement stairs she starts to run, runs to her office, shuts herself in and draws the curtains which have come halfway off their hooks and won't close properly, but let in a dusty slant of sun. Pulls the photograph out from its envelope and stares at it as if into a mirror. *Don't be confused by surfaces: in the depths everything becomes law.* Then she shoves the photo back into its envelope; locks it into the top drawer of her desk. Wants to get up, leave, go back to her house where she can be alone and let none of this in. But finds she can't move from her chair: legs dead, arms bound. Presses the heels of her hands into her eyes.

"You bastard, Bertrand. You blithe little bastard—you think no one and nothing can touch you. You barge into this place, into my house, into my careful little life—into hers. Oh, we'll see what we can do, we'll just see—." Claire unpeels her hands from her eyes, looks up at the Japanese poster on the wall, and smiles as charmingly as she'd done the day Halyna first walked into her office. *Hinx, minx, the old witch winks: the fat begins to fry.*

ON EITHER SIDE of the ditch a profusion of weeds, wildflowers, for some of which Halyna can find Polish names. Wild strawberries— she bends and picks some on the side farthest from the highway, tasting dust in the gritty little seeds, but pressing the sweet red flesh with her tongue, licking the juice off her fingertips. Careful not to stain her dress, crouching there in the puddled dust of the ditch while cyclists wheel wearily by, handkerchiefs knotted round their heads. They smile at her, calling hello. And then she springs up and starts walking again, slowly, lazily—it's a good quarter of an hour too early to arrive at Claire's. Instead of going up the walk to the house, she takes the path down to the shore and sits on the dunes, cross-legged, her oboe resting in the hammock of her skirt, her hair tucked down the collar of her dress so the wind won't whip it into her eyes.

Fishing boats in the bay—white specks against inky water. Halyna's seen the fishermen come into Wagner's store for cigarettes and twine and those stiff rubber gloves they wear. She likes the way they look, the dark, hard faces, as if sun and wind have stripped away everything inessential and pared their eyes down: direct, open. Not, she sighs, like Bertrand France. His is inescapably the face of a city-dweller, a face that would look absurd in all but the most civilized of country places. And yet she quite likes the fussy touches that make up the sum of him here—the precise parting of his hair, the bow ties, the scratched but still beautiful leather shoes—even his glasses, if only he'd polish them. Or, more to the point—if he'd take them off once in a while so that his scruples would become diffused, unreachable, and he could give in, at least to his desire to kiss her. After all the walks on the beach, the blushes over verb tenses and vocabulary, the conspiratorial glances at the cafeteria table, their evening at Claire's—they were still like brother and sister. As if, while he had on those abominable spectacles, there were some crystal shield around him, so that he could look at her without so much as undressing his eyes. As if she were a difficult piece of music he'd consented to study, but which he'd never perform.

Now that she's been here at Spruce Harbour for a good two weeks she can laugh at that Halyna who'd thought she could step off the train and into the arms of a lover, when all she'd done had been to walk into the solicitous, black-serge embrace of Père Gilbert. And into the house of Claire Saulnier about whom the priest had spoken with such respectful reserve. Halyna sighs. If she's not going to meet any rakes or roués during this little spurt of liberty, then at least she might be vouchsafed a scarlet woman instead of Claire, with her tea and ginger biscuits, her theory papers and bare white house. Hardly a sink of sin, a den of delicious iniquity.

Halyna jumps up from the sand, brushing her skirt, pulling her hair from out her collar so that it flies like gold spray about her. She runs down the path, up the back steps to the porch and peers in through the kitchen window. No light on—Claire's away. She bends down to the mat in front of the door, pulls out the key— they say no one needs to lock their door in a place like Spruce Harbour, but Claire does, all the same.

Half an hour later, just as Halyna has finished her scales and tone rows Claire comes in the front door—so quietly that Halyna cries out when she finally notices the stranger in the doorway of the sunroom. For this woman seems ashen, extinguished—for the first time since Halyna has known her, Claire looks old. But she speaks in her familiar voice.

"Sorry, I didn't mean to frighten you. Go on, you're improving—definitely better than yesterday. Keep this up and we can showcase you at the Evangeline Beverage Room before you go."

"No thanks. Really, my fingers will fall off if I play another note. Don't you think I deserve a break? Do you mind if we just sit and talk for a little?" Halyna follows Claire into the parlour, putting her oboe carefully into its case, and then depositing it on the empty mantelpiece. She takes the chair next to Claire's, kicks off her shoes, stretches out her bare legs, then folds them up under her so she's sitting cross-legged, chin in hand, meditating on the woman next to her.

"Claire? What's the matter?"

"What do you mean?" Claire gives herself a little shake, sits up straighter in her chair.

"You look like death. Or at least as if you'd seen a ghost."

Claire folds her arms across her chest, as if barring a door. She distrusts this intimacy Halyna has assumed. After all this business with Mariette, Hector, the photograph, Bertrand, all Claire wants is to be on her own. And yet there's something contagious about the sociability Halyna has assumed, sitting so casually in the armchair, bare-legged, twisting her long, loose hair like a skein of silk round her hand. Inviting Claire to confide, confess.

"I challenge you to spend an hour with the good father who runs the finance bureau and not to emerge as though you've seen a whole tribe of ghosts, or at least had your brain put through a blender. They do it on purpose—it's almost as bad as being jesuitical, that precision-tuned inability to follow the simplest idea. If you want the arts, you have to pay for them, you can't expect scalpers and a mile-long line-up to subsidize every concert we put on. And it's all on your behalf—yours and your fellow students. You know—that gala concert, talent show, whatever you're all supposed to be putting on the at the end of the session. For the delectation of the general populace, who will all be out at bingo or in watching Dallas, anyway. And they want me to turn a profit out of it? Sweet, bleeding heart of Jesus—but this isn't of the slightest interest to either of us. Let's change the topic. Come on, into the kitchen—let's break out the tea and ginger biscuits. No, Halyna, I'm not about to start corrupting you. Your Bertrand never lets anything stronger than *eau de source* pass his lips."

"Why do you call him my Bertrand?"

"You did confess to more than a pedagogical interest in him last time you were here. How obscene that prefix is: pederast, pedophile, pedagogue. Lapsang Souchang all right? Here—take a biscuit—sit down."

Halyna raises the ginger biscuit to her lips, licks it tentatively, then puts it back on her plate. "How many lovers have you had, Claire?"

Claire doesn't even falter, pouring out their tea, letting the steam cloud the space between their faces. "I told you I wasn't about to corrupt you, Halyna. Why on earth do you want to know a thing like that?"

"I wish to God someone would corrupt me." Halyna leans forward, eyes like sparklers, hand circling the tea cup, pressing the china as if she were intent on cracking it. "Tell me, Claire.

Am I hideous—do I repulse you? Is there something totally lacking in me?''

''Whatever are you talking about?''

''About—about love—well, then sex. About taking a lover. All right, Bertrand—for want of anyone else. And do you have something stronger than this tea?''

For a moment Claire looks as though she's going to burst out laughing, but instead she reaches behind her to a corner cupboard; pulls out a bottle of sherry and two glasses. ''Here—'' she fills it to the top. ''You'll be late for dinner at the cafeteria.''

''I don't care.''

''Your father-confessor will.''

''I don't *care.*''

''All right then.'' Claire goes over to the refrigerator and pulls out various packages of cheese, a huge bunch of grapes and an even bigger bottle of white wine. From various cupboards she produces bread, olives, smoked mussels (from Japan—the only local produce Spruce Harbour sells is dulse and dried fish) and lays it all on the table. ''Here''—and she slides a knife across to Halyna. ''Start cutting some bread and cheese. And while you're at it start thinking of a good reason for being here instead of in the bosom of Sacré Coeur.''

''Does it matter?''

''Oh—in a way. My job depends on not ruffling the feathers of such fussy little hens as Père Gilbert. Wine?''

''Yes, please. Do you need the job?''

''Pass the butter. Of course I need the job. One has to buy groceries, even in Spruce Harbour. Now, what will we tell them?''

''That you were—accompanying me. In a piece I'm going to play for that concert or talent show you talked about to the priest this afternoon.''

Claire considers the mussel she's put on a cracker: examines its oily, yellow softness, turning the cracker round and round before she finally pops it into her mouth. ''I see. You've been planning this little attack, haven't you? How do you know my playing's up to scratch?''

''Oh, if we choose the right piece no one will know if it isn't—

they'll be listening too hard to me." Halyna takes a long sip of wine and Claire breaks into a laugh.

"I don't think you'll have any trouble carving out a career for yourself, Miss Radowska. You've a healthy sense of your own worth, at least—did you know that? I thought so. But it's not a bad idea—playing something together. What about—"

"I was thinking of something from the Franck sonata—we'd have to fudge a transcription for oboe, but that shouldn't be too difficult. Do you think you could manage?"

Claire shrugs. Halyna is absently pulling the enormous purple grapes off their stems, piling up what look like miniature cannonballs on her plate. She peers at Claire out of those slanted amber eyes which so disconcert Père Gilbert during confession, wrinkles her forehead, licks at her lips, as if they were the reed of her oboe. "I don't care what we play—or if we come up with any excuse at all for my being here. But since I am here, I want you to tell me—just how do you go about it?"

"Oboe transcriptions? Oh, sex, of course. Didn't you cover all that in health class in grade ten?"

"I don't mean that. It's not the anatomy, it's the business of getting somewhere—with someone. This is the first chance I've ever had to get away from my parents and find myself a lover. I've been here for two weeks and all he's done is pay me compliments on my labials and aspirates—"

"So you've got some little scheme for killing off your viginity, like a Roman soldier falling on his sword? And with Bertrand, Bertrand of the clogged spectacles and bow tie, Bertrand the bionic Encyclopedia of Art? My dear child—"

"Don't call me that—you sound exactly like Père Gilbert. Just give me an answer—can't you?" Squeezing the grape in her fingers so that it bursts out of its black skin, oozing sweet, translucent pulp down her hand. Her eyes practically pounding into Claire's. "What do you do—how do you get him up against the wall—except that's not how it's done, is it?"

Claire refills Halyna's glass; her own sits untouched by her plate. "But why Bertrand—surely there are easier marks, and more rewarding ones. I shouldn't have thought he was what you'd call a practiced lover. Unless that's why you want him?''

Halyna finishes the wine in her glass, rakes the hair back from her face, tugging through knots the wind has tied. Refuses to look at Claire, addressing the grapes on her plate instead. ''It has to be Bertrand—and it has to be now. I can't go back to my parents the way I left—little white lamb—I might as well seal myself into a tomb, or turn into that concrete virgin in the parking lot. Bertrand—all right, he's not exactly Don Giovanni, but then I wouldn't want to end up like Donna Elvira. I want a lover, not an Evil Seducer.''

What you want, thinks Claire, is to be the Great Don yourself. Luring butterflies over the abyss. She sweeps bread crumbs off the table onto the shabby linoleum. Delima will be in to clean tomorrow. Delima.

Halyna pushes her plate away from her and leans across the table. ''I don't want a quick screw in a sandbox, Claire. I don't want some stupid thug using me for target practice, and then wiping his hands and going off for a beer with the boys. And I don't want to fall in love—I thought you'd understand. I want a lover, someone I can be on equal terms with—I want to get as much as I give. Is that so awful, Claire? Isn't that what you wanted, what you had?''

''You've had far too much wine already—don't you dare touch that bottle. I'm going to put on the coffee, sober you up before sending you back. For heaven's sake, Halyna, leave the dishes— just go into the living room, sit down for a moment and collect yourself. Go on.''

Slowly, tipsily, baby steps all the way from the kitchen to the armchair into which she flops, fish into net, damp hands over flushed face. *Have you no shame?* Her mother's refrain, whenever she found Halyna hiking up her skirts, unbuttoning a blouse to expose her throat. No shame. She shuts her eyes tighter against the palms of her hands, thinking of Bertrand, his lank, clean, awkward body in the eternal corduroys and brilliantly-white shirt. Absurd bow tie which must be the height of Paris fashion but which, among the overalls, checked shirts, sweat-suits and short shorts to be seen in and around Sacré Coeur, seems as incongruous as a chandelier in an outhouse. But then his hands—beautiful hands, fingers long and fine, thumbs spatulate—the fine black hairs curling up from the wrists. Those hands on her breasts, between her thighs—her own hands unbuckling his belt, reaching down into the soft darkness over his belly, into his groin. And then his sex, soft, helpless under her fingers as a sea urchin without its shell, or else arched, primed? Images—Saint Sebastian limp and bound; illustrations in the *Joy of Sex* book she'd found while cleaning Mr. da Silva's apartment. Blood booming in her veins, her hands clasped in her lap, knuckles white—

"Here—watch you don't spill it. There's milk and sugar in the kitchen, if you want—but I think you'd better take this black." They sit sipping bitter coffee, silently. And then Halyna starts shivering; rubs her arms and eyes, as if she's woken from a spell.

"This isn't getting me anywhere. I'd better go back."

But before she can move from the chair, Claire reaches forward and puts her hand under Halyna's chin. She smiles, her beautiful, slow, seductive smile.

"Halyna, listen to me. You're always talking about getting places—away from Halifax, your parents, your virginity—all of that. Then why are you being so silly about Bertrand? Let's forget that he's not exactly the best material for—let's call it 'erotic experiment.' But he is, on the other hand, a perfect candidate for marriage."

Claire drops her hand from Halyna's face. The girl stares at her, then whispers, "Mother of God. You're crazy, Claire— you're absolutely out of your mind." But she sits on the edge of the chair, her eyes on Claire's lips.

"Not crazy, just pragmatic. Inspired. Oh Halyna—can't you see any further than the end of your nose? You've told me all about your family and their plans for you, the obstacles they keep throwing in your way. The fact you haven't any money to take you where you want to go, as far as you want to go. So it seems perfectly clear to me that what you need at this point is a husband."

"I can't even get the fool to kiss me—how do you propose I drag him to the altar? And which altar, I'd like to know? St. Alphonse, with Père Gilbert saying the nuptial mass and my mother drowning in her tears? And then what, Claire? Be a house-wife and mother in —Paris?''

Claire puts her hands behind her head and looks up at the cracks in the ceiling. ''So you have got the brains you were born with, after all. You don't have to do anything excessive—like having babies or keeping house, Halyna. You'll be the wife of a *Parisien.* You'll become a French citizen. You can go off to France to study, teach—get medical care, bursaries, be sponsored for competitions, whatever you like, without any need for those ridiculous cards and permits they've made it almost impossible for foreigners to get. And you can have it all within the space of a few weeks—if you use your head. Fly off to Paris with Bertrand at the end of the immersion, get married, enroll at the *Conservatoire* for master classes with Duclot—''

''And then?''

''Haven't you any imagination at all? Besides, that's your business, not mine.''

''And what about Bertrand's business?''

Claire drops her arms to her sides—her face takes on that extinguished look it wore when Halyna had first noticed her in the sunroom. Claire rubs her face with her hands, as if she wants to press her eyes deeper into her head. And then rams her hands into her pockets. ''I should think it would be very good for Bertrand to fall in love. I mean really fall—get his knees scraped, the glasses knocked off his head, his nose bloodied. Maybe more than his nose.'' She laughs, a hoarse laugh that makes Halyna think of the crows in the spruce trees behind the college.

''But if Bertrand really falls in love—with me—then what happens when I don't want him anymore?''

Again, Claire laughs. ''You mean when you can't use him anymore? Oh, he'll have to manage—as other people do. There are such things as divorce, you know—even annulment. Don't tell me you're actually worried about how this—hypothetical marriage—will ruin Bertrand's life? My dear Halyna, he doesn't even have a life to speak of—this might just start him off on one. You know, giving as much as you get. More. Really, I think this might just be the making of Bertrand France.''

In the silence that drops its stone between them, Halyna rises from the big chintz chair, goes over to the mantelpiece and picks up her oboe. She fingers the case for a moment and then turns back to Claire. "When I first met you, you said you were a selfish person. Then why are you going out of your way like this? Just why do you want to help me at all?"

Claire gets up from her chair and goes to Halyna, standing so close to her that her words seem like little hammers on Halyna's ears.

"Because it's all I can do—'those who can't, teach.' Remember? And because I want to. Does it really matter? What if I told you that when I was a little girl my mother made me promise that I'd do all the things she never did—get back to England, study, perform, have a brilliant career. All the things I'd sworn I would never do—I was going to stay with my father, take care of him; we were going to live together forever. And in the end I broke all my promises. So you can make up for that; you can do what I couldn't—you can do it for me. As for Bertrand, well—. Ever since I met him, I promised myself that I'd do what I could to—shake him up a bit. Admit it, he's all bound up in himself, like a clumsy parcel with a big blue bow. Why shouldn't we help him get out before he completely dries up inside, turns to a fine green dust, like Christmas pudding that's been left to age too long? There—that's reason enough. Beside, Halyna—you don't have to listen to a word I say—you're free to walk out that door and confess your little heart out to Père Gilbert. Do as you please—I've simply made a suggestion. I'm really very tired; I think you ought to go."

Halyna holds her oboe tightly in her two hands. The pupils of her eyes are huge, as if the coffee she's drunk has been poured into them. Claire sees herself reflected in them: an infinitesimal ghost of herself, locked in Halyna's eyes. And then the image drowns, because Halyna is bending forward, kissing her formally on both sides of her face, as if she were already in France.

"Good night, then. I'll come back tomorrow afternoon—we can start rehearsing the Franck sonata—and talk some more about—how to get places. All right?"

Before she can get to the door, Claire calls out to her.

"Halyna—be careful. If you really want Bertrand—for more than fifteen minutes in the dunes, that is, then just do everything your mother's ever told you. For now. *A la guerre comme à la guerre.* You know?"

"Oh, I know." Halyna slips outside as swiftly, lightly as if she were a scrap of paper blown by the wind.

SATURDAY; LATE-AFTERNOON, the hottest day on record in Spruce Harbour since 1924, or so the A.M. radios proclaim. Halyna threads her way through the dying spruce trees on the college's front lawn and enters the asphalt sea of the church parking lot where she comes upon Bertrand, staring up at the statue of the Virgin. Hands jammed in his pockets, tapping his toe—not in the best of moods. She begins to creep up behind him, slowly, slowly, till she's close enough to clap her hands round his eyes and cry, "Guess who?" as if they were children playing games at recess. She keeps her hands over his glasses till finally he has to reach behind him, grab her arms and tug them down to free himself.

"Really, Halyna—what if someone sees you?"

But she just blows him a kiss and whispers, "Don't forget Claire and I need you for an audience tonight. *A bientôt.*"

He watches her fly along the path, skim over stones and roots exposed by this stupid, static sun. Imagining the cotton blouse sticking against her skin, her skirt clumping about her legs. Hot, unbearably hot all this week—the college grounds filled with students in short shorts, bathing suits. The priests have shut themselves up in the cool fastness of the church and let the Québécois instructors handle the sight of all that flesh soaking up God's light. But among the browned and baking bodies Halyna's is never to be found—all that week he'd searched in vain for her upon the blankets and folding chairs. Before and after classes she's been incommunicado—shut up in the library, in confession with Père Gilbert or praying in St. Alphonse church, a scarf over her head, watching candles drip into nothingness on their tiered brass trays.

But most often, too often, she's been at Claire's, rehearsing for the farewell concert. Not only afternoons but evenings as well, and he, Bertrand, suddenly cast out, denied access to the house he'd come to think of almost as his own, a haven on this fogbound, truck-torn, spruce-struck coast.

Halyna stops at Wagner's store on her way to Claire's and buys herself something cold to drink. She ignores the other immersion students practising their colloquial French on the patient Acadians behind the counter. The man lined up in front of her does the same. He's got a can of pipe tobacco and a package of ball point pens in his hands. He's not a fisherman, though he looks like he belongs here. No baseball cap, thank God. He's bearded, dark-haired—attractive, wearing a tracksuit that's been washed and worn so many times it looks as though the air might puncture it. Not much taller than she, a good four inches shorter than Bertrand, but so much more at ease in his body that he makes Bertrand seem a gangly adolescent, in comparison. She can't make out what the man behind the counter says to him—they seem to know each other well. She wishes they'd say each other's names, just so she'd know who he was, this Adonis in Adidas. As she pays for her drink she watches him go out the door—he turns on the steps to talk to someone coming in and she realizes then where she's seen him before. On campus—he works at the college—Bertrand knows him.

She hurries, after she's paid for the drink—down the steps, over the gravel driveway into the ditch. Too hot to run, but she's late, Claire will be waiting for her. He's directly ahead of her now, hears her steps beside him, stops to make room for her to pass him. He nods hello. She should nod back and walk on, but instead she stops.

"Bonjour."

Smiling at her—he reminds her a little of men in Renaissance paintings—the clipped beard, the narrow eyes. He should have gold earrings, a knife at his belt. They start to walk again, and to talk, easily, casually.

"Can't get much hotter than this."

"No, I suppose not."

"You're one of the immersion students, aren't you? I've seen you around the campus."

"Do you work there?"

"Yes. Are you enjoying the session?"

"No." She should have said yes, or simply smiled. She shouldn't have used that tone of voice, declarative, definitive—demanding a response.

"It's that bad? Your French sounds pretty good, though."

"It's not my French I was talking about."

"No?" Imperceptibly, they slow their pace—the pathway to the beach is only a few hundreds yards away. "Maybe it's the weather?"

She frowns at him for a moment; she can't bear the thought of anyone making fun of her. The path narrows here. Their shoulders touch as they walk along: they catch the scent of dust and heat on each other's skin. Hector switches to English, for which she feels absurdly grateful. "They work you too hard, is that it?"

"I don't mind lessons—that's all right, it's—I hate living in residence—too many people—it gets on your nerves."

"I suppose."

They stop at the turnoff to the beach—he has a towel rolled up under his arm; she's swinging her oboe case. Claire will wonder what's keeping her. She should say goodbye and walk on. Opens her mouth to do so, but it comes out differently.

"Do you live around here?"

"Half and half. I've a little shack at the back of the Kwikway store—and I'm building myself a place out in the woods."

Silence, except for the faraway buzz of a three-wheeler blasting up and down the beach. Finally he adjusts the towel under his arm, and turns towards the path. "It's a great day for sunbathing. Why don't you come along—take the afternoon off."

"I've got to—yes, I'd like to. But—I can't, I've got an appointment." She holds up the oboe case. "I'm rehearsing for a concert—at the end of the session. Will you—will you be there all afternoon?"

He smiles again. "Depends on the weather. Anyway, maybe

another time. Have a good practice." Makes his way down the lane, waving as she calls out.

"Yes—I will. Maybe—another time. *Au revoir.*"

She can hear the piano as she runs up to the front door. It's going to be much, much better than she'd believed possible, this performance they've planned. Claire nods as Halyna puts her oboe down on the dining table and runs upstairs to the bathroom. Recklessly, she splashes cold water over her arms and face and neck, feeling it dribble down her back, soaking the bleached-out cotton, turning it almost transparent. Too hot to do anything more than sit somewhere cool, without a stitch on, fanning yourself and sucking ice cubes. She opens the bathroom window, pokes her head out and looks across to the beach below. The merest breeze picks at the waves sliding into shore—she can see all of Spruce Harbour on the sand: children jumping in and out of stinging salt water, mothers patrolling for jelly fish or rubbing oil on their husbands' backs, teenagers with ghetto blasters staking out the dunes, or blurting their three-wheelers over the sand. She cranes her head so she can get a better view of the beach—thinks she can see him lying stretched out on his back on a red blanket, alone. She could have said yes; she could have gone with him (what would she have done with her oboe?). She could have spent the whole afternoon at the beach, lying beside him on the blanket (she didn't bring a bathing suit); she could have gone off with him behind the dunes, the way all the other couples did (what would she tell Bertrand, or Claire?).

"Halyna? Are you coming down—we haven't got much time, you know."

For two hours they practise, going through the last movement of the sonata, phrase by phrase. Claire insists that it isn't good enough, that it has to be as near perfect as they can get it. She refuses to let Halyna treat the whole thing as a sub-dress rehearsal. The concert is only two weeks away, and Claire is determined to make it pay off. Père Gilbert has been confronted by a very different Mademoiselle Saulnier from the one he knew. She had come to his office with a palpable degree of meekness in her demeanour, wearing, miracle of miracles, a skirt instead of those detestable trousers. She'd asked his permission for Mademoiselle Radowska to spend even more time at her house this week—afternoons and evenings—rehearsing for the concert. In French, of course—it would be an excellent opportunity for Halyna to add to her vocabulary those musical terms she'd need were she to study or perform in Québec, for example. Yes, they could have practised in the old chapel—except that the immersion students had booked it for aerobics—and as for the gymnasium, it was full of volley- and basketball players. Père Gilbert had taken Claire's point and, recalling Halyna's innocent confessions (one of which had focussed on her poverty of spirit in not feeling more than the merest politeness toward this woman who had so generously allowed her the use of her house), had ended by acceding to Claire's request. It was, after all, better to have Halyna in a spinster's keeping than to let her loose for that pack of wolves to devour. He was not unaware of how the male students, even some of the teachers—particularly that co-opérant whom Père Philippe thought such a feather in the college cap—lusted after her, if only in their looks. Mere lust, the intolerable itch in the groin; they would have used that poor child to scratch themselves with, if he hadn't been there to stop them. Well, he would use whichever of God's instrument was to hand—even the piano of Claire Saulnier.

At quarter to seven Bertrand sets out, bow tie squarely in place, his freshly pressed shirt and trousers a rebuke to the sloppiness the heat wave's engendered; his spectacles looking, at last, as though he's lifted a handkerchief to them. The ill temper Halyna had noticed in him that afternoon hasn't been helped by the interview he's had with Père Gilbert, for whom he'd been waiting by Our Lady of the Lightbulbs, when Halyna had played her guessing game with him. Tantalizing, the feel of those rounded, warm, bare arms about him; unbearable, the thought that Père Gilbert might even then be peering out his office window, spying on them, putting his nasty two and two together, when all along Bertrand hasn't the slightest intention of doing more than admire Miss Radowska's musicianship. As if he'd fall to that—taking up with a student, sneaking out to the sand dunes as if he were just another campus lout. As if he didn't possess scruples, principles, pride, quite distinct from those embedded by his childhood faith.

As it was, he'd had to listen to half an hour's worth of priestly admonition and upbraiding; damn the Eudist Fathers for seeking out this Siberia in their flight from Godless France—Sacré Coeur must be the last bastion of Complete Catholicism—Bertrand had heard they weren't allowed to teach Voltaire. He'd have to ask Hector about that—except that Hector was never to be found in his office, even though his holidays were over. And that he'd been less than civil to him those last times they had met—hadn't offered even a word of congratulation on the last photograph of Mariette.

Frogs cheeping in all the ponds and marshes along the ditch, though not so vigorously as they'd done those first few weeks of spring. All the stars are out—the single redeeming feature of life in this wilderness: were he not so intent on preserving the immaculacy of his trousers, he would have looked up as he walked along, risking the chance of tripping over rocks and roots. He contents himself with stopping at the gravel path to Claire's front door; looking to see if anyone's watching, and then throwing back his head to gaze up at the stars. All the constellations are visible, steaming, sizzling light as if they, too, feel the heat that has bombarded the coast this week, parching the fields, withering the wildflowers along the ditch. Only the wild roses are able to resist—there's a clump of them here, by the split rail fence. He has a charming inspiration—he will pick a bunch of them, white and pink, to offer the two women inside. But his fingers meet a multitude of small and vicious thorns—they make him think of hairs on a weightlifter's arms. The stems are unexpectedly tough—he'll turn his hands to a bloody pulp trying to snap a few twigs off those branches. So he surrenders his idea, consoling himself with the thought that they wouldn't have known how to deal with *gentillesse*. Stealthily—he never knows when one of his students may be watching—he stoops to smell these blossoms, like rosy hands stretched out to give him anything he wants. Their rich, ponderous scent makes his head wheel slowly, heavily, like the constellations over him.

Betrand hurries up the path, knocking three times at the door before he finally pushes it open and stumbles inside. Liquid, scalding laughter—have they seen him trip over the rug? No, they are perfectly ignorant of his presence. Sitting side by side on the bench in front of Claire's Bechstein, hands collapsed on the keys, their heads together, one dark, one fair, just like a Victorian mezzotint. But now Halyna's head is resting on Claire's shoulder, as though she were weak with laughter and has to be supported lest she slide right down to the floor. Immediately his eyes travel to a silver tray on the dining room table, a tray with three glasses and a bottle of cognac. The bottle's full, thank God. For a moment, just a sliver of a moment, he's been imbecile enough to—he's had a hideous vision of Claire getting Halyna drunk and—he didn't know. Shipping her off on one of those Japanese freighters that occasionally pull into the local harbour—opium dens, the spicy brothels of the east. Ridiculous. He was starting to think just like that cretinous Père Gilbert. And yet—they don't get up from the bench where they sit together, even when Claire finally notices him and calls hello. And Halyna—she meets his eyes only to shift closer to Claire, putting her arm around her waist, casually, playfully—looking him up and then down, eyes like hot honey. He feels a tight metallic string being plucked inside him. What if she were to put her arm round him like that? Her arms around him this afternoon, in the parking lot. He marches over to the piano and shakes hands hello, forcing the women to sit up straight, apart.

"Bertrand—so good of you to show up after all." Claire stands up to greet him, looking, for the first time since he's known her—feminine. She's made herself up. It's not just the makeup and the fact that her hair's arranged rather than merely combed, but she's sporting cologne, a pearl necklace, and—a dress. He finds himself staring down at her, as if her legs were a newborn miracle, as if she'd worn trousers all this time to hide the fact that she had wood from hip to heel, instead of—really, a rather fine pair of legs.

"You must be thirsty after your walk—it's blazing out there, isn't it? We've opened all the windows and it's still like a Turkish bath in here. Lucky we knew you were coming—it's kept us decent, we might have stripped down to our knickers just to keep from melting away. Don't blush so, Bertrand, I'm only joking.

Here, have a drink—just once in your life; come now, Bertrand, you have to help us celebrate. I've worked this poor girl to the bone and we've finally managed to go through this bitch of a sonata without any major disasters. I really think we're going to do ourselves proud on the night of the concert. Come join us, Halyna—we'll have a little break and then go through the whole damn thing for Bertrand. Take a chair by the fire—nothing like the sight of a totally empty fireplace to make you feel cold as November.''

Halyna refuses the chintz armchair Bertrand is offering her, saying she prefers to sit on the floor, between them. Claire pours out a huge slosh of cognac for Bertrand, who is too distracted by this sudden revelation of Halyna to refuse the glass. Amber cognac, the exact colour of her eyes. He moves the glass gently in his hand, sending the liquid into a steady whirl—just like his senses. For if Claire were looking as attractive tonight as any woman one might meet in the right kind of café in his native city, then Halyna is—miraculous. Somehow that faded skirt and prim white blouse, open at the throat, suits her better than any splashy silks. She's done her hair differently too; pinned up from her face, but cascading down her back, deliciously tangled, so that his fingers ache to stroke it smooth. She looks—so Slavic, like a character out of a Turgenev novel; her cheek bones make him positively dizzy. To steady himself he takes a great gulp of the cognac—don't they give it to shock victims to bring them round? But it makes everything worse—or better; the room seems to glow as if there really is a fire lit, and it's a Dickensian Christmas eve, with all manner of frogs—no, crickets chirping on the hearth.

''I hadn't known it was going to be so difficult,'' Claire was saying. ''Of course it's an outrage to play that sonata on anything other than the violin for which it was written. But why not be outrageous for once in one's life?'' And she launches into something terribly technical about transposition—he can't follow, though Halyna's nodding her beautiful head at Claire, and occasionally contradicting her. He takes another sip of the cognac and ends by downing almost the half of it. This time it doesn't burn his throat but slips down like a lovely warm mist, almost purring as it goes.

"—though they never let any of us do that at the Conservatory—it's probably changed by now. Britten used to say—"

Claire is on about her years in London and Halyna's drinking it all up, the names and places Claire's dropping—rather vulgarly as anyone less naïve than Halyna would see at once. Bertrand notices that Claire has poured herself some more cognac—how flushed she looks, her face like a sheet of white paper held up before a flame. Smiling at him—mockingly?—at the glass, half-full in his hands. He'll show her—he takes another gulp and swallows it whole. She goes on talking, casually leaning across to him and refilling his glass. He means to refuse—but it looks so lovely, the colour, lambent in this swirling globe of a glass. He feels his shoulders give way and he's suddenly reclining, no, lolling in the overstuffed chintz armchair, resenting the vivacity of Claire's voice, holding the glass up to his lips—drinking in the fumes and then just drinking. Halyna is the only one who hasn't taken anything, not even water. There she sits on the floor, cross-legged, like a child at nursery school, looking up at Claire as if she were the sun and moon and every star.

He mops at his face with the linen handkerchief he always carries—confoundedly hot in here. Claire ought to bring in a fan, you could faint from heat like this. Tropical—there are damp patches on Halyna's blouse, under the arms, and—. He buries his nose in his brandy snifter, buries his blush, furious, fire-engine red; those are her nipples showing through the thin cotton of her blouse. She has nothing on underneath. He waits for a long moment then, stealthily, looks again. Halyna's eyes still fixed on Claire's face, unaware that he's anywhere in this room, this house. Cannot keep from staring at her, his eyes like animals grazing on a world of sweetgrass. Nipples. What an ugly word, utterly lacking in poetic association. *Tétine*—that wasn't any better—what did the Germans call them? The Italians? Why did one never learn that sort of thing when studying a foreign language? Not nipples but—roses, like the flat, duskily pink ones he'd tried to pick by Claire's door: four petals stretched wide from a golden centre.

Aureoles—that was better. Like rose petals, a whole meadow of roses—he has a foolish, yearning desire to throw himself on his knees; press his head between her breasts, only to drink in the scent of roses, roseflesh. Another long pull of cognac—the glass is empty; he leans over and puts it on the tray and Claire refills it immediately, as if she's been monitoring him all this time. Refills his glass and then gives it to Halyna to give back to him. He knows that his hands are trembling violently as he bends to take the glass from hers. She's leaning towards him, a waterfall, a cataract of roseflesh as his hands stretch out to take the glass, one inch more and he could be caressing her. But gently she pulls herself back, lifting her hands to her hair, coiling its pale fire round and round at the nape of her neck, adorable neck. *O saisons, O châteaux.* . . .

"Halyna, be an angel and fetch some chocolate from that cabinet over there—Bertrand looks a little peckish."

He watches Halyna get up—not quickly, airily, but languorous, as if she were underwater, weighted down by her own round, rich flesh. And he thinks suddenly of Chagall's paintings of his wife, of her floating towards windows against brilliantly blue air, her breasts white doves. Voluptuous—he repeats the words over and over to himself, feasting on the hypnotic combination of the vowels, as Halyna comes back, kneels down before him, unwraps the chocolate from its thin silver foil and lays a slab of it like a witch's wafer on his tongue. Smiling all the time, the smile of a child, a lamb, a dove. Père Gilbert had been quite right to go on and on to him about her purity, her modesty, her chasteness . . .(if she had nothing on under her blouse, what, then, about her skirt? *oh dark declivities*) her God-given innocence, but the trouble was that these qualities do not tame, but rather inflame, so that—

So that he is suddenly aware of two things—that his glass is inexplicably empty again. And that he is pinned to his chair by an erection so magnificently painful it makes him catch his breath. Immediately he puts his glass down between his legs, cupping it with his hands to try and hide, as best he can, the irremediable state of his groin. Claire, thank God, has left the room—she's gone off to put a record on the stereo: Janet Baker—*Ariae*

Amorosae—the one she'd played for him some weeks, years, millenia ago. But she is here, now, looking down at him, head tilted, the lines of her lips evil as in a Beardsley drawing. She knows, she knows the exquisite humiliation his own flesh is inflicting on him. If he could only get out, away, into the soothing, cooling blackness of the night. But no, he is fixed here, bayonetted by his own lust, helpless as he watches Claire settling down in her chair, stretching out her leg, bare leg, so that it touches the small of Halyna's back. And the girl, who looks suddenly sleepy, eyelids drooping, leans back against Claire's knees, as Baker sings, throaty, tremulous, declivitous. Claire is stroking Halyna's hair, lifting it up like sheaves of wheat; letting it fall over the girl's shoulders, hiding her face, sleeping rose face, age of innocence. Claire's fingers butterfly over Halyna's neck and throat, over the golden chain as it hangs down between—

Outrage conquers lust, turns him acrobat as he leaps up from his chair, knocking the empty snifter to the floor. Startled, Halyna opens her eyes. Claire is leaning back in her chair as she always does—as she had been? Had he really seen what he thought—or was it the cognac, the heat of the room, the toll of the day, long day that has somersaulted into night, this night. "Halyna!" His voice as well as his hand pulling her up to her feet, away. And then, in a voice even he can tell is ridiculously slurred, "I think it's time I took Miss Radowska home."

Claire smiles, inclines her head and walks to the mantel where Halyna's oboe lies in its plum-velvet shelter, as if it's never been played. She tucks the case under the girl's arm. "Yes, you do that, Bertrand. She's exhausted, poor thing—I've been working her like a devil. You can always hear the Franck another night. Go on—good bye. Watch out for the transport trucks."

Night warm, black, glistening as fur. They walk in silence, Bertrand holding Halyna's arm paternally, protectively—he feels completely revived, is about to make some sort of casual remark to banish the hothouse images this evening's bred, when Halyna looks him straight in the eyes and begins to laugh. Not nervously— uproariously. He drops her arm and steams ahead, so that she has to run to catch up with him. When she reaches his side he relaxes his pace, meaning to say something honed and devastating as a scimitar. But he explodes instead.

"She's nothing but a dried-up, drunken, disgusting old witch. Of course you wouldn't have noticed how she was hitting the cognac, how she was—. What a perfect product of Spruce Harbour, a *fine fleur*—carnivorous, just like those hairy plants that grow in all the bogs around this excuse for a landscape, this—"

Halyna lets him speak his piece, until he falls petulantly silent. As they reach the church parking lot, they can hear the Virgin's halo crackling through the emptiness of the air, over the tips of the spruce and hawthorn clotting the lawn between church and college. It makes Bertrand remember the electric clock on the wall of what used to be his refuge; remember the calendar with crosses stabbed through the days of each month. "Only two more weeks and I'll be on the plane, bound for Texas, and then Paris, and free, home-free," he thinks. Entering the spruce grove, Halyna presses up against him—she's shivering; he should offer her his jacket. Two more weeks—he can do without Halyna, without Claire, without anything but the thought of Antoinette, waiting for him at Charles de Gaulle, driving with him down to see the old Comtesse. *O saisons, O châteaux.*

The spruce are ancient, diseased, tufted with Old Man's Beard. Dead branches sticking out like spikes—he's seen it before in a film, *The Seventh Seal*—the girl burned as a witch in the forest? He can't remember; it's been so long since he was within fifty miles of a cinema, he's forgotten so much. Moon swimming in and out of shallow clouds: confusion, conflation of branches, moss, moons—a thin white mist thrown up by the heat. Shallow roots disturb the powdery soil, like a dowager's cheek bones through inches of rouge. Not a dowager but a man, a strange man, he's coming for them, he has a knife in his hands. Halyna starts to shriek and Bertrand claps his hands over her mouth, lest the intruder be none other than Père Gilbert making his rounds.

No stranger, no priest, just the statue of St. Alphonse, holding his crucifix like a dagger before his great, vacant, upward-rolling eyes. Halyna falls back against Bertrand in her relief. Bertrand lets his hands fall from her mouth, to her hips. And is pulling her towards him; she is pulling him to her; they are both enclosed in mist, in a cognac-laden cloud, staggering back against the marble statue of St. Alphonse. They kiss, tongues pushing and shoving like quarrelling children, then slow, soft, as his hands leave her hips and move up, pulling out the blouse from her skirt, reaching up under the white blouse, gleaming like another, unfocussed moon, because she has taken his glasses off, and he doesn't care. Even if she should throw them to the ground and trample them he doesn't care, for she is unbuttoning her blouse and he can see his fingers on her breasts, holding them like warm white doves that will beat wings and fly out of his hands if he does not hold them down. Doves brooding, shaking wings round his face, sheltering him; covering eyes, ears, mouth as the moon dives up from under the sea, raining gold and silver, over them, over and over.

FINALLY THE DOOR SLAMS. Halyna waves to him from the back porch. Bertrand jumps up from the dune on which he's been perching, brushes the sand from his trousers, adjusts his spectacles—the extra pair he'd brought with him to the New World, just in case—and makes his way cautiously through scrub alders to the clearing between house and beach. At last they meet, kiss briefly, their lips mis-matching so that the kiss takes on all the charged frustration Bertrand has felt this past half hour, waiting for Claire and Halyna to finish their rehearsal. He takes her hand for the short walk home—short enough, but they'll be drastically late if they stop for even a few moments. Moments in which they might take shelter under tall clumps of Japanese knotwood, as they'd done ever since that night at Claire's; moments they've been able to snatch from classes, meals, his marking of papers and making of summer travel arrangements, her practice sessions with Claire and closetings with Père Gilbert. Moments as tenuous as the hollows they make in the uncut grass as they lie down together, kiss and—forebear. She'd let him bury his face in her breasts, but as soon as his fingers stray under her skirt she'd push him back, locking her legs and staring up at him, her eyes like

mortars fired at close range, his groin some great, unlaunchable
bazooka.

She was afraid, she said. Her parents—they would die of shame
if anything should happen to her—that way. Die of shame. But
didn't she, wasn't every girl her age on the pill? She'd shaken
her head, burying her face in his shoulder; she'd been raised a
Catholic, a Polish Catholic—there was no help for it. Of course.
So how could he do anything short of marrying her, as if they
were minor characters in some Victorian novel? He couldn't
exactly swagger into Wagner's store, slapping a package of condoms and a ten dollar bill on the counter, as Hector undoubtedly
did. Everyone in Spruce Harbour would know who, with whom,
and how many times. Was he supposed to ask Claire to pick him
up a supply when she drove into Falmouth, as she seemed to do
most days now? He couldn't force himself on Halyna any more
than he could marry her—the whole affair was impossible, out-
rageously, unjustly impossible.

Halyna hums part of the sonata as she walks. Her hand in his
seems amazingly strong, for all its roundness, softness. It comes
from playing an instrument, he reflects—thinking now of her lips
and the way they play him when they kiss. Thinking of her lips,
her breasts, having just to think of them, not to have them under
his hands, even though she's here, walking with him. All the time
they've wasted—she's wasted, working on that damnable sonata
with Claire. Going overboard, the both of them, as if they were
about to début in Carnegie Hall and not the chapel of Collège
Sacré Coeur. He digs his fingers into Halyna's palm, hard enough
to make her give a sharp little shout of surprise and try to pull
her hand away. But he holds on to it, firmly, masterfully, desperately. He wants her enough to lie, steal, cheat, kill. What if he
were to wrestle her to the ground, right now? She would wrestle
back, and probably win. They are nearly at the end of the path—
he will have to let go in a moment, whether he likes it or not. Let
go—in a few days' time, simply let go, fly off, never see her
again. Never having had her.

They drop hands just before they leave the clearing. Halyna
goes first, Bertrand some five minutes later. He scowls and kicks

at the stones in the ditch as he walks, quickening his steps as he
goes past Wagner's store where the children lie in wait for him,
their bicycles making small circles in the gravel. Round and round
they wheel, chanting: *Shame, shame, double shame. Now we
know your girlfriend's name.* He flushes his usual boiled-lobster
hue, keeping his fists in his pockets, but it's no use—the children's
words are hornets buzzing in the locked room of his skull, long
after he's entered the cafeteria and devoured his floury chowder
at the table farthest from Halyna's. Long after he's armed himself
in his residence room in his purple silk pyjamas, with the Rilke
Halyna gave back to him this morning.

"Sex is difficult, yes." Bravo, Rainer Maria!

> Bodily delight is a sensory experience, not any different from
> pure looking or the pure feeling with which a beautiful fruit
> fills the tongue; it is a great, an infinite learning that is given
> to us, a knowledge of the world, the fullness and splendour of
> all knowledge . . . .

Fullness. Splendour. If he could have only one night with her,
not writhing under a clump of knotweed but in a bed, her body
free of clothes—free like that first night he'd kissed her. He closes
his eyes and pictures again Chagall's women: the Beloved in the
paintings for the Song of Songs, airily voluptuous, floating like
a richly fleshed and scented cloud through enchanted air. He
thinks of himself, weighted, leaden—as much by the tidy package
of his future—Antoinette and the *château*—as by the torment in
his loins, sperm kicking, curvetting like wild horses, penis some
great mystic finger pointing upward to the heaven of his unreachable bliss. Firmly, he grasps his Rilke:

> And in fact the artist's experience lies so unbelievably close to
> the sexual, to its pain and its pleasure, that the two phenomena
> are really just different forms of one and the same longing and
> bliss . . . .

What if he were to seize her, steal her away from the octopus embrace of her father and mother, from the unctuous care of Père Gilbert? To leap up into that blue air where she floats so far above him; to seize her and fly to anywhere that was not Spruce Harbour, or Paris. What if he were to ask her to come on holiday with him—this little trip he was planning to the southern states and to Texas, to see the Gernsheim Collection? But then, when he made the connecting flight to Paris—what would he do with her—what would her father do with him—for she'd told him enough to make it clear that her father was Polish in temperament, passionately Polish. . . . Her father, black-suited, his lips set like granite slabs as he chases the seducer of his only daughter over highways and through alleyways all the way to Dallas. Besides, Texas isn't the proper setting for Halyna. He pictures her instead against a back-drop of turrets and roof tiles the dreamlike, blue-grey colour of ancient slate. Agnès Sorel—that portrait at Chinon, Agnès Sorel, the King's mistress, painted as the Virgin, in a scarlet dress, the bodice slit open and one alarmingly circular breast presented to the Child's astonished mouth . . . She belongs among the *châteaux* of the Loire, that was where they should consummate this affair. In a small hotel somewhere, an old-fashioned hotel with wrought-iron balconies on which she'd stand in her peignoir, stretching out her arms to ease the stiffness of sleep while he comes up behind her, puts his arms around her, holds her as they look out over the river, rooftops and towers half-obscured by chestnut leaves and mist.

Tears prickle his eyes as he shuts his book, removes his spec-tacles and lies back on his pillow: institutionally lumpy—he longs for the down-filled pillows of Commereau. His eyes pop open; that brute next door is playing his ghetto blaster again, not to disguise but to accentuate the heaves and groans and unabashed shouts of pleasure radiating from the ridiculously short, narrow bed. He could get up, throw on his dressing gown and slippers, bang at the door—even use the skeleton key, but what would be the use? They'd simply laugh at him—the girl would no doubt stick out a tongue red and slippery as a lollypop and invite him in. If only Père Gilbert had let him keep his own room in his own house, instead of insisting that he live here with the students, teaching them a more colloquial French in his out-of-classroom hours. The groaning stops—the ghetto blaster bleats alone—they've probably finished and fallen asleep. Thank God. He folds his arms behind his head, lies back, shuts his eyes again and tries to knit up the loose threads. Where had he been? Commereau, Commereau, the Comtesse—Antoinette.

Antoinette: his eyes pop open. How many times has he written to her since his arrival here? Half a dozen? Letters that were the equivalent of a *nuit blanche:* dreamless, tedious—almost impossible to bring to an end. Because after the "My dear Antoinette" what else was there to say except, "fondest love, Bertrand." It could have been the chance of a lifetime to write letters filled with passionate longing, mere sexual desire sublimated into image clusters, thickets of metaphor, radiant, stellar prose—if only he'd had an Héloise for his Abelard, an Héloise instead of a weight-lifting, tennis-playing, rabbity redhead with an expensive sports-watch on her wrist. Who would expect a formal declaration of marriage from him the moment he stepped off the plane and into her much too masterful arms.

Arms he'd been locked in, that first visit to Commereau. Her parents watching a *roman feuilleton* on television, an entire wing away. The Comtesse dreaming of artists scattered like birds over the lawns of the *château*, pecking after the crumbs she scattered. Antoinette had suggested they have what she called a preliminary screw; it might have been a set of tennis, for all the casualness with which she proposed it. To salvage some remnant of romance, he'd insisted they seek out the ruined part of the *château*. Moonlight scalding his buttocks, bats fumbling about his ears as he'd finally engineered himself into her taut body. Afterwards she'd complained about how cold the stone floor had been, even with his sweater spread under her: how cold and hard. She'd brought a package of tissues with her; her remembers her methodically wiping her thighs, as if she'd tidied herself this way hundreds of times before. Whereas with Halyna that night under the spruce trees—

"Intellectual passion drives out sensuality." All very well for da Vinci—*he* had intellectual passion to spare. And *he* hadn't felt

Halyna's hands over his eyes, breasts at his lips—white like milk foaming in the pan, like hawthorn blossom, *jeune fille en fleur.* It wasn't as if she were throwing herself at him, snaring and scheming, like some Slavic Lola-Lola. Yet whenever they parted after those desperately innocent fumbles in the dunes, he felt as if a sledgehammer had hit him in the loins, as devastated, as loose about the knees as if he'd done a walkabout of a harem . . . .

Shame, shame, double shame. He disdained to ease the lust that had jumped up to attention in him once again—to pump away his longing for that knowledge and splendour Halyna promised him. What if he asked her to come away with him—to the Loire—just for a little tour, a fortnight—even a week? Surely she could think up a convincing excuse for a week's absence? He'd forgo the trip to Texas (he'd never been too keen on the idea of a Greyhound bus) and buy a one way ticket to Paris for himself and a round trip for Halyna—he could draw on the inheritance money from his grandmother. One could live for practically nothing if one stayed at the smaller hotels, the lesser-starred ones—he wouldn't want them to run into anyone he knew. An exquisite interlude— for both of them. He'd be in a position to take proper care—she need have no worry on that score. They could travel third class on the trains—she wouldn't mind, trains were inherently romantic no matter what the price of one's tickets. And she'd never been to France before. He could be a guide, shepherd her into her first sexual experience as he'd shepherd her through the *châteaux* of the Loire. He wasn't like those Neanderthals slobbering round this campus, dragging not only the backs of their hands but their groins as well as they lumped over the ground. She will come with him—how can she help it? She loves him, he knows she does. Hasn't he felt her whole body tremble under his hands when they kiss—isn't she like some wonderful sea anemone, waiting, aching to loosen its fronds, wave them undulantly in slow, soft, balmy seas? He is sure of her, sure—it only remains to tell her in the morning and phone the travel agent in the afternoon . . . .

Bertrand falls asleep while working out exchange rates between French francs and Canadian dollars. He sleeps fitfully and dreams, just before waking, that he's in the old orchard at

Commereau, leaning against a cherry tree as Halyna, perched high above him on a rustic ladder, pits the cherries with her own teeth and then tosses the slashed red fruit, one by one, down to his outstretched tongue.

THE AFTERNOON BEFORE the concert Halyna and Claire are not bruising their fingers on their respective instruments but are sitting upstairs in Claire's room, looking at a dress spread out over the bed. Purple, polyester bridesmaid's dress which Aunt Sabina had passed on to her niece along with other of her daughter's hand-me-downs. Cousin Gail had been a thin, small-breasted, long-waisted girl. The passion-purple which had salvaged some trace of colour in her cousin's cheeks clashes violently with Halyna's golden skin, her amber coloured eyes. Or so Claire decides, picking up the dress and cramming it back into the plastic shopping bag in which Halyna had carried it over.

"You're finished with your exams?" she asks of the girl sitting disconsolately on the edge of the bed.

A shrug—yes.

"Good. We'll go on a shopping expedition—if you don't mind."

"I've no money to spend on clothes. I told you that ages ago, don't you remember?" Halyna as her mother has so often seen her, sullen, obstinate, sitting with her legs spread wide under her skirt. Claire has to keep herself from rapping Halyna's head, telling her to sit properly—like a lady, that's what her mother had told *her* in this same room, years and years ago: *You must have presence, dignity on the concert platform. People are always watching you, you can't afford to make a single mistake.*

"How can I have presence wearing a thing like that?" Halyna pounds a fist into the plumped plastic bag.

"I never said—"

"You said a musician must have presence, dignity—"

"Never mind what I said. Let's go. And don't worry—you won't need much money for this shopping spree."

It's a fifteen minute drive to the best Frenchy's on the shore. Claire's car joins the pick-up trucks, aged sedans, and the few new splashy cars in the parking lot. The women walk through weather- drubbed plywood doors past the ads for Cheap and Easy Taxidermy, Reliable Baby-Sitting, Satellite Dish Decoration, and Kittens Needing Loving Homes. Into the sanctuary: clothes, hats, shoes, gloves, handbags, belts dumped onto enormous wooden tables according to the age and sex of the potential wearer. Children are running up and down between the tables, laughing, throwing tantrums, being slapped and kissed, trying on snowsuits in the nicotine-scented heat. One of them comes careening into Halyna who squeezes even closer to Claire. Through heaps of white and coloured, printed and striped and floral blouses women shove their hands, sifting, burrowing, churning so that the clothes they discard are pushed as if by some textile volcano the edges of the table while the treasures at the very bottom of the pile heave into view. There is an art to this, Halyna decides—there are women here who can tell in seconds whether that silk blouse is hopelessly ripped in the armpits, whether that's indelible ink or just a season's smudges on that cotton shirt. Claire seems to hold her own among the others. Halyna watches her work the tables, moving from shirts to skirts to belts, accumulating half a dozen blouses, four skirts, a long, hideously orange dress with ivory-lace trim, and three flannelette nighties. "For polishing silver," Claire explains, shoving the items into Halyna's arms and going back to sift for more.

Halyna seats herself on a narrow bench against the wall, next to the old men and women who've come to Frenchy's with their daughters, to be outfitted for the hard winter ahead. They speak to one another in a French nothing like the language Halyna's had drilled into her these past five weeks at Sacré Coeur—she can make out hardly a word of it, except for the English terms they scatter into their speech like candy wrappers on a sidewalk—*les* groceries, *le* TV, *la* babysitter. Claire has disappeared behind a mountain of bedspreads and curtains—whatever can she want with them—hasn't she enough already? The doors bang open, shut, open, as more and more people come in to scrounge for clothing.

She tucks the clothes Claire's given her under the bench, then sits up to stretch her legs and finds herself staring across a table of men's shirts straight into his eyes.

"Hello again."

"Hello."

"Shopping for souvenirs?" He speaks in a teasing, familiar voice, as if he knows she likes him, as though they'd spent that afternoon on the beach together, after all.

"I'm not going yet—"

He tightens his grip on the shirt in his hand, stares down at the label. But he can feel her eyes on him still, the warmth and weight of them.

"Halyna—where are the things I gave you—Oh—Hector."

"Hello, Claire. How are things?"

"Which things? Halyna, we'd better get on our way—have you still got those clothes I picked out?"

Halyna stoops down to retrieve them from under the bench. Hector watches her as he speaks to Claire. "Haven't seen too much of Bertrand lately—what's he up to?"

"You mean what am I up to, with him? Don't worry, Hector, everything's going to roll on wheels. Speaking of wheels, Delbert tells me you're on the road a lot, going down to Falmouth—he seems to think I'd be interested in the subject of your health."

"My health?"

"Yes, because of all the trips you're making to the hospital. Don't you think you'd better watch yourself a little? Halyna, you've taken forever—where's that horrible orange thing—look, you've dropped it. Pick it up, for heaven's sake. Now, let's pay for all this and get out of here—I don't want to be up all night putting this costume together."

Halyna, having retrieved the clothes, looks round for Hector, but he's moved on to another table, turning his back to them. She lets her hand fall to the shirt he'd been holding when he spoke to her. Claire puts out her hand and takes it.

"Ralph Lauren. Not quite Hector's style. But it's wonderful, the irony of it—some of Spruce Harbour's poorest families clothe themselves year round in castoffs from the ancestors of people who booted them out of Grand Pré. Really, Halyna—I've seen pig farmers in Bill Blass jackets—cashmere, no less. Fishplant workers in Anne or Calvin Klein—lovely, isn't it? Now, is this everything? Halyna, do pay attention—we need something else, something to pull the whole thing together. Wait, I've got it."

And she pulls Halyna to another table, one full of hats and bags, untufted wigs, souvenir cushions from Niagara Falls. Digs her hand into the pile and draws up a black straw hat—crushed, punched through at the crown, and with a yellow velvet rose like a drowning victim at the brim. "This is it!"

By the time they've slapped down a five dollar bill for their heap of purchases, Hector has disappeared. The women climb back into the car and are rolling down the highway, past the rappie-pie take-out trailer, the U-'n-Me Fishery Company, Thibault's Mink Farm and a hand-painted sign pointing to the turnoff for the Fish and Game. Claire is chattering about what they can do to create a dress from the rubbish they've found—taking the lace from this, the buttons from that, making a sash out of the skirt, clipping the rose from the straw hat—

"You know him?" Halyna asks as they pull up in front of Claire's house.

"Know whom?"

"That fellow you were talking to at Frenchy's."

"Hector? Let's say I used to know him."

"How?"

"Oh, he used to be a student of mine. Gone to the dogs—or the drains. Fixes them—at the college. You must have seen him around. He's the janitor there."

"The janitor. He doesn't look—"

"The only janitor in Nova Scotia with a Master's Degree in philosophy." Her eyes like flints, chipped to a cutting edge. "Now, are we going to chat away about Hector, or are you going to help me with your costume? As I was saying, we could do something with that rose—do hurry, we've still got to squeeze in some practice time."

They go through the last movement of the Franck sonata while the clothes go through the washer and dryer. There is no more talk of Hector while Halyna washes up the supper dishes and Claire steams the dark yellow rose over the tea kettle. They'll have to hurry—Halyna has been given permission to spend the whole afternoon and evening at Claire's preparing for tomorrow night's concert. Claire has arranged for the local papers to cover it—excellent publicity for the college, Père Gilbert agreed. But it's seven-thirty already, and Halyna will have to be back at the residence before eleven, and this costume will take time.

She stands like a dressmaker's dummy as Claire walks round her, draping her with bits and pieces of the things they'd bought that afternoon: pinning, snipping, trimming. "We'll make you look like—a starlet, a goddess, a princess, whatever it takes to make Bertrand throw himself at your feet and beg for your hand in marriage."

"Just like in a fairy tale," Halyna says, listlessly, holding her arms out so Claire can adjust the sleeves.

"Exactly like a fairy tale," Claire chides. "Don't lose heart now. I know my Bertrand, and you've nearly got him where you want—pinned and wriggling against the wall. Didn't you say he's asked you to go away with him?"

"For a week—a little fling—isn't that what they call those things?"

"It doesn't matter what they're called. He's paying for your ticket, isn't he? That's as good as a proposal. Just keep on with the *jeune fille en fleur* business—you can't be that impatient—"

Halyna steps out of the reach of Claire's scissors and pins. Scraps of material flutter from her shoulders over the bare arms she folds across her chest. "What if I am impatient? What if I've changed my mind and don't want Bertrand anymore, don't want this little scheme you've dreamed up? It's impossible, I've had enough of it. You don't know what it's like, playing Ice Maiden in the dunes, wrestling with Bertrand, pleading wide-eyed innocence till I'm afraid I'll go permanently pop-eyed. It's all been a mistake, Claire. I've been stupid. It's not your fault but I don't want to go through with this anymore—"

"Stand still, don't wriggle so, you'll do yourself to death on these pins. That's better. Now, let me unpin you, and then you can get to work with the scissors—I want all the lace off that dress.''

While Claire sews the white blouse to the skirt of a dismembered wedding dress, Halyna tears off yards of cotton lace—there is no sound but the shriek of slit stitches. When there's enough to make a ruffle round the neck which Claire has decided is scooped too low—"Nothing brazen, no flaunting"—she flings down the scissors and lies back on the bed, watching Claire sew at the little machine in the corner of the room; listening to Claire's projections of her brilliant future.

"Master classes at the *Conservatoire,* to start with, and you can always try to get into a woodwind ensemble, and from there, recording contracts—not *Deutsche Grammophon* of course, and not solo pieces—but with time and the competitions you'll win, who knows? Especially if you go to study with Duclot himself— I gather he takes very few pupils. You'll have to amass some pretty impressive credentials, but you've certainly got the talent, and you've a lot of the technique. Here—it's ready—slip it back on. It's really just a matter of focus and discipline—letting nothing get in the way of your music.''

"You make it sound as easy as blowing your nose." Halyna is struggling into the dress. Claire does up the back, fingertips cold like little pins against Halyna's bare skin.

"Do I?" She fastens the last button of the dress, puts her hands on Halyna's shoulders and turns her round so that the girl's face— flushed, angry, anxious—is directly opposite hers. "Look, Halyna—there are only two ways of getting through your life with any kind of success. You aim yourself straight ahead at what you want and you don't stop moving till you get it. Or else you realize you're open to attack every step of the way, that you're never going to get what you want. So you make up your mind to want what you're going to get. There's nothing in between, except confusion and disaster—for yourself and everyone around you.''

Claire reaches down to the bed and picks up the velvet rose that she's steamed until it's opened out like an entire bouquet. She pins it to the bodice of Halyna's dress, right where the lace cascades, hiding the cleft between Halyna's breasts. "You're one of the ones who will get wherever they want to go. You're nearly there, Halyna. You can't stop now, it's the only way for you to get out—you'll be miserable if you don't." She puts her hands around Halyna's neck; unfastens the gold chain, and gently tugs up the cross. Puts it in Halyna's hand, closing the girl's fingers over it, holding them, for a moment, in her own. "You don't need that. You certainly don't need me. Right now you need Bertrand—and no one but Bertrand. Good God it's late—quick, get changed—I'll drive you back."

"No. I'd rather walk."

"Don't be idiotic. It's pitch black out there—all we need is for you to trip over a root and break your leg."

Halyna straightens her skirt, fastens up her blouse, pulls on her sandals. "I'm going to walk. Good night."

It takes fifteen minutes to get from Claire's house to the residence. Along the ditch, under stars which have absconded, taking with them any pattern or direction, Halyna walks, almost runs. She knows this path by heart, she's travelled it so many times over the last five weeks. Transport trucks barrel past her; the stench of the exhaust seems to clog her eyes and ears as well as her lungs. Finally a light comes into view—the Kwikway sign. She stops in front of the store window, peering at the ghostly lights of the freezers, the foil packets of chips glimmering in the darkness. "In a shack at the back of the Kwikway store," he'd said. She can see her reflection in the window, just the bare outline, can smell the heat and dust on their skins as they walk in the ditch together, brushing shoulders. Why hadn't she gone with him to the beach that day? Why couldn't she be with him now— give in, give up. Her body heavy in the cotton dress, her skin prickling against the cloth, even her hair a weight she can no longer carry.

She creeps past the window, round the store, to the addition at the back. The lights are on—a small yellow square at the very back, moths bumping the glass. She hangs back, unable to decide what to do—go to the window? Knock at the door? If someone should be with him? Bertrand—didn't they play chess together? But Bertrand was chaperone tonight at the discothèque—she'd go to the door. And if he had someone else with him—a woman? He was the kind of man not to be alone on a Friday night—she'd known that about him, right away. As she'd known that day walking to Claire's, that it would be the easiest thing in the world to make love with him. *A quick screw.* She doesn't want to love anyone, to be held under, fastened tight. Claire, fastening the back of her dress, sealing her into that focussed, perfect future: Paris, the *Conservatoire.*

Through the window she can see a bed—empty, unmade. A kitchen table with a book propped up against a beer bottle. The room seems empty—he must be in the bathroom—perhaps in the tub. She wants to laugh out loud—puts her fingers over her mouth—he mustn't hear her. His body shaped so differently from Bertrand's. *Men are like that. Like what? You'll find out.* But her mother would never tell her. Perhaps if she tapped at the window, knocked at the door? Should she just walk in? *Have you no shame?* None—she had pride, instead. She would never, never let any man lord it over her. With Bertrand that would be easy, he wouldn't so much as touch her hair if she didn't want him to. But this man, Hector, the man Claire doesn't like, or likes too much—there was something peculiar in the way she spoke about him today.

Why doesn't he come into the room, look up at the window, see her crouched there in the dark, waiting. For what? Is this what she wants—this man, in the dark, just this one, first time. Something she wants without any calculation, can feel herself wanting, needing now. If it hadn't been for Claire she would have gone with him that afternoon to the beach, or this afternoon, at the store—could have asked him then and there to take her away. Could have taken herself away with him, slammed the door on this hateful little scheme of Claire's, slammed it so hard the whole house would fall down. If she can muster the courage to go into this room, now, turn the handle and walk inside—even to show herself will be enough. Shake the house down, stay an hour or the whole night, go in, go on. . . .

But the handle won't give—the door is locked, and no one comes to answer her knocking. She knocks so hard her knuckles scrape against the wood, until she realizes that the truck is gone and nobody's home—that she will hurt her hand so badly she won't be able to play at the concert. And that it is not tomorrow she will be performing, but tonight.

BERTRAND SHIFTS in his chair. These "comic" recitations the students are giving—rusty nails, shattered glass would be pleasanter in his ears. How can Père Gilbert sit there with that look of bland beatitude on his face? Perhaps it's the effect of the light—day just giving over to dark, spent rays tumbling through the stained glass like aging acrobats, burnishing here a scarlet toe, there the cerulean robe of the saints placed side by side, as if in some kind of celestial identification line. As if the hyperactive use of one of his senses could annul the others, Bertrand focusses intently on the spots of colour—amber, emerald, amethyst—that fall like airy, insubstantial rain on the polished floorboards. But the assault on his ears continues; now it's a guitar and a small chorus of singularly graceless-looking girls thumping through *A la claire fontaine*. Faces beaming to the point of imbecility—voices a full tone flat. Really, he preferred the *boîte de nuit* the night before, for all that it had been so raucous, even vulgar. Once Père Gilbert had left, the skits had become positively indecent and he'd found himself applauding Halyna's wisdom, her inherent good taste in staying away from such a grotesque performance. If he hadn't been obliged to attend he would gratefully have passed his time in Claire's living room, reading Flaubert while they rehearsed the Franck sonata. *Au clair de la lune* now—dragging out all the old warhorses, just for the benefit of the reporter in the front row. One reporter, the rest of the students, and all the locals who could be mustered, including Hector in the seat right behind him. Hector in mufti—no overalls or baseball cap. Trying to impress—whom? It doesn't matter—he and Hector haven't spoken for weeks, but that doesn't matter, either—he will soon be an ocean away from this terrible place and its people.

How many more before Halyna's piece? Could he excuse

himself and go out? For a smoke, except that he never touched tobacco. The toilets were just down the hall—that would give him a mere five minutes' reprieve. If he feigned a coughing fit? But she would be dreadfully offended if he missed her performance. She'd come back so late last night, he'd waited up for her, pretending to watch a late film on the residence TV, but fastening his eyes on the window. All for a glimpse of her; she'd promised to stop by and say good night after her session with Claire. Now that his plan to carry Halyna off has been set in motion he finds himself jealous of her every movement, each glance that does not respond to his own. Even though she'd been away from him all yesterday, all she'd done last night was to gesture vaguely through the glass and run off to her room. He'd felt just like a wakeful goldfish in a bowl, after everyone's turned off the lights and gone to bed. He would have followed after her, but some students had walked in just then—they would have seen him, word would have spread, just when they had to be most careful. The slightest whiff of suspect behaviour and Père Gilbert would be down on him like a cleaver.

Good Christ, no—surely not tap dancing? In the chapel—even if deconsecrated? But yes, here are a whole row of his students in Acadian costume (completely bogus, of course: no seventeenth-century *paysan* would have been able to afford to dress in black-and-white polyester, even if it *had* been invented then). They are tap-tap-tapping his head into incipient migraine. This qualifies as aesthetic atrocity—how can Halyna even appear after this? She shouldn't debase herself by sharing the stage with these sub-amateurs. Besides, Claire had lost her head over the whole thing; it wasn't fair to either of them. The sonata was a demanding piece, not the sort of thing one performed for a lark, and certainly not for an audience of adolescent baboons. Poor Halyna had worked like a slave at it, but for what reward? And that nonsense of staying up till all hours to make a dress—though it would make a charming picture, a perfect Renoir: Girl Sewing. Halyna's golden head bent over some white, filmy material. She was quite like a Renoir—such marvellous skin tone and what a pleasure it was, aesthetically speaking, to see a young woman who wasn't shaped like a coat rack but—like a lazily flowing river, a soft-plumed bird, a perfect piece of fruit ripening on a branch. He shifts his body in the metal chair, bites his lip—has a sudden recollection of Mariette that one time she'd posed for him in the nude—her body rigid, fierce, her eyes—. He hasn't seen her for ages, hasn't even told her the photo was coming out in *Photography Today*. Well, he would send her a copy as a way of saying goodbye. He really ought—

But here at last is the piano being pushed closer to the centre of the room. Claire walks out in a long black dress—good God, she's made up as she was that other night—she looks quite striking. Applause—stilted—this is the last number on the programme, and everyone else is as tired of the whole thing as he. Now—Halyna, in a white dress—wherever had Claire found such a marvellous dress? It suits her perfectly. Someone flicks a switch and the room becomes crystalline with hard, white, electric light that flares into every corner of the chapel.

Halyna stands where the altar used to be, clasping her oboe, waiting for Claire to signal the beginning. Her hair is braided round her head, catching white fire, like the electric halo round the Virgin in the Parking Lot. Except that Halyna is flesh and blood and beautiful. That rose—golden-yellow, colour of the cognac he'd drunk at Claire's that night, that blessed night they'd finally kissed. Passionate and modest rose concealing the shadowy cleft between her breasts and yet signalling its presence more vividly than the most daring décolletage would ever have done. Now, lifting the oboe to her lips, licking the reed—too bad it wasn't the violin, wind-players always look so undignified—and they begin. He closes his eyes, not wanting to see the contortion of Halyna's face as she plays, her cheeks as they puff in and out.

Music slipping down him like the cognac that night at Claire's. Not fire but light—and ice. Softest, most sensuous well-being and yet an exquisite alarm, somewhere—so beautiful, and therefore so sad, that it cannot last, that it cannot always be this. Stop time, stop world, let there be just this music. As if he were still a small boy on that path in the Luxembourg gardens. Delicious darkness, his lids pulled down against the light, surrendering to the oboe's sinuous and swaying tone: round, dark, deep—

Until the music is Halyna, Halyna's round and moonlike flesh. Floating high over him, away from him like Chagall's women floating tangibly out of opened windows, out of his arms. Unless he pulls her back to him, holds her down, fixes himself inside her so that she will not get away, not now, not ever. And without any preparation, like a great bird swooping down by him, startling him so that his heart begins pounding and for a fraction of a moment he does not know where or who he is: the idea, the image of an idea for fixing Halyna forever beside him, under him, his. He will—he will marry her—take her away with him to France, sign the necessary papers and marry her, *fait accompli*. Halyna his wife—little tremors shake his lips—it's impossible, he's out of his senses, he can't give up—and yet the image of Halyna, naked on a bed: his bed, his wife, whenever he wants her—touch of fruit upon his tongue, in his mouth, a feast—

Clapping all around him. He blinks his eyes open, wincing at the shrillness of the light. Halyna bowing, a goddess, a queen inclining her head toward her audience and to Claire, applauding her from the piano. Halyna walking toward Claire, extending her arms to her, raising her up from the bench and both of them bowing as the saints and martyrs in the blackened windows glower over them: his parents' faces, the Comtesse, Antoinette. Hector is clapping, whistling behind him: barbarian. Bertrand looks fiercely at Halyna, willing her to return his stare, to acknowledge him, his possession of her as if she were already his wife. And at last she does raise her head, looks into the audience and—it is to answer him, it could only be for this—she smiles. Steps right into his eyes, her image locked here, inside him. Always, already and only his.

5

Here everything's white, so clean it hurts to look, to smell. At first they let her stay in bed, sheets ironed stiff, tucked in so tight she felt chained between them. People coming with charts, needles, glass pens under her tongue, ball points scribbling notes to take down everything she doesn't say. How can she talk to them when they're not, this is not real, everything so stiff with light, everyone separate and all the same in white coats and dresses, white words they say: "How are you feeling today? Time for your pills. The doctor will be coming round this morning at ten." At first they let her stay in bed, but not anymore; now she must get up, brush her teeth and wash her face, get dressed in clothes that don't belong to her: skirts, blouses, stockings, shoes with little plastic bows on them. Comb her hair in a mirror that shows her a face that isn't hers, no more than the moon's face is hers.

They tell her to go into the TV room; she goes. If you do everything they want, they smile at you: the nurses, the social worker. They like her to smile; they like her to talk, too, but she can't. There's a hole in her throat, slit right across so her neck flips open like the lid on a tin can, held on by a tiny metal thread. Words come up from the pit of her stomach and fall out the hole in her throat; it hurts so much she's stopped trying to close the hole and make the words come out her mouth, the way they used to. When Frère LeBlanc comes to sit with her, he says it doesn't matter—God hears the words we say in our hearts; He listens even to our silences. He gave her a medallion, silver with a cross and a circle of stars on one side, blue glass with Our Lady on the other. And a picture of Jesus sitting in a field of green grass, and children all around Him, like stones on the beach there are so many. Except that Paul isn't there, and so she takes the picture after Frère LeBlanc has gone, takes it and tears it into as many pieces as there are children, and flushes it down the toilet. The medallion of Our Lady she puts into the little drawer beside her bed, the drawer in which she keeps the toothbrush, toothpaste, washcloth and soap they'd given her the day she came here.

After she has sat in the TV room the nurses come up to her and say, wouldn't she like to take a little walk around the ward: wouldn't she like to go down to the children's wing and help the play ladies there? She doesn't know what a play lady is—she knows that Paul isn't with those children; she shakes her head, no. But she goes for a walk, since that makes the nurses smile at her; she goes to the other ward where there's a big window and babies inside glass boxes, babies sleeping or screaming and nurses running in between the boxes, looking after them. She wants to knock on the glass, ask if she can come inside and help look after the babies, but the words are little blades scraping her throat. No one says to her, ''Come on in, come and help us, you look like you know how to take care of babies,'' so she just stands and looks at the glass boxes, and doesn't leave till one of the mothers comes by to collect her child.

When Delima came to see Mariette they sat in the TV room. For a while Delima talked at her, and then at the other people in the room, and then shut up and watched the TV. Mariette doesn't have to cover her eyes or ears to shut Delima out—she can do that without lifting a finger, close herself off so no one can get inside her, anywhere. When Claire comes Mariette closes off her ears and just looks at her; sometimes she thinks it's that other time: she is thirteen, and Claire has driven her to hospital; she is afraid she's going to bleed all over the back seat of Claire's pale blue car, blue as Our Lady on the medallion. Claire doesn't look any different now, except that she's taken a pocketknife and nicked the skin at the edges of her mouth and eyes: long, shallow cuts, so no blood shows. Claire sits with her and doesn't say anything, and each time she comes she stays a shorter and shorter time, until finally she doesn't come at all. Just like the last time, all the other times.

Hector comes instead. If she's in the TV room, he comes up to her and holds out his hand, pulls her up from the sofa and puts her arm through his. They're going for a stroll, he says, taking her along the corridors, up and down the elevator, all across the lobby downstairs. He brings her saltwater kisses from the Kwikway store; she doesn't eat them, but puts them away in her night table drawer, along with her toothbrush and medallion. She would like to tell him, "Thank you," but she can't. He doesn't try to make her talk; he just puts her arm through his and takes her walking, all the way downstairs, where people come in and out, wearing their real clothes, and the light isn't so sharp or white. Once he came in the evening and stayed till late at night; it was the time she couldn't sleep, couldn't swallow the pills they gave her, because the floor under her bed had fallen away, the ceiling caved in, even the stars dropping from the sky like glasses from a kitchen shelf: falling and breaking into pieces so small that everything goes black, outside and in, and she can't tell where her eyes stop and the world begins, where her hand stops and his begins.

Mariette's seen the doctors, shut off her ears and eyes while they talk, talk, talk; she's sat with the social worker, counting the buttons on her blouse till the social worker says, "Would you like to go home—to your family?" No, no, no, the words cutting her open but no sound comes out. She shakes her head, no, and the social worker stops asking things and just writes them down in a notebook, as if she were at school. And then looks up, and just like a teacher, in a teacher's tired voice says, "We'll have to find somewhere for you to go, Mariette—you can't stay at the hospital forever. We'll have to see." While Mariette smiles at her, smiles and thinks how, if they send her back to the trailer she'll just wait till the middle of the night and slip out to the highway. Hitch a ride so far away he'll never be able to catch her, so far away she'll find where they put Paul and steal him away, just like she was one of the mothers coming to get her baby, take her baby out of the glass box and hold him high on her hip. Like

Our Lady carries Her baby, so high even the fire at Her feet won't scorch him, so high even the black inside her won't so much as dirty his shoes.

CLAIRE STOPS at the Post Office on her way home—home from the hospital at Falmouth, where she was invited to meet with doctors and a social worker and Delima (who didn't show up); home from a meeting with Père Gilbert at his office (in which she protested ignorance of Bertrand's gross abuse of trust in running off with Halyna); home from a stop at Wagner's Kwikway store, to buy groceries for supper and dodge questions, comments, insinuations and innuendos on this, the greatest fountain of gossip in Spruce Harbour since Père Delphis Deveau went mad at Mass, fulminating over the presence of condoms on the shelves of Wagner's store until he was quietly led away by Frère LeBlanc. She is careful to arrive at the Post Office long after Delbert has gone to any one of his sixteen female relations for supper. Letting herself in through the huge glass door with her pass key, she empties her post box of several fliers and free offers, a catalogue from an exclusive American mail-order store, a dentist's bill, and a letter from Bertrand. She imagines Delbert's short, fat but sensitive fingers handling the slim bluish envelope and stroking the stamps—the head of Delacroix's *Liberté*; the severe, navy-blue *par avion* sticker—as if to glean secrets from their very surfaces. But there are no secrets at all in this affair. She simply dumps Bertrand's letter into her briefcase, throws the fliers and free offers in the wastepaper basket, and bangs the door of the Post Office shut behind her.

Bertrand's letter remains in her briefcase as Claire eats her supper: poached eggs on toast, black coffee (she must have forgotten the milk in her rush from Wagner's store). She would like to forget Bertrand as well; his letter will only distract her from decisions she must make, excuses she must find to justify her actions to herself, now that she has thought up enough reasons they should satisfy others. Halfway through her meal she gets up from the table and walks out to the hallway. She thinks she must have left the radio on upstairs, she could hear people talking— some sort of interview. But there's nothing amiss in her room; the radio's off, with only the luminous digits flashing. Poison green: how she hates that colour. Perhaps it was children who'd made the noise, sneaking up on the house, trying to break a window. One day she'd set the RCMP on them. Or it could have been a couple having an argument behind the dunes. She waits for a moment, looking out the window for signs of fleeing children, a lovers' quarrel. But all she can see is the sun still high overhead, the water blue-black, like the ink she once used for writing out sums at school. A world simplified to basic elements, everything extraneous cancelled, expunged. Bertrand's letter is buried in the bottom of her briefcase, as is the formal letter of reprimand from Père Gilbert. These things don't matter, are already dead, burned-out like stars that only appear to glow across vast distances. She takes a last admonitory look at the radio before she leaves the room. Things will return to the way they were, everything locked up, silenced and distanced.

By the time Claire has washed up the few dishes and sat down in a chair with a book and a glass of port, she's decided exactly what she will do. Tomorrow morning she will not return to the hospital. She will merely telephone Doctor Salter and tell him that she feels she can be of no further help with his case. She will then phone the Social Services number and speak to Mrs. Cottreau, who had pleaded with her so earnestly this morning. "No," she will say. "No, I can't possibly take Mariette in—even for a few weeks, never mind the length of time it will take her to get completely well. She needs the company of people her own age— lots of them; and I lead a solitary kind of life—it would be worse for her than the hospital ward." She will say this in so firm and final a voice that Mrs. Cottreau will not come back at her with— "But you can't expect her to go back to the trailer—especially now that the little boy's gone." Or, if she does, Claire will answer, "I don't expect her to go back there at all—I expect you to find a better placement for her than I can provide." And hang up the phone.

As for Mariette—how could she help her? How could one person ever help another without botching things up past mending—or without, as in the case of Halyna, securing someone else's ruin at the same time? Claire refuses to look at Bertrand's letter—she cannot cope, at the moment, with anyone else's catastrophe—though perhaps the letter is just a little crow of "look what we've gone and done!" There hasn't really been time for anything to happen yet—and she doesn't want to know when it does. That is their business—they are simply two people who've walked off the edges of her world, and are floating in the thin air of elsewhere.

Yet Mariette's face keeps surfacing on the page of the book Claire's trying to read—the face she saw on her first visit to the hospital: no longer the face of the girl who used to push her mother's children in a battered stroller up and down the fishplant road, but a mask: blotched, pasty, bloated. The effect of the anti-depressants she'd been given: large blue pills with a Dixie Cup of water, four times a day. When Mariette had entered hospital she'd weighed only eighty-six pounds; they'd had to feed her intravenously. Now, with the medication she'd been given, she looked as though she'd put on water, not flesh. Delima says they're not feeding her properly; if they'd let the kid come back home, she says, she'd be good as ever. And there's room at home, now that Paul's been taken off to the Centre, where there are specialists who can take care of him, teach him things Mariette can't. She wouldn't understand, Delima said—wouldn't believe how it was hurting Paul, keeping him at home—doing him harm.

But Delima hadn't shown up for the meeting this morning, leaving Claire as the only "family" member present, though she'd explained to them that she was no relation, that she merely happened to be Delima's occasional employer. Then why had she come to see Mariette so often, they'd asked her—why was she here now? And she hadn't had an answer for them, not then. I am not anyone's keeper, she should have said—and walked straight out. But hadn't. The girl's face, swollen and stained, the hair that been sleek, iridescent as a raven's wing now matted, brittle as dead leaves. Not Claire's fault: Bertrand's. Though as far as she could figure out it wasn't what Bertrand had done, but what he'd refused to do, that had sunk Mariette into this black, black hole. No doubt Delima had filled her daughter's head with ideas about Bertrand marrying her, carrying her off with him to Paris, or else settling down with her in Spruce Harbour in a house painted turquoise and lemon-pie yellow, with butterflies crucified over the door. Delima's fault. Claire closes her eyes to erase the image of Mariette; sees instead the face from the photograph, limitless holes of eyes and mouth. Feels again as she had when Hector first showed her the picture—as if she's going to be sick to her stomach. No, she is merely going to open her eyes, focus on some distant object. She reaches for the briefcase and Bertrand's letter.

Hôtel du Balcon
Sully sur Loire

Dear Claire,

We thought you would prefer a letter to the formal announcement I'll have printed up later. I wonder if you ever guessed what we were up to? I imagine there must have been quite a little—stink, to put it bluntly, given the moral excesses of which Père Gilbert's capable. As if Halyna weren't of age and perfectly entitled to make her own decisions. But it's all water under the bridge—her parents, and mine too, will simply have to come round to the fact of our marriage. I still feel strange, using that word. Everything's happened so fast, I feel just like a character in a nineteenth-century novel, where people do momentous, serious things.

You must be dying to know how we managed everything—it was a close shave, as you can guess. After Halyna slipped away from the reception—by the way, did her picture get into the local paper, as that reporter promised?—and changed her dress, she came back to the chapel and mingled, as I did, with the audience. Did you notice her chatting with Père Gilbert? Quite a nice touch, I thought. She was quite a favourite of his—he'll probably be howling still at the way things worked out. As I was saying, we mingled. Halyna left first, pleading headache—she was sorry she couldn't give you a proper farewell. As you'll remember, I stayed right through to the end, to throw you all off track. I shouldn't think either of us slept much that night—we both had packing to do and, after all, elopement isn't the thing to steady the nerves, is it?

The next morning we greeted each other briefly at breakfast—again, diverting suspicion. And then she boarded the bus with her suitcase and was driven down to the eight o'clock train, while I waited for Jean-François—that insufferable immersion teacher who never stops talking about Québec's new language laws: that man is terminally boring, I warn you. He'd offered to drive me to the airport right before lunch. Anyway, Halyna got off the train at Kentville, where there's a longish stop, to telephone her parents that she'd missed the train and would be taking the bus instead—so that they would be there at the bus depot, and not at the railway station, to meet her. It's not pleasant to think of them waiting around for her, worrying when she didn't show up—but then, all's fair in love. Isn't it? All the way to Halifax I listened to Jean-François talk politics, occasionally dropping remarks about my flight to Dallas. We parted ways at the ticket counter at the airport—what a barbaric place. Luckily I was too excited to be hungry—the only source of food I could see was a frozen yogurt machine, and *that* was out of order.

You can imagine how nervous I was, waiting for Halyna to show up. I'd made sure she'd have enough money for a taxi from the train station to the airport—extortionate fee that it is—but I couldn't help envisaging disaster. I worried that her parents hadn't been there to receive her phone call, and would be waiting for her at the station or that she might, at the last moment, fall prey to her own anxiety and guilt about leaving them and coming with me. You wouldn't know it, but she's unbelievably shy—she's been raised in a very old-fashioned way. I needn't have worried—she did show up, even if it was five minutes before the boarding call. Five hours later we were in Paris. There was a little delay in clearing customs—I had to have words with, and, I'm ashamed to say, grease the palm of a minor customs official. But that doesn't matter; of course I'm not counting pennies in any of this. It's so wonderful, Claire, you must understand.

Naturally, the first thing Halyna did was to phone her parents. They must have been so relieved to hear her voice. I couldn't understand what it was Halyna said. The line was bad and she's written to them since—the morning of our wedding, as a matter of fact. Luckily we found people very understanding of our situation—the paperwork was unbelievably complicated, as it always is. You can imagine our impatience for everything to be over and done with, and for us to be legally married at last. As I've said, Halyna has certain very strict and old-fashioned ideas about certain things—maddening at the time, but now that I've survived it, one of the things I absolutely adore about her.

So here we are, a million kilometres from Spruce Harbour, and a healthy distance from Paris, where there are a number of puzzled people waiting for explanations. I don't mind admitting that at times I feel as though the ground under my feet has turned into—something like honey. Sweet enough, but hardly solid. Of course, I haven't mentioned to Halyna all that I've given up for her so that we can be together like this, always. She, after all, has only left her past—I've lost a future. Not that a future without her would have been worth embracing—I can't begin to tell you what she means to me.

My father has written to us—a short note, but civil—barely. My mother, of course, was rather more unrestrained. And that person of whom I spoke to you—the one with whom I had an understanding—well, she's been quite good about the whole thing. As well she might—she admitted that she'd also found someone else during our separation. I can't say much for her choice—a tennis coach who works part-time as a gardener on her grandmother's estate. But that's hardly to the point. What matters is the way in which things have turned out, that what I thought was going to be the most uneventful year of my life—about as savoury as a boiled egg—has yielded this. The most important thing is that I can see, now, how terrible it would have been— truly catastrophic—to have married the wrong person, and to have lived out my life not knowing what Rilke calls "the fullness and splendour of all knowledge." (By the way, I forgot to leave the *Letters* in your post box at the college—they ended up in my suitcase—I'll mail them back to you as soon as I have time.)

We have a full half of our honeymoon left. The Loire is at its very best for us—halcyon weather. We even spent some time on the beach—there's a charming section of the river behind our hotel, and not a single spruce in sight. It's amusing to play tour guide for Halyna—I want us to take in only the cream of the *châteaux* (the Americans have overrun all the common-garden ones). She's still terribly serious about her music—she insists on putting in a good two or three hours every day, while I read the papers or stroll about. She's even thinking of enrolling in the *Conservatoire* in the autumn—we'll have to think about that. She says it would give her something to do while I'm studying for my exams. I've set my sights on a university post, you see, and one has to jump through a thousand academic hoops to get one here. Not like Sacré Coeur—not at all.

Well then, Claire—it remains only to write what I was in too preoccupied a state to say that day I left Spruce Harbour. I did enjoy our talks together—I think they did you good. If ever you decide to quit that dreary coast and come to Paris for a holiday, we'd be glad to show you around. Take care and, *Courage*!

Amitiés
Bertrand

"And so they'll live happily for—perhaps another week?" Claire folds the letter back in its envelope and goes to the cabinet in which she keeps her cognac and whatever chocolate Bertrand did not devour. She pours herself a drink and makes her address. "No need to say goodbye to you, Bertrand—I did that some time ago. And so, farewell Halyna. One day I'll order one of your records from the catalogue—sit here with the jacket in my hands and stare at your photograph. I'll be able to say that I was once your accompanist. So will Bertrand—"

"I said, I brought your milk—you forgot it at the store." This time it's not the radio, or children playing pranks, but Hector, standing in the hallway, watching her, listening—for how long?

"Since when have you started breaking and entering—or is that one of your sidelines, now?"

"I'm sorry, Claire—I did knock. The door wasn't locked, you know."

"I didn't know. And don't put that thing down on that table—it'll leave a ring."

She controls herself enough to take rather than snatch the carton from Hector's hands. He'll have a fine story to tell the Kwikway gossips—old maid Saulnier talking to herself—worse, talking to her bottles. By the time she returns from the kitchen she half expects him to be gone, as if he really were just a delivery boy who'd accomplished his day's errands. But Hector is standing right where she left him, standing there like some piece of unwanted furniture too heavy to move out of the room. She'll have to let him stay till he's got what he came for—she simply hasn't the energy to boot him out. He takes the chair beside hers, removes his baseball cap, putting it down on the table between them, lights his pipe, and it is suddenly as if he's been here a dozen times in as many days. As if he possesses rights she never granted other visitors. He is looking round for an ashtray—gets up and finds one on the mantelpiece.

"You didn't come here just to deliver milk, Hector. And I don't believe I issued you an invitation. I've had an impossibly long day, and I don't need company for, oh, about another fifteen years, I'd say. Tell me what it is you want, and then go home."

He has Stella's fine, dark features—all of his sisters are big and blond and raw-boned like their father. "Look, Claire, I don't mean to—"

"Of course you do. People always disclaim responsibility when they're about to make some particularly nasty comment or request. I suppose you want to know about Halyna and Bertrand—as it happens, I just received a letter from the happy husband. I'll get it for you."

"No, I'm not here to talk about those two." He's leaning against the mantel, looming over her.

"And I thought you'd be burning with curiosity to know all the details of Bertrand's just deserts. It's delicious, really—he still thinks of Halyna as a cross between a little girl taking her first communion, and a Polish Aphrodite, washed up on Spruce Harbour beach along with the Javex bottles and rubber gloves. He's head over heels in love with her—or at least with his idea of her. But it won't be long before he's—what shall we say?—disabused of his illusions."

"Poor kid."

"I thought you were out for his hide."

"I don't mean him—I was talking about the girl."

"Halyna? Oh, she'll come through all right—she knows just what she wants—and it's not wedded bliss with our *Français de France* . . . ."

"What, then?"

"Why ask me, Hector? Besides, I thought you didn't want to talk about Halyna or Bertrand."

He relights his pipe, watching her turn her glass round and round in her long, white fingers: bloodless, they look. "I was down at the hospital this afternoon. I saw Mariette."

She drinks what's left in the glass. "How very kind of you. I'm sure she was beside herself with excitement—did you bring her flowers?"

"Look, Claire—I know you were there this morning. Annette Cottreau told me—"

"Social workers are the worst gossips of all, I'd forgotten that. And she's your cousin, isn't she?"

"She told me that Mariette could be discharged if someone would take her in—and that they'd asked you."

"Good God, man, what business of yours is it to—"

"I didn't say anything to her. In fact, I'm talking to you, now, because I want you to promise me you won't have anything to do with Mariette. Just wait a minute, let me finish. It's about time you gave up all this tinkering with other people's lives, Claire—it's done no one any good. Look, I'm willing to take full responsibility for screwing up my own life; I'm just starting to put the pieces together again—''

"Bravo!"

"—but Mariette's not in any kind of condition to think for herself—and I don't want you doing her thinking for her. Look, Claire, I don't give half a shit for what you've talked Bertrand into doing, or undoing. He deserves whatever he gets. But Mariette—''

"You talk about her as though you owned her. What gives you the right?"

"She belongs to this place, and I happen to think I belong here too. And if I can help her—''

"She never asked for your help—no one's asked for it. If anyone's meddling with people's lives, it's you, Hector. And if anyone has a right to help Mariette—." Claire stands up, but doesn't face him—she walks across to the piano, the Bechstein her father ordered from England, after the war was over. She strokes the keys gently with her hand: perfect rows of black and white, black and white, black and white—precise, unchangeable order drowning out even the most distant voices. She plays a series of diminished sevenths, then starts speaking—to the keys, so he has to creep forward to hear her.

"Surely you've heard the gossip, Hector. How Delima was keeping house for my father that last year before I came back. Keeping house and warming his bed, too. Not that that proves anything. Delima—being Delima—was warming more than one man's bed. Do you think I didn't know what people were saying when I came back—and when Mariette was born? Do you think I enjoyed the thought that my father probably died screwing Delima—or whoever else was available along the Shore that year? There's an excellent chance that Mariette's no more my sister than she is yours—and she could be, couldn't she, Hector? Delima being Delima, and men in these parts no more faithful to their wives than they should be." She looks up from the piano now, a smile like a crescent moon on her lips. Smiles into his eyes. "If Mariette comes to live with me the whole Shore will nod their heads and cluck their tongues. Do you think I care about that now? You know, it's a big house, Hector. And I seem to have got used to the idea of having company. Not that Mariette's very talkative these days. Actually, I hate noisy people, hearing them talk and shout all the time. So Mariette would be the perfect companion, don't you think? I ought to thank you for coming round to see me tonight—you've saved me from making a mistake—not a grave one, just a minor error. I appreciate your interest in Mariette's well-being, I really do. Now, don't you think it's time you went wherever it is you call home, and let me go up to bed. I'm tired—you must be too.''

Her voice is quiet, still as a cup of cream. He cannot believe what he's just heard her say, the acknowledgement she's just made. What, how can he say anything after this, do anything but pick up his cap from the table, and make his way out her door?

Only when she hears his truck start up, gravel crunching under its wheels, do her hands begin to shake, shake so badly she has to put her head down, arms over the piano, jangling the keys. Noise, she must make enough noise to drown everyone out, keep them out. Even if she must take Mariette in. Nobody home. How else can she keep silence?

MRS. COTTREAU, in navy skirt and severe white blouse, sensible shoes and shiny vinyl handbag, shakes Claire's hand. ''That's wonderful—you know, I was afraid, the other day, that you weren't going to be able to help us.'' She leans across the kitchen table, bringing her face close to Claire's—a little conspiratorial display. ''We think it best that she see very little of her mother and step-father, just for now. She seems to need a little insulation from family life, you know how it can be? But we'd like her to have visitors. Frère LeBlanc, for example—he came to see her quite a few times in hospital. Oh, and Hector Wagner, he seems to have done her some good, really taken her out of herself. She's almost back to normal, now, except for her speech, and that will come with time.''

''Sorry, I don't understand you. Am I supposed to be keeping open house for Mariette's visitors? You do know that I work for a living, Mrs. Cottreau—I can't have people running in and out—''

"No, of course not. But if someone should happen to call—as I'll be doing from time to time, and Frère LeBlanc . . . . Besides, you won't want to be tied up with Mariette all the time, I'm sure. As I was saying, we think she's going to do just fine here; and it won't be forever, Miss Saulnier, don't worry about that.''

"I won't.''

From an upstairs window, Claire watches the social worker's car pull out of the drive. It is the window of the room she's always kept locked—she's decided to put Mariette in her parents' old room. Delima has cleaned it out for her—Delima will come every Saturday to visit Mariette while she cleans the house—it seems the best possible arrangement. On the top of the old pine chest of drawers, Delima has left a paper bag with dried fish from Wagner's store—a coming-home present. Claire takes the bag and throws it into the wastepaper basket. Then she opens the bureau drawers, one after another. In the top one are socks, underpants and nightgowns Mrs. Cottreau's bought at Frenchy's for Mariette. No brassières—does she think of her as a child, still? In another, sweaters and blouses and trousers—it will be a little like having a life-size doll to dress and feed. Claire shuts the drawers, picks up the wastepaper basket and leaves the room. She pauses before closing the door, turns to take one last look. It will do, she decides—it will not be impossible. If Mariette belongs anywhere, it's in this room that's been cleaned and aired for her. Cleared of voices, noises, ghosts. It had been so easy after all, unlocking the door, gathering up the dust sheets, opening windows to let in air like a flock of hungry birds. *Nobody home but jumping Joan.* A children's rhyme.

She lets the door bang shut behind her. Gets rid of the dried fish in the kitchen garbage and goes to her desk. A formal reply to Père Philippe's letter of reprimand—she will need it for her files. They have never given anyone tenure at Sacré Coeur—it is assumed that, like death itself, one's going or staying will be at the discretion of Higher Authorities. They could end her contract, such as it was, with a snap of Père Philippe's spatulate thumbs—

which would leave her—and now Mariette—in less than ideal conditions. But she can't sit down to write the letter—can't keep herself still. She goes over to the piano and plays through the first movement of the Franck sonata, looks up at the cabinet where Bertrand's letter can just be seen behind the glass. By now she knows it by heart. And she suddenly wishes, with all of that heart which she feels, now, like some scratched stone inside her, that she'd never had anything to do with either Bertrand or Halyna. Yet she has dreamt of them, all the same, far away on that "other side" she'd promised herself never to want or miss: the two of them nocturnal creatures, now, no more illuminating, no more reachable than dead or fallen stars.

ON THEIR WALKS down to the beach, Claire and Mariette take the path from Claire's back door down through the spruce grove to the top of the dunes—the same path Bertrand and Halyna used for their clandestine walks back to the college. Those lovers have left no traces along the way, no white pebbles or bits of bread by which to find their way home again, reflects Claire—those two are on their own. Unlike Mariette, who follows her as closely as if she were holding Claire's hand. Follows slowly, making sure of her steps over the undergrowth and through the mat of beach pea vines on the lee side of the dunes. Neither speaks—it's as if they've outgrown the need for mere words between them, as though they're as close as an object and its image in a mirror.

Not a perfect autumn day, but adequate for the outing which the doctor's prescribed as a necessary part of Mariette's routine. Claire stops by a driftwood log pushed up to the highwater mark— they will sit down here and take the air. Air spongy, swollen with moisture it will not let fall. Indistinct from the thick grey surface of the sea, water that the sun, meshed-in by clouds, cannot warm or light. Like Mariette's eyes when she'd first come out of hospital, eyes like parched stones. Under water now, colours and patterns visible, even if too small to read. Claire shifts on the log to look at Mariette who is watching a small green fishing boat

chug through the porridgy sea to harbour. Looks with the satisfaction of a gardener who has spent an entire season coaxing leaf
out of a blasted branch. At the beginning she'd come into Mariette's room each morning to find the girl awake but inert: still,
silent, curled up in herself like the skeletons of fish you find on
the wharf—blank rings of bones, tail stuffed in mouth, eye sockets
shallow, vacant. Had to shake her out of bed, lay her clothes on
the counterpane each morning, remind her to put on her socks,
comb her hair, eat what was put on her plate. She'd had to accept
Hector's help in taking Mariette for walks, since the girl seemed
to have forgotten how to put one foot in front of the other. Had
become thin, frail as a wishbone—needing to be walked back,
Claire on one side, Hector on the other. At first he'd come faith-
fully, each afternoon, except for those days he was working on
his shack, hut, whatever-in-the-woods. Claire shoves the hair out
of her eyes, but Mariette lets hers blow around her face, little
black whips. Before Claire had cut it, Mariette's hair had looked
dead, like a hangman's rope down her back.

Mariette sits placidly on the log Claire has chosen, like a child
on her best behaviour, exquisitely intent on doing whatever
pleases the adult who has charge of her. Her skin is no longer
blotched and swollen; she sleeps at night without sedatives. And
she's begun to talk enough to appease the social worker, who has
told Claire she won't leave the girl on her hands forever, that
arrangements can be made for Mariette to learn some sort of
trade. There is, of course, no question of her going back to the
trailer; Mariette simply looks right through Delima when she
comes to clean—she doesn't even see the boys who say hello to
her if they should pass her on the beach. Since her speech is
somewhat restricted, Claire hasn't expected Mariette to talk about
anyone or anything—not about Bertrand, certainly, nor the
brother who has been "put away" as Delima calls it. Nor has
Mariette responded with anything like enthusiasm to Mrs. Cottreau's plans for her. "If you want," was all she'd said to the
idea she apprentice as hairdresser's assistant to Régine's House
of Beauty down the road.

No. Mariette seems, Mariette is content to stay with Claire

here, now, just as she is, keeping things as they are, and this has been, Claire realizes, watching Mariette watch the fishing boat fight the stupidly resistant wind—this has been her own deliverance. The girl's silence, her quietness fill up all the empty corners of the house, drown out all the whispers and shouting. It's as if Mariette's presence eases the pressure of the past, absorbs those ghosts compounded of absence and memory till they are stick, stock, stone dead, sunk to the bottom of some deep black pool. Claire has finally given them what they want; she and Mariette are two glass transparencies which have come together to make one image. Foreground, background, all unravelled edges now complete and closed. Claire no longer dreams of her mother's burial, of her father choking on his own vomit by the foot of the bed in which Delima does or does not lie, with Mariette curled in her womb, transparent, helpless as a sand shrimp.

For half an hour or more they sit together on a driftwood log rubbed to soft silver in the sea, casually rolled up on this particular stretch of sand to serve as the equivalent of a park bench. Claire, who has sat on such benches in Regent's Park, the Luxembourg gardens and Chamonix, thinks now that they might as well be make-believe, that she has really never travelled further than this spot, a stone's throw from the house in which she grew up and to which she has now brought Mariette. Time is a perfect circle; Claire at forty is the same as Claire at four. This girl beside her is the same Mariette who tagged along when Delima came to clean, years and years ago, when Hector had been the brightest, the most promising of all her protégés. Only the life within this circle is real; everything else has fallen off the edge of a world small and flat as the stones children skip across the water. Bertrand, Halyna: postcard figments. The letter in her pocket from the Administrative Council of Sacré Coeur, informing her that her contract will not be renewed after this semester, due to financial constraints as well as certain disturbing events having to do with the Summer Programme. Claire looks out to sea, then back at Mariette; there is no difference, everything diffuse, porous as the air around her, the sand which dribbles through her fingers. Except where once there were three, father, mother and child, now there are only two: sisters. Not just sisters, twins. Siamese twins joined not by a strip of bone or blood, but by a plenitude of silence that comprehends everything and everyone. And they need never speak a word. They are already spoken.

SOMEONE SITTING *on the end of his bed, the way his mother used to, watching over him when he was a small child and ill with fever. But this round, golden face swimming slowly into focus, this fragrant and voluptuous body in the stiff white dress that would have suited a Spanish Infanta is not anyone's mother. "Hector," she says, that one word a small glass ball suspended in black air between them. It is the middle of the night, so dark you cannot see your hand in front of your face, and yet her face is luminous as the full moon, as bright as a mirror tilted at the sun. "Hector."*

He sits up in bed, raising his hands to touch the glass ball floating towards him: his name. The girl reaches forward, pockets the glass ball, shakes her head. "Over here," she says, and this time the air is empty of everything except his own eyes, drawn to where she gestures. There is something in the corner of the room, by the window, where the wind riffles the curtain, revealing and concealing a shape beneath it. "Go and look," she says. He reaches toward her, putting his arms not around but through her shoulders, trying to press her to him, but grasping nothing, being pushed forward through a long, clear, icy tunnel until he is finally standing at the window. This time the girl is not there, though her voice continues, part of the wind teasing the flimsy curtains. "Choose," she says. "Which one?"

Wind like icicles scribbling across his face, as the curtains blow open and he sees two women, or rather, a woman and a girl, standing side by side. A mother and daughter: two sisters, one older, one almost a child. The younger one has holes where her eyes and mouth should be, holes flooded with dark. The older one smiles red-lipped at him, showing the small, sharpened knives of her teeth. "Choose," but as he stretches out his hand to the younger, tugs at her hard to draw her away, she brings the other with her; he looks closer and sees that the women are joined from ankle to hip. Siamese twins he cannot separate without a knife. "Choose," and suddenly there's a blade in his hand, and he's severing the skin and bone and flesh that knits them together. Not blood but light pouring out the wound he makes, blazing light, blinding him so the knife falls from his hand and he cannot see to find them.

HIS DREAM a sparkler crackling in the night. Hector wakes with a last glint of light under his lids before dark devours the story, leaving only random bits of bone and hair behind, bits that, however hard he tries, he cannot shape into a body. He sits up in bed, checking the fluorescent dials of his Chinese-made alarm clock, the one that sirens him awake each morning. Four o'clock. Hector props himself up against the pillow, shuts his eyes and listens to the clock doing battle with the belch and blare of trucks along the highway.

Descartes' dreams: whirlwind, thunderclap, and finally the spirit of truth descending to him, dictating terms. Whereas his own dreams, the important ones from which he wakes with his throat parched and his body drenched with sweat; these ones he can no longer, in any coherent way, remember. It was different when he was younger, when he was living away. But now his nights and days are held in separate arms by this world he's chosen; no way they can touch, come together, even though it was for this he came back, for some simple continuity, harmony between who he was, what he wanted.

He tries to salvage, reconstruct something from the night. Tomb sealed up, no stone to roll away. He thinks of Mariette, not as she looks now but as he'd first seen her at the hospital. Was she, like him, always in pursuit of vanished dreams—or is her life a dream too well-remembered? What went on inside her silence; was she speaking to herself, shouting out in ways no one could hear? Or was this her truest state, before or beyond speech, living in and to herself, like those Things Rilke speaks about: plants, animals, all patient and humble and willing . . . . So that it didn't matter whether she ever spoke more than the few words Claire had managed to coax out of her: "yes," "no," "if you want." Perhaps she really was at home at Claire's, though surely she needed someone who'd do more than use her as a kind of mirror in a dark room, catching unseen reflections, fastening invisible images. Images of what? Only Claire knew—. He wonders, just for a moment, if his own interest in Mariette is simply a means of intruding into Claire's life, opening doors she has never let anyone so much as glimpse. . . . Just for a moment, and then the thought burns out, leaving only a slight, scorched smell behind.

His own interest in Mariette. Visits at the hospital almost every day, visits in which they would walk the corridors and he would ramble on about anything and everything to her perfectly uncomprehending ears. And now that she's at Claire's, he takes walks along the beach when they're sure to be there—on weekends, or else late afternoon, after work. Sitting with them, talking to Claire of nothing at all, while Mariette sifts sand through her fingers or watches children digging traps and moated castles by the shore. Claire not wanting him with them, but not making any move to leave, preferring to out-sit, out-talk, out-wait him, knowing her house is just behind the dunes, and that she can retreat there any time she likes, taking Mariette with her like a banner signalling her own strength, mastery—over him, if not the girl. For when winter comes Claire will shut up Mariette like a prisoner in that house, will let no one but Frère LeBlanc and the social worker near her, slamming the door in his face if ever he came—. To do what? Sit, cap in hand, and stare at her? What does he want from her? What can she give him that he hasn't yet discovered, either in Montréal or all the length and width of the French Shore?

Hector picks up the clock off the night table, catching the tinny pulse within his hands. He'd meant to do so much this past summer—finish his cabin, move in before the winter storms, begin rewriting the first chapter of his thesis for that publisher in London, the one Delbert had so distrusted. Instead, he'd driven back and forth to Falmouth hospital, lain on the beach in the unfamiliar

arms of that summer's sun. . . . Remembering, in the way he
sometimes recalls figures from films whose names and plots he
has long forgotten, that girl with long hair, pale yellow hair and
a white dress, the girl he'd met on his way to the beach, on her
way to Claire's. The girl who'd played at that last concert and
given him that extraordinary smile, a smile which had made him
think she'd mistaken him for someone else. And he couldn't even
recall her name—the girl who was now Bertrand's wife, if Claire
was to be believed. What would Bertrand do with such a girl—
and what could she do with him? Take pictures, pose for photographs. . . . He has no trouble remembering every detail of Bertrand's photograph of Mariette.

Hector puts the clock back down on the dresser, pulls on his
jeans and walks over to the window from which he can make out
the lights of the fishplant like a chain of small and tidy stars,
defying dawn. Claire, Mariette, Bertrand, himself, that girl—
such an unlikely mix: random stars strung together into a constellation, making up a picture like a child's dot-to-dot drawing—
but of what? How were you to connect them? Not that there was
ever more than a fictive correspondence between the names and
shapes of constellations: Ursa Major, Orion's Belt, Charles'
Wain. He and Claire used to argue over them, years ago, when
he was, he supposed, still a child, and she—. What was she then?
What is she now? His former mentor, Mariette's guardian,
nobody's daughter, mother, lover. Perfect, impregnable, complete—nothing would ever touch her. Not even Mariette, who was
so much her ward, now, people had almost ceased thinking of her
as Delima's kid or even Claire's half-sister—she was really
Claire's child.

As he stands there looking across at the bay the fishplant lights
blink out, abscond. Day, already, but there is nothing for him to
do here or at the college for another four hours or so. He could
try and go back to sleep—or he could get the hell outside. Early
October, the light flirting with frost, milky mist rising from the
ponds fenced off along the ditch, ponds which the firemen use to
fill up their hoses whenever someone's barn or house burns down.
Hector pulls on his shirt, a sweater. His cabin—it's become a

reflex with him now to anticipate disaster. Suppose someone broke in and switched on the kerosene heater—left without turning it off? That had happened to Albert Thibodeau's camp; the whole place had burned down as quickly as a piece of construction paper. He had time enough to make a quick run out and check that things were all right. Perhaps he could even take the canoe out for a while—what would it matter if he were half an hour late for work? Was Père Philippe going to catechise him in his office, under the drooping crucifix and the over-varnished painting of the Deportation? Who knew, maybe it was time to launch a guerilla war to secularize the college, kick out the priests and become Generalissimo and Recteur all at one.

On the way to the lake Hector drives by Claire's house, sees a light burning downstairs, in the room she uses as a study. Claire, too, cannot sleep—does she have bad dreams? Does she have any dreams at all? Or is she up pacing the floor? The gossip at Wagner's store has it that Claire's being shown the door at Sacré Coeur, and all because of that *Français de France* and the Polish girl he ran away with. Hector resists the temptation to beep his horn at Claire's house; he continues down the road, wondering for the few moments before he makes his turnoff how things are going for Bertrand: whether his happiness—if one can call it that— is worth the price Claire may have to pay for it. At any rate, Bertrand has a wife, and Claire, a child: fair enough exchange. As for himself, he has nothing out of all of this, except a minimal acquaintance with Mariette. And in his dreams at night, the negative of a photograph, an image he cannot remember, only the sound of it burning out, tracelessly, in the sudden dark of waking.

STILL NOT MORNING. Mariette has to wait another hour, two hours till she can get dressed and go downstairs. Trucks going by all night: last thing she hears before she falls asleep, first sound in the morning. Truck going past, now—Hector's truck. She can see the Kwikway sign. Hector's her good friend, they told her that at the hospital. They said, "You're lucky to have such a kind man to come see you: all men aren't like that, you know?'' Claire doesn't like him coming by—Claire's the woman who looks after her. Mariette can ask her for anything she wants and Claire will make sure she gets it; they told her she would. Claire buys Mariette clothes at Frenchy's, everything but shoes—they wear the same size; Claire gives her the pairs she doesn't want anymore, her closets are full of shoes, she says. She gave Mariette a room with a lock on the door—asked her, ''Do you really need one?'' and Mariette said, ''Yes.'' Claire locks her door at night. She can hear the click. Claire calls out to her on the stairs, ''Good night, Mariette,'' but Mariette's supposed to be asleep and pretends not to hear. Claire says she needs lots of sleep, so she sends her early to bed. Mariette lies awake listening to the trucks go by: going to Whitby, going to Falmouth, some even to Halifax.

Paul's in Halifax, in a treatment centre, Claire says. Like a hospital and a school mixed together. Somewhere near Halifax. Too far for Mariette to visit him; sometime, when she's all better—not now. Better means saying ''yes'' and ''no,'' saying ''please'' and ''thank you.'' So she makes the words come out when Claire wants them. Making noises that scrape against her throat and cut her tongue, but Claire hears ''yes'' and ''please'' and ''no thank you.'' She doesn't want Mariette to go. She says, ''You don't have to leave, ever. If you don't want to go to Régine's just say so.'' Mariette doesn't know. Maybe she could make some money and go on the bus to see Paul, go by herself. Maybe she could just hitch a ride up to Halifax—people do it all the time, up the highway, all the way to Halifax, all the way across the sea to France.

He took her picture, lots of pictures. Claire keeps them locked in a drawer. Mariette found them. When Claire was out shopping, she looked in all the drawers like Delima used to do. She found the picture he took that time in the trailer with Luc, before she got sick, so sick she was bleeding in Claire's car and she wouldn't look at her, wouldn't talk to her. Claire knew what Mariette did with him, she knew. Praying to her, eyes shut and hands open, asking Our Lady to help her, make him leave her alone. Again and again, but it was too late by the time Claire listened. Even when Mariette shuts her eyes it burns through, black fire, black like the car in the woods, car with brambles punching through and the windscreen smashed, like he says he'll do to her face if she tells that he took the photograph. Claire keeps it in the drawer, locked, but Mariette found the key and she knows Claire knows.

Claire's awake, she's walking downstairs—Mariette heard the floorboards crack as Claire went by her room. He drives by in his truck, she can see the Kwikway sign on the door. Claire won't let him talk to her; she doesn't want him around, but Mariette doesn't say a word. She sits there and listens to them talking. His name is Hector. He comes to see her in the hospital; he goes for walks on the beach, sits down beside Claire and watches Mariette. He wears glasses, and his hair is black, like hers, but he combs it so you can see the part, straight and white as a line on the highway, all the way to Halifax, near Halifax. He is a kind man, the nurses say so when he comes to see her in hospital.

In the hospital there are women in white dresses who come and see the babies in glass boxes, carry babies in their arms the way she used to carry hers, carry Paul everywhere because he wouldn't walk, he couldn't, it wasn't her fault. *You be smart and hook him good, pin him down he'll marry you for sure. He's the kind that does and you feel that good with a kid in you, like the sun's risin' up in your belly.* And he'll take her away with him, and they'll live together, her and him and the baby, she won't ever be alone anymore. It'll be her kid, her own and no one can take him from her. Not even Claire, watching when he talks to Mariette, watching to make sure she doesn't say anything to him. He never comes to see her when Claire's out; at the beach he talks to Claire, talks so Mariette can't understand what they're saying. She says, "yes," "no," "if you want to." She never wants to.

When she first came to Claire's house, Claire would tell her stories, all about witches putting spells on people so they turn into animals, can't cry for help or explain to the ones who could save them. Claire is magic, she's not like any other woman. Skin so white Mariette can see through it, blood white as her bones. They eat meals together. She helps Claire clean the house, dust the books—not the piano. Once Mariette sat down and tried all the keys, black, white, black and Claire came up behind her; she wanted to hit her, but instead she just closed the piano, pulled the lid over the keys as if they were dead. At night, after Claire thinks she's asleep, Mariette hears her play, so soft she doesn't know if she's hearing or dreaming the music. Sad music, empty like a room with no furniture, and no windows, just walls and doors.

Every night Mariette has dreams—night after night, as many dreams as there are cards in a pack, but only one she can remember. They're at a dance, at the club—together, she and Claire, and Hector comes up and asks Mariette to dance. Claire says, "No, she can't, her shoes are too tight; they're my shoes." And Hector says, "She can take them off, can't she?" and he goes to pull off Mariette's shoes, Claire's shoes, but he pulls so hard that her feet come off with the shoes, blood pours out black and thick and hot like fire. And it covers Mariette till she's inside her own blood, black as the sky at night, when there are no stars and no moon, and they can't see her or hear her. No one can find her. She's inside her self where no one can get her. Just like the baby he shoved inside her. They cut it out, put it away somewhere and she can't get him back, safe inside her, like the sun rising up, if she can get him inside her. This time, one time it won't hurt and she'll keep him safe, take him away where no one will find them, just Mariette and her baby and some kind rescuer. If Claire forgets to lock the door, if she ever forgets.

CLAIRE IN HER STUDY, on her desk a mug of untouched instant coffee smelling of mushrooms and the cold, damp dark. She drums with her fingers on the package that came in yesterday's avalanche of mail, the package she'd thrown out, unopened, as soon as she'd glanced at the postmark. Thrown it out and gone to bed and dreamed of the concert, the Franck sonata spilling out the fissures of her sleep till she'd finally woken at four o'clock. Waited an hour before pulling on her dressing gown and creeping carefully downstairs, so as not to waken Mariette. Retrieving from the wastepaper basket in the study a slim brown packet with her name and address marked on it. No sign of the sender—Delbert wouldn't have been able to tell which one of them sent it. But he'd know, the whole shore would know, from Père Gilbert to Louis à Pepsi. "It doesn't matter anymore," she tells herself. "It really doesn't matter."

The package lies like a sleeping child in her lap—one she'd prefer not to waken, fearing a tantrum, or tears. This wasn't part of the bargain—she wanted nothing else ever to do with the two of them; she'd cancelled them out, sent them off like the children in fairytales who are commanded to wear out seven pairs of iron shoes, eat seven iron loaves before they find their heart's desire. Yet here is a fat letter from Halyna, surely a confession, accusation . . . . She takes the paperknife and carefully slits the edge of the padded envelope: it's only a book—but with a letter inside it, two tissue-thin sheets covered on both sides with large, strong, slanted handwriting:

Paris, 1 November

Dear Claire,

I'm sending back the book you loaned to Bertrand—it somehow got mixed up with my things when I moved. As you might have guessed, things have changed between Bertrand and myself—in fact, we are applying for a divorce. There are a thousand things to tell you, and then again, there is nothing you won't already know.

I don't imagine you've heard yet from Bertrand. I saw him a few days ago—in the Luxembourg gardens, sitting at one of the wrought-iron tables up on the *terrasse*. Do you remember how you said all this would help shove him out of his shell, make him start living at last, instead of just cataloguing people and events as they went past him? When I saw him he looked like a man who'd just had his house burn down, a man sitting in a pile of cinders on the ground. I didn't go up to him, or call to him—not because I was afraid, or ashamed—it's not the loss of me he's mourning, but an idea he had about me. For the funny thing is that by the time we finally came to Paris he knew he'd made as complete a mistake as it's possible to do. He showed me a photograph of the girl he said he should have married. Do you know, she was holding a child? I didn't know what to think. But he doesn't care anymore what anyone says. I honestly think he'd be happier back in Spruce Harbour than in Paris—he doesn't even go to the museums or read the newspapers anymore, and his parents expect him to fail his exams. I'm telling you all this partly because I think you may hear from him at some point, and be able to—finish helping him. You helped me, didn't you Claire? I suppose I should thank you.

At any rate, here is the book Bertrand called his Bible. I've thumbed through it—there's a passage in it that makes me think of you. Do you remember it?

Loving, for a long time ahead and far on into life is—: solitude, a heightened and deepened kind of aloneness for the person who loves. Loving does not at first mean merging, surrendering and uniting with another person . . . it is a high inducement for the individual to . . . become world in himself for the sake of another person; it is a great, demanding claim on him, something that chooses him and calls him to vast distances.

You never really told me much about yourself—not a fraction of what I confessed to you. There's something I should tell you, though, something I only learned through Bertrand. I'm someone who finds it very very difficult to love, and rather easy to hurt people. My mother will never forgive me for what she thinks I've done to our family—my father still begs me to come home in his letters. But now that I'm no longer under his thumb, he seems—no longer my father, but just a helpless old man who writes me letters in Polish. I don't really want to see either of them again. Does that make me some kind of monster? I wonder sometimes if there might have been other possibilities for me—human, I mean, not musical. If I hadn't gone off with Bertrand, if I'd somehow sabotaged your wonderful scheme. But that hardly matters now, does it?

You'll be sitting in your parlour, in one of those enormous, faded chintz chairs, reading this. In your white house with the rail fence round it; the doors and windows shut tight. I'll think of you, from time to time, alone in your vast distances—and then I suppose I shall forget you altogether.

There doesn't seem anything more to say.

Halyna

Claire reads the letter only once; she folds it into a small square and then puts it, along with the book, into the drawer in which the photograph of Mariette is locked. Turning the key is like sprinkling earth on a fresh grave. "Finished," she says. And then, "She knows absolutely nothing. Least of all about herself." Leaving the room, going up the stairs to wash and dress, she pauses for a moment on the landing, listening, as if for an intruder in the house. But there is nothing—perfect silence from Mariette's room; she'll have to knock on her door in a moment to wake her—it isn't good for her to sleep too long. She needs something to occupy her, the social worker had said, suggesting quilt-making—you could even make money at it, and there can never be too much of that, now can there? "No," Claire had answered, refusing to be drawn into any conversation on her fallen fortunes, now that the college had let her go. There would be quite enough to keep the both of them, once she'd picked up a few new pupils. She was driving down to Falmouth later today, to be interviewed for a part-time position at the high school. Fallen, indeed.

"It doesn't matter," she repeats to herself, staring at her face in the bathroom mirror. Her skin feels tight, as if it's plaster, not cream she's smoothing under her eyes, at the corners of her mouth. "Not now, not anymore. Amen."

"IT'S NOT SUCH a great day, but I thought we could go for a walk anyway. Would you like to? Claire's still out? I saw her at the college this morning. Better put on some boots, and take something for your head, it looks like rain. Tell you what, we could drive down to the woods back of Deer Lake—I've got a canoe out there—we could go for a ride if it doesn't rain.''

Mariette goes to get her boots and scarf—she makes no sound when she walks; she's like air going through air. Hector scribbles a note to Claire, telling her they'll be back in a couple of hours— with any luck she won't be back till suppertime. With or without luck it's time this happened, Hector insists. Claire can't expect to go on forever with Mariette like some houseplant in her keeping. And Mariette is better now, Hector's sure of that. If she's to recover completely, she'll need to get out of this house—dead and stale in here, the air spongy with dead time, old memories.

She comes back, dressed for rain—Hector looks out the window and sees fine strings of it, like fish wire in the air. ''Let's run for it,'' he shouts and suddenly he's at the truck, holding open the door for Mariette who's walking slowly, deliberately, as if she hasn't heard or understood him—or just refuses to take any suggestions at all. There's no one outside to see them, but there's no accounting for the long-range vision of people who sit all afternoon at their parlour windows, watching the cars pass along the highway, knowing the make and date, the repairs and paint jobs done on every vehicle in Spruce Harbour. They may see Mariette sitting beside him in the Kwikway truck—may telephone Claire, except that no one calls her; she is *persona non grata* in the gossips' world. It doesn't matter, he's already told her in his note: ''Taken Mariette for a ride.'' But not the sort of ride Claire thinks—not the kind she's taken Mariette for, all this time.

''Would you like to listen to some music?''

''If you want.''

''What do *you* want?''

She's not looking through the window at anything. Just staring at the rain as the windshield wipers smear it in broad crescents: click, clack, click. What if that's the way her mind sounds, now— what if there really is nothing more than yes, no, yes, no, her head empty, impenetrable as a windshield? What would she think if he were to put on a tape right now—something easy like the *Symphonie Fantastique* or Pachelbel, the People's Choice? That's right, patronize her; why not give her a Kleenex in case she drools? No music—not because she'd feel stupid, not knowing how to listen, but because he can't trust himself not to lord it over her, instruct her in the rudiments of culture, like the late-lamented Bertrand. What, then? What is there to say to her?

"Are you cold in that slicker? Would you like my sweater— you're sure? Okay, then. It won't be too much longer. It's beautiful in the woods now—nicer than the beach. I hate it there at this time of year—a whole summer's worth of pop cans and chip bags. Anyway, I thought the woods would make a nice change."

'I talk, therefore—she isn't.' What did he expect? A miracle cure occasioned by a country drive? The main thing is that she didn't say no; she could have refused to come along—she must know that she's taken an action, made a decision, to come with him instead of waiting for Claire. Even if she doesn't know, yet, what it could mean. Claire knows. Coming to his office late this morning, handing over the keys to her own: *I thought I should let you know, Hector. I just had a letter from Halyna—she's left Bertrand. To his own sad devices; it seems he's going through rather a rough patch just now. Are you satisfied? I am, for my part—and for Mariette's. So I think it's time we called it quits, you and I. There's no need for you to come round anymore; we've already all the company we need.*

"We're here—it's just down the path, along that line of alder. You sure you're warm enough? Watch the mud—it'll be better a few yards in, under the shelter of the trees. Here, take my hand."

Her hand cold, small, like a pebble picked up out of the water. He'd like to put it in his pocket. They walk side by side on the path—Hector is not a large man, but she seems no bigger than a child beside him. *She's not a child, Claire; I think it's up to Mariette to decide if she wants to see me or not.* What he could have said, but didn't—she'll find out soon enough what he has to say—what Mariette wants or doesn't want.

"Look, here—have you ever seen this kind of moss before?" He crouches down and she bends with him, till they are hunkering over a clump of small green stars, sprung up between the roots of a stunted birch. As if she's blind and deaf he takes her hand, moves it into this tiny, rooted sky, stars thick and soft, entangled. Her face is no more than a hand's breadth away from his: beads of mist caught in her short black hair, even on her eyelashes. He reaches his fingers up to her face, touches it as gently as she's pressing the starry moss. Her face doesn't change—she doesn't move to touch his hand or to push it away; it is as though she were a branch or a pool of water, receiving him . . . *the deep, simple needs in which life renews itself* . . . He leans towards her, kisses her face where he'd touched it with his fingers. She's watching him out of eyes like black curtains drawn against the light. What light—his feeble scenario? Hector Wagner meets Rima the Jungle Girl, Trailer Girl, lovely loony Mariette.

She's standing up, over him—starts to walk ahead quickly, on her own. The path's too narrow for them both. She disappears around a bend in the path—gone—into the lake, dear God—. Hands in his pockets, he has to keep himself from running after her, turning, stumbling to where she sits, cross-legged, waiting on the dock beside the canoe.

Too wet, too late to go out but he asks her all the same. She says "yes," and so he shoves the canoe into the water, helps her climb inside, gives her a paddle which she holds in her arms like a child. No life jackets; he doesn't bother asking her if she knows how to swim, that's all part of the risk, isn't it? Claire won't be home yet. Claire's gone all the way to Falmouth, she won't even have telephoned. With any luck—. They've cut into the cold, black water, its stillness pitted by random but persistent drops of rain, their clothes getting heavier and heavier the further they go. She sits looking not at the woods on either shore, but straight ahead of them, as if they were heading out to sea instead of circling this small, land-locked lake. He tells her that if they're lucky they might see a deer come down to the shore to drink. She shakes her head, and at that very moment both of them jump, rocking the canoe. Gunshots: hunters in the woods, and there they were, walking around without anything to mark them off from trees or rocks; one kind of animal among all the rest, as silent and vulnerable. He tells her they should head back, and she says no, not even turning her head. And so they go on, until the lake narrows into a dead end of pickerel weed and water lily leaves looking like great, blind eyes on the surface of the water.

All the way back they ride in a silence broken by hunters' guns and the churn of water under his paddle. They have crossed this lake only to return—there is no passage here. And yet it does not feel like the same shore onto which they step. Both of them soaked to the skin, but it's Hector who shivers, leading the way into the cabin where there's a kerosene heater they can warm themselves by. He leaves her sitting by the stove, rummages in the kitchen for two mugs of instant coffee, a tray on which the Blue Boy and the Age of Innocence Girl simper side by side. The transfer's been crookedly applied; it is not one of his mother's better efforts. Sitting alone there, her hair damp, her eyes dark with rain; silent and calling forth not desire but tenderness—*And even if they have made a mistake and embrace blindly, the future comes anyway . . . on the foundation of the accident that seems to be accomplished here.*

Here.

Accomplished.

THE HOUSE IS LIT up like one of the Loire *châteaux—silence et lumière*. Hector presses Mariette's hand after he helps her out of the truck. He would like to kiss her, but everyone in Spruce Harbour will be looking on from their kitchen windows; surely Claire has alerted the R.C.M.P. by now or at least every social worker from Falmouth to Whitby. He takes Mariette, who is wearing his sweater under her raincoat, up the gravel path to Claire's front door. It is open, for a wonder—he calls hello as they walk inside. No answer. For a fraction of a moment he has a vision—acrid, sulphurous as match-spurt into flame—of Claire lying stretched out on her bed, ten bottles of aspirin in her gut. But Mariette hasn't so guilty an imagination; she walks in past Hector, hangs up her coat, takes off her boots, and then makes her way into the living room where Claire is sitting in one of the large chintz armchairs, with a book in her hands and a slender gold-tipped cigar burning in an ashtray beside her. No greeting is exchanged between the women; Mariette sits down on the edge of the piano bench, rubbing her arms as if she's cold. Claire looks hard at Mariette, at the sweater she's wearing, then over to Hector who's joined Mariette at the piano bench. She makes no room for him to sit down beside her, so he stands, hands in pockets, an involuntary grimace on his face.

"Mariette, you must be starved—I left some stew for you—it's on the stove. Why don't you go into the kitchen and help yourself. Well, if you're not hungry, you must be tired—why not go up to bed?"

Mariette rises from the bench and is about to walk up the stairs when she turns, pulls off the rough grey sweater, and then gives it, all in a ball, to Hector. He lets it fall to the floor, reaching out to her, instead, putting his hands around the close-cropped head. Kisses her. "Good night, Mariette. I'll come round tomorrow afternoon—after work. That will give you plenty of time."

Claire doesn't seem to have noticed Hector's embrace, or his words—she's reading her book as Mariette goes up the stairs. Lights a slender cigar, turns a page, says to Hector, who's dropped the crumpled ball, "Lock the door when you leave, will you? And do take your Frenchy's best when you go—Mariette's got plenty of her own sweaters upstairs. Besides, it clashes horribly with the carpet." She turns another page.

"Thanks, I'd love one—now, where do you keep your Scotch? Nice cabinet, this. Rocks are for barnacles. I'll take it straight, thanks all the same." His voice low, convivial; were Mariette listening she would hear only the most amicable of tones from Hector. And from Claire, the accelerated turning of pages. Hector sits down in the chintz armchair next to Claire's, and takes slow sips of his drink. He could be, he reflected, one of the cabbage-roses on the upholstery for all the attention she's paying him. But there's a certain ferocity in the way she smokes the cigar—it gives her away. So he leans back in his chair, his arms behind his head and waits. He'll stay all night, if he has to. Hector's stomach begins to growl—he could help himself to her Scotch, but scarcely her stew.

Book snaps shut. Claire's voice low, like his—though Mariette must surely be asleep by now—she'd looked as though she were drowning in her own exhaustion as she'd gone up to bed. Voice low, but tipped with glinting little spikes. "Are you going to leave my house, or do I have to call the police?"

"Call who? Joe à Willie, constable in the RCMP? You forget he's my second cousin."

"And you forget that my father delivered him."

"Many long years ago, Claire. I'm surprised at you trying to play that card. Look, this is a waste of time for both of us—I might as well tell you—"

"I haven't the slightest interest in anything you might have to say."

"Don't you want to know what's happened?"

Claire stubs out her cigar, throws her book onto the coffee table, goes up to the cabinet and pours herself a cognac. "The last of the bottle," she says. "Now that I'm no longer on Sacré Coeur's pay roll, I'll have to descend to brandy."

"Look, Claire, I'm sorry about your job—but that's why it's important you should listen to me now. You aren't going to—"

"Oh shut up, Hector, and go home." She's smiling at him, a generous, wide smile that seems to put arms about him, draw him in. Like a crocodile.

"I'll go home as soon as you let me tell you what it's only common decency to let you know."

"Common decency? Really?" She comes back to her chair, pulls up her feet, folds her arms and looks at him with exaggerated intensity. He's suddenly, uncomfortably aware that she's dressed up for this—her speech as well as her face. Her intonation has become viciously British, and there's something aggressive in the way she's put on lipstick, rouge, shadow over eyes that shine like crumpled tinfoil. He puts down his drink; puts down, too, the sweater he's been holding like a dead cat on his lap.

"Mariette's coming to live with me."

"Wonderful. Marvellous. All right, now you've told me—I

don't need to show you the way out, surely?''

"Claire, you don't understand. Tomorrow I'm coming to pick up Mariette and her things, and she's moving in with me. To put it bluntly, she needs to get out of this house—and she wants to live with me."

"And how do you know all this—let me guess. She told you. Our little chatterbox Mariette has poured out her heart-of-hearts to you. No? Then how about this: you took her off into the proverbial woods, asked her if she'd like a quick screw, and she said, 'If you want.' ''

If it weren't for the thought of Mariette upstairs he would shove his fist into her face. "Claire, you are a fucking bitch."

"Bitch maybe—fucking, thank God, no. There's not much to choose from round here. I'd recommend abstinence, Hector, particularly regarding young girls who've been under the care of psychiatrists as well as social workers."

"She's doing all right, Claire—and it's not thanks to you. Christ, you've been treating her like some sort of domesticated imbecile, wrapping her round with cotton batting, expecting nothing more from her than you would from a table or chair. Look, I don't care if the gossip is true or false, I don't care if she's your father's kid, or Luc-Antoine's kid, or—''

"Keep my family out of this." Her voice has risen, now, to match his; she's clenching and unclenching her fists, as if she, too, would like to use them.

"So we won't discuss that. I'm not saying you haven't done good things for her, helped her to get better. But she needs more than that—''

"More? A cock jammed up her cunt every hour on the hour until you get tired of it?''

They both stand up from their chairs. Claire is walking towards the stairs as Hector grabs her by the arm.

"That's how you think of it? Poor Claire."

Wrenching herself free. "Go. Now. Do you want her to hear this?''

"I love her."

Claire's hand goes to her stomach, as if she's been hit there.

But she's laughing, doubled over with laughter—she finds her way to the piano bench, sits down and wipes her eyes. "I'm sorry. It's just that you sound—so Victorian. The Repentant Seducer."

"Come off it, Claire—you make it sound as though she were some thirteen-year-old maiden sweet-and-pure that I've dragged down to the mud—violated. Isn't it a bit late in the day for you to start worrying about Mariette? You didn't give a good goddam for her when you could have helped her; you just sat on your own clean hands, right?"

"You don't know—"

"Look, let's forget what I know and don't know about Mariette's past. That's her own business. But her present is mine."

"Very neat. Can I just ask you what that present involves? Let's see—connubial bliss in a shack in the woods; you spend your day unblocking sewers at the college while Mariette—makes quilts? Gathers firewood? Grates potatoes for *râpure*? And then, you're so well-matched—you'll have so much to talk about together. After all, you're only a good ten, or is it eleven years older than she; you're a near-Ph.D. and she's a kid who quit high school at the age of sixteen, has had a breakdown and, though good-natured, even docile, isn't up to more, intellectually, than changing diapers and mixing Pablum—"

"So why not let her do just that? It would be the best thing in the world for her. That she's as uncomplicated, even simple as she is—doesn't it occur to you that I might love her just for that, for bringing home to me everything I'm not, letting me into a world that's maybe more substantial, more important, than this paper universe you've built around you here—"

Hector goes over to the coffee table, starts slapping its accumulated magazines, newspapers, books, records onto the floor as Claire watches, arms folded, her face impassive. "You're a great one for giving advice, Claire. Launching your protégés out into the world you couldn't stick, and then, when your mistakes come back home to you, refusing to see them, stepping over them as if they were something the dogs have left behind in the ditch. You know who's given me the best advice of all? Dear old Delbert. He's been telling me ever since I came back just what I should do—build a place of my own, right here, marry, have kids. Just like every one of my ancestors has done for the last two hundred years. So that's what I'm going to do, and take care of Mariette in the bargain, and leave you to your own solitary devices, vices, whatever you want to call them.''

He is out of breath, his face flushed. Standing in a pile of heaped magazines and papers, he feels like some soldier who's just captured the enemy's stronghold. And the enemy sits, so pale that the red on her lips and cheeks seems to be slashing her skin. When she speaks, it's like a capitulation. Except that Hector is the one who falls.

''Mariette can't have children. The abortion she had when she was thirteen took care of that. The doctor said her uterus had been too badly scarred. Mutilation was the term he used.''

''She can't have—?'' Hector stands there for a moment, head bowed, as if he's paying his respects to the death of an idea. Then he bends down, trying to pull his sweater out from under the avalanche of papers. Still squatting on his heels, he looks up at Claire, her face a flag hoisted over him. Quickly, he gets to his feet.

''I don't believe you—why should I? Anyway, it doesn't matter. I care for her, and I'm going to get her out of this dead place—I could go right up to her room and bring her down now, if I chose. I brought her back tonight to be fair to you—and because I'm not carrying anyone off—she'll come of her own free will. You've had your chance, Claire—years and years ago, when you first came back. Or maybe you never had a chance—never had the courage to take one.''

Claire walks up to him, her face inches away from his, so that he senses a blur of red and white around the glittery eyes: a smell like dust and roses. She's smiling at him again, gently this time, her voice a cradle slowly rocking her words. ''You're taking your chances now, are you? You say it takes courage? Hector—why not be honest with yourself—with all of us—and call it by its proper name. You don't love Mariette, you just feel pity for her—selfish pity. You want to play backwoods Pygmalion, redeem all your failures by embracing the small and simple things of life—

wildflowers, singing birds, children. And you think you'll have it all in Mariette and your cabin-in-the-woods—you think the whole world will suddenly come clear to you and take you in its arms and say, 'There, there, Hector, everything's fine, we're all one happy family.' As if love were as easy as patting a dog on the head. Wake up, man. I give you three weeks—and that's generous—before you dump her back on my doorstep. Take her, if you want—if she wants. But don't bring her back to me when you're finished this little experiment. Because she won't belong here after that—not to me, not to this house. And you'll be responsible—for the first time in your life you'll be responsible for ruining someone else's chances, instead of just your own. So, *courage, mon coeur.*"

She turns to go upstairs, away. Thinking she's won, that what she's just told him about Mariette—about himself—will matter. What Claire doesn't know—how can he begin to get across to her the worlds and worlds outside her head she doesn't know? And he has to tell her, or else she will have won, and he'll never have the courage to come back tomorrow.

"Claire—." Urgently, so that she'll stop and turn to him, just long enough for him to put his hands out. He pulls her towards him and kisses her on the mouth that's half-open, as if to answer back or ask a question. Kissing so hard the red on her lips begins to taste of blood, so hard that everything's contained within a brute lock of lips and tongue.

When Claire speaks her words sound like paper tearing. "Get out. Get out. Get out." Shutting her eyes so she can't see his face. Till she hears the sound of his truck starting up, and runs to the door, shoving the whole weight of her body against the wood, fastening the bolt, tightening the chain. She stumbles upstairs in the darkness, locks herself into the bathroom and scrubs at her lips, even her tongue, till she gags. Then lets the tap run till the water comes out so cold it scrapes her skin as she splashes it over her face, her hair, her throat.

Five minutes later she returns to the landing, her hair combed, her hands still. Listening for a moment outside Mariette's door, she tries to call good night. But no words come. She will talk to

Mariette tomorrow; in the morning everything will be different, none of this will have happened, go on happening. She goes to her own room and undresses, putting away every item of clothing, making sure her dress hangs scrupulously straight on its hanger. Gets into bed, pulls the covers up tight. And cannot sleep. For the first time, she feels like a stranger in her own room, in a bed too small and narrow, a house that no longer belongs to her, now that she's let so many strangers inside. *Blind man can't see. Every knave must have—.* And the slave is she.

FOUR IN THE EARLY November morning; sun slowly pulling back the dark, like the covers off a bed. Trucks pounding up from Falmouth on their way to Whitby, to Halifax: headlights dull in the emergent light. Coming through Spruce Harbour, Louis ticks off the landmarks: college towers, the Disney spire of the church, Our Lady, gently rusting under the sputtering bulbs of Her halo. Wagner's Kwikway, its fluorescent sign half-on, half-off, so the only letters that stand out are KWIK. Lonesome time: night not over, not yet morning. Still, people out, bent on God knows what kind of business. Coming round the curve he slows the truck— someone on the road ahead. Could be a boy or a girl—getting into a car. Stupid kids, hitch-hiking—he'd half a mind to blow the horn at them, pull up on the shoulder and give them both a piece of his mind. If they knew what he'd seen, on this road—might just as well holler out for trouble as get into a car with a stranger. The car starts off again—he overtakes it as soon as he can. And drives on straight for Halifax—no, the car never passed him, he's sure of that, he would have seen it. For all he knows it might have pulled onto a side road, up towards the falls. Or gone on to Whitby and taken the ferry to New Brunswick, on into Québec, or down into Maine. He doesn't know. But he feels bad, not having stopped, not having tried to interfere—though God knows if he acted on his impulses, and what he knew of the road, he'd never get to his delivery-points at all. All kinds of crazy kids on the roads these days—how was he to know?

IN THE MORNING, her bed empty, never having been slept in: all the clothes still hanging in the closet except what she'd been dressed in the night before. Not even a quarter missing from the change box kept on the kitchen counter. In her dressing gown, Claire sits on the bench in the hallway, waiting, in case Mariette has just gone out for an early walk, though she's never done so before. Sitting and staring at the little table on which she keeps her car keys, house keys. An hour—two hours?—and still Mariette hasn't come back. If she had spoken to her last night, called out to her, at least. What had she heard, or seen? Calling the social worker at last, asking her to go round to Delima's to make sure Mariette hasn't just run away home—though Mariette would as soon have run back to the hospital as the trailer. And then the police: to keep an eye out, just in case. And then Hector—only then. Not that she thinks he could help, but because by then she knows it's too late, for him as well as herself.

Past noon when he gets to the house and finds Claire, still in a dressing gown, hair uncombed, mouth slack. Hearing the news, feeling it like a blow to the gut, knowing, without having to ask, that Mariette heard them, saw them last night. The flatness of Claire's voice that doesn't seem to belong to her, anymore than does the sagging dressing gown.

"She could be anywhere—she didn't take anything with her, you know that? The police seemed disappointed—they figured she'd taken money from my purse, maybe the silver teaspoons. But everything I'd got for her since she came here—she left it all. Neatly hanging in the closet, folded in the drawers. Just took the clothes she had on and walked out the door. They figure that means she's coming back—Christ, they're stupid. She's not coming back. Not to you, not to me. A good night's work, don't you think?"

He shakes his head. Too late. As though the whole affair were some book from which the last hundred pages have been razored out, so that you know nothing of how or why things come to an ending. That there's been an end—of that at least he's certain. Twisting his cap round and round in his hands, suddenly furious at the plastic that will not break or tear. Claire standing with a hand on each wall, to keep him from coming any farther than the hallway.

"They think she took off—joyriding. After all, she's Delima's kid, right? But she just may have, too—taken off, I mean. Got the hell out. Or she could be hitching her way up to Halifax, to that Centre, to find her brother. She may be there right now—if she got the right kind of ride. They'll phone here, if she shows up. I'll let you know."

"I'm going to find out."

"What?" Claire pulls the lapels of her dressing gown closer together, as if she's just realized that she's standing here like this before him—dishevelled, distressed. A surrender—if only of appearances. *Nothing's happened, nothing could happen. Not to her—to me. He doesn't say a word about last night. Doesn't he remember; has he made it unhappen?*

"I'm going to look for her. I'll take the truck."

"But I said they'd phone."

"I'm taking the truck."

And he goes. Claire hears the truck pull away from the house—reaches a hand up to her hair, combing it back from her face. She must look like a scrubwoman in this dressing gown. She'll trash it, right away—order something decent from the catalogue, before her severance pay runs out. Something durable. Must smell like a scrubwoman, too—better go straight upstairs, have a bath. Water so hot it will scorch her, burn off the closeness, muskiness of the last day and night. Put on a white shirt, black trousers—sharp, clear definitions, separations. Not her fault. How can you be responsible for something you can't even imagine happening? It was all his doing, this time she hadn't lifted a finger; she had stood there like the newel-post on the stairs and let accidents happen. They would find Mariette, she wouldn't be able to get very far. Nothing could happen, nothing had.

Claire runs the water for her bath, watching the mirror cloud with steam, erasing everything in the room, even her eyes.

HECTOR STARTS UP the truck, sending a shock of gravel into the blue afternoon air. He's careful not to exceed the limit as he heads north along the coast road—if he goes too fast he may miss her, she may be sitting on the shoulder, or in the ditch, waiting for a ride. The road's practically empty—if he's careful, alert enough he will find her, he will be able to undo everything that has happened from the moment he stepped inside the door of Claire's house last night. He should never have taken her back there; he should have stayed with her, taken her back with him. He should never have listened to a word of Claire's; he should never, he should never, he should—. *The heart has reasons that reason knows not.* Tell that to Mariette. He will never tell anything to her, he wouldn't presume; he hasn't the right. Claire was right, she was always right, he should never have come back.

Slams on the brakes. But it's a man about his own age, jeans and a checked shirt, and hair that hasn't been cut in months. Shaking his fist at him as Hector drives on, a little faster now, at least until he's left the man far enough behind. Past the turn-off to Whitby, down into the Valley. Baptist churches, Kwikway stores, gingerbread verandahs, on none of which sits Mariette. Make a mistake, take the consequences—but which? If she hadn't said what she had—. *We love our children—drive carefully.* Had she lied to him about Mariette not being able to have kids? Had he lied to her when he'd said it didn't matter?

Miles and miles of spruce, now. Would she have stayed on the small roads—does she know it's easier to hitch on the highway? Suddenly he's sure she's come this way, getting a ride all the way to Halifax—that she's wandering round Halifax right now, lost, confused, too scared to ask anyone directions. Can't ask directions, she doesn't say anything—but to hitch a ride in the first place? A birch tree here and there, to break the monotony of green. He drives as fast as he can, knowing she's not anywhere on this road, wanting to get to the city before she gives up, before the wrong person stops to talk to her. Under his hands her bones as small, her heartbeats fierce as a bird's. Crows: hundreds of black beaks, tearing into sacks of rotting garbage. Chases the image away by reaching for a tape—he will put on Mozart at top volume—*Così fan tutte.* But she wouldn't know that music; it would hurt her if he played it; he would have to get rid of his tapes, at least when she was riding with him in the truck. No Pygmalion, thank you very much—he wouldn't change a hair on her head; he wanted her just as she was, for what she was. *If you trust in Nature, in what is simple in Nature, in the small Things that hardly anyone sees and that can so suddenly become huge, immeasurable . . . .*

But he doesn't see her, anywhere. Past the watershed area, the sandy stretch of soil with beautiful pines rearing up in rows either side of the road: past the industrial parks, the sleek waters of the basin with their even sleeker boats and houses. Through the rotary and into the city. Everywhere everyone but Mariette. Late afternoon—university students possessing the sidewalks, arms burdened with books, talking, talking. Himself, years ago in Montréal: possessing his future, the future Claire had unrolled like a moving carpet in front of him. He parks the car along a street bordered by faculty buildings: Anthropology, French, Spanish, Philosophy. Wanting to get out and walk with them; talk the way he'd done all those years ago. Not talk, ask; ask them if they've seen a girl in jeans and a checked shirt, looking—small, maybe even a shade simple? *The small Things that hardly anyone sees.* Curses himself, starts up the truck again and drives down the main streets, down to the Public Gardens where there is no Mariette: not even on Barrington, the rough side of Barrington. Doesn't even think of driving down to the Centre, of phoning Claire to ask if there's any word. He doesn't trust Claire, doesn't trust himself with Claire; later, he will think about all that later, after he's found Mariette, talked to her—

You're so well-matched: you'll have so much to talk about together. About the children they wouldn't have. *What do you expect her to do all day while you're out unblocking drains at the college?* Listen to the loons on the lake. Collect specimens of moss and lichen. Sharpen his pencils for him. *If you have this love for what is simple and try very simply, as someone who serves, to win the confidence of what seems poor: then everything will become easier for you, more coherent and somehow more reconciling.* Claire again, Claire's book he'd once learned by heart to please her, words he can't shake out of his head even now, looking for her still, even though he knows by now—each corner he turns takes him further away from her. Streets emptying of schoolchildren and mothers with strollers; filling with hookers and sailors who materialize out of a darkness that hoods the face of evening. He hasn't eaten since breakfast—he hardly slept the night before; he can't go on driving like this all night, no one would expect him to. Perhaps she's already home, perhaps they've found her, perhaps they'll never find her. Almost, but not quite without knowing he has crossed the long suspension bridge over the harbour, headed the truck in the direction of the Valley: set out on his way home.

Halfway to Spruce Harbour he reaches into the box on the seat next to him for a tape. *Così*; he listens with painful pleasure to the *Addio* in which the women bid farewell to their lovers. It is the most purely poignant music he can imagine, and it is all a joke, a trick played on willing dupes by a professional cynic. He stops the tape, rewinds, and listens again to the trio, remembering in acute detail what Claire had said and done the night before: how he had thought to knock down her arguments, her glittery-hard eyes and smile, with a kiss, for Christ's sake, that kiss he had dreamed of giving her when he was a kid of thirteen. Queen Christina on her wildly rearing horse, slashing his face with her whip. She had known, she must have known all the time that Mariette would be listening, would hear every word they said. Keeping their voices down so as not to wake her, but hoping all the time that she'd hear, crawl out of bed like a child banished from the grown-ups' party; crawl out of bed to the landing and listen. He must have known, too—and hadn't stopped, had only wanted to get back at Claire, get Claire, and in such a way that he'd get rid of Mariette. Remembering, again, how small and yet how open she'd been under his hands and the weight of his body; seeing, for the first time, that what he'd been pleased to call his own tenderness had been evasion, displacement of his desire to get back at, free of, Claire.

The lights are on in Claire's house, but he doesn't stop the truck in front of her door. He needs more time before he sees her again—

he doesn't want to find out anything more, not yet. He'd thought himself free of her, but he's only tied tighter and tighter. What's happened is his responsibility—his and Claire's, and in a random way, Bertrand's, who was by far the most innocent of Mariette's tormenters. And before Bertrand, the man who'd got at her first and left her—what had Claire said? Mutilated inside. And Mariette? She's paying the price for them all. He thinks for a moment of the immersion student, the girl who ran off with Bertrand, who has left Bertrand and is now free of everything, everyone in her way. Then he sees Mariette's face. Then the girl's, then Mariette's, like neon signs blinking back and forth, signalling senselessly from light to dark.

He halts the truck, not at his apartment in back of the Kwikway store, but in the parking lot of St. Alphonse Church, before the statue of the Virgin. He can see the tired bulbs of Her halo leaking a little light into the dark around Her, mopping up the unacknowledged sins of the world like so much brackish water at Her feet; using Her own hair and robes to do so. *Bowing to necessities that are greater than pleasure and pain, and more powerful than will and understanding.* The eyes of the statue as blank and null as Mariette's face those times he went to see her at the hospital; rust stains from the metal supports for the halo dribbling down the plaster, indelibly. And he suddenly feels that if he were to get out of the truck and kneel down before this statue, he could concentrate his guilt and desire so fiercely it would crack the plaster, topple the shell from the pedestal and reveal what and whom he'd been searching for all these miles and hours along the highway. If he could get out and kneel, if the sky would break and all the stars fall down, if he could push that much farther and deeper inside himself, so that he'd know what to do—. But the sky stays solid as steel, the stars are strung on wires no prayer of his will ever cut.

6

The glass door between the letter boxes and the post office counter has been propped open—Delbert makes sure of his prey. But I won't go in to the counter, even though I have letters to mail, and Delbert is watching for me as he calculates the change due to another customer. Nothing in the letter box but bills, ads for Kut-Rate Kosmetics and Exotic Dancers at the Evangeline Beverage Room. Junk mail to be crumpled decisively, thrown in the wastepaper basket under the counter. Except that even throwing away junk mail you come face to face with Mariette. The photograph of Mariette the police have stuck up behind the glass, on the bulletin board. It's one of Bertrand's photographs, one of those Delima found under Mariette's bedclothes almost a year ago. The delicacy and clarity of her features, even the slight shadows under her eyes are like paper cuts; they sting your eyes. I've heard Frère LeBlanc telling Delbert that Mariette looks like a little madonna in that photograph—it should be under glass on the vestry wall, he says, not displayed in every post office and general store along the 101.

It's hard to take your eyes from her picture, hard not to see that other photograph beneath this chaste, mild pose. But I have to pick up my mail from the ledge and slip out the door so quickly Delbert won't have a chance to walk over to the glass door and start to question me. I have no answers for him—no one has any answers. It is mid-March; Mariette has been missing since November, and even Delbert will admit at the end of a particularly long day that Mariette may never be found, though a body in jeans and a checked shirt might be recovered one afternoon in any one of the woodlots or waste fields on the back roads between Falmouth and Halifax. She never showed up at Delima's trailer, in Frère LeBlanc's church, or at the Centre, though Delima will tell you that her Mariette's high-tailed it out west to Toronto or maybe even B.C.; gone with some good-looking guy who's got eyes in his head and knows a looker when he meets one.

I've had to leave the engine running—the car's even more temperamental now than it was in the days when I used to chauffeur Bertrand round the Shore. Teaching piano in Falmouth all day—Three Blind Mice and Jingle Bells till I want to belt out obscene songs at the top of my lungs. Tomorrow is Saturday—six local students, one by one, doing scales and practising movie themes; it's what they want to play, and I have no pride left, mother. The house needs to be repainted, badly—tiles have blown off the roof during the winter storms, and there are new cracks in the plaster, under that rose-patterned paper you so carefully put up. I don't know yet whether I'll be able to make enough money teaching piano to keep the house—I'd get almost nothing for it if I sold it—old houses like ours are too hard to heat—everyone's buying shoebox bungalows, putting them up side by side along the soggy sideroads. And without the house there's really no reason for me to stay, is there? No defence against anything. ''Nobody blames you,'' Delbert told me the last time I went in to mail a letter. Concern and respect in his voice like the lead weights you put into curtain hems to make them hang straight. ''No, we all know it's not your fault. You were good to her—but she's not to blame, either, she wasn't right in the head, or she'd never have run away like that. But I tell you, these things happen, and then they pass away. Don't let them ruin your life, your chance for happiness.''

Even the garage is falling apart—why didn't you make me take care of this before? Whole boards need to be replaced—the snow drifts in during storms, so that some mornings I have to dig the car out. Don't let them ruin your car. Your life. He meant Hector, you see. Delbert has the notion—God knows how Delbert puts two and two together and comes up with minus one—the notion that Hector had been courting me all this time, that he'd got cold feet and run off at the last minute. The first time I went into the post office after Hector moved away, Delbert kept me waiting at the counter till all the other customers had left: riveted grave and steady eyes on me. "Don't worry, Claire. He'll be back. Halifax isn't such a long way away—it's not Montréal; it doesn't have those big buildings like Montréal, you know—we won't lose him. And just when he'd gone and built that nice house for himself—I know he sold it, but that doesn't mean he's not coming back. You'll see—you just have to have patience."

"I see no need for patience," I told Delbert, "except with the service at this post office." I haven't spoken to him since, though he lies in wait for me, sad-faced and heavy-eyed, reconciled to my rudeness, which he construes as heartbreak.

The house is cold, dark. I hate going down to the basement to stir the ashes, cram in logs over the embers. It was something you always refused to do—you'd say you had no intention of ruining your hands; you forbad me to help him. So it was always you, *papa*, who handled the furnace, stoking it before you went out on night calls, carrying out boxes of ashes, heavy boxes. I could never understand how something could be soft and yet so heavy. You never explained anything to me, did you—I was always supposed to anticipate and accept whatever mystery you forced my way: accept your love and your hate, your sending me away, your summons to return to this house. Your deaths and your refusal to die. When I was little you'd never let me talk. "Listen," you'd say, "listen to this piece of music, this explanation of the stars, this quarrel, this passion, this silence." They say that children are born to language the way they are born to a particular set of parents, that our speech speaks us, and our possibilities are enclosed in a set of rules as arbitrary and fixed as grammar itself. But you are a language all of your own and you are still speaking me—I can put my hands over my ears and still I hear you, dream you, utter you in every move I make. When Mariette was with me for those few months she silenced you. I was the only one home, at last. But Hector was right, you know—it was too late; I lost her and now I have you back again, for good.

Too tired to eat anything—I'll just have a drink—but there's no cognac left, or brandy either. A thimbleful of sherry from a bottle I've been meaning to throw out for weeks. If they could see me, Stella Wagner, Delbert, Père Gilbert—drinking from the bottle, licking the rim. Garbage collection tomorrow—they'll have been keeping track of how many bottles I've thrown out over the last couple of months. The news will spread all the way from Falmouth up to Halifax—the social workers will be coming after me, next. Quite a comedown, but then, like house, like daughter—both daughters. Disintegrating like your house, our skulls like the roofs of abandoned homes, slowly, surely caving in. You'll have noticed how bad things are in the house—yes, I know, the piano needs tuning, the dust's like fur over your books and prints. But I've had to cut corners; Delima no longer comes to clean. Think of it, *papa*—Delima's pregnant again, at her age. But have you ever realized that Delima and I are almost the same age? If I'd shacked up in a trailer with a Luc-Antoine, if I'd gone out to clean house or gut fish instead of playing scales, I'd look Delima's age, wouldn't I, mother? But you wouldn't know—you didn't live to be the age I am now, though you are always older, wiser, better than I. *Hinx, minx, the old witch winks/The fat begins to fry.*

I said I wasn't hungry. I don't want anything to eat, I'd like just to sit down. Read a book, flip through a catalogue, choosing records I can't afford to buy. Not piano, not vocalists, not woodwinds—but there it is, after all, the Franck sonata. Of course it should only be played on the violin; we made a mistake, Halyna and I. Not Halyna. She got away, after all—Halyna's my one success. I launched her, perfectly. As for Bertrand, however melancholy he might be for the moment—he's at least on his own home ground. Bertrand and Halyna—stars that have burned out and fallen to some other earth—I don't want them in my house, in my head again. It's bad enough having Mariette there, Mariette and Hector slipping into my thoughts, slipping in through slashes and holes; sharper for the fact of their absence.

All day I fence them out, with every lesson I give, every mile I drive, every record I play or book I pick up. But at night I dream; Mariette's in the room across the hall, crying out that someone's

trying to hurt her. I fly across to help, only to find Mariette and
Hector bloodying each other in your bed. I try to pull them apart
and find it's not Mariette but myself in the bed with Hector, using
my arms and legs like blades against him, fighting so hard my
mouth fills with blood. I am drowning in a cup of blood—. And
then I wake to the slur of traffic over the highway, lessons to be
taught, bills to be paid. The days like loaves of dry bread to be
eaten through. And I will, I will eat my fill until the house or I
give way. I won't run away like the others. I can't run anywhere,
this is the only place I know.

It's cold in here, even with all the lamps lit. I'll have to go
downstairs again and stoke the fire. But I'm tired, and it's too
dark down there. I'll hurt my hands. I burn wood until May—
sometimes June, it can be that cold here, with the wind blowing.
One person alone in a house gets colder than a family, even a
couple would—I can't remember it being so cold for us. You
wouldn't know that, either—you always had someone with you;
the babies curled up, blood-warm inside you; Delima in your bed,
her child inside her—your child. I'm the one who's been solitary—
words don't keep you warm, and you always lock the door at
night, you never let me in. *We are solitary.* You underlined that
in your book, the only thing—besides me—that ever belonged to
you both. I lost the book. I gave it away—but I got it back, she
sent it to me, and I put it—not there, not in the cabinet with
Bertrand's chocolate, not on the mantel but in your study, in the
desk drawer, here. She sent it back with a letter, with a photograph; you marked the passage: do you remember?

> We *are* solitary. We can delude ourselves about this and act as
> if it were not true. That is all. But how much better it is to
> recognize that we are alone; yes, even to begin from this real-
> ization . . . A man taken out of his room and, almost without
> preparation or transition, placed on the heights of a great moun-
> tain range, would feel . . . an unequalled insecurity, an aban-
> donment to the nameless . . . . He would feel he was falling
> or think he was being catapulted out into space or exploded
> into a thousand pieces . . . That is how all distances, all

measures change for the person who becomes solitary . . .
Unusual fantasies and strange feelings arise, which seem to
grow out beyond all that is bearable. But it is necessary for us
to experience *that* too. We must accept our reality as *vastly* as
we possibly can: everything, even the unprecedented, must be
possible within it. This is in the end the only kind of courage
that is required of us: the courage to face the strangest, most
unusual, most inexplicable experiences that can meet us.

We *are* solitary: *father, mother and I.* But I would have helped
her, I wanted to help her—all of them. If I'd spoken to Bertrand
about her—if I'd warned her, there would never have been this
photograph, this photograph in which I can't tell where I stop and
Mariette begins. And Bertrand, and Hector, too. They are here,
even if they don't know it. In the film itself: invisible, yet powerful, as if they were holding the woman's arms and legs, bending
them into the shape they want them to take; a kind of embrace.
The portrait of a couple, fused in an intensity that could be love.
Love is difficult, I find it difficult to love. Halyna's letter, Bertrand's photograph of Mariette, your volume of Rilke I once
loaned to Hector, who has gone because he could not bear his
solitude. It is too cold in here; the air is like ice; it is like being
on a mountaintop in a summer dress. I must make us warm. I
cannot go down to the basement. I will build a fire here, where
we sit, where we most need it to keep us warm. You had it sent
all the way from England, after the war, but I have no desire to
play it; there's no one to accompany except the stupid children
who come and stumble through Three Blind Mice, and movie
songs. One, two, three matches before the letter burns, a spurt of
crimson flakes, then black, while the photograph shrivels. But
nothing seems to happen to the book—it's too solid for the fire to
do more than blacken its covers. Five, six, seven matches, the
pages so slow to surrender themselves, as if the air's too cold for
them to burn. More paper, any papers—magazines, books, record
jackets . . . . Varnish sizzling, crackling at last. The wood's
begun to smoke, bitter and black so we can't breathe, I must open

windows, I must get us some air, but the windows are sealed up tight.

Too hot, too bright—I have a fever; my throat's singed, even my words. Outside, I must get my breath, don't you feel it, how can you sit there talking, don't you feel anything? The windows won't open—the curtains are flares, a red curtain in front of the door. Kitchen, I can try the kitchen door, there's time still, I can undo the bolt, the chain, *get out, get out, get out.* They're all outside, waiting, nobody home but the two of you fighting, talking, talking me, making me listen here, looking out the window at the wind blowing. Night sky a black pond, ice your eyes can skate on. All of them there, in a line, hands linked, whirled up from earth, icy configurations reeling and frozen while everything burns and falls. Catapulted into space, exploding into a thousand pieces, around me, inside me, now.